THE MURDERERS
OF KATYN

THE
MURDERERS
OF
KATYN

VLADIMIR ABARINOV

FOREWORD AND CHRONOLOGY
BY
IWO CYPRIAN POGONOWSKI

HIPPOCRENE BOOKS INC.
NEW YORK

For information, address:
HIPPOCRENE BOOKS, INC.
171 Madison Avenue
New York, NY 10016

Library on Congress Cataloging-in-Publication Data

Abarinov, Vladimir.
    [Katynskii labirint. English]
    The murderers of Katyn / Vladimir Abarinov ; foreword and
chronology by Iwo Cyprian Pogonowski. -- 1st ed.
    Includes bibliographical references and index.
    ISBN 0-7818-0032-3 :
    1. Katyn Forest Massacre, 1940. I. Title.
D804.S65A2313 1993
940.54'05'094762--dc20   92-36852
                                                CIP

Printed in the United States of America.

CONTENTS

In his capacity as a special correspondent of the weekly *Literaturnaya Gazeta,* the author of this book spent several years searching for and systematizing evidence and archive sources relating to the circumstances in which a group of Polish officer prisoners met their end on Soviet territory. Until quite recently, the Katyn Case has been one of the blank spots in the history of Soviet-Polish relations. That is why Vladimir Abarinov seeks to reveal as many fresh details (up to 1990) as possible, for it is these details which, together with facts that have been established beyond doubt, can throw light on a tragedy that took place in the Katyn forest where nearly 15,000 people lost their lives. The work uses materials from Soviet archives, letters received by the author from readers in response to his publications in the Soviet press, reminiscences, documents and writings by foreign historians and publicists, and daily records of the author's meetings with eyewitnesses of various episodes of the "Katyn Case."

FOREWORD

The Murderers of Katyn by Vladimir Abarinov was published in Russia in January 1991. The author describes the largest execution of officers, prisoners of war, during World War II, committed by Soviet security forces -- a fact officially denied by the government of the USSR for 50 years. The mass execution was an international crime committed in the Spring of 1940 on 15,000 captured Polish military, intelligence, police, and territorial officers by the Soviet NKVD officers acting on Stalin's orders. It has been known by the name of Katyn, the place in which a part of the graves of the victims were first found by the Germans and investigated in 1943.

The origin of the Soviet mass murders of Polish officers goes back to September 28, 1939 when the German-Soviet Boundary and Friendship Treaty was signed. It contained secret provisions for the mutual extermination of potential Polish opponents of both Germany and USSR. Both governments were to take all the necessary measures to contain and prevent the emergence of any hostile action directed against the territory of the other side. Germany and USSR would liquidate any signs of agitation within their own territories and inform each other of measures taken to achieve this aim.

The Soviets implemented their program by executing 15,000 Polish officers. Katyn, with graves of 4443, became just a symbol of the execution of all Polish officers, whose sites of mass murder and burial are listed in the main text and in the Chronology. The circumstances of this war crime are described by Abarinov in great detail. His research was brought up to 1990.

Since then additional information about this mass murder of the pre-war Polish officer corps has been established by the Ministry of Justice of the Republic of Poland in preparation of indictments against the Soviet war criminals surviving in Russia. These recent Polish findings are included in the Appendix I (p. 365) in the *Chronology and Annotations on the Mass Execution of 15,000 Polish Officers by Soviet Security Forces*. Appendix II (p. 395) includes 16 sample biographies of the murdered Polish officers. Appendix III (p. 409) contains 26 moral principles of Russian revolutionaries also known as *Nechayev's Catechism of 1869*. Such principles of ethics and morality were practiced on a gigantic scale in Soviet Russia and led to the international crime committed on Polish officers in 1940.

In retrospect it is obvious that the pre-war Soviet government was aware that the essence of the policies of the Nazi-German government at all times was the implementation of the doctrine of *Lebensraum*, or a huge German living space which, eventually, was to include the great agricultural lands of the Slavic two-thirds of

7

Europe, located mainly in Poland and the Soviet Union. After Germany and Japan signed the Anti-Cominform Pact in Nov. 1936, the Soviets feared the possibility of a two-front war at the time when Stalinist purges were severely weakening the Red Army.

Japanese attacks on Soviet territory started in 1938 near lake Chasan and continued in 1939 in Mongolia. At the same time the government of the Soviet Union was aware that the German drive towards a war for Lebensraum at any cost resulted in steady progress towards an eventual signing of a common defense treaty by Great Britain, France, and Poland. By encouraging and eventually joining in an attack on Poland, the USSR could entangle the Germans for years on the western front in a war of attrition, while the Soviets could annex half of Poland, the Baltic states, and Romanian Bukovina. The very fact of German cooperation with the Soviet Union would also constitute a betrayal of Japan by Germany at a time when the Japanese were in combat with the Red Army in Mongolia.

The conclusion of German-Soviet treaties on Aug. 23 and Sept. 28, 1939 together with Japanese failures on the battle field drove Japan to negotiate an armistice with the Soviet Union. It was signed on Sept. 15, 1939, two weeks after Germany attacked Poland on Sept. 1. As soon as the government of the Soviet Union disengaged itself militarily in the Far East, it issued on Sept. 16, 1939 an order to the Red Army to invade Poland. The Soviet forces crossed the border of Poland on Sept. 17, 1939. By that time the Germans were already at war with Great Britain and France, neither of which felt strong enough to declare war on the Soviet Union, in retaliation for the Red Army's invasion of Poland. As the Soviets got out of combat with Japan they deflected the Japanese forces against the United States and the European colonies in Asia. In their calculations the Soviets did not expect the fall of France in 1940.

The Polish people suffered undescribable terror during the Soviet-German alliance. Some of the German war crimes committed in 1939-1941 are mentioned in Appendix I, which includes the updated facts of Soviet mass murders committed on Polish prisoners of war as these facts, gradually, are being established.

Vladimir Abarinov made a pioneering effort to present the truth about the Soviet mass murders of 15,000 Polish officers to the Russian people. His book was written to free the Russians from half a century of lies fabricated by the government of USSR in order to blame the Germans for the hideous war crime which, in fact, was perpetrated by Soviet security forces early in 1940.

Iwo Cyprian Pogonowski   Summer 1992.

AUTHOR'S NOTE

The blank spot which is the subject of this book is one of the most inveterate and painful. It is no less thorny or significant than the issue of the Soviet-German protocols of 1939. The Katyn syndrome has been an obstacle to normal, good neighborly relations between the two countries for nearly half a century now. There was a moment—already in the period of glasnost—when it seemed that a lot of things, perhaps even our relations with the whole of Eastern Europe, depended on our confession. The crisis of confidence was resolved by a unilateral statement of the Polish government, which laid the responsibility for the massacre of the Polish officers at the door of the Soviet repressive organs. Yet even after this statement was made, the Soviet side kept silent on the matter for more than a year.

Displeasure with historians about this issue, however, is not quite appropriate, for we were all fully aware that full scale research work could not be carried out without an appropriate political solution. We could only try to get things moving by uncovering more and more fresh information; I hope that this subject, which is quite dramatic in its own way, has yet to find its final chronicler.

When I began to study the Katyn issue, my plans did not include writing a book. It was at a time when the very word "Katyn" was taboo for the party ideologists. Almost no one dared to uphold Stalin's version any longer, people speaking from high rostrums called on their audiences to be patient, because active searches for fresh material were under way, but nothing had been discovered so far. I had no reason not to trust these statements. I simply believed that there was not a moment to lose waiting; the witnesses, if any of them could still be found, were not long for this world, and the truth would die with them. No archive sources could make up for what these people knew. Any detail impressed on an eyewitness' memory is unique. There cannot be too many such details if we really want to know the whole truth. And the *whole truth* is a matter not only of *who*, but also of *how*.

Quite a few months passed before I got down to systematizing a massive pile of individual facts. They resisted systemetization and contradicted one another, and my searches brought me time and again to deadlock or made me return to the starting point. There were several successes which I am inclind to ascribe to sheer good luck. On the whole, my work consisted of conducting a systematic study of archives, writing and double-checking each piece of evidence. Only rarely did this work bring any appreciable results.

I am quite aware that here and there the book is difficult to read and overburdened with figures, names and dates. Someone could certainly make a best seller out of Katyn, but I will leave to others the opportunity to cross this moral boundary. Today there is no shortage of people who have a way with words, but Katyn is not a subject for belles-lettres nor perhaps is it a subject at all. The miasmata of Katyn have been dissolved in the air which we breathe, the earth on which we walk, and the blood which courses our veins. Yes, the book is difficult to read during a tram ride, but then it was not conceived for this kind of reading.

The mail which I have received from readers vividly illustrates the fundamental change that has taken place in Soviet public opinion over the past three years. At first, many people simply had no idea what it was all about. Not infrequently, letters came from frenzied Stalinists such as one S.V. Aganezov from Ashkhabad, who wrote to me that, instead of eliminating blank spots, I was reviving the White Movement. There also came more placid and pacifying letters. "Is it really possible that our Polish friends cannot assess what happened from a clear-cut class standpoint?" reasoned D. I. Ovchinnikov from Yuzhno-Sakhalinsk in his letter. "After all, these people were the top echelons of the old Polish army that was in the service of the bourgeoisie. Why, then, are the Polish comrades beginning to lose their class intuition and slip into nationalist arrogance? I believe that it is essential tactfully and as comprehensibly as possible to carry out explanatory work among them in this area." How can you explain to Ovchinnikov that appealing to the class intuition of those whose fathers lie buried in the Katyn forest is senseless and amoral? Characteristically, Ovchinnikov does not waver in the slightest in determining the culprit of their death. And this is just it: almost none of the readers, even those who justify this crime, have any doubts that massacre *could* have been carried out by the organs of the People's Commissariat of Internal Affairs (NKVD).

The bibliography of Katyn runs into hundred of titles, and yet the issue is far from being exhausted. Nor does this book claim to be the last word on the subject. Several things were not included in it for lack of space, but there are many more things which are yet to be discovered and made public. I felt happy, having received two hundred letters in response to my publications in *Literaturnaya Gazeta*, because this was very nearly a record-breaking figure for materials published by the weekly's international department where I was working at the time. Later on, however, we did two programs for Polish TV with the journalist Andrzej Minko. When I subsequently came to Warsaw and Andrzej opened a cabinet in his office, I saw in it *fifteen hundred* letters from Poles addressed to us. And almost every single envelope contained copies of documents, photographs, and requests to help establish the fate of someone's father, husband or brother... All of them needed a reply, and each of them was an unwritten chapter of the *Labyrinth*.

The Katyn tragedy is not an isolated episode from the past. My dossier on Katyn keeps growing and parallel subjects are being added to it. These new shoots intertwine, forming a powerful root system which runs through the whole of Soviet history of the last 50 years.No one will pull up this rotting stump for us. Telling the whole truth about Katyn is a painful, difficult and sickening task. Yet it is impossible not to tell it. The time has come not just to speak,but to speak out directly.

It was not my intention to give a chronological description of all the events relating to the Katyn case; this task has already been carried out by other authors whose books simply have to be translated and published in the USSR. I have told only of things about which I had something new to relate, while making the accounts of universally known facts as brief as possible. For the same reason there are almost no primary sources in this book; the only exceptions were hard-to-obtain or recently published texts, and also testimonies whose reliability is contested by my interlocutors. In any case,these documents have never been published in Russian. Archive materials having no references to printed publications are being published for the first time. This, certainly, also applies to the information given by participants in or eyewitnesses to the events being described. A number of selected fragments of the book have previously been published by me in periodicals.

When collecting materials about Katyn, I kept coming across people who were ready to help me, and this was the case not only with private individuals, but also with officials. I would like to extend my warmest thanks to all of these, namely, Boris Bespalov, Vladimir Birshtein, Arkady Brodsky, Yelena Butova, Lyudmila Vasilyeva, Andrzej Werner (Poland), Suren Gabrielyan, Tamara Gusarova, Marek Drażewski (Poland), Eugeniusz Duraczyński (Poland), Yuri Zora, Alla Kallas, Boris Karpov, Leonid Kotov, Sergei Kryzhitsky (USA), Vladimir Kuznetsov, Bożena Łojek (Poland), Czesław Madajczyk (Poland), Inna Martoya, Andrzej Minko (Poland), Albina Noskova, Sergei Olyunin, Leonid Okhlopkov, Alexei Pamyatnykh, Yelena Perelevskaya, Revolt Pimenov, Anatoli Rubinov, Nikolai Ryzhikov, Masha Slonim (Britain), Edmund Stevens (Britain), Gabriel Superfin (FRG), Olga Tabachnikova, Maren Freidenberg, Whitney R. Harris (USA), Zinaida Shatalova, Yekaterina Shukshina, Yelizaveta Shchemeleva, and Klavdia Yaroshenko. I would also like to thank most cordially everyone who deemed it necessary to respond to my publications. Their letters and telephone calls not only led me to fresh information, but also provided invaluable moral support. An exceptionally important part in this work was played by the late Natan Eidelman—may he rest in peace. My thanks to all those who worked on this book.

INTRODUCTION

The fate of a vast number of Polish servicemen captured by the Red Army invading Poland in September 1939 remained unknown for a long time despite persistent inquiries made by the Polish government in exile. Finally, on April 13, 1943, German radio announced the discovery of mass graves by the occupying authorities in the Katyn forest near Smolensk. It was determined that there were graves of 10,000 Polish army officers shot and killed by the "Jewish commissars" in the spring of 1940. Worried by this news, the Polish government in exile asked the International Committee of the Red Cross to conduct an investigation on the spot. Moscow's response was extremely sharp: on April 26, 1943, the Soviet Union severed diplomatic relations with Poland.

We will discuss the circumstances in which the German occupying authorities uncovered the mass graves in the Katyn forest, as well as subsequent developments later in this book. Now let me simply remind the reader of the principal milestones of the Katyn Case.

September 1939. The outbreak of World War II. The independent Polish state ceased to exist. On the territories incorporated into the USSR under the Soviet-German treaty of friendship, some 250,000 Polish servicemen were taken prisoner.

March-April 1940. Correspondence from Polish officer POWs with their relatives in Poland was interrupted. All mail was returned marked "Addressee has left."

June 22 1941. Germany invaded USSR.

Introduction

July-December 1941. Diplomatic relations were established between the Soviet Union and the Polish government in London; a treaty of mutual assistance was signed and an agreement was reached on the formation in the USSR of a Polish army. Of the Poles released by amnesty, none were from the officer camps.

Summer 1942. The Poles who worked in the Todt work team in the environs of Smolensk learned from local inhabitants that Polish POWs shot dead by the NKVD had been buried in the Katyn forest.

February 1943. The German secret field police became interested in the graves. A number of local residents were interrogated. The resulting report reached Alfred Jodl and his copy was given to Gerhard Butz, professor of Breslav University, who subsequently supervised the exhumation.

March 29. The beginning of excavations.

April 13. The Third Reich authorities officially announced the discovery of the graves.

April 17. The BBC aired a communique from the Polish government in exile with a request to the International Committee of the Red Cross to send its experts to Katyn.

April 26, 12:15 a.m. A note on the severance of diplomatic relations between the USSR and the Sikorski government was handed to the Polish ambassador in Kuibyshev.

May 8. A statement on the Soviet leadership's consent to the formation under the aegis of the Polish Patriots' Union of the Tadeusz Kościuszko Division, not subordinated to the Polish government in London, was published.

May 30. The international commission of experts convened by the Germans in Katyn gave the date of the execution as Spring 1940.

Introduction

January 24, 1944. A statement by the Soviet Special Commission headed by Academician N.N.Burdenko, which established that the Poles were executed by the Germans, was published. The execution date was given as Autumn 1941.

June 1-2, 1946. The International Military Tribunal in Nuremberg interrogated witnesses to the Katyn case. The Katyn massacre was excluded from the final text of the sentence for lack of proof.

May 1987. In keeping with the Soviet-Polish Declaration on Ideological, Scientific and Cultural Cooperation, a bilateral commission of historians was formed to examine blank spots in the history of relations between the two countries.

April 1990. USSR President Mikhail Gorbachev admitted the NKVD's responsibility for the killing of the Polish POWs. The Katyn issue entered a new phase...

Chapter 1

THE PROSE OF DEATH

Echelon, Special and Through Convoys

Among the responses to my publication "Beliye pyatna: ot emotsiy k faktam" (Blank Spots: From Emotions to Facts; in: *Literaturnaya Gazeta,* May 11, 1988) was a letter sent on to me by the Secretariat of the Main Directorate for Internal Troops of the USSR Ministry of Internal Affairs. It was addressed to A. V. Vlasov, then the Minister of Internal Affairs of the USSR. Its author, Alexei Lukin, a resident of the city of Kalinin (now Tver), called on the minister to help historians clear up the Katyn issue.

In his day, Alexei Lukin was the communications officer of the 136th Separate Internal Security Battalion of the NKVD of the Byelorussian SSR, which was reformed to accordance with the wartime table of organization into the 252nd Regiment of Escort Guard Troops of the NKVD of the USSR, on June 22, 1941. The battalion, based in Smolensk, was involved in the escort and guarding of Polish POWs confined in the Kozelsk and Yukhnov camps. According to Alexei Lukin, the Kozelsk camp existed until the beginning of the war and early in July was evacuated. "Neither during their transportation nor during their confinement in the camps," writes Alexei Lukin, "were any violations of "human rights," as they call it today, ever allowed. Any attempt to violate them entailed severe punishment. I took part in escorting many POW parties, both scheduled and unscheduled. There were no complaints against me or my subordinates. "In addition to the

Chapter 1

letter, Alexei Lukin told me in a telephone conversation a number of valuable new details, including, in particular, the fact that a notable figure, I. A. Serov, the future Minister of State Security, who was People's Commissar of Internal Affairs of the Ukraine holding the rank of State Security Commissar 3rd class in the period under discussion, came down to Smolensk from Moscow to supervise the evacuation of the Kozelsk camp.

What made Lukin's letter particularly valuable was that it gave the exact name and number of the military unit; this was a key to the archives. Wishing to help Soviet historians, I handed over a copy of the letter to Natalia Lebedeva, a research associate of the Institute of Universal History of the USSR Academy of Sciences, who had been recommended to me quite favorably, on condition, however, that the results of her investigation would be published in *Literaturnaya Gazeta*. Having waited in vain for an answer for quite some time, I went myself to the Central Archives of the Soviet Army, where it took me surprisingly little time to find all the documents relating to the Katyn Case.

Incidentally, soon after Natalia Lebedeva received the xerox copy of the letter, her boss, Oleg Rzheshevsky, a member of the bilateral commission, telephoned me. He was very courteous. He asked me if I had anything new on Katyn and offered me his full cooperation. I knew perfectly well what Rzheshevsky's stand on the Katyn Case was[1], and so I evaded his questions and asked for a week to think over his proposition. It was quite obvious that Rzheshevsky would try to use the letter as an argument in favor of the Soviet version of the events. He did not wait for a week as we had agreed; instead, he contacted the weekly's editors. I still cannot see what he was trying to achieve: could it be that he wanted to block my work in this way? Anyhow, he was turned down, and I continued to investigate the Katyn Case without hindrance, though admittedly, in my time off.

Nonetheless, Oleg Rzheshevsky circulated the text of Lukin's letter. In April 1989, Professor Marian Wojciechowski, a member of the Soviet-Polish commission, gave an interview to the newspaper *Sztandar Młodych*, in which he said, in particular:

"One Soviet historian said that General Serov came to Kozelsk early in 1941 to make arrangements for the evacuation of Polish army officers. This is quite possibly true. They were not, however, the Polish army officers taken prisoner in Lithuania in July 1940. There were only about 1,000 of them."[2]*

The inconsistency of attempts at a biased presentation of the information provided by Lukin are visible to the naked eye. Nevertheless, I became aware that subsequently I would have to use extreme caution in my contacts with representatives of official Soviet historical science.

---

* The professor is mistaken. Documents show that 2,353 persons were confined in the Kozelsk camp, having been brought there from Lithuania. Another 2,023 privates and NCOs from Lithuania were put in the Yukhnov camp. The data are given as of July 23, 1940 (Central State Special Archives, stock 1/п, inventory 3a, file 1, sheets 89-90). Here and further on documents of the Central State Special Achives are quoted from A. S. Prokopenko and Yu. N. Zorya's publication in *Voyenno-Istoricheskiy Zhurnal*, 1990, No.6.

This episode came to an end in March 1990, when Natalia Lebedeva published her sensational material in *Moscow News* and then, in the *MN* issue of May 6, corrected some of the errors made in the previous publication. The strange thing was that not only did Natalia Lebedeva not offer her article to *Literaturnaya Gazeta*, but she also did not consider it necessary to even mention its editorial board, which had given her such vital help; this, however, is not what really matters. (As a matter of fact, she did mention my name in her publication of May 6, 1990, but still there were no apologies in it.) Naturally, any struggle for individual pre-eminence in covering such a theme as Katyn is completely out of place, to say the least, and I would most probably have kept silent if considerations of momentary advantage had not prevented Lebedeva from displaying the necessary impartiality.

Let us now, however, take a closer look at the documents.

ESCORT GUARD TROOPS
OF THE NKVD OF THE USSR

A Historical Outline

The history of the escort guard troops began on April 20, 1918. On that day, the Russian Republic's escort guards, incorporating *gubernia* (province) and *uyezd* (district) escort guard companies, were formed by Order 284 of the People's Commissariat for Military Affairs. At the same time, Chief Inspectorate of Escort Guards was set up under the Chief Administration for Places of Confinement of the People's Commissariat of Justice.[3] This structure did not exist for long. As early as July 23 of the same year, the Chief Administration for Places of Confinement was transformed into a Punitive Department of the People's Commissariat of Justice, and the Chief Inspectorate into an 8th Section of the Punitive Department (circular letter of the People's Commissariat of Justice of May 24, 1918, [4] and Order 466 of the People's Commissariat for Military Affairs of June 18, 1918).[5] On September 9, 1919, by Resolution 168 of the People's Commissariat of Justice, the Punitive Department was renamed the Central Punitive Department[6] and its 8th Section, the Department for the Administration of Escort Guards. "It was only in July 1924," writes Alexander Solzhenitsyn (I have not verified this information), "that military discipline and manning through the People's Commissariat for Military and Naval Affairs were introduced in the escort guard corps by a decree of the All-Union Central Executive Committee and the Council of People's Commissars." In any case, as of July 19, 1924, there existed a USSR Administration for Escort Guards under the Head of the RSFSR Administration for Places of Confinement. On October 30, 1925, it was named the USSR Central Administration for Escort Guards and in March 1930, the USSR Central Administration for Escort Guard Troops under the Council of People's Commissars of the USSR.[7]

By a resolution of the Central Executive Committee and the Council of People's Commissars of September 17, 1934, the Central Administration for Escort Guard Troops was disbanded and its duties entrusted to the Chief Administration for Frontier and Internal Security Guards of the NKVD of the USSR. Finally, on March 16, 1939, a Chief Administration for Escort Guard Troops of the NKVD of the USSR was installed.

From the moment of its establishment, the Chief Administration for Escort Guard Troops of the NKVD was headed by Brigade Commander (subsequently Lieutenant General) Vladimir Sharapov, who, together with a number of other top executives of the NKVD, was decorated with the Order of the Red Star in April 1940. Everything seems to indicate that Vladimir Sharapov was an able commander who coped excellently with the tasks set before him, making it possible for him to continue at his post until July 1941. At a conference of operations section commanders with the participation of representatives of a number of People's Commissariate of the USSR, on the escorting and transportation of prisoners under guard, held in Moscow in November 1940, one of Sharapov's subordinates, by the name of Shelgunov, said: "Our task is to find fundamental questions in reorganization of our work. We also have sufficient conversation and even some to spare when we hear that there is an established order, a tradition which should not be broken. This is wrong. And Major General Sharapov often rebukes us for our lack of daring and creative thinking."[8]

By that time, the escort guard troops were a complex, highly organized and well-adjusted mechanism with its own infrastructure, a system of ranks and reporting. It was a mechanism which never stopped working and which functioned with the greatest precision. In January 1941, escort guard troop units were stationed in 130 locations. They stood guard over 113 NKVD prisons and 23 POW camps. Every day 60 echelon convoys, 176 scheduled convoys and an average of 30 special convoys (those for the transfer of particularly dangerous state criminals) started out. People were brought under guard to the court sessions of 154 judicial organs, to 113 railway stations and landing stages to be exchanged for other prisoners from convoys in transit (data from the 2nd quarter of 1940), and to construction sites and industrial enterprises. Besides, escort guard troops guarded the storage facilities of the Chief Administration of Military Supply of the NKVD, of which there were 27 in the middle of 1940.

As of September 1, 1939, the numerical strength of the escort guard troops was 28,800.

An extract from Order 31 of December 10, 1939, to the escort guard troops reads as follows:

A high level of organization and mobility was displayed by the units of the 13th Division and the 15th Brigade, which managed within a very short space of time to switch over to the escorting and guarding of prisoners of war. The task set by the People's Commissar of Internal Affairs of the USSR was performed excellently, without allowing a single escape, by the units of the 13th, 14th, 15th, 17th and 19th brigades. Full marks to them for that.[9]

An extract from a service state report of the escort guard troops of the NKVD of the USSR for the 1st quarter of 1940 reads:

Chapter 1

The 1st quarter of 1940 was characterized by heavy work load for the 11th, 12th, 14th, 15th and 16th brigades and for the 13th Division. The increase in the work load of the troops of the said informations is due to their performing special missions assigned to them by the People's Commissar of Internal Affairs of the USSR, i.e., guarding the reception stations and prisoner-of-war camps and escorting special resettlers from the Western regions of the Ukrainian SSR and the Byelorussian SSR."[10]

An extract from the log of the 15th Separate Rifle Brigade of the escort guard troops of the NKVD of the USSR states:

In 1939, in connection with the setting up of the Byelorussian Front (September 17), the brigade was assigned the mission of guarding and escorting White Polish prisoners of war. Over the period of the existence of that front, 58,796 prisoners of war were transported under guard. Before the beginning of the war the units of the brigade continued the transportation of prisoners and special resettlers under guard in echelon and by convoy from the Byelorussian and Lithuanian SSRs.[11]

As a matter of fact, the 136th Battalion was part of the 15th Brigade directly subordinated to the Main Administration for Escort Guard Troops of the NKVD of the USSR.

What was the total number of Polish POWs held on Soviet territory? At a session of the Supreme Soviet on Octber 31, 1939, Vyacheslav Molotov reported that Red Army units had captured about 250,000 Polish servicemen in the course of the September campaign. Zawodny and Lojek give a more accurate figure of 230,670, which was raised to 250,000 as a result of mass arrests conducted on

26

the territories that were incorporated into the Soviet Union under the Soviet-German treaty on friendship and the border. (See also Stefan Zwoliński's work giving the following data on Polish army losses in the defensive war of 1939: over 70,000 killed and died of wounds, about 130,000 wounded, and more than 400,000 captured by the Germans and over 230,000 by the Soviets.)[12] According to Lebedeva, the number of POWs held on Soviet territory was 130,242.

In point of fact, however, the very same records of the Main Administration for Escort Guard Troops to which she refers give another figure, 226,391.[13] As we can see, this figure practically coincides with the estimate made by Polish experts and with official Soviet information. The difference between this figure and the one given by Lebedeva is 96,149. And yet, and I will stress once again, both she and I used the same archive documents.

In addition to Molotov's address, there is yet another Soviet source, the newspaper *Krasnaya Zvezda* of September 17, 1940. The editorial in that issue, devoted to the first anniversary of the liberation campaign, says: "Within the space of 12 to 15 days the enemy was completely defeated and destroyed. During that period the Nth group of troops of the Ukrainian Front alone captured 10 generals, 52 colonels, 72 lieutenant colonels, 5,131 commissioned officers, 4,096 NCOs, and 181,223 privates of the Polish army in the course of the battle operations and encirclement," a total of 190,584. In quoting these datum, Józef Mackiewicz notes that this figure does not include members of the police force, gendarmerie, and frontier guard corps, or persons arrested individually. It should be added that, together with those who were allowed to leave for their homes (42,400), the total number came to some 233,000 and, together with those shot and killed, to 248,000. I will refrain from any further manipulations with figures. Yet there is a striking coincidence here, namely the 5,131 captured officers (*Krasnaya Zvezda*) and the 15,131 persons shot dead (Central State Special Archives). You get the impression that *Krasnaya Zvezda* simply left out a figure, and that this is an ordinary misprint. It should also be noted that in the process of calculation, a difference of several hundred or even one or two thousand may arise; there are persons who were convicted or held on espionage and other charges in Article 58 of the RSFSR Criminal Code. These people dropped out of the category of prisoners of war and subsequently appeared in the documents as particularly dangerous state criminals.

The Red Army command was for the first time faced with the need to transport and house huge numbers of prisoners of war. We can assume that even professionals in whose care they were soon placed were nonplussed. It was not in vain, however, that Brigade Commander Sharapov called on his subordinates to display more daring and creative thinking. By September 22, 1939, as many as eight prison camps and also 138 transit camps were set up in European Russia especially for prisoners of war. Each prison camp was designed to accommodate 10,000; the fact, however, that, say, the Putivl camp was overcrowded[14] seems to indicate that the prisoners were "packed tighter" whenever the necessity arose. In July 1940, there were already 17 POW camps and, by the end of 1940, as many as 23. By that time, the numerical strength of the escort guard troops had already reached 38,280.

All the POWs were placed under the authority of an Administration for the Affairs of Prisoners of War of the NKVD of the USSR especially established for the purpose. It was headed by State Security Captain Pyotr Soprunenko. Among other things, the exchange of prisoners with Germany fell within his competence. The exchange was launched in keeping with a resolution of the Council of People's Commissars of October 14, 1939, and in accordance with a resolution of November 14, 1939, a joint Soviet-German commission for exchange was set up. The exchange was continued through the Brest checkpoint until June 1941.

While they waited for their fate to be decided, the POWs worked, in particular, on the construction of the Novograd-Volynsky-Lvov highway, at the Krivoi Rog and Zaporozhye integrated iron-and-steel works and in the Donbass coal mines. At the time, quite a number of escapes were made, and in the documents of the Main Administration for Escort Guard Troops, it was noted that their number was growing. Thus, for example, in the first quarter of 1940, a total of 112 prisoners escaped from the construction of the highway, which was guarded by the 229th Escort Guard Regiment; out of this number 18 were apprehended, five wounded and two killed. Between April 1 and April 26, again from the same place, 23 persons escaped (five of whom were apprehended and one wounded while being arrested). More often than not, successful escapes were made during the transportation of prisoners. Here is a description of a typical incident given in an

Chapter 1

operative information summary of the Main Administration for Escort Guard Troops dated October 7/14, 1940:

On June 10, 1940, at 1:00 am 6 km from Vilno 2 interned corporals of the former Polish army being transported under guard in a convoy escorted by servicemen of the 226th Regiment of the 15th Brigade (convoy commander Battalion Commissar Comrade Peisachenko) jumped out of a freight car through a manhole while the train was moving.

An operative party headed by Section Commander V. I. Smirnov, with his patrol dog Lux, was immediately detailed to pursue the escapees. The patrol dog got onto the scent and, having followed it for 2 km, came to a main road and refused to proceed further.

The escapees were not apprehended.[15]

There is a record of a number of cases where escapees were harbored by the population of Eastern Poland. The operative information summary of November 10, 1940, made it incumbent upon the personnel of escort parties to "assess critically the statements of local inhabitants, in particular, of those living in the western regions of the Ukrainian and Byelorussian SSRs." Let me also quote a description of an abortive escape attempt, which was mentioned in Order 2 of January 10, 1940, to the escort guard troops:

On December 21, 1939, four prisoners of war working at construction project No.1* tried to make an escape from the escort guards of the 229th Regiment.

---

*Construction of the Novograd-Volynsky-Lvov highway.

One of the escapees was shot dead by the escorts, another was wounded and the rest continued running to escape.

Red Army man Zhukov rushed off in pursuit of the escapees. In spite of the frost, he threw off his greatcoat and boots to make progress easier and, 7 kilometers from the place of work, he killed the first of the escapees with a shot from his rifle, then apprehended the second and returned him to the camp.

As a reward for his worthy performance of duty I award Zhukov, Red Army man of the 229th Regiment, a citation and bonus to the sum of 200 rubles.

This order shall be announced to the entire personnel of the units of the escort guard troops of the NKVD.

> Colonel Krivenko, Acting Commander of the Main Administration for Escort Guard Troops, Chief of Staff of Escort Guard Troops of the NKVD Brigade Commissar Shnitkov, Chief of the Political Section [16]

You can well imagine what would have been in store for Red Army man Zhukov if he had been a less enduring runner and a worse shot. Could anyone have brought himself to say that Zhukov ran his seven-kilometer race without boots and greatcoat out of lofty ideological considerations? Or that he ran in order to get a bonus? Because he wanted to distinguish himself? Because he hated the enemy? Anything is possible, but there is a limit to everything. He was driven by the fear of punishment: I cannot find any other explanation for his behavior.

It was this document which shook my attitude to the escort guard troops of that period. Having realized its true meaning, I went again through the entire archives of the

Chapter 1

Main Administration for Escort Guard Troops and now I can state with good reason that the conditions of service in the escort guard troops of the NKVD were unbearably hard. I do not mean the commanding officers (they were professionals), but the rank-and-file Red Army men who were drafted into the army and who, by the will of the high command, found themselves playing the part of prisoner guards of which I am now speaking. Any one of them might have found himself on the other side of the barbed wire if he had displayed insufficient enthusiasm for his work or showed ordinary sympathy for those held under guard. This was exactly what a *Summary of Breaches Committed in Performance of Duty* noted. Besides such minor breaches of duty (quite common in the army) as falling asleep while on guard, absence without leave or the loss of one's weapon, it had a special paragraph (it was a printed blank form) headed "Contacts with Prisoners and Display of Sympathy for them." Which means that such "displays of sympathy" were not a rare occurence. This is what happened to those who could not stifle the voice of mercy:

On June 27 of this year (1940—*Author*), one Shkolnikov, Red Army man of the 152nd Separate Battalion of the 17th Brigade, while standing guard in a prison, established contact with a prisoner under investigation accused of a counter revolutionary crime and had long talks with her.

Not confining himself to this, while standing on June 30 and July 3 of this year, Shkolnikov once again established contact with the prisoner and imparted to her certain information which must not be divulged, and was given by her an assignment to communicate certain information to her acquaintances.

To do this, Shkolnikov personally, on behalf of the prisoner, wrote a letter to her aquaintances, which was found on him during a search and confiscated.

This is how it was: "established contact," "was given by her an assignment to communicate information". . . . What kind of state secret could be divulged by an ordinary Red Army man assigned to guard a "counter revolutionary" under investigation? Not much other than the date of his next watch: on the third day after two days off. And yet a voluntary informer appeared who was unscrupulous enough to inform on him. Shkolnikov was neither reprimanded nor detailed for an extra duty nor confined in a guardhouse cell.

...The Chelyabinsk Regional Military Tribunal of the Troops of the NKVD sentenced Shkolnikov to 3 years of imprisonment.[17]

Don't you dare sympathize with prisoners!
Following is a story whose ending is less harsh—perhaps because the main character in it was a commanding officer (summary of June 13, 1940):
"In escorting an echelon convoy by the 148th Separate Battalion (convoy commander Captain Asiryan) a guard, wishing to frighten a woman prisoner who persisted in attempting to get into conversation with passers-by, scratched her eyebrow with a bayonet.
"The brigade command proposed penalizing the culprit."

Chapter 1

This extreme accuracy seems to me very suspicious. Could it not be that the guard took aim at her eye? The story, however, does not end here.

"The improper conduct of the convoy commander, Captain Asiryan, should also be noted. The latter, having found out what had happened, sent the Red Army man to apologize to the injured prisoner.

"The brigade commander imposed a penalty on the captain for his improper conduct."[18]

Do not play gentlemen before passers-by! Characteristically, the proper authorities were once informed, this time by someone from among the captain's subordinates. It appears that not only was it the case that senior officers educated their juniors, but also the other way around.

Documents of this sort can be quoted endlessly. Does the reader not find, however, that his perception becomes less acute and that he instead develops a cool academic interest? Let me remind you that we are now talking about things which are tragic.

Naturally, there were occurrences of an entirely different sort as well. There is no sense, however, in dwelling upon them, because they have been described more than once in memoirs, whereas the summaries of the Main Administration for Escort Guard Troops only recorded emergencies that were not characteristic of the overall picture. As a rule, prisoners did not bring any complaints against escort guards, of which an appropriate record was made in prisoner transfer papers.

For fairness' sake, it should be noted that escort guards treated prisoners of war more leniently than they did their

The Prose of Death

own compatriots. It can be presumed that there existed appropriate instructions to this effect, although I have not found any trace of them in the archives. Persons being deported from the USSR were treated well. Among documents of this category I came across a text which may even be regarded as funny. Here is an extract from a summary dated October 7/14, 1940:

> On August 31, 1940, a special escort party of three men from the 236th Regiment of the 14th Division (escort commander Junior Political Instructor Yakushev) was in a passenger compartment on its way from Moscow to Odessa. During the journey, the escort commander warned the passengers against conversing with one another, since the escorted woman was going abroad. He also told some of the passengers that she was French by nationality, that she had been in prison in Moscow for 2 years and that now she was being deported. He asked the passengers whether there were escort guard units in Odessa.
>
> Thereby a military secret was divulged during the carrying out of an important assignment.[19]

You can well imagine Junior Political Instructor Yakushev, who had just broken out of the gloomy world of prison convoys and punishment cells, was now brimming with pride over the assignment given him! In this particular case, it was probably someone from among the passengers who displayed this vigilance. Once again, a woman was the cause of trouble. Incidentally, it should be noted that she was being transported under guard in an ordinary train compartment. The description of the same occurrence

35

is to be found in another document, the minutes of the conference that was mentioned above:

Comrade Vorobyov (1st Special Section): The case is as follows: in the month of August a certain Vertkovskaya was being transported under guard from Moscow to Odessa. It was simply an outrageous case. Perhaps the escort guards were insufficiently instructed, and so began telling everyone not to speak to the woman, saying that she was being deported from the Soviet Union and that she was a dangerous criminal. This gives rise to a belief that what the NKVD does is arrest people and deport them from the Soviet Union. This escort guard appears to be quite an experienced one: so why did he start talking like this? This seems strange.[20]

So this is what Political Instructor Yakushev's sin was: he put the idea into the passengers' heads that the NKVD banished people instead of punishing them. As a result, the reputation of this formidable people's commissariat suffered. In effect, Yakushev slandered the punitive organs! This unprecedented case was brought to the notice of the NKVD's leadership; it was mentioned as an example during briefings and used as a bugaboo to frighten newly-drafted servicemen. What kind of punishment Yakushev underwent is still not known.

And it certainly goes without saying that the most privileged prisoners were the Germans, who were transported to Brest to be handed over to the German authorities. As a matter of fact, they were fully aware of this. Here is a paper which opened an exhausting exchange of official letters:

Top secret
To Comrade Krivenko,
Brigade Commander,
Deputy Chief of the Main
Administration for Escort
Guard Troops of the NKVD,
City of Moscow

March 7
No.9/10/0109

The German embassy in Moscow has applied to the NKVD with a request to return to Konrad Kinder, a German national deported from the USSR, his underclothes, confiscated during his arrest.

The suitcase with the underclothes (an inventory of same is attached hereto) was handed over to Junior Lieutenant Gursky, commander of an escort party from the 236th Regiment, who signed for it, on December 20, 1939, during Kinder's transportation under guard from Moscow to Brest. During a check made in the prison and at the Brest checkpoint the suitcase with the underclothes belonging to Kinder was not found.

In order to report to People's Commissar of State Security of the USSR Comrade Merkulov, you are ordered to establish immediately when and where the underclothes belonging to German national Konrad Kinder were handed in by escort party commander Comrade Gursky.

Advise of the results.

State Security Major Bashtakov, Head of the 2nd Department of the USSR People's Commissariat of State Security State Security Junior Lieutenant Kruglov, Head of the 5th Section.[21]

Chapter 1

Just imagine: People's Commissar Merkulov himself looked into the matter concerning the suitcase of an obscure German, a suitcase which contained nothing but underclothes! Could it really be that they were afraid to anger German ambassador Count Friedrich von Schulenburg with the loss of some underwear? What we see here is a case of Big Time Politics in which even the least detail is of tremendous importance. Stern messages flew around to the command of the 11th Brigade and from the regiment; Junior Lieutenant Gursky wrote explanatory notes, trying to call to mind the ill-fated suitcase which he had held in his hands more than a year before. Moscow, however, was not satisfied and Gursky was summoned to the capital in person. What's more, the order was given to interrogate the Red Army men from that same escort party who, naturally, had been demobilized by that time.... All this nonsense took up no less paper than all the Soviet-German treaties along with the corresponding protocols.

Let us, however, turn to the Poles. As I have already mentioned, their treatment was initially quite correct (which is confirmed by A. A. Lukin in his letter). Later on, however, it became harsher. One of the proofs is to be found in the operative information summary of November 10, 1940:

On August 12 of this year, while searching a prisoner of war being transported to a prison in Moscow, 2,322 grams of gold was found to be in his possession. The gold was sewn into two linen belts. Before that, the prisoner of war was several times transported under guard. First, from the Shepetovka Station to the Starobelsk camp and then from Starobelsk to the Yukhnov camp, from the Yukhov camp to Gryazovets, and from Gryazovets to Moscow.

The said fact shows that searches made by the escorting personnel are of poor quality, for which reason the concealed gold was not found earlier.

Indeed, this was an unprecedented case: what was that gold, in what form and where did it come from? There is no point in making conjectures and there is no additional information. Also of note is the fact that the prisoner of war has been transferred so many times from one camp to another. As a matter of fact, prisoners were actually quite often transferred from one place to another; in each camp and also in the regional departments of the NKVD, in Moscow, Kiev, and Minsk, investigators worked with the Poles, instituted proceedings against them and searched for their accomplices; intelligence and counterintelligence also took an interest in the prisoners (more on this subject will follow later). On the other hand, the prisoners were sorted, for example, according to occupation.

The command personnel of the troops must pay attention to making more thorough searches of prisoners of war being received from camps.

Future search of prisoners of war are to take place on the same basis as that of other prisoners.[22]

From which it follows that before the middle of November 1940, prisoners of war were searched on some special basis.

Chapter 1

Fate of Prisoners

Let us now concentrate on those prisoners whose tragic fate is the subject of this book. I am referring to those in the Kozelsk, Ostashkov, and Starobelsk camps of the NKVD.

Officers were separated from soldiers even in transit and they were kept in harsher conditions. Here is an excerpt from a letter by Michail Dobrynin from Brest:

> In 1937-1941 I lived in Smolensk. My house was situated near a railway crossing and I remember well how trains carrying Polish prisoners of war used to pass by. Quite often the trains stopped at our crossing and stood there for quite a long time. We boys and some of the adults came close to the trains and spoke to the Poles. Our people brought them food. They gave us Polish coins and joked with us. They were rank-and-file servicemen. On the other side of the tracks temporary barracks were built where the 'nobles' were led under guard. They were mostly army officers but also civilians, including women and children. Contact with them was forbidden, but you could take a look at them from a distance.

First, here are some more figures. It is useless to try to determine the exact number of prisoners held in each camp, because these figures varied all the time. Let me refer to Professor Madajczyk, who had studied all the sources known to exist by the time he began writing his book. His data match in principle the data found in archive documents to within a hundred men, and for Starobelsk, are accurate to a man. According to Madajczyk, approximately 4,500 officers were held in the Kozelsk camp, including four generals, one rear admiral, 400 senior and 3,500 junior officers, and 500 cadets.[23]

The prisoners held in the Starobelsk camp included some 3,900 officers (8 generals, 380 senior and 3,450 junior officers, and 30 cadets) and between 50 and 100 civilians. About 6,570 policemen were confined in the Ostashkov camp. Such was the outcome of the game of patience played by Beria; the camps in Kozelsk and Starobelsk became officers' camps, while the Ostashkov camp specialized in policemen.

As I have already mentioned, the camps were under the jurisdiction of the Administration for the Affairs of Prisoners of War of the NKVD of the USSR. The commandant of the Kozelsk camp was State Security Senior Lieutenant V. N. Korolyov; its commissar, Senior Political Instructor Alexeyev; and its special section head, State Security Senior Lieutenant Elman. An important part in the camp was played by A. Ya. Demidovich, head of the 2nd section.*
Polish sources also mention V. K. Urbanovich, who, according to the documents, held the position of deputy camp commandant for supply and maintenance. Writers of memoirs refer to him as a colonel because of his insignia. In actual fact, however, the three rectangular collar pins of a Red Army colonel corresponded to the rank of state security captain. The commandant of the Starobelsk camp

---

* The 2nd sections of the camps and, accordingly, the 2nd Section of the Administration for the Affairs of Prisoners of War kept a record of "contingents".

was State Security Berezhkov (there is a similar misunderstanding here as with the case of Urbanovich; he is also referred to as a colonel in literature on the subject) and its commissar was Kirshin. The commandant of the Ostashkov camp was State Security Senior Lieutenant Borisovets.

Since we are now talking about personalities, let me also name other characters mentioned in literature, whose names and ranks I have checked against the appropriate documents to give their correct spelling and eliminate errors in the lists made up by the students of the Katyn tragedy (Janusz Kazimierz Zawodny, Louis Fitzgibbon and Leopold Jerzewski).

The commandant of the Gryazovets camp was Senior Battalion Commissar N. I. Khodas; the commandant of the Yukhnov camp, State Security Major Kadyshev; and the head of the Smolensk Regional Department of the NKVD, State Security Major Ye. I. Kupriyanov. State Security Major V. M. Zarubin (referred to as a brigade commander by Polish sources), who is mentioned by all authors without exception, was an operative commissioner of the 2nd Special Section of the NKVD. There was also a man by the name of Rafail Leibkind, who held the rank of state security senior lieutenant; the part that he played in the fate of the POWs is not as yet clear. Documents also mention State Security Lieutenant Filippovich, assistant head of the 1st Special Section of the Smolensk Department of the NKVD. It has been hard to identify Colonel L. Rybak; perhaps this is what Colonel Rybakov, the former commander of the 15th Brigade and in July 1940 Chief of Staff of the Escort Guard Troops of the NKVD of the USSR, is called in the lists. Besides, mentioned among those awarded the medal "For Valiant Labour" by a Decree of the Presidium of the Supreme Soviet of the USSR "On the Decoration of NKVD Workers with USSR Orders and Medals" of April 26, 1940 (*Pravda*, April 27, 1940), is State Security Senior Lieutenant Josif Rybak, whose functions are also unknown. We will go back to the Polish lists later on. Now I would like to give a number of names that have so far not been known to specialists. I confess that the structure of the organs remains a mystery to me in many ways, but I will reproduce the names and numbers of units exactly as they are given in the documents; as for the pecking order, I give it the way I understand it to be.

NKVD Department for the Smolensk Region:
Deputy head of the department—State Security Captain Ilyin
Head of the 1st special section—State Security Lieutenant Karavayev
Head of the 3rd special section—State Security Sergeant Bobchenko
Staff members of the 3rd special section—Lelyanov and Aibinderov
Head of the operative section—State Security Lieutenant Krasinets
Operative commissioner of the department of the NKVD— State Security, Sergeant Razgildeyev
Head of the prison section—State Security Lieutenant Zhamoido*
Deputy head of the prison section—State Security Lieutenant Malov
Head of the detention prison—State Security Lyusy
Commandant of the inner prison—State Security Lieutenant Stelmakh

---

* *In Natalia Lebedeva's publication "The Tragedy of Katyn" (International Affairs,* 1990, No. 5) he is erroneously described as the head of the detention center and his name is incorrectly spelled 'Zhomaido' instead of 'Zhamoido.' In August, 1944, Lieutenant Colonel Zhamoido held the post of deputy head of the NKVD Department for the Smolensk Region.

Chapter 1

Ostashkov Camp:
Inspector of the 2nd section—Galkin

Yukhov Camp:
Commissar—Lavrentyev
Head of the 2nd section—State Security Junior Lieutenant Shul-
zhenkov

Gryazovets Camp:
Head of the 2nd section—Lieutenant Shakhov

Later I shall supplement this list with the names of staff
members of the central apparatus of the NKVD-NKGB.
The persons listed above held positions mentioned in the
list and could not be ignorant of the POWs' fate.

The Kozelsk Chronicle

The archives of the 136th Battalion are not small, nor
are they complete. Some of the documents relating to the
period under discussion were destroyed early in July 1941
by a commission especially set up for the purpose. Incidentally, there is a strange discrepancy between the dates here.
On July 9, 1941, Major General Vladimir Sharapov wrote
to Lieutenant General Maslennikov, Deputy People's
Commissar of Internal Affairs:

In keeping with Order 53 of the People's Commissariat
of Internal Affairs of the USSR of July 6, 1941, on the
disposal of archives, current records and correspondence,
submitted here with your consideration is a statement of
the commission of the Administration for Escort Guard

Troops for selecting archive materials, current records and correspondence which have lost their operational and scientific-historical significance.[24] ("Scientific-historical significance" indeed! General Sharapov must have had second sight.)

It should be noted that Order 157 to the 136th Battalion, by which the commission for selecting documents was set up, was issued on July 5, 1941, and the commission was ordered to begin its work also on July 5 and to finish it on July 6.[25]

It follows that the battalion began destroying its archives before the order from Moscow was received. Or perhaps there was some special instruction for the battalion? In any case, the 1939-1941 archives of the escort guard units which guarded the Starobelsk and Ostashkov camps have not survived at all.

Colonel Terentii Mezhov was in command of the battalion; in January 1941, he was replaced by Major Porfirii Reprintsev. The commissar of the battalion was Senior Political Instructor Mamakh Snitko (Snytko) and its chief of staff was Captain Nikolai Yavorivsky and later, at the beginning of the war, Captain Vladimir Olovyanov.

The battalion had its headquarters in Smolensk at 19 Smirnov Street. Here it kept guard over two NKVD prisons—a detention center and inner prison—and a storehouse. Besides this, the battalion was engaged in echelon, scheduled, in-town (to law courts and to the railway station) and special escorting, and also drew inner guard duty. Its numerical strength was 404 men in the first quarter of 1940, and this did not change a great deal before the end of the year. In the second half of the year, there was a substantial increase in the number of echelon convoys (53 in the fourth quarter as compared with 10 in the first quarter of 1940), whereas the number of scheduled convoys varied between 32 and 46 throughout the year. This maximum figure was recorded in the second quarter of the year, which is quite significant.[26]

In 1939 the battalion escorted 9,956 POWs, an indication that this was not its main task. As of September 25, however, one company was detailed for guard duty in the Kozelsk camp. Besides, as I have already mentioned, the battalion kept guard over the Yukhov camp which is more often than not referred to as Pavlishchev Bor by Polish sources.* In the first quarter of 1940, a total of 60 men were employed to guard the camps and in the second quarter, 100 (14 posts, which were probably taken in three shifts).

The 136th Battalion had an excellent reputation with the command. During the period in question, its escort parties did not allow a single escape, nor was any other more or less serious breach of duty recorded. There is, however, one mention of a negative fact. "During an inspection," Skorobogatov, secretary of the YCL committee, stated in his report of June 24, 1940, "the YCL members did not demonstrate their superiority in firing submachine guns and Nagant revolvers."[27] The number of awards was far greater. Thus, to mark the 22nd anniversary of the escort guard troops Battalion Dispatcher M. F. Goryachko

---

*In Yukhnov there was a TB sanatorium called Pavlishchev Bor and in Gryazovets a resthome of the Council of Forest Industry, before the POW camps were set up there.

and Assistant Platoon Commander A. I. Plakhotny were presented with valuable gifts and Political Instructor D. G. Zub received a citation in an order to the brigade of April 19, 1940.[28] In the same month (note the dates) I. Ulyanov, a patrol dog guide, was awarded a citation in an order to the brigade "for the skillful use of patrol dog Orka in escorting an echelon convoy on the itirerary Smolensk-Kandalak-sha."[29]

Optina Hermitage

The Optina Hermitage of the Presentation in the Temple has an absolutely exceptional place in the history of Russian culture, theology, and philosophy. There is a huge amount of literature about this cloister, including a number of recent publications such as, for example, a detailed article by Vadim Borisov which appeared in the magazine *Nashe Naslediye*, 1988, No. 4, so the reader may well have some idea about the phenomenon of the Optina Hermitage without any assistance on my part. There is no point in repeating things that are well known; it is enough to clear up obvious misunderstandings and rectify the mistakes which are to be found in present-day publications and which are essential to the subject under discussion.

One of the mistakes concerns the original purpose of the skete,* and another is made by Natalia Lebedeva, who

---

*skete (New Greek), a settlement of Eastern Orthodox monks inhabiting a group of small cottages around a church and dependent upon a parent monastery.

writes that "pilgrims stayed" at the skete. This statement is at variance with the very etymology of the word "skete." The skete of St. John the Baptist, founded in 1820's, housed the cells of famous Optina *startsy.*** The Optina Hermitage also had eight hostel buildings, pulled down after the revolution, which were, of course, situated outside the skete or cloister grounds. It could not have been otherwise, because women were not admitted into the skete. Having opened the appropriate chapter of *The Brothers Karamazov* ("On Arrival at the Monastery"), we will find a topographically accurate description of the road to the skete: the novel's characters are on their way there for a meeting with Starets Zorima, whose prototype was Starets Amvrosy of the Optina Hermitage. Amvrosy's cell has survived to this day, as has another structure of a similar type. In 1939-1941, it accommodated the camp's commanders and in 1943-1956, it housed a special children's home for the children of victims of repression. The escort guards' barrack was in the building which now houses the monastery refectory. In the NKVD documents, the skete was referred to as "territory No. 2." According to former prisoners of the Kozelsk camp, people from the Western Ukraine and Western Byelorussia were confined there.

**starets, pl. startsy (Russ. lit., 'venerable old man'), a spiritual director or religious teacher and counselor in the Eastern Orthodox Church, a spiritual adviser who is not necessarily a priest, but who is recognized for his piety, and who can be approached by monks or members of the laity for spiritual guidance.

There are even more substantial errors than this. I still cannot see what made Nina Chugunova, the author of a first-rate article about the Optina Hermitage (*Ogonyok*, 1989, No. 34), write that this former monastery housed a Young Pioneer camp before the war. Indeed, there was a camp in it before the war, but it had nothing to do with Young Pioneers. I cannot confirm that there was never any Young Pioneer camp on its grounds at all, but then, when speaking about the Optina Hermitage, it is simply impossible not to say even a word about the other camp. In the context of the Katyn issue, this appears tactless, to say the least.

Before the NKVD camp, the monastery buildings housed a sanatorium named after Maxim Gorky. According to Professor Stanisław Swianiewicz, after the POWs were given permission to correspond with their relatives, it was the sanatorium which they were to give as the return address, and the professor views this as some kind of black humor by NKVD officers. Perhaps, initially, some directive to this effect was actually issued. Soon, however, the address of the Kozelsk prisoners was changed; written on envelopes and postcards disinterred from the Katyn graves is "P. O. Box 12, Kozelsk, USSR." A facsimile reproduction of one of these postcards can be seen in Janusz Kazimierz Zawodny's book.

The atmosphere and living conditions in the Kozelsk camp have been described in sufficient detail, including even the schedule of film shows (see *Pamiętniki znalezione w Katyniu*, Editions Spotkania, Paris, 1989), so I will not repeat them; instead, let me describe my own trips to the Optina Hermitage.

Chapter 1

Quite a few people living in the settlement of Optino in the vicinity of the cloister remember the Poles, but their recollections are rather vague. To get more detailed information, I was sent to Klavdia Yaroshenko, née Levashova.

Having listened to my questions, Klavdia Yaroshenko first of all showed me the service record book of her mother Olga Levashova, born 1910, who worked as a laundress first at the sanatorium and then at the NKVD camp. This is confirmed by corresponding entries in her service record book: "July 4, 1939. Hired for work in the laundry... September 20, 1939. Dismissed because of the liquidation of the Gorky Sanatorium." Following which Olga Levashova "worked as a laundress in the NKVD organs" and her discharge is recorded as follows: "July 27, 1941. Dismissed in conformity with Para. A of Article 47 of the Labor Code, Order No. 97. Commandant of the NKVD Camp, State Security Senior Lieutenant (signature)." This is precisely the date of the final liquidation of the Kozelsk Camp.

Klavdia Yaroshenko's elder brother, Valentin, who was subsequently killed at the front, also worked at the camp. He was a projectionist and in the winter of 1939/40 rarely spent his nights at home, staying at the skete most of the time. This means that there were living quarters for enrolled civilian personnel not far from the cottages of the NKVD officers.

According to Klavdia Yaroshenko, the conditions that were created for the POWs were quite good. For example, the bread ration was 800 grams per day (which exactly corresponds to what Swianiewicz said), quite a substantial quantity in those days of scant supplies; at any rate, no one among the local population saw such an abundance.[30] Several of the Poles were given a free rein. This fact has not been noted by a single one of the Polish authors. Yet next to the monastery there stands a water tower, still functioning, designed and built by a Polish engineer from the camp. It is not by hearsay that Klavdia Yaroshenko knows about the water tower; her other brother, Yevgeni, who is still alive today, used to work with that same Pole at the local mechanical plant. In reply to my question about where films were shown, Klavdia Yaroshenko showed me a group photograph of the entire Levashov family at the coffin of her father. The coffin was lying in the Church of St. Mary the Egyptian, naturally a former church. In the days of the sanatorium, from which the photograph dates (1937), it housed a social club. This fact is supported by a quotation from Kosarev, the then YCL leader, written in white letters on a length of red cotton, which can be seen above the relatives of the deceased: "Self-criticism is a Bolshevik way of strengthening our relationships."[31]

While I am about it, here is the repertoire that I copied from Józef Zentina's diary, found among the Katyn graves on the corpse of its owner: *Alexander Nevsky, The Poet and the Tsar, Volga-Volga, We Are from Kronstadt, A Great Citizen, The Year 1919, Mother, The Seagull, The Man with the Gun, Childhood, St. Jorgen's Miracle, My Apprenticeship, Maxim's Return, Lenin in 1918, Chapaev, The Vyborg Side, A Girl of Character, The Circus,* and so on.

Films were shown every other day and, sometimes, two days running. In addition, there is a record of a concert held on February 23, 1939, in which local schoolchildren took part. There is no notable bias in the choice of films, the only exception being *Alexander Nevsky*, completed by Eisenstein in 1938. It was taken off the screen right after the conclusion of the Soviet-German non-aggression pact and put back on only after the outbreak of the war. It can be inferred that this was a kind of a "closed show," probably aimed at enhancing the Poles' anti-German sentiments. If this was actually the case, it cannot be denied that the camp's management was quite far-sighted, as the position of official Soviet propaganda was positevely pro-German at the time.

The late Valentin Levashov was on good terms with the camp's inhabitants. One of the POWs made a mandolin and gave it to him as a gift; he took the mandolin with him when he went to the front, where it was lost in 1943 together with Valentin himself. Klavdia Yaroshenko used to have a small wooden bench, painted many times over, which was also made by one of the POWs, but half a year before we met she gave it to some Poles who came here on a visit.[33]

None of the Optino natives could recollect anything about the events of the spring of 1940, and as for the execution of POWs, they believed it to be quite possible and, considering those hard times, even natural.

The POWs worked in the forest, felling trees for firewood, and in the spring of 1940 they cut down an apple orchard destroyed by frost. Klavdia Yaroshenko also remembers how the Poles were led in file from the camp in the summer of 1941. According to her estimate, there were about 50 of them.

Thus, the sanatorium existed in the Optina Hermitage until September 20, 1939, and the prisoner-of-war camp from September 25, 1939 (the date of sending an escort guard company there), until July 27, 1941. Subsequently, during the war, there was a military hospital in it. Both Olga and Valentin Levashov continued working there: she as a laundress and he, until he was drafted, as a projectionist.

Some details remain to be added to Klavdia Yaroshenko's story.

Most of the Polish POWs held in the USSR were reserve officers mobilized at the beginning of the war. In particular, among the Kozelsk prisoners there were 21 college professors, over 300 army and civilian doctors, more than 100 writers and journalists, many lawyers, engineers and teachers, and also about ten chaplains and one civilian priest. The regime in the camp was rather liberal, although as Swianiewicz writes, "any public worship was strictly forbidden in the camp, therefore our divine services on the appearance of early Christian worship in catacombs." It was precisely this which later prolonged the life of priest Jan Leon Ziółkowski by nearly four months. At the time when priests were being taken out of the camp, he was confined in a punishment cell for performing occasional services; they simply forgot that he was there. The prisoners regularly listened to Soviet radio and read Soviet newspapers, in particular, the Smolensk regional paper *Rabochy Put*. Judging by their diaries, they closely watched developments in Europe. Stanisław Swianiewicz mentions an oral magazine organized by prisoners and edited by Second Lieutenant Leonard Korowajczyk, a student of Vilno University, and First Lieutenant Janusz Libicki, an associate professor of Poznań University (both of these were identified among the Katyn corpses). On March 19, 1940, the feast day of St. Joseph, the magazine was entirely devoted to the memory of Marshal Piłsudski.

"In the camps," observes Leopold Jerzewski, "particularly so in Kozelsk and Starobelsk, the atmosphere was quiet and even optimistic." The transfer of POWs to the allies via one of the neutral countries was regarded as the most likely prospect. At the worst, the Poles believed, they would be handed over to the Germans. In the meantime, the NKVD officers who had arrived from Moscow got to work.

The main content of the NKVD officers' activities in the camp was the processing of the POWs for their subsequent, so-called "operative intelligence processing." A dossier was opened on each POW. The prisoners were interrogated, often several times. Their interrogators were surprisingly well informed about their subjects.

The highest-ranking commanding officer in the team was Brigade Commander Zarubin. He was distinguished from his other colleagues by rare erudition. He spoke several languages and he had a suave manner. "The attitude of these officers (NKVD interrogators—*Author*) towards the prisoners held in Kozelsk was more or less correct," writes Swianiewicz, "but the brigade commander was not only faultless in this respect, but he also had the manners and gloss of a man of the world."[34] Zarubin brought with him a small, but well-selected library of 500 volumes in Russian, French, English, and German, and willingly let the prisoners use it; the library included, for example, the book *The World Crisis* by Winston Churchill, which was extremely popular in the Kozelsk camp. It is interesting to note that State Security Major Zarubin was the only NKVD officer whom the POWs saluted, by order of Division General Henryk Minkiewicz, the highest-ranking officer confined in the camp. The camp command carried out the orders of the brigade commander without question, in particular, those on the transfer of POWs from one barrack to another. Zarubin played his own, minor game of patience. "He reminded me of well-educated gendarme officers of tsarist Russia," notes Swianiewicz and this is, perhaps, the most expressive description of Zarubin.

Zarubin did not just study the contingent carefully, but also made decisions in a number of cases. It is probably he that professor Swianiewicz has to thank for his life. Another Kozelsk prisoner whom the brigade commander liked, law professor Wacław Komarnicki, who subsequently filled the post of Minister of Justice in the Sikorski Cabinet, also survived.

Early in March or in February (according to Lebedeva) Zarubin disappeared from the camp, presumably having completed his mission. Jerzewski believed that he might have become a "victim of yet another Stalin's purges," being a dangerous eyewitness of the "final solution" of the Katyn issue, or that he "successfully survived the war and Stalin and continued to live under another name." Neither of these two hypotheses corresponds to reality. Vassili Zarubin died in Moscow in the mid-1970s under his own name; this information was supplied to me by Lietenant General P. A. Sudoplatov, a former high-ranking NKVD-NKGB officer. He spoke about Vassili Zarubin in the most complimentary terms and confirmed both Zarubin's excellent command of a number of foreign languages and his high erudition. Sudoplatov, however, denied Zarubin's as well as his own involvement in the fate of the Polish prisoners of war.

After Zarubin's departure, the life of the Kozelsk prisoners entered its final stage. None of the camp's commanding officers concealed the fact that a decision had been made, but what the decision was remained a mystery.

As early as December, priests were moved out of the Kozelsk camp, and out of the other camps as well. None of them, with the exception of Ziółkowski and Kantak, has been found either among the living or among the dead. As has already been mentioned, Ziółkowski's corpse was exhumed in Katyn. Kantak survived; he was a citizen of a free city of Gdańsk, which had become the German city of Danzig by then. On March 8, another 14 officers, including Colonel Stanisław Libkind-Lubodziecki, procurator of the Supreme Court; Cavalry Colonel Starzeński, the former military attaché in Belgium; Captain Radziszewski, adviser to a drafting commission; and a Navy First Lieutenant Graniczny. They were brought to the prison of the Smolensk Department of the NKVD and here their tracks were lost. Out of this group only one, who was sent from Smolensk to Kharkov, was lucky enough to survive. On April 3, regular transfers of POWs under guard began, lasting until May 12. Two of the escorted batches, with a total of 245 prisoners, were destined for the Yukhnov camp (Pavlishchev Bor); these people remained alive. The rest of the prisoners lie buried in the Katyn forest. In any case, 2,730 of the 4,143 corpses exhumed in 1943 have been identified. All of them were prisoners of the Kozelsk camp.

Here are a number of significant details. Before their departure, all the POWs were inoculated against typhoid

fever and cholera, apparently in order to calm them down
and suggest to them the idea of their forthcoming transfer
to the West ("which, considering the geographical situation
of Kozelsk, was indeed quite true," notes Jerzewski). Each
party was given dry rations: 800 grams of bread, some
sugar, and three herrings. Judging by the quantity of
bread, this was a day's ration; it took about one day,
including numerous stops and delays, to get to Katyn.
Second Lieutenant Władysław Furtek recalls a mysterious
phrase uttered to him and his fellow prisoners by Demidovich: "Well, this means that you got into good company."
Furtek was taken out of Kozelsk on April 26 in one of the
two escorted parties sent to Yukhnov.

Such is the Polish version of the developments that took
place in the Kozelsk camp in the spring of 1940.

Let us now open the logbook of orders to the 136th
Battalion for the year 1940.

On March 14, Battalion Commander Colonel Mezhov
was requested to go on a mission to the headquarters of the
15th Brigade, stationed in Minsk. On March 18, he
returned to Smolensk and on the same day left for Kozelsk.
It was also on March 18 that Battalion Dispatcher Goryachko, Assistant Platoon Commander Plakhotny, Political
Instructor Zub,* and a company of 48 led by Lieutenant
Khotchenko, commander of the 2nd Company, went to
Kozelsk, to be joined a day later by a company of 45
(commanding officer Junior Platoon Commander Nidelko)

---

*These are the very same three men who received awards a
month later in honor of the 22nd anniversary of the escort guard
troops of the NKVD.

and, in another 10 days, by a company of 12 (commanding officer Sergeant Major Afanasenko).

During the period of Colonel Mezhov's stay in Kozelsk (he returned to Smolensk on May 14), 9 convoys were organized. Of these three were sent to the Yukhnov camp, two to Smolensk, one from Smolensk to Kozelsk, and three from Kozelsk to Gnezdovo, departing on April 8, 16 and 17 (the convoy commanders being Junior Lieutenant Bezmozgy, Section Commander Korablyov and Sergeant Major Gridnevsky, respectively). There was definitely no camp in the environs of Gnezdovo. On the other hand, in those parts there was, and still is, the Katyn forest or, rather, the part of it known as Kozyi Gory (Goats' Mountains) where the mass graves of Polish POWs were subsequently found.

Let us first take a look at the Kozelsk-Yukhnov convoys. All three of them departed from the camp on May 12. This date coincides with the date mentioned in Polish sources. It was precisely on that day that the last prisoners, who were transported first to the Yukhnov and then to the Gryazovets camp, were moved out of Kozelsk. There were about 95 of them. According to documents, there were 30 prison guards plus three commanding officers. This was more than enough. While studying some other papers, I established that normally there were about 15 prisoners per guard when they were transported in a prison car, that is, a Stolypin car. The situation with the convoys headed for Gnezdovo appears to be more complicated. The dates also coincide, but the numbers in the convoys are too few. The convoys travelling from Kozelsk to Smolensk should also be included among them, yet even in this case the numbers of prisoners and guards will remain incommensurable. Here is a table in which I have combined data from Polish and Soviet archive sources:

Polish sources			Documents of the Central State Archives of the Soviet Army		
Date	Destination	Number of prisoners	Itinerary	Number of prison guards	Convoy commander
April 8	Gnezdovo	277	Kozelsk - Smolensk	8	Koptev
			Kozelsk - Gnezdovo		Bezmozgy
April 9	Gnezdovo	270	Kozelsk - Smolensk	1	Ardelyan
April 16	Gnezdovo	420	Kozelsk - Gnezdovo	7	Korablyov
April 17	Gnezdovo	294	Kozelsk - Gnezdovo	4	Gridnevsky
May 12	Yukhnov	95	Kozelsk - Yukhnov	7	Bogdanov
			Kozelsk - Yukhnov	12	Tikhonov
			Kozelsk - Yukhnov	11	Tatarenko

Chapter 1

Whereas the escort parties of the two convoys that departed on April 8, numbering 16 persons, could handle 277 prisoners, the escort parties of the convoys with departures on April 9, 16, and 17 simply could not accomplish the task.

There was also a convoy under the command of Junior Lieutenant Tikhonov, traveling in the opposite direction from Smolensk to Kozelsk, which departed on April 9 and returned to Smolensk on April 21. It can be presumed that prisoners were transported in this convoy out of rather than into the camp. On April 19 and 20, convoys of 304 and 344 persons respectively departed from Kozelsk, and there were 20 Red Army men in Tikhonov's escort party. Yet there still remain 14 Kozelsk-Gnezdovo convoys recorded in Polish sources but not confirmed in any way by the archives of the 136th Battalion, not to mention the small number of prisoner guards in three out of the nine escort parties which I identified. No part of the logbook of orders could have been removed from it, nor was anything crossed out, so it has to be assumed that the battalion was assisted by another escort guard unit. There is some information to indicate that it was the 226th Regiment of the 15th Brigade, stationed in Minsk (regiment commander Major Nikifor Sukhovets). It has not been possible to verify this information, since the earliest surviving archives of the regiment date from 1941.

Among cases of transporting particularly dangerous state criminals, a mention of Colonel Lubodziecki was found. This is a separate subject and a separate mystery. On the night of March 3, an escort party of 15 led by Junior Lieutenant Koptev departed from Kozelsk Station. They were ordered to deliver and put at the disposal of the commandant of the Smolensk prison a convoy of 202 POWs. According to a receipt signed by the officer of the day at the prison on March 11, however, only four POWs and two parcels were actually delivered. What became of the rest of the prisoners and why it took the escort party so long to get to Smolensk is not known.

Who were those four men? They were Colonel Stanisław Lubodziecki, born 1879, file No. 1153 (the register even has his home address as 20 Mickiewicz Street, Apt. 3, Warsaw); Captain Leopold Lichnowski, born 1894, file No. 3806;* Julian Wansowski (or Wąsowski); and Marian Gowiak (or Gawiak). Thus, the date that Lubodziecki was sent from Kozelsk is March 3, not March 8, as memoir writers indicate. From the Smolensk prison, Colonel Lubodziecki and Captain Lichnowski were sent on March 14 by way of Kharkov to Kiev to be put at the disposal of the 3rd Section of the State Security Department of the Ukraine NKVD (escort commander Military Technician 1st Class Shifrin) and Wąsowski and Gowiak were sent on March 15 to the Ostashkov camp (escort commander Junior Lieutenant Pikalev).

Finally, we have yet another document available, Battalion order 119a of May 21, 1940. Here is its full text:

In the period between March 23 and May 13, 1940, the 2nd Company and the 1st Platoon of the 1st Company carried out one of the main tasks set by the Main Administration for Escort Guard Troops and the brigade command for déconcentrating the Kozelsk prisoner-of-war camp of the NKVD. Despite all the intensity and complexity of the work both in escorting prisoners

---

*In Adam Moszyński's lists Captain Lichnowski is shown among the prisoners of the Starobelsk camp.

Chapter 1

and in guarding the camp itself, the task of deconcentrating the camp without allowing a single escape by a prisoner of war or any breaches of duty, was achieved and the work carried out was highly rated by Colonel Comrade STEPANOV, a representative of the Main Administration for Escort Guard Troops of the NKVD of the USSR. Particularly exemplary performance of the task of guarding and escorting prisoners during that period was displayed by the following comrades: TATARENKO, Section Commander of the 2nd Company, who exceptionally, efficiently, thoroughly and ably carried out the serious and important role of operational team commander which he was commissioned to perform in this operation. Comrade KORABLYOV, Section Commander of the 2nd Company, who served splendidly as a convoy commander. Junior Lieutenant Comrade BEZMOZGY, Platoon Commander of the 1st Company, who coped with the task perfectly despite performing the duties of a convoy commander for the first time ever; in addition, the entire personnel of the platoon commanded by Junior Lieutenant Comrade BEZMOZGY took part in performing this task and carried it out excellently, without a single breach of duty. Junior Lieutenant Comrade KOPTEV, Platoon Commander of the 2nd Company, acting as a convoy commander, coped excellently with the task set before him. For this I am awarding them a citation and a bonus: Comrade TATARENKO, 70 rubles, Comrade KORABLY-OV, 50 rubles, BEZMOZGY, 70 rubles, KOPTEV, 70 rubles.

Red Army men of the 2nd Company, Comrades PAVLENKO, GAVRILOV, DUBROV, PROKOFIEV, PANOV, ZACHAROV, and SHARIN, and Red Army men of the 1st Company Comrades ANTROPOV, KHRAMTSOV, PONOMARYOV, SHCHUKIN and KUCHUMOV performed their duties excellently, and for this I am awarding them a citation plus bonus of 50 rubles to PAVLENKO, and 10-day home leave to ZAKHAROV, SHARIN, ANTROPOV, KHRAMTSOV, PONOMARYOV, KUCHUMOV, and SHCHUKIN. I am also awarding a citation and a bonus of

25 rubles each to Comrades GAVRILOV, DUBROV and PROKOFIEV.

Battalion Dispatcher Comrade GORYACHKO carried out his work exceptionally efficiently, seriously and ably, and for this I am awarding him a citation.

> Colonel MEZHOV,
> Battalion Commander
> Senior Political Instructor SNYTKO,
> Battalion Military Commissar
> Lieutenant UGLOV,
> Deputy Battalion Chief of Staff[35]

And so for the *deconcentration of the camp*. (In the report by YCL secretary Skorobogatov, which was already mentioned above, we can read: "the task of *partial* deconcentration of the camp was performed well," though this, however, could be understood as partial participation in its unloading).

Note the names which are already familiar to us: Tatarenko,[36] Korablyov, Bezmozgy, Koptev, Goryachko. As for Red Army men Pavlenko, Gavrilov, Prokofiev, Zakharov, and Dubrov; they were members of the teams which left for Kozelsk after the battalion commander on March 18 and 19. The Colonel Stepanov mentioned in the order was the head of the 1st Section of the 1st Department of the Headquarters of Escort Guard Troops of the NKVD of the USSR. In Lebedeva's opinion, it was the very same "tall black-haired NKVD colonel with a big, fleshy face," described by Swianiewicz, who supervised the deconcentration of the camp upon Zarubin's departure. One might agree with this if we had a portrait of Stepanov at our disposal. I will only note the following. As I have already mentioned, the Poles had a vague idea of the special ranks of state security officers. There was no such rank as "NKVD

Chapter 1

colonel" and the collar pins of an army colonel corresponded to the rank known as "state security captain." Thus, it
might have been, for example, Kupriyanov, the head of the
Smolensk Department of the NKVD, or a colonel, Mezhov
and not Stepanov.

What happened at Gnezdovo Station, not far from
Smolensk, is described in his reminiscences by Professor
Swianiewicz, who was brought here from the camp along
with the April 29 convoy. On April 30, at dawn, the train
of six Stolypin cars reached Smolensk and then, after a
brief stop, continued on its way. "Having traveled several
dozen kilometers, the train came to a stop. The sound of
commands, noise created by the movement of many people
and the sound of automobile engines were heard outside."
About half an hour later an "NKVD colonel" entered the
car and ordered Swianiewicz to follow him.

Having got out of the car, I smelled the pungent smells
of spring from the fields and coppices where snow still lay
here and there. It was a wonderful morning, and a skylark
was singing its song high up in the sky. There was a station
not far from where we stood, but there was not a soul to be
seen there. Our locomotive had already been uncoupled
and had moved away. Some sounds were heard from the
other side of the train, but I could not see what was
happening there. The colonel asked me if I would care for
a cup of tea...."

Having locked Swianiewicz in a compartment of one of
the cars that had already been vacated, the colonel ordered
a Red Army man to keep watch over the prisoner and
bring him some boiling water, after which he went away.
Swianiewicz climbed up into the upper berth and began
watching the scene outside through a ventilation slot. (The

prison car, dubbed the Stolypin car, was described in detail by Solzhenitsyn in *The Gulag Archipelago*, to which the reader is referred). He saw that the area next to the train was surrounded by Red Army men wearing NKVD uniforms.[37]

At half hour intervals, a bus whose windows were painted over with white paint pulled up to the train and stopped alongside the carriage so that the prisoners could get into it without stepping on the ground. In the center of the area of ground stood the NKVD colonel and, a bit further on next to the Black Maria, an NKVD captain, who was subsequently identified as the commandant of the inner prison of the Smolensk Department of the NKVD. Soon guards came to fetch Swianiewicz and then, accompanied by the captain, he was taken to the prison and from there, on May 5, to the Lubyanka. (Here the same kind of misunderstanding in respect of ranks is to be observed. The commandant of the inner prison was State Security Lieutenant Stelmakh, who wore single, rectangular collar pins, the same as an army captain).

Some of the memoirists mention inscriptions left by Kozelsk prisoners on the walls of the prison cars. One of them, scratched with a pencil or a match, was found by Władysław Furtek, who is already familiar to the reader; he left the camp on April 26. It read: "Leaving the train at the second station after Smolensk and getting on trucks," followed by a date which he could not make out—April 12 or maybe April 17. Another incription was found in his prison car by R–cz, a lawyer from Vilno, who was transported from Mołodechno to Połotsk on June 27, 1940. This time the text was written with an indelible pencil: "We are leaving the train not far from Smolensk and put on trucks." Naturally, both inscriptions were in Polish.

Chapter 1

I must say that at first sight these stories seemed to me slightly implausible—they could hardly be added to a file—and I hesitated about making a mention of them in this book. Fortunately, an archive document turned up which not only confirmed the fact that such inscriptions actually existed, but also explained their origin. A political dispatch addressed to Merkulov says:

It has been established that the top-ranking officers of the former Polish army being held in the camp gave instructions to the officers who departed in the first batches to write inscriptions in the carriages indicating their destination so that those who would be transported after them could find out where they were headed.

On April 7, on the return of the first carriages, an inscription in Polish reading "Second batch: Smolensk, April 6, 1940" was found.

(...) An order has been given to remove all inscriptions and in the future to inspect the cars.

There is yet another testimony, a diary of Major Adam Solski (member of the convoy departing on April 7). The entry dated April 8 reads:

At 12:00 o'clock we are standing on a side track in Smolensk. On April 9, a command for reveille and preparation for departure was given in the prison cars. We are being transferred somewhere by truck. What next? Ever since the break of dawn things have been developing rather strangely. A transfer in the boxes of a Black Maria (it's frightening). We were brought somewhere into a forest like an out-of-town resort. We were searched thoroughly. They were interested in my wedding ring and took away the rubles that I had, and also my belt, my penknife and my watch, which showed the time to be 6:30...

The entry ends abruptly at this point. Major Solski lies buried in the Katyn Forest. The diary was found on his corpse by Gerhard Butz, Professor of Forensic Medicine, who was the first to open the Katyn graves.

This, in fact, is all there is to it.

Let us now try to analyze and, if possible, supplement these texts.

To begin with, here are some facts about Swianiewicz. The professor is still lost in conjectures as to why he was left alive and why, for that matter, he was not taken out of the camp together with one of the two convoys sent to Yukhnov. There are some documents on this subject.

On April 27, Soprunenko, the head of the Administration for the Affairs of Prisoners of War, received an order from Deputy People's Commissar Merkulov to prevent the transporting of Swianiewicz to Smolensk immediately. On May 3, he also received an instruction from Kupriyanov, the head of the Smolensk Department of the NKVD, which reads as follows:

> Transport detainee Stanisław Swianiewicz, now being held in the inner prison of the Department of the NKVD, on the first prison car to depart and place him at the disposal of State Security Senior Major Comrade Fedotov, the head of the 2nd Section of the Main Administration for State Secutiry of the NKVD of the USSR.

On May 4, yet another paper on the same subject, ordering the transportation of Swianiewicz under guard to the inner prison of the NKVD of the USSR, was received. The professor was escorted to the Lubyanka prison by three guards led by Lieutenant Voloshenko. On May 6 the escort party commander telegraphed to Smolensk: "Material delivered Moscow. Voloshenko."

What need might Soviet counter-intelligence (it was counter-intelligence that Fedotov was head of) have of a professor of economics?

Wishing to retain the status of a foreign national, Swianiewicz had previously concealed the fact that he was a professor at Vilno University. This fact became known to Zarubov shortly before his departure from the camp, and then by pure accident. The brigade commander, writes Swianiewicz, became greatly interested in this circumstance and immediately invited him for a talk, during which he questioned the professor in particularly great detail about his recent trip to Germany.

It was probably this very conversation which saved the professor's life. By that time Swianiewicz already had the reputation of an authority on the economics of totalitarianism. During his confinement in the Lubyanka prison, Swianiewicz wrote a treatise on the methods of financing the German armament policy. I venture to presume that Swianiewicz's personal contacts in German university circles were also of interest to counter-intelligence. In particular, he was on good terms with Theodor Oberlaender, professor of Koeningsberg University. The latter was a friend of Erich Koch, the future Gauleiter of the Ukraine, and an ardent champion of Soviet-German friendship. In 1934, Oberlaender had visited the USSR, where he met with Bukharin and Radek, who expressed their full support of his views.[39]

The Prose of Death

What happened at Gnezdovo Station was fully confirmed to me by Arkadi Kostyuchenko from Vitebsk. In 1940, he was nine years old, and at the time lived in the settlement of Sofiyevka, one kilometer from the station.

"In 1940," he writes, "one or two passenger cars with barred windows arrived at Gnezdovo Station from time to time. A truck called a Black Maria drove up to the cars. From the car, Polish officers (wearing military uniform) were taken under guard to the truck and driven away to the Katyn Forest. The forest was fenced off and no one saw what was happening there. There was a rumor, however, that shots were heard. At the time, as far as I remember, no one doubted that they were being shot there. Not much was said about it, however, because it was such a serious and dangerous matter. That is why people tried somehow to take no notice of it."

In response to my additional questions, Arkadi Kostyuchenko sent me still another letter:

When thinking over the answers to your questions it begins to seem to me that my recollections of those years are somehow fading, and dissolving in later memories. The more so that we, who were boys then, were living our own lives and had our own interests at the time, just as always, and we perceived the affairs of the adults only insofar as they were taking place before our eyes.

Of course, I do not remember which month it was, but I know it happened in summer. The weather was warm and sunny and we were running about barefoot. The Poles were wearing tunics;

69

Chapter 1

some of them carried greatcoats or trench coats on their arms and some had traveling bags with them.

Why am I referring to them as Poles? Because this is what everyone called them and their tunics were so beautiful, with their badges and stripes. They looked well and it seemed to us that they behaved with pride and dignity.

Whether their guards were changed I do not know. They were driven into the forest in a Black Maria. The guards stood on both sides as the Poles were moved from the carriage to the truck. In all probability, the guards had come in a car, because there was not enough room for them in the truck. I personally only once had a chance to see such a transfer, and even then only from a distance, but as for the green carriages with barred windows on the station tracks, I saw them quite often. These carriages had obviously come with some train, were uncoupled and then, after unloading, coupled to the next train.

I recall the following case. The boys brought something unusual to the settlement which greatly surprised all of us: shoes shaped and hollowed from a piece of wood. The boys had got them from the Poles. How this could have happened I cannot imagine even today. But I remember quite well that they were wooden shoes and that they were taken from the Poles. This I know for sure. Later on I saw similar shoes in Western Byelorussia, in Grodno, in 1944. They were quite common there.

No one displayed any hostility towards the Poles. As I remember, they were not even regarded as prisoners, let alone as enemies. Officially there had not been any war with Poland.

At the time it was not just dangerous to speak about the Poles. People were afraid of everything. At night neighbors were not infrequently arrested. I do not agree that all this was accepted as a manifestation of some necessary justice. Quite a few people felt

70

that something terrible and unjust was happening and . . . kept silent.

I, for example, well remember my boyish thought of those days about this, but I could not understand it at the time: this understanding communicated itself to me from the adults. Certainly, there were some who, aiming to profit by it, cried hurrah, but then there always were scoundrels and, unfortunately, there will always be . . .

Kostychenko's testimony can be trusted for the following reasons. Firstly, he does not say anything unnecessary. Secondly, he makes reservations about possible slips of the memory. Thirdly, his letter includes one uninvented detail, wooden shoes. It should also be noted that our correspondence dates from the time when there were practically no publications about Katyn in the Soviet press and anyway no detailed descriptions of the developments at Gnezdovo have appeared to this day. Incidentally, such is the case with other letters as well. All of them date from the second half of 1989 or January 1990, at the latest.

The second letter begins with facts which are completely at variance with the facts given by Polish sources. Arkadi Kostyuchenko maintains that what he saw happened in summer, although he notes right away that the POWs had winter clothes with them. (Futher on, we will see that the presence of greatcoats and scarves somewhat upsets the well-balanced theory advanced by Burdenko). My correspondent was certainly confused by warm weather, which is still more psychological proof of the reliability of the testimony. Somebody telling lies would never have made such a gross mistake.

The other details all coincide, with the exception, perhaps, of the shoes which somehow do not seem to fit in with the atmosphere of deconcentration at Gnezdovo. The Poles simply had no opportunity to exchange souvenirs with anyone. The transfer in Smolensk described by M.A.Dobrynin is, on the other hand, a different story altogether. Such an aberration would seem to be quite possible. Nor is it to be ruled out that the shoes could have been given to the boys by one of the NKVD officers who carried out searches on the site of the execution.

The striking thing is that Adam Solski's impression that the place where the Black Maria brought him looked like an out-of-town resort fully corresponds to reality. At Kozyi Gory, there was actually a *dacha*, or a summer residence, of the Smolensk Department of the NKVD and the forest range where it was located had been fenced off at least since 1934.

I. I. Titkov, a former driver of the head of the Smolensk Department of the NKVD, recalls that in the spring of 1940 he drove Kupriyanov to Gnezdovo. Upon reaching there, he stayed in the car after Kupriyanov got out, watching the disembarkation from the train and chatting with escort guards.

Finally, rumors about the shooting of Poles were circulating among the local population in the spring of 1940. This fact is confirmed by the authors of several letters that I have received.

The Prose of Death

In the environs of Kozyi Gory, false testimonies are not unknown. For example, I happened to hear a colorful description of a group of prisoners brought to Gnezdovo among whom there were two priests with dogs on leashes. Despite the fact that out of all the priests held in the Kozelsk camp only one ended up in Katyn, the existence of dogs appears quite impossible. Besides, telling a chaplain from an army officer, and from a distance at that, is a difficult task for a person not conversant with the subject.

The question of changing the quards is of fundamental significance, and here is why. Such a large-scale execution could not be carried out by escort guards, if only because they did not have enough revolvers (and we know that it was revolvers which were used in Katyn). Only convoy commanders and sentry dog guides were armed with revolvers. In general, the Katyn action demanded exceptional professionalism on the part of the men who carried it out. The convoys numbered 92 to 420 POWs. According to Swianiewicz, the bus had room for not more than 30, and the interval between its trips was about half an hour, which barely left enough time for handling each batch. This had to be done so that the next batch would not guess until the last minute why they were brought here. If all this were not enough, searches were also quite prevalent. This was clearly not the work of escort guards; this had to be done by professionals. Let us recall Swianiewicz's words: he said that the ground next to the train was surrounded by "NKVD soldiers" which means that the escort guards

73

were changed. When was this done? Was it perhaps during the brief stop that he mentions?

The organs used to have special units known as a commandant's company and a commandant's platoon. They were real professionals. In one of Zhavoronkov's written accounts, there is a phrase to the effect that it was Stelmakh who displayed particularly great skill. One must allow, however, for Zhavoronkov's boundless opportunism when reading his writings. What's more, Stelmakh, if I identified him correctly, did not take part in the executions. He arrived at Gnezdovo specifically in order to fetch Swianiewicz. In a word, the facts here come to an end and what begins at this point is not even guesswork, but divination.

True, there is something else on which we might work, even though it would not be of much help. It was only on April 30 that the convoy under the command of Section Korablyov, which departed from Kozelsk on April 16, arrived in Smolensk. Where Korablyov and his unit were and what they did in the period between April 17 and April 30 is not clear.

* * *

Colonel Rybakov, Head of the 1st Section of the Staff of Escort Guard Troops of the NKVD, who came to the Kozelsk and Yukhnov camps on an inspection tour in July 1940, was dissatisfied with what he saw there. "Alongside individual shortcomings affecting the quality of service," reads an order to the escort guard troops of July 22, 1940, "the lack of appropriate discipline was observed in the companies of the 136th Battalion of the 15th Brigade. Such essential elements of discipline as military bearing, smart appearance and the ability to salute one's commanding officers and higher ranking commanders in accordance with the new wording of Article 27 of UVS-37* and Article 42 of the Infantry Drill Regulations are lacking."[40] This was the reason why he was not happy with the 136th Battalion.

The Kozelsk camp continued to exist, but now it was already Kozelsk-2; confined in it were Poles interned in Lithuania and Latvia.

Dating from that period of the camp's history is a document found by the Germans in the archives of the Byelorussian NKVD and published in June 1943 in the occupation newspaper *Nowy Kurier Warszawski*. Since the original text of this document has recently been found in the rooms of the Central State Special Archives, there can be no doubt about its authenticity. It is a top secret report of August 20, 1940, submitted by State Security Lieutenant Starikovich, member of the staff of the Smolensk Department of the NKVD, to the department head, Kupriyanov. Starikovich reported from Kozelsk:

> All the interned persons are aware that they are in the camp of Kozelsk, Smolensk Region, and that previously confined in this camp were also Polish prisoners of war.

---

* Internal Service Regulations adopted in 1937.

Chapter 1

As proof of this assertion, I state the following: 1. People arriving at the station in transports, can after having got out of the cars, see inscriptions with the name of the railway station. 2. During the march from the station to Kozelsk the road passes through the town where the interned persons have an opportunity to read the names of institutions and organizations, and also of streets and localities. 3. The camp command has not removed the inscriptions on the walls made by the prisoners of war who left the camp. This makes it possible for a new group of interned persons to learn that there already were prisoners of war in the camp.

Taking this opportunity, I must bring to your notice the fact that there were cases of a breach of secrecy by the camp's personnel. In July a sentry said in a conversation with one of the prisoners of war that there had already been people in the camp.

The interned persons showed particular interest in the tower next to Barrack No. 15, which previously housed the local prison and on whose walls various inscriptions were left. From them it could be understood that prisoners of war awaiting their trial had been confined in it. On the walls of the barracks they also saw traces of shots, from which it could be inferred that it was here that executions had been carried out.

The boards with inscriptions in the walls of the barracks must be replaced, for it is from them that the prisoners learn about Polish officer POWs' stay here. I was advised about this by an informer.

In February 1941, about two hundred interned servicemen belonging to the French, British, and Belgian armies were sent in several batches from the Butyrka prison to Kozelsk.

Here is some information about the final evacuation of the camp.

On May 22, 1941 a convoy led by Major Reprintsev arrived in Murmansk from Kozelsk. In it, 1,000 POWs came to NKVD Construction Project No. 106.[41] Another large convoy was sent from Kozelsk to the Gryazovets camp (convoy commander Lieutenant Katelyan). On July 2, on arrival at the destination, the escort party handed over 1,224 "interned servicemen and civilians of former Poland," and also 181 Frenchmen, Englishmen and Belgians (the original number indicated in the papers was 195, which was subsequently amended). Late in July, a convoy of 10 led by Junior Lieutenant Murashov left Kozelsk for Potma. Finally, still another convoy of 80 POWs led by Katelyan departed from Smolensk to the Angara area in July; I strongly doubt that they were Germans. Alexei Lukin was absolutely right when he informed me about the evacuation of the Kozelsk camp in July 1941.

The subsequent developments were as follows. On July 5, a convoy of 1,300 POWs was sent from the Yukhnov to the Gryazovets camp. On August 6 or 7 ("to regard as available as of today," says an order of August 7, 1941), Junior Lieutenant Pikalev and, together with him, the 3rd Company numbering 122 men arrived from Kozelsk to join their unit which had by that time been named the 252nd Regiment and was now stationed at Vyazma.

Thus the Kozelsk and Yukhnov camps of the NKVD ceased to exist.

Chapter 1

When working in the archives, it is hard to determine immediately the value of the documents one finds there. Perhaps there are researchers who are led by their intuition; as for me, I simply copy all texts without exception until my hand grows numb. Thus, added to my file on the Katyn issue were the lists of those Poles who fell under the category of particularly dangerous state criminals and who were transported under guard by the 136th Battalion at the request of investigators in the second half of 1940 and the beginning of 1941. I do not know what made me check them against the list of Katyn victims compiled by Adam Moszyński (Lista Katyńska, GRYF, London, 1989), but then this is no longer of any significance. What really matters is the astounding fact which was established as a result: people who are listed as executed in the spring of 1940 were transported from camp to camp and to Moscow, Minsk, and Smolensk months after the Katyn executions . . . . Let us, however, look at the events in chronological order.

September 1940. Convoy traveling from Yukhnov to Kozelsk (convoy commander Quartermaster Technician 1st Class Arkhipov). Number of prisoners being transported was 12, including Antoni Michałek, who is on Moszyński's list.

October 1940. Same itinerary. Number of persons being transported was six, including Sergeant Aleksander Rozmyzł, who was supposed to be dead.

It gets worse and worse as it goes on.

The Prose of Death

October 1940. Smolensk—Minsk (convoy commander Political Instructor Permyakov). All the seven prisoners being transported were listed among those executed. They were Police Major Hugo Zemler, Captain Leon Jaszczukowski, Police Sergeant Piotr Majewski, Police Commandant Witold Skrętowski, Major Józef Olędzki, Police Major Konstanty Worono, and Infantry Captain Eugeniusz Wojciechowski.

October 1940. Kozelsk—Minsk (convoy commander Political Instructor Zub). Number of prisoners being transported was seven; four of them, Captain Władysław Piko, Captain Leonard Lutostański, Captain Eugeniusz Płociński, and Captain Stefan Mańkowski, are listed among the Katyn victims.

November 1940. Kozelsk—Moscow, Butyrka prison (convoy commander Political Instructor Zub). Three out of the six prisoners being transported, Second Lieutenant Józef Kownacki, Captain Józef Pilarski, and First Lieutenant Włodzimierz Prokopowicz, are in the list of the Katyn victims.

December 1940. Emil Stefaniec, a police officer confined in the Kozelsk camp, was ordered to be transported and placed at the disposal of the head of the district department of the NKVD of the town of Święciany. Senior Police Sergeant Emil Stefaniec is included in Moszyński's obituary.

December 1940. Kozelsk—Smolensk prison (convoy commander Section Commander Vassilyev). Prisoners being transported: Hilary Urbanowicz and Antoni Witko-

Chapter 1

wski. Police Sergeant Hilary Urbanowicz is listed as having been executed in Katyn. There are two Witkowskis, both without initials, on the Polish list.

December 23, 1940. Sixteen men were transported from Kozelsk in isolation from one another, to be placed at the disposal of the head of the NKVD Department for the Vileika Region. Among them were Sanitary Service Captain Marian Ziembiński, Police Sergeant Augustyn Milczewski, Senior Patrolman Stanisław Sawala, Police Sergeant Major Stanisław Klenowski, and Senior Patrolman Józef Ogonowski. They are in Moszyński's list; there are also another two names which give rise to doubt (they are probably misspelled).

December 30, 1940. Yukhnov—Smolensk, inner prison of the NKVD (through convoy Smolensk—Kozelsk—Yukhnov —Kozelsk—Vileika—Kozelsk—Vileika—Smolensk, convoy commander Lieutenant Stolyarov). Two out of the five prisoners being transported, Second Lieutenant Wacław Nowak and Gendarmerie Sergeant Major Włodzimierz Łukowski, are listed among those executed.

Finally, on February 5, 1941, Police Sergeant Julian Chmielewski was transported from Kozelsk to Minsk to be placed at the disposal of the head of the 2nd Section of the State Security Department of the NKVD of the Byelorussian SSR (convoy commander Junior Lieutenant Tankov). He is also listed by Moszyński as being among the Katyn victims.

This brings the total to 26 persons, and these notes pertain only to Kozelsk.

The Prose of Death

In addition to the first names and surnames, military ranks also coincide. Certainly, individual mistakes and coincidences are possible in this list, but then there are too many of the latter. Individual discrepancies are also possible. For example, a request might be received to send off a person who no longer was in a camp or had never been there at all. Naturally, in such a situation no one was transported anywhere, and an appropriate note was made in the request. As for the convoys listed above, however, there is a complete set of documentation pertaining to each of them, including a receipt signed by the addressee and a telegram confirming the fulfillment of the assignment. The fact that these people were alive at the time is not to be doubted.

However, they were not found among the living. The only hypothesis that comes to mind is that they died later on, after the Katyn executions. Establishing their fate ought to become the subject of a special study. Whatever the case, these names must be made into a special list to be dealt with separately.

* * *

Here is yet another episode from the early days of the Soviet-German war.

On July 10, that is a few days before German troops entered the city, a convoy of 43 led by Junior Lieutenant Sergeyev set out from Smolensk for Katyn. There can be no doubt that this was the liquidation of a prison. Similar evacuations of prisons were carried out in numerous towns in the forward area in the early months of the war. Judging by the number of escort guards, there were no less than 600 prisoners transported under guard at this time. Who were they? Where are they? Nothing is known about them.[42]

Should anyone venture to argue that their execution is not an established fact, I have still another document at my disposal.

A report by State Security Junior Lieutenant Kompaniyets, head of the 3rd Section of the 42nd Brigade of the Escort Guard Troops of the NKVD,* to State Security Senior Major Belyanov, head of the 3rd Section of the NKVD of the USSR:

On June 26, about 2,000 prisoners, escorted by a sniper company, were evacuated from Minsk prison, but, in view of systematic attacks on the column of prisoners, by agreement with the prison command 209 political prisoners were shot near the township of Cherven and nonpolitical prisoners were released."[43]

Who can guarantee that there were no Poles among those prisoners who were shot and, even if there were actually no Poles among them, are we not morally obliged to clear up the circumstances in which these crimes were committed?

---

*In December 1940 the 15th Separate Rifle Brigade of Escort Guard Troops of the NKVD of the USSR was renamed the 42nd Separate Brigade of Escort Guard Troops of the NKVD of the USSR.

Ostashkov

Much less is known about the Ostashkov camp than about the Kozelsk camp. According to Madajczyk, about 6,570 people were confined in it. They were mostly police, gendarmerie and frontier guard officers, and also members of courts-martial, priests, a group of civilians, and about 400 army officers. Lebedeva gives a much smaller figure, whereas an information report signed by Soprunenko says that 6,168 police and gendarmerie officers were being held in the NKVD camps as of March 1, 1940.[45]

Whatever the case, the Ostashkov camp was the biggest of the three. The camp was housed in a former monastery known as St. Nil's Hermitage.

ST. NIL'S HERMITAGE ON STOLBNY ISLAND

A Historical Outline

The monastery is situated on Stolbny Island 10 kilometers to the north of Ostashkov. It was founded in 1590 in honor of the hermit St. Nil (secular name, Grigori), who settled on Stolbny Island in 1528 and died there in 1555 at the age of 65. The original wooden structures of the cloister were destroyed by a fire in August 1665. The assemblage which has survived to our day was built in the period between 1669 and 1863. Taking part in its construction were the architects I. F. Lvov and I. I. Charlemagne as well as master stonemason Angelo Bottani from Switzerland. The churches were painted by Ostashkov master Boris Utkin and the stucco moulding was executed by Sergei Vassilyev. On July 1820, Emperor Alexander I and in May 1889, Grand Duke Konstantin Konstantinovich came to the cloister in order to venerate the holy relics of St. Nil of Stolbny Island. The monastery received large donations from tsars Michail Feodorovich and Alexei Mikhailovich, Empress Anne Ioannovna, princes Trubetskoi and Pozharsky, and from many others. On average, about 100,000 people visited St. Nil's Hermitage every year. By May 27, the feast day of the invention of the holy relics of St. Nil, up to 15,000 people gathered there. During the Lent, that number doubled.

On December 20, 1917, all the valuables that were at the cloister were seized and confiscated. A total of 539,480 grams of silver and 824 grams of precious stones set in gold were subject to confiscation. Later on, 1,392 kg of old-minted copper coins were confiscated, as were linen, church plate and furniture. In 1920, an iron grillwork fence was dismantled at St. Nil's Hermitage to be put up at the cemetery of victims of the revolution on the Zhitenny Peninsula. The last divine service was held at the cloister on June 9, 1928. Its 12 monks headed by Gavriil, supervisor of St. Nil's Hermitage, and Archimandrite Ioanniky, father superior of the monastery, were tried by a proletarian court. What sentence they were given is not known.

From 1929-1935, St. Nil's Hermitage housed an almshouse and in 1935-1939, a children's labor colony, whose wards lived and worked according to A. S. Makarenko's method. A shop for the manufacture of blowtorches was built at the colony and it had its own brass band, a theater, a cinema hall in the former Cathedral of the Epiphany, and in its park there was a Ferris wheel, swings and a sports ground. It was in that period that the construction of the dam now linking Stolbny Island with the Svetlitsa Peninsula was launched. To this end, the colonists pulled down the Church of St. John the Baptist (1771-1781) on the hermitage grounds and the Church of St. Michael the Archangel, dating from a later period, in the village of Svetlitsa on the lake shore. The brick and broken stone thus obtained, however, was not enough for the dam, and so a narrow channel was left across which only a pedestrian overpass was built. The only cargo transport facility linking the island with the shore in summer was the motorlaunch *Chapaev*, which operated here until 1973. As B. F. Karpov (more about him is to follow) said about the demolition of the churches, "this foolishness resulted from our poverty and our poverty was a result of our foolishness." He observed, however, that the channel ensures the necessary ecological balance between two neighboring bays. In 1939, the labor colony was disbanded.

Guarding the Ostashkov camp was the responsibility of the 135th Battalion of the 11th Brigade of Escort Guard Troops of the NKVD (Brigade commander Major Michail Ishchenko), stationed in the village of Bogorodskoye in the environs of Moscow and subsequently, from May 1940, in

Chapter 1

Baranovichi. Incidentally, it was the very same battalion which guarded the Lefortovo, Butyrka, and Taganka prisons. In the battalion's service record card for 1939 there is an entry saying: "In the 4th quarter a company was detailed for guard duty at the Ostashkov camp."[46] Besides this, it is also known that on June 28, 1940, a convoy of 323 escorted by guards from the 236th Regiment of the same brigade left Ostashkov for Severonikel. The following fact is also mentioned in the archival documents:

"On December 19, 1939, sentry dog Murka died at a sentry post guarding the Ostashkov prisoner-of-war camp. It would seem impossible to establish the cause of the dog's death from the material on same submitted by the command of the 135th Battalion."[47]

This, in fact, is all that I was able to find in the archives of the Main Administration for Escort Gq'r' Troops, and as for the archives of the 135th Battalion for 1939-1940, they are missing from the Central State Archives of the Soviet Army.

On the other hand, I am in possession of two rather interesting testimonies. One of them is by Boris Karpov, an Ostashkov old-timer, formerly a teacher of geography and now a pensioner. Here is a text which he wrote at my request:

In September and October 1939, trains bringing Polish POWs began to arrive at Ostashkov. The POWs were marched before a vast assembly along Volodarsky Street to the landing stage which formerly used to belong to the monastery. There they were put on wooden barges that were tugged by the S/S *Maxim Gorky* to St. Nil's Hermitage.

That their life at the camp was hard is confirmed by such facts as this: many of them gave gold watches in exchange for a loaf of bread. Those who died were buried in the Troyeruchitsa graveyard on the territory governed by the Zaltsovo Village Soviet.

Some time around the end of March or the beginning of April, I saw prisoners being marched under guard on the ice across Lake Seliger. They were moving in small groups so as not to break the ice. They were taken to a place in Ostashkov known as Tupik, now Splavuchastok. There they were put into stove-heated freight cars.

When I asked him about the color of the tunics that the Poles were wearing, Boris Karpov said with confidence that the officers were clad in blue and the soldiers, in grayish-green ones. He also added that never in his life had he seen such a beautiful uniform, except in pictures showing officers of the Russian tsarist army. According to Karpov, the Poles were bearing themselves with pride and he believes that they did not regard themselves as prisoners of war.

The color of the tunics is a significant detail: it was the police uniform which was of blue color.

Boris Karpov went to see the Troyeruchitsa graveyard. It is situated on a hill and the grave fences stand close to one another. In its very center, however, is a rather spacious plot, overgrown with weeds, where no traces of any graves can be seen. Karpov maintains that this is the place where the bodies of prisoners who died of "natural cause" lie buried. Boris Karpov also told me that they were buried not in coffins, but in wooden boxes; according to him, two corpses were put in each box of this type.*

The other testimony is by Maria Sidorova; in her day she, just like the Levashov family, was "provided with agent service." It was Karpov who found her, and he not only found her, but he also recorded her words on paper which he subsequently legalized. He made the chairman of the village Soviet certify Sidorova's signature. I did not have a chance to meet with Sidorova personally, for she was ill at the time. I will therefore reproduce the document written down by Karpov:

In 1939, I, Maria Sidorova, born in 1909 in the village of Tverdyakino, Zaltsovo Village Soviet, worked in the canteen kitchen at the children's labor colony housed in the former monastery known as St. Nil's Hermitage. In the autumn of that year, the colony was disbanded and began urgently to be prepared for receiving Polish prisoners of war. How many of them would arrive no one knew. In October trains with Poles began to arrive by way of the town of Ostashkov. At first they

---

*Boris Karpov seems to be right, for Solzhenitsyn writes about one of his heroes that he spent the winter of 1941/42 doing light work "packing naked corpses in coffinlike crates of four boards head to feet, two in each."

were given regular meals, but later on, since St. Nil's Hermitage was not prepared to accommodate such a number of people, they had to be given "mash" made of rye flour.

There were a total of 14,000 of them. Using the POWs as labor force two bakeries were urgently built. In the buildings 3 to 4 tier bunks were put up. The Poles had their own medical personnel. Senior officers even had their families with them. The Poles were polite and cultured people; they were very clean and paid great attention to their clothes and appearance. They were not sent to work. Their labor activity was confined to serving themselves.

In March and April 1940, the Poles were sent in large batches on the ice across Lake Seliger to the town of Ostashkov. The last to be moved out were the sick, who were transported on carts in May. I do not know what subsequently became of them.

October 8, 1989.

The first thing that hits the eye is the striking discrepancy in figures. Sidorova maintains that there were 14,000 POWs, which is more than twice as many as the figures given both in Polish and in Soviet archival sources. There exists, however, yet another figure. Historian Igor Klochkov, a member of the Polish section of the Moscow society Memorial, who has devoted much of his energy to studying the Ostashkov issue, says that the number of the POWs held in St. Nil's Hermitage, at least at one time, was 16,000; he obtained this information from a man who was in charge of bread supplies to St. Nil's Hermitage at the time. I have no reason not to believe Sidorova and Klochkov. I think that they are simply under a misapprehension.

Chapter 1

It would seem that their information dates from a later period when the monastery housed a military hospital. The presence in the camp of families also seems to me scarcely probable, although, as has been mentioned, a certain number of civilians were held there.

As for the circumstances of unloading the camp described by Karpov and Sidorova, these are quite plausible. The winter of 1939/40 was severe with a hard frost. By April, the ice had definitely not yet been broken on Lake Seliger. As for transportation by trucks on the ice, it might have been hazardous. This is where riddles begin.

According to Polish sources, the evacuation of the camp began on April 4 and was completed on May 16. Three convoys, which departed on April 29, May 13, and May 16, had the Yukhnov camp as their destination. The number of POWs in the convoys was 60, 45, and 19, respectively, totaling 124. Later on, they, just as the surviving prisoners of the other two camps, were transferred to Gryazovets.

Where were the rest of them moved to?

Two hypotheses exist on this: Senior Patrolman A. Woroniecki, who was held in the Ostashkov camp and who found himself in one of the convoys sent to Gryazovets, spoke about a talk that he had with an escort guard. "You will not see your comrades any more," said the escort guard and then, in response to Woroniecki's questions, he added reluctantly, "They've been drowned."

Gendarmerie Sergeant Major Józef Borkowski was on friendly terms with Nikitin, head of the camp bakery. "Do you know where they will take us?" the sergeant major asked him. "To some place in the north," was the answer. The sergeant major was moved out together with the April 29 convoy, which, as it was, was headed northward. At the Bologoye Station, the car in which Borkowski was travelling was uncoupled and directed to Rzhev. The train with the rest of the POWs remained at Bologoye.

Finally, there is the testimony of Katarzyna Gąszczecka, who, together with a number of other deportees, was transported on a barge across the White Sea from Arkhangelsk to the mouth of the Pechora River.

"Looking at the receding shore," tells Gąszczecka, "I suddenly felt an overpowering longing for freedom, for my homeland and my husband and for life itself and began to cry. All of a sudden, a young Russian member of the crew appeared before me and asked:

"Why are you crying?"

"I am crying over my life. Is this also prohibited here, in your 'free' state? I am crying over my husband's life, too . . ."

"And what was he?"

"A captain," I replied.

The Bolshevik laughed derisively. "Your crying will be of no help to him. All of your officers have been drowned here in the Barents Sea."

He stamped the deck with his heel. Then he, quite unabashed, told me that he personally had taken part in a convoy which transported some 7,000 people and that there had been many former Polish police and army officers among them. Two barges were tugged. When they were out at sea, the barges were released and sunk. "All of them went to the bottom," he concluded and went away.

An old member of the barge's crew who happened to be nearby waited for the NKVD officer to leave and then fully confirmed his story.

These three testimonies are all that Polish sources have to offer. In analyzing them, Józef Mackiewicz admits that this information is definitely not enough to draw any final conclusions. Assuming that Ostashkov prisoners were transported to Arkhangelsk, their route would take them through Bologoye. Mackiewicz, however, reminds me that late in 1941 there were rumors about an accident on the White Sea and also about the transfer of Polish officers to the northern islands. As we will see later from a report by Captain Czapski, these rumors were spread by NKVD officers. This clarification is quite appropriate, and yet I think that the possibility of an information leak should not be ruled out.

I will quote another two testimonies relating to the subject.

The first letter came to Polish TV after a broadcast of a program about Katyn that Andrzej Minko and myself had prepared. Its author, I. Wychowski from Gdańsk, writes:

In 1954, I was working at the Petrozavodsk Shipyard in Leningrad, at the chief technologist's department. Its head was engineer Tsytrin and its power plant technologist engineer Basov. Working together with them was a ship's mechanical equipment technologist whose name I forgot. This friend of mine told me the following story which I give in his own words:

92

The Prose of Death

As a lad I landed a job as a ship's boy on a tugboat which sailed in the country's northern water areas - the White Sea, Lake Onega, and the White Sea Canal. Early in the spring of 1940 the tugboat was assigned to take several scows at moorage and tow them out to sea. Together with ourselves, a number of NKVD officers embarked on the tugboat. I saw that in the open scows there were several thousand Polish prisoners of war, among whom I saw some people wearing a black uniform. My friend, a sailor, who was older than I, told me that they were Polish policemen. On top of the scows stood NKVD soldiers with bayonets. The tugboat towed the scows into the open sea. When we were several dozen miles from the shore, we were told to stop. The NKVD officers got from the tugboat to the scows. We left the scows and sailed back to the moorage. A day later the tugboat returned to that spot. The officers embarked on the tugboat once again. I noticed that there were only the NKVD guards on the scows and not a trace of the POWs was to be seen. I asked my sailor friend where the POWs had gone. He pointed a finger at the sea bottom and said: "Do not ask me and do not tell anyone that we know or our fate will be the same." The NKVD officers' faces showed that they were very nervous. When we returned to the shore, the entire crew was instructed not to tell anyone about this under threat of severe punishment.'

The second letter was kindly placed at my disposal by Professor Madajczyk. The letter, written by Tadeusz Czyz from Sopot, had been received by the history department of Jagellonian University.

The letter opens with the words: "In 1954, I was in the USSR, working at the Petrozavodsk Shipyard in Leningrad . . ." And then follows the same story told by an anonymous technologist. The author of the letter explains that a scow is a barge with an opening bottom.

The method of transporting prisoners in open barges, or scows, widely practiced by the Gulag,* was described by Solzhenitsyn. I will recall these lines for the benefit of the reader: "People were thrown into the troughlike holds and lay there in piles or crawled around like crabs in a basket. And high up on the deck, as though atop a cliff, stood guards." And then, further on: "Prisoner transport by barge on the Northern Dvina (and on the Vychegda) had not died out even by 1940, but, on the contrary, it livened up quite a bit; it was a route along which the *liberated* Western Ukrainians and Western Byelorussians were moving." To this I will add not so much Ukrainians and Byelorussians as Polish deportees, or special resettlers, who will be the subject of the next chapter.

The story seems quite credible (in twilight or from a distance dark-blue tunics might well appear to be black), and as for the version involving special barges with an opening bottom, it has to be declared highly questionable. Even if the POWs were drowned, they had to be sunk together with the barges, locked in their holds, so that the dead bodies should not come up to the surface.

I. S. Klochkov advances his own hypothesis. He positively maintains that the POWs were moved out of the mo-

---

*Gulag is the Russian acronym for the Main Administration of Corrective Labor Camp.

nastery in barges at least one of which sank, or was sunk, in one of the Seliger straits. This version seems to me absolutely implausible, above all, because the ice could not have melted on the lake by the beginning of April. Or, perhaps, the information supplied by Klochkov is about one of the last May transports? By that time Lake Seliger, as a general rule, becomes free of ice and navigation is in full operation. (Exact information about the spring of 1940 could be found in the archives of the local meteorological service, but I have not been able to uncover appropriate documents as yet). Even in this case, however, certain doubts still remain. The maximum depth of Lake Seliger is 50 meters and the lake is a popular spot with tourists, fishermen, and yachtsmen, so it is hard to imagine that not the slightest trace of the sunken barge has come to light during all these years. Karpov, at any rate, being a seasoned fisherman, definitely denies such a possibility. True, Klochkov mentioned a handful of Polish coins found on the shore by local residents; in my opinion, however, this fact does not mean anything at all and cannot serve as serious proof.

Finally, quite recently, when I was already finishing my work on this book, still another version, which, in my view, is the most convincing, came up.

After our May trip to Kalinin and Ostashkov, Maren Freidenberg, D. Sc. (History), co-chairman of the Kalinin (now Tver) branch of the Memorial Society, published a small article in the bulletin brought out by the society in which he called on readers to relate to him everything they knew about the fate of the Ostashkov prisoners. As a result, he received information containing a reference to the late Colonel A.P. Leonov, a staff member of the Special Inspectorate of the NKVD, who died in Kalinin in 1965. According to Leonov, the Poles were transferred from Ostashkov to the prison of the Kalinin Department of the NKVD. From there, they were taken in small batches to the NKVD Department's *dacha* near the village of Mednoye, where they were shot and killed. In the same year, 1940, a cottage for the *dacha* commandant was built on the site of their burial.

It should be noted that reports about the shootings at Mednoye appeared earlier, but there was nothing to corroborate them. I also mentioned this address in a conversation with Freidenberg. The *dacha* or, rather, a sports center of the local department of the KGB still exists at Mednoye today.

Having hardly finished reading the letter, Freidenberg found in the newspaper *Kalininskya Pravda* (May 30, 1990) an interview with Colonel V. A. Lakontsev, head of the Kalinin Department of the KGB (it is interesting to note that the interviewer was Yu. Burov, *Sovetskaya Rossiya's* own correspondent, who for some reason did not publish it on the pages of his paper; true, during those days nearly the entire space in *Sovetskaya Rossiya* was allotted to a verbatim report of a Congress of People's Deputies of the RSFSR), in which among other things there is mention of the burial site at Mednoye. According to Lakontsev, lying buried there are not only Poles, but also "active henchmen of the

Germans" (as is known, they were publicly tried and hanged), and also Soviet servicemen who died of wounds. As it transpired, the Kalinin Department of the KGB had already been carrying on these searches "for many months!" True, no documents had been found. Now Lakontsev was calling on everyone who could supply any information about the burial site at Mednoye. It is strange that he did not make such an appeal earlier, for it was not yesterday that the documents quoted in this book were found; perhaps if he had, this period of many months would have been reduced. The information that the dead bodies of Soviet servicemen were thrown in the same pit containing the corpses of executed Nazi henchmen also sounds monstrous. Why were they not turned over to their families? Why were they not buried in a proper manner? Naturally, any vile thing might be expected of Beria's butchers, but then military hospitals, thanks be to God, did not come within their jurisdiction. Lastly, if no documents had been found, how could one know that it was Nazi henchmen who were buried at Mednoye?

Taking his own experience as a basis, Maren Freidenberg concludes that this is a well-tried method of blocking the excavations. At any rate, it is not the first time that it has been used to hamper the activity of the Tver branch of the Memorial Society.[49]

A day after the appearance of the publication, Yu. Burov called up Freidenberg and suggested that they visit Mednoye together. Naturally, Maren Freidenberg consented right away.

Chapter 1

On his arrival there, Freidenberg easily found the house on the *dacha* premises in which he was interested. It is a typical peasant log house boarded up with deals. Dwelling inside, just as before, was the *dacha* commandant. Next to the log house, the visitors saw what was clearly a man-made sand mound. When questioned about the origin of the mound, the commandant answered without hesitation that it was earth dug up when laying the foundation. According to Freidenberg, at this moment the visitors exchanged a meaningful glance. Every rural resident knows that the classical Russian peasant log house is built without a foundation.

Freidenberg's version strikingly corresponds with the circumstances of the Katyn shootings. In both cases there was a "dacha of the NKVD department" and POWs were brought to the place of execution in small batches. At this point I will refrain from any further comments; additional materials are needed and, in case of their absence, excavations are required.

* * *

As I have already written, late in June 1940, the last 323 prisoners were transported from St. Nills Hermitage to Severonikel. The report of July 23, 1940, on the number of POWs present in the camp says:

"Ostashkov camp: vacant."[50]

A Historical Outline
(Concluded)

Between 1940 and 1942 some military units were stationed at St Nil's Hermitage. In 1942-1944 it housed a total of six military hospitals. In 1944, a children's labor colony, this time for juvenile delinquents, was once again set up on the monastery grounds. In the late 1950s, there was a mutiny at the colony, which was brutally repressed by the authorities. A few members of the colony management were put on trial for abuse of authority and for battery and the colony itself was liquidated.

Between 1961 and 1971, the monastery buildings housed a home for the aged and between 1973 and 1988, the Rassvet tourist camp.

From 1974, restoration work has been under way at the monastery; its progress, however, is rather slow. To this day, only 1,157,000 rubles out of the estimated cost of 13,000,000 rubles has been used. In March 1989, the architectural complex was turned over to the Kryukovo casting production administration of the Mostransgaz gas main and the Nilova Pustyn tourist camp began operating on Stolbny Island. Finally, in 1990, on the insistence of local inhabitants and at the request of Bishop Viktor of Kalinin and Kashin, the head of the local diocesan administration, the monastery ensemble was turned over to the Russian Orthodox Church.

Chapter 1

I have been to St. Nil's Hermitage twice, in January and May of 1990. The architectural assemblage of the monastery is wondrously beautiful and harmonious, although, perhaps, not absolutely singular. There was, however, a structure on its grounds which attracted the attention of researchers, a multi-tiered wooden church which is regarded as the prototype of a whole style. This church has not survived to our day.

The completion of the restoration work is still a long time off. All the monastery buildings are scaffolded and there are heaps of rubble in the courtyard. Instead of sheet copper, the domes of the churches are covered with tin. The wrought iron grilles on the cell windows are being wrenched out and replaced with ordinary wooden frames. In the middle of the courtyard stands a "lice killer"—an iron cabinet in which clothes were steamed in order to disinfest them—a thing which was quite common at one time and which now is a relic, almost a museum piece.

Inside one of the buildings traces of a canteen that it used to house—a dilapidated oven, a stove and a serving window—can be clearly seen.[51]

When taking a look at the environs, I felt sorry that I had come here on business, very sad business at that, and not as a tourist.

Starobelsk

The third officers' camp was the Starobelsk camp situated in an area which was then part of the Kharkov Region and now part of the Lugansk Region and was also housed in a former monastery. According to Polish experts, 3,920 people were confined in it, including, as reported by Jerzewski, about 20 college professors, about 400 doctors, some 600 airmen, and also a number of lawyers, engineers, teachers, public figures, writers, and journalists. The entire staff of the gas protection research institute without exception, nearly all staff members of the Polish army's institute of armaments, and Baruch Steinberg, rabbi of the Polish army, were held in this camp.

From the documents of the Main Administration for Internal Affairs, it follows that the Starobelsk camp was guarded by the 230th Regiment of the 16th Escort Guard Brigade (regiment commander Major Ilya Shevtsov), stationed in Rostov-on-Don. An order to the escort guard troops of December 31, 1940, commends escort guards for the vigilance they displayed:

"In guarding the Starobelsk camp, comrades Shcheg- olkov, Zhilin, Yelnikov and Kalinichenko, Red Army men of the 4th Company of the 230th Regiment, excellently fulfilling the Guard Regulations, prevented and thwarted a number of attempts at escape made by prisoners confined in the camp."[52]

Chapter 1

Here is a description of still another attempt to escape, quoted from an overview of the operative use of sentry dogs by the units of the escort guard troops of the NKVD in the 4th quarter of 1939:

> On October 10, 1939, at 19:00 hrs., one prisoner of war escaped from the Starobelsk camp guarded by the 230th Regiment of the 16th Brigade. A sentry noticed the escapee at a distance of 300 to 350 meters from the camp. The escapee managed to reach a populated locality and hide in a ditch amid trees.
>
> Comrade Velichko, a sentry dog guide, who was at the camp, made timely and skillful use of sentry dog Elsa and thus prevented the POW from hiding in the populated locality.
>
> The escapee was apprehended and returned to the camp.[53]

Besides this, there is a report by an NKVD operative team (Trofimov, Yefimov and Yegorov) of November 25, 1939, addressed to Beria, from which it follows that an anti-Soviet organization was exposed at the camp. The authors of the report give an unflattering opinion of Kirshin, the camp's commissar, who, "instead of organizing through the political apparatus cultural and educational measures which would make it possible to carry on the political indoctrination of junior and reserve officers as well, (. . .) by his inactivity enabled the anti-Soviet activists among the officer POWs to take over the initiative." And not only this: "No sooner had we begun taking out the members of the organization marked out for arrest than Commissar Kirshin, acting at his discretion, went to the POWs' barracks and, speaking with individual activists of the underground, began 'exposing' their activity, demonstrating the illegal, anti-Soviet character of their work, etc., having thus blurted out the fact of our being informed about the existence of the organization and made it possible for the participants in the organization to prepare themselves." Finally, "Comrade Kirshin does not enjoy prestige among the personnel of the camp and from the very first days he compromised himself by the fact of cohabitation with one of the camp's medical nurses."[54]

Soon, however, all this furious activity was brought to an end.

There is more information about the events that took place at the Starobelsk camp in the spring of 1940 as compared with the developments at the Ostashkov camp. Much of this is due to the fact that among its prisoners was Captain Count Józef Czapski, a noted artist and writer, who subsequently published his *Wspomnienia Starobielskie* (Starobelsk Reminiscences) and then, later on, still another book about the USSR, *Na nieludzkiej ziemi* (Living in an Inhuman Land). Fragments of Czapski's reminiscences were at one time submitted to the Nuremberg tribunal as a document for the defense in trying the Katyn case.

This is how Czapski describes the beginning of the camp's evacuation:

As early as February 1940 rumors began to circulate that we were to be moved out of that camp. Our camp authorities spread rumors that the Soviet Union would turn us over to the Allies, that we would be deported to France so that we could fight there. There was even an official Soviet paper showing the itinerary of our travel by way of Bendery, which was being put stealthily among us. One night we were awakened and asked whether any one of us spoke Romanian or Greek. All this gave rise to such an atmosphere of hope that, when in April they began moving us out first in smaller, then in larger batches, quite a few of us were totally convinced that we were being released.

It was absolutely impossible to understand by what criteria the groups of POWs being moved out of the camp were formed. The age groups, draft contingents, ranks, professions, social origin and political convictions were all mixed up. Each new prisoner transport showed the falsity of the various conjectures. There was one thing about which all of us agreed. Every one of us was feverishly waiting for the moment when the next departure list would be announced.

On April 25, a transport of 63 prisoners departed from the camp. During a stop, one of the prisoners looked out through a hole and saw a railwayman tapping the car wheels with a hammer. "Comrade!" the prisoner asked him. "Is this Kharkov?" The worker answered in the affirmative and added: "You'd better get ready to disembark. Here they unload all of you people and take you somewhere by trucks."

I, on my part, will supplement the above with a testimony by one of my readers, Anatoli Zaika from the town of Sumgait.

I remember this camp the way it was in 1940-1941," he writes. "During those years my stepfather, Nikolai Fedorenko, brother of Yakov Fedorenko, Marshal of the Armored Command, was assigned by the Party to this camp as its supply manager. He often travelled in a truck about the Donbas area and sometimes took me along. For this reason I visited the camp two or three times and each time was surprised at the good order and calm which I saw at the camp. There was quite a mass of people there, but there was no crowd and the people looked quite decent, I do not remember hearing any talk about any kind of emergency at the camp. It was like this till August, 1941. At the time, refugees from the western regions were streaming into the quiet and not very populous town, and the situation at the fronts deteriorated sharply. Apparently, the supply manager's nervousness and anxiety with the sending of Polish prisoners from the camp to some other place increased. Late in September, I was called up for military service and some Poles from the camp sewed me a superb greatcoat. I went there a couple of times for a fitting. The camp looked almost entirely deserted. At the end of September I went to serve in the Black Sea Navy and lost touch with my relatives. Soon I learned that they had been evacuated. Fedorenko was transferred to a similar camp in the environs of Moscow. He died in 1943.

The first prisoner transport departed from Starobelsk on April 5, and the last on May 12. Two of them, which departed on April 25 and May 12 and contained a total of 79 persons, came to Gryazovets.

Subsequent developments with those who escaped execution were as follows (the quotation is from Czapski):

I was one of the last to leave Starobelsk. As soon as we came to the station unpleasant surprises began to happen: our batch was shoved in groups of 10-15 persons each into the narrow compartments of a prison car which had almost no windows and was filted with heavy grates instead of doors. The escort guards were extremely rude. On principle, they let us use the toilet only twice a day. We were fed salt herrings and water. It was unbearably hot in the cars. People lost consciousness and the indifference of the escort guards, who had obviously got used to this, was particularly noticeable. Our transport was brought to the Pavlishchev Bor camp. There we met several hundred of our comrades from Kozelsk and Ostashkov. In all, there were about 400 of us. A few weeks later, we were all moved further on, to Gryazovets, near Vologda, where we stayed until August, 1941.

We were given the right to write to our families once a month. Our living conditions were now better than at Starobelsk and at first we were convinced that the same thing had happened to the rest of our comrades, that they had been sent to other camps, similar to ours, scattered all over Russia. We lived in an old building of a former monastery, though the old monastery church had been blown up with dynamite.

Thus, at Gryazovets, the POWs were also held in a monastery (incidentally, today it is still used as a transit prison). How many prisons, political detention centers, colonies, and special homes for the children of "enemies of the people" have been housed in former monastery buildings and churches, beginning with the famous Solovki! Alexander Solzhenitsyn observes on this subject: "As had been the custom since as early as the Civil War, monastery buildings, which are by their very location ideally suited for isolation, were mobilized on a wide scale." Indeed, as a general rule, monasteries are situated in secluded spots, they are surrounded by walls, their cells can easily be converted into prison cells, and they have communications and service blocks. There is not even any need to build watchtowers, for their bell towers and over-the-gate churches can be quite readily used for the purpose. And yet, I think it is not their practical advantage alone which explains the NKVD's partiallity for church buildings. I am quite sure that the repressive organs pursued an ideological goal as well—that of desecrating the nation's sacred places.

One day I had a strange dialogue with Archimandrite Evlogy, Father Superior of the Optina Hermitage. I requested him to bless the film we were going to do there. "And you have applied to the town executive committee?" he asked me in reply. "That's not our level," I said with an air of importance and, I believe, my answer duly impressed him. We were granted permission to film, but the father superior declined an interview. What kind of clergyman is it that refers you to the secular authorities in response to your answer to your request for his blessing? While I am about it, I will add a couple of observations not related to the subject under discussion: the very same Optina Hermitage was built by the monks themselves, for hired labor was not allowed at the cloister, and now it is being restored by contract builders . . . . And the church hierarchs keep on about the need to revive the spiritual traditions of the Russian *startsy*.

Until quite recently, all attempts to get any fresh information about the Starobelsk camp were to no avail and so it seemed an almost helpless affair. In June 1990,

107

however, the press group of the Kharkov Department of the Ukrainian KGB reported:

"In the course of the searches yet another mass burial site of victims of the Stalinist repressions has just been found. According to preliminary documentary data and eye witness reports, it is located in District No. 6 of the Forest-Park Zone. Buried there are over 1,760 Soviet citizens executed in accordance with sentences by law courts and decisions by extrajudicial bodies, and also Polish servicemen unlawfully executed in 1940, whose number is being established." (The Kharkov newspaper *Krasnoye Znamya*, June 3, 1990).

I was immediately put on guard by the date; the Kharkov and Kalinin departments of the KGB seemed to be acting in collusion with each other, as if they were carrying out the same command.

On the ninth day after the appearance of the first publication, it was followed by another, an interview with General Georgi Kovtun, Deputy Chairman of the Ukrainian KGB, by the newspaper *Izvestia* (June 12, 1990). As it transpired, a criminal investigation in connection with the finding of the burial site was launched as early as autumn 1988. And now, at last, its results were published: "In the 6th District more than 1,760 of our innocent compatriots, as well as over 300 defectors from prewar Poland were shot to death, in a number of German POWs died in an infection camp in 1943, and also Polizei* and traitors were executed in accordance with sentences passed by a tribunal."

---

*Polizei is the German word for police; designation of Russians who served as police under the German occupation in World War II.

The Prose of Death

Attentive readers ought to find this text familiar to the reports on the burial sites at Mednoye and in the 6th District of the Kharkov, which seem to look like carbon copies of each other. True, there are certain differences between them: in place of Soviet servicemen who died of wounds, the latter report mentions German servicemen who died of contagious diseases, and also defectors. It is rather ambitious in respect to the fate of these defectors; it may be presumed that they were also shot to death. The presence in the grave of traitors' corpses does not give rise to objections in this case, because in Kharkov, in contrast to Kalinin, an open trial of a group of members' punitive squads was held in December 1943, following which they were publicly hanged and, according to US journalist Richard E. Lauterbach, left hanging for three days. General Georgi Kovtun also reported that "no information about the Starobelsk camp was found in the archives of the country's KGB"; there are, however, statements on the destruction of the appropriate documents, for which reason "experienced Kharkov investigators" were sent to the Central State Archives of the Soviet Army and the Central State Archives of the USSR. Here they had a stroke of luck: "the KGB staff members working in the archives succeeded in gathering, bit by bit, a number of materials indirectly testifying to . . . ." And then General Kovtun offered the data which Lebedeva had already published in March. In conclusion Nikolai Gibadulov, head of the KGB Department for the Kharkov Region, assured the readers that the truth about the tragedy in the 6th District would be revealed to its full extent and definitely made public.

I do not feel particularly enthusiastic about this text, above all, about the phase concerning the absence of necessary documents from the KGB archives . . .

It seems only natural that a few days later Gennady Zhavoronkov, a *Moscow News* correspondent, who regards the official Soviet acknowledgement of responsibility as his personal achievment, made his appearance in Kharkov. Incidentally, the material published in *Moscow News* (No. 24, June 24-July 1, 1990) says that the report by the press officers of the Kharkov Regional KGB Department appeared *after* Zhavoronkov's trip to Kharkov, which makes the story even more interesting. What are the fresh details concerning the burial site in the 6th District that he published?

"Covered loaded trucks lined with zinc sheets used to rumble into the camp; once relieved of their cargo they quickly sped back to Kharkov. Watchdogs used to howl at night, as if trying to tell the world about this horror story."

I envy Gennady Zhavoronkov his skill at writing stories with expression. He speaks of watchdogs howling at night and trucks quickly speeding back after being relieved of their cargoes; he certainly has a way with words. Let us, however, divert ourselves from Zhavoronkov's exercises in belles-letters and turn our attention to an obvious contradiction. He writes that the bodies of the executed people were brought by trucks to the 6th District. However, didn't General Kovtun tell us that it was not they that were shot?

No, it was not. Witness Ivan Dvornichenko* testifies: "They were shot inside the NKVD building in Chernyshevsky Street." Alongside other gruesome details, Zhavoronkov reports that in the 1970s, when human bones and skulls showed above ground in the 6th District after showers, the local KGB department built a holiday home and a number of *dachas* there, which have been today handed over to the city.[55] As for the KGB, with whom the *Moscow News* correspondent spoke, he only shrugged his shoulders, meaning to say that there were no documents and no witnesses. Why do Kovtun and Gibadulov have both and Nessen has neither? The lack of materials notwithstanding, however, Nessen states that the case of mass burial has been passed on to the procurator's office. What exactly has been passed on and in what form? Was it documents of the Central State Archives of the Soviet Army and of the Central State Special Archives? It is all very elusive when there is nothing to work on. And Zhavoronkov goes on singing his sepulchral song:

"There are hillocks in the forest, as if the earth is going through wild convulsions each autumn and spring. As if the buried are crying out for help." Crying out for help, presumably, to Gennady Zhavoronkov.

---

* By the way, Zhavoronkov did not mention that Dvornichenko's letter was recieved not by him, but by the editors of the Kharkov newspaper *Novaya Smena*, who published the letter in its issue of March 3, 1990. See also Leon Bójko, "Czarna droga Starobielska," *Gazeta Wyborcza*, May 29, 1990.

Chapter 1

Right at that time I happened to be in Poland and there I read in the newspaper *Trybuna* of June 24, 1990, that General Golushko, Chairman of the Ukrainian KGB, and his deputy, Kovtun, had visited the Polish Consulate General in Kiev and handed over to Włodzimierz Cimoszewicz and Lech Kozaczko, deputies to the Sejm, a list of 4,031 names of Starobelsk prisoners. While in Warsaw, I heard an intriguing story about finding some papers, which had survived literally by some miracle, in the archives of the Kharkov Department of the KGB. And yet I know for certain that these lists were obtained by the Kharkov KGB from the staff of the Central State Special Archives without any particular effort.

And yet, however, I am coming to the conclusion (or, rather, the feeling) that, all the logical discrepancies and omissions notwithstanding, the location of the Poles' burial site is indicated correctly. There is one thing that worries me: I am not very much inclined to believe in the absence of appropriate documents from the KGB archives.

As follows from the service record card of the 230th Escort Guard Regiment, the company which guarded the Starobelsk camp was recalled in the second half of May 1940. On May 20, 1940, it returned to its permanent station in Rostov-on-Don.

Then, on July 3, 1940, Klok, a political controller (or censor, as I understand it) of the camp's special section, Sysoyev, head of its 2nd section, and Kuryachy, secretary of the camp's management, "carried out the destruction of incoming correspondence addressed c/o the camp for the POWs who have departed from the camp," about which fact an appropriate statement was drawn up. The statement includes a reference to Directive 25/5699 of the Administration for the Affairs of Prisoners of War. In all, Klok, Sysoyev, and Kuryachy burned 4,308 items of correspondence—letters, postcards and telegrams.[56]

Then, in September 1940, the camp's special section received instructions to burn the personal files on the POWs who had departed the camp, excepting those who had been transferred to Yukhnov. Their files were to be forwarded to the Administration without delay. The same paper specified: "The lettered files containing material on the POWs and also on the population residing round the camp are effective and shall remain at the special section of the camp." This document was signed by P. K. Soprunenko and State Security Senior Lieutenant Marlyarsky, head of the 2nd section of the Administration.[57] The instructions were duly carried out. On October 5, 1940, Pismenny, an assistant inspector of the Administration's 2nd Section, and State Security Sergeant Gaididei, acting head of the special section of the Starobelsk camp, drew up a statement certifying the destruction of 4,031 personal files (so this is where the figure named by Golushko and Kovtun comes from; there is a list attached to the statement), of the same number of personal record cards, and of other documents which, in their opinion, had lost their operational significance.

113

Chapter 1

* * *

How the departure of prisoners from the three camps proceeded is described in detail in the already mentioned political report submitted to Merkulov. It was signed by Regiment Commissar Nekhoroshev, commissar of the Administration for the Affairs of Prisoners of War, and senior Political Instructor Vorobyov, deputy head of the Political Department.

Here is some brief information about each camp.

Starobelsk:

"There have been no escapes nor attempts to escape. No negative sentiments apart from those described in report No.25/3301 of April 14 of this year have been revealed."

Kozelsk:

"Most officers feel at ease and are happy that they have at last been released from slave captivity."

Ostashkov:

"Most POWs, above all, rank-and-file policemen who believe that they are going home, are in high spirits."

Nekhoroshev and Vorobyov also reported on a large number of applications received from reservist servicemen (regular officers did not write petitions). The following texts are reproduced by way of an example:

I request you not to turn me over to any German or neutral authorities, but to let me stay and work in the Soviet Union. I have the following reasons for making this request:

1. I have so far been apolitical; of late, however, I have become better aquainted with and more strongly drawn by the ideology of a socialist country. I have no doubt that I will personally be able honorably to fulfil the duty of a Soviet citizen.

2. I am a textile industry engineer by profession and education and I have no doubt that my knowledge and experience will be of substantial use to the Land of the Soviets.

3. I am a Jew and I have so far been subject to national oppression, which has enabled me to fully appreciate the Soviet Union's policy of national freedom.

Georgi Altman.

I request that on leaving the camp I be permitted to stay in the USSR. Do not send me to any other countries. I am a doctor, a medical specialist, and, while living in a capitalist country, I saw all the injustice of that system and the terrible life that poor people led there; that is why I always sympathize with the communist movement. I dreamed of living in a free socialist state in which there would be no national oppression which I, being a Jew, always felt.

Yakov Tanenbaum[58]

Characteristically, the Jewish POWs do not write explicitly why they do not want to be sent to Germany (simple souls! They were afraid to "libel" the USSR's ally!), yet they manage to mention their nationality seemingly unintentionally. Sure enough, the Soviet government complied with the requests made by these men: they remained in the Land of the Soviets forever . . .

How many Jews were there among the 42,492 people turned over to the Nazis during the pre-war years?

Chapter 2

THE END
OF THE "POLISH EXPERIMENT"

The final result of the operation to disperse the officers' camps is well known today: 15,131 persons were turned over to regional departments of the NKVD and 395 were transferred to the Gryazovets camp.

15,131 and 395. This is the proportion of the dead to the living, of death to life, the cannibalistic accounting of the NKVD.

What became of the rest of the Polish soldiers who were made slaves of the Gulag?

In January 1940, at the Krivoi Rog camp, only one-third of the total number of prisoners, and at the Zaporozhye camp, about half, went to work, and at the end of January the prisoners of the Zaporozhye camp went on a hunger strike. In describing these developments, Natalia Lebedeva apparently does not suspect that these were not simply refusals to work, but actual strikes, for the POWs knew that the coal they were mining was being exported to Germany. The camp authorities responded to the strike with reprisals, yet they never succeeded in achieving the desired effect. Immediately after the completion of the action at Kozelsk, Ostashkov and Starobelsk, the soldier POWs began to be transferred to Siberian and polar camps.

Chapter 2

One of the destinations was the Northern Railway Camp on the Chibya River. The section "Special Tasks for the 2nd Quarter" of the *Review of the State of Service of the Escort Guard Troops of the NKVD in the 2nd Quarter of 1940* includes the following paragraph: "Transportation under guard of 33,585 prisoners and 7,910 POWs to the construction of the Northern Pechora Main Line (NKVD Order No. 0192)."[1]

I have already mentioned the 1,000 POWs tranferred to the Murmansk Region for the construction of an aerodrome in May 1941. To complete the story, let me quote, in chronological order, three documents, which will make it clear what subsequently became of them.

May 28, 1941

Top secret
To: Comrade Orlovsky
Copy to: Comrade Frenkel*
Copy to: Comrade Soprunenko
Copy to: Comrade Sharapov

In accordance with Order No. 00358 of the People's Commissar of Internal Affairs of the USSR of April 8, 1941, 4,000 internees will be forwarded to you in the period between May 15 and June 15 of this year to work on the construction of aerodrome at Ponoi.

---

*In 1941 Frenkel, Naftali Aronovich, was a corps commissar, and Head of the Main Administration of Railway Construction (cont.)

In this connection I order that you take the following as guiding principles:

The End of the "Polish Experiment"

1. All the internees must be accommodated in one camp separately from the prisoners.

2. Guard duty inside the camp shall be the responsibility of the watch personnel.

3. The external guarding of the camp and guard duty at the construction site shall be carried out by escort guard troops.

4. The inner-camp regime among the internees shall be established by the head of the camp in accordance with appropriate instructions by the NKVD Administration for the Affairs of Prisoners of War and Internees.

5. The use of the internees in production activities shall be made in accordance with the instructions of the head of the construction project.

6. The head of the camp shall share equal responsibility with the head of the construction project for the fulfillment by internees of the set production norms.

7. The setting up of a camp for the accommodation of escort guard troops, the camp's personnel and the internees shall be the responsibility of the head of the construction project.

8. The supply of the internees and the camp's personnel with all types of allowances both from Murmansk and at the place of

---

of the NKVD of the USSR. It was for Kandalaksha that Frenkel was awarded his second Order of Lenin (he received his first in August 1933 for the construction of the White Sea Canal); see the decree of the Presidium of the Supreme Soviet of July 20, 1940, "On the Decoration of Railway Construction Workers (the Far East and Kandalaksha—Kuolajarvi)." For more information about him see *The Gulag Archipelago*.

119

work shall be the responsibilty of NKVD Construction Project No. 106.

Note. The supply of the escort guard troops with all types of allowances shall be the responsibility of the Administration for Escort Guard Troops.

9. The working day of the camp's personnel, internal and external guards and the internees was set by Order No. 00368 of the People's Commissar of Internal Affairs of the USSR of April 8 1941.

10. The feeding of the internees shall be effected depending on the fulfilment of production norms in accordance with the instruction attached hereto.

11. Monetary remuneration to the internees shall be paid in accordance with Order No. 298 of the People's Commissar of Internal Affairs of the USSR of April 2 1941.

12. Considering the brevity of the navigation season, NKVD Construction Project No. 106 shall lay in the necessary supply of foodstuffs sufficient in the case of the intemees being left in the camp for the winter.

> Chernyshov,
> Deputy People's Commissar of Internal Affairs of the USSR
> Copy validated by Lebedev, Senior Operative of the Secretariate of the Deputy People's Commissar of Internal Affairs of the USSR[2]

I would like to return the reader's attention to the paragraphs 6 and 10. Let us recall what *Izvestia* wrote about working in the harsh climate of the North, about the record breaking construction time and about the builders who "with characteristically Bolshevik persistence and energy overcame the difficulties which faced them."

From an operative dispatch of the staff of the 41st Brigade of Escort Guard Troops of the NKVD of July 6, 1941:

" As reported by the head of the NKVD Department for the Murmansk Region, 4,000 POWs working at Ponoi have been evacuated by sea to Arkhangelsk. No reports on same from the convoy chief have been received to date. The information is being double checked."

Signed: "Major Gusev, acting brigade commander."[3]

From an operative dispatch of the staff of the 41st Brigade of July 14, 1941:

" The 2nd Company of the 225th Regiment under the command of Captain Patrakeyev with Polish POWs from the locality named Ponoi on the Kola Peninsula have arrived in Arkhangelsk. Am awaiting exact information on the POWs' further iternerary."

Signed by the same person.[4]

One of my readers, A. V. Sidorov from Zaporozhye, gives yet another address:

"In the winter of 1940/41, my father was sent to the town of Obdorsk (now Salekhard) to inspect an electronic power station which had been (or almost had been) built there. Having returned from there, he told his family in strict confidence of the terrible fate of the Poles confined in the camp. I remember him describing Polish men and officers working at the construction site at 50 degrees below zero centigrade without gloves and wearing summer caps, fainting from hunger and back-breaking work and dying, their bodies stiffening in the snow. It was also then that father said that local residents had told him about even greater atrocities being committed in other camps situated in the mouth of the Ob river and along the entire coast."

The destinies of the surviving Polish POWs are closely intertwined with the fate of the civilian population deported from the territories incorporated in the USSR in September 1939. This is an entirely separate major topic which we will touch upon here only in order to complete the picture as much as possible and try to make some corrections in the treatment of the Katyn subject.

I will begin by recalling my conversation with Alexei Lukin.

I met with the former communications officer of the 136th Battalion at his home in Tver (still Kalinin at the time) on May 2, 1990. Together with me, a filming team headed by Andrzej Minko, an editor from Polish TV with whom we had already made two programs came to interview him. I cannot say that Alexei Lukin was particularly enthusiastic about posing in front of a camera. Yet, for fairness' sake, it should be noted that he did not look for an excuse to refuse the interview, either. Being clearly a naturally gentle person, he was uneasy (and who does not feel uneasy, when they find themselves in front of a TV camera for the first time in their lives, the more so since

The End of the "Polish Experiment"

this was a Polish TV camera) and recalled details and chose his words carefully, and yet he bore himself with dignity and did not change his stand in the least, although our talk was already after the official Soviet acknowledgement of responsibility. Considering this, greater attention must be paid to his testimony.

Below follows a verbatim record of our conversation without any omissions or rearrangements. I spent a great deal of time on this test, trying to choose an appropriate place for it in the book and reshaping it this way and that. At last, I decided not to touch on anything in it so as to avoid any unintentional bias. I hope that my comments will to a certain extent make up for the somewhat haphazard nature of our conversation. The gaps in the text are for technical reasons.

V. Abarinov: Alexei Alexeyevich, please tell me, what scheduled itineraries did your battalion have?

A. Lukin: We escorted prisoner transports to Ursatyevskay and at Ursatyevskaya we turned them over to another escort party, or else we took them to Sukhobezvodnaya in the Kirov Region. And then there was a convoy that I took to a place 12 kilometers from Kuibyshev, where a large aeroplane building works was being built. And also another integrated aeroplane building works was being built north of Kandalaksha in Karelia: this was where we took them.

V.A.: But you were a communications officer. Why were you engaged in escorting POWs? You had your own duties.

A.L.: It follows that the battalion had so much work to do. We, all of us, almost to the last officer, took part in escorting prisoner transports. I traveled less than the others. I escorted

123

some 4 or 5 convoys. That is, regular convoys where I was convoy commander or assistant convoy commander.

V.A.: Does this mean a total of five convoys or five Polish convoys?

A.L.: A total of five.

V.A.: And those with Poles?

A.L.: All of them were with Poles.

V.A.: Over what period, from the end of 1939 until when?

A.L.: Until the very beginning of the war. By the way, candidate member of the Party; I was given recognitions as soon as I joined the battalion, but it seemed that I would never have a chance to be admitted. Now I was on a mission, now the entire Party bureau was on a mission. Thus it went on up until the beginning of the war, and the recommendation was sent to the Main Administration for Escort Guard Troops, and it was at the front, near Oryol, that it finally caught up with me.

V.A.: Alexei Alexeyevich, please tell me about the Kozelsk camp. What was it like?

A.L.: About the Kozelsk camp . . . . I was there only once. They reported to me on how communication was provided with the sentry posts and I checked on the report.

V.A.: Which was precisely part of your duties.

A.L.: Yes, it was as a communication officer that I visited it. And so I checked the communications . . . . What could I notice there? The bunks were normal, two-tiered; I cannot say that it was bad or cramped there. The feeding was normal. As a matter of fact, the soldiers were given the same food as the prisoners. So I was told by the communications men.

V.A.: And how did the Poles look, how did they bear themselves?

The End of the "Polish Experiment"

A.L.: I had little contact with them . . . . I met with those who spoke Russian. They asked me and Sharapov . . . . [5] No, Sharapov was not there, he was at Yukhnov, and as for Kozelsk.

V.A.: The head of the camp? That was Korolyov.

A.L.: No, why, it was not Korolyov . . . .

V.A.: Demidovich was the commissar.[6]

A.L.: Demidovich . . . . Yes, Demidovich was the commissar. That's right. So it was with them that I went to see the camp. They asked us mostly about how they could get in touch with their relatives. When we began moving people out of Poland, we were told that we were moving out the *osadniki* (repellers)[7], the officer corps, representatives of the foreign ministry, and civil servants. That is, people who might have been potential enemies and potential collaborators with the Germans. This was what General Serov explained to us; have you heard about him?

V.A.: Yes, I certainly have. He was the one who later became minister of state security.

A.L.: Yes, of the KGB.[8] I cannot say anything negative about him and I do not agree . . . . They say that he was Beria's henchman. I still cannot see how he could have been Beria's henchman. He was his subordinate... And take the stories of how he briefed us and how he tore us off a strip, as the phrase goes, if we committed a violation in escorting prisoners! No, that wasn't true, that was a lie.

V.A.: Was it he who came to the camp in 1941?

A.L.: No, I think he was there from the very beginning. From the very beginning of the operation to move out the Polish population. He was in charge there. He briefed us for the first time, I think, in Minsk at the end of 1939. This was in winter, either in December or in January. We did not celebrate the New Year's Day then; we had no time for celebrations, the work load was very great . . . . And, besides, he gathered us for a briefing in Baranovichi. That, I believe, was early in 1940. I think he supervised this operation... those operations for moving out the Polish population all the time.

V.A.: Please tell me, do you remember a certain Colonel Stepanov from the Main Administration in Moscow?

A.L.: No, I don't. I remember that General Lyuby[9] came to our unit in the early days of the war. As far as I remember he replaced General Serov and at that time took over the command. He went to Katyn together with the regimental commander and left us behind. I took all my men along and wedged myself in an infantry regiment. Or, rather, not wedged myself, but was taken into it, and that was that. And thus I served in the infantry regiment until July 21, when I was wounded.

V.A.: Was that during the defense of Smolensk?

A.L.: It was in and beyond Smolensk. We were in Smolensk till July 24, but now they write that Smolensk was surrendered on July 16. That is not correct.

V.A.: Why did the regimental commander go to Katyn?

A.L.: He went there because the Germans were already in Minsk, were already approaching Minsk; therefore, the evacuation had to be speeded up. It was a very complicated business: people had to be evacuated, German planes were flying over the highway at an altitude of 10-15 meters and all the roads were thronged with refugees, and not only motor roads, but cart roads as well. Things were very hard and there were too few trucks. We used the trucks which we stopped; we took out the refugees, requisitioned the trucks and loaded them with Poles from the Katyn camp.[10] I met a man, let me see, this was at the very end of July, around July, I believe, I've forgotten his name, the name of that lieutenant.

The End of the "Polish Experiment"

V.A.: You said that he was probably a political instructor.

A.L.: That's right, I just cannot remember his name. But he was one of the comrades who . . . . You know how we formed the regiment? It was made up of those who had been called up for retraining in the spring before the war. They were chairmen of collective farms and shop superintendents: they were retrained at our unit. When the war began, they were made NCOs and commissioned officers and mostly went into the officer corps. All of them were advanced in years . . . .[11]

V.A.: Alexei Alexeyevich, let us go back to the beginning. What facilities was the battalion guarding? There were two camps . . . .

L.A.: Three camps.

V.A.: Three?

L.A.: Yukhnov, Kozelsk and Katyn. This I know.

V.A.: Well . . . .

A.L.: And I don't know about any other camps.

V.A.: And in the city itself?

A.L.: We had a prison in the city, but it was guarded by a unit which, when the KGB was set up, was subordinated directly to the KGB, and we remained subordinated to the Main Administration for Escort Guard Troops, which was part of the Ministry of Internal Affairs, that is, of the NKVD.[12]

V.A.: I see. Well, now, you said that you checked communication with the sentry posts at Kozelsk. How many posts were there?

A.L.: I believe there were about 10 posts there.

V.A.: And was there barbed wire round the camp?

A.L.: Yes, there was.

V.A.: And were there any civilians confined in the camp?

Chapter 2

A.L.: Yes, there was.

V.A.: And were there any civilians confined in the camp?

A.L.: Well, quite a few of them were former servicemen who had dressed up as best they could. Very few of them were wearing Polish military insignia, very few indeed.

V.A.: You were in charge of the convoys which left on April 10 and, I believe, on April 17 for the western regions of the Ukraine and Byelorussia. Were the convoys going from a camp or to a camp?

A.L.: They were going from a camp. And one of the convoy; that I took was from Lida and not from a camp. I took it to Kuibyshev.

V.A.: Who were in it?

A.L.: Mostly dames. From whorehouses. From red light districts.

V.A.: And so it was to that very construction project that you took them.

A.L.: I don't know. I turned them over to another escort party. I was met there by a commissioner, who turned my team out of the car and asked all the prisoners whether they had any complaints. By the way, as a general rule, they checked on us two or three times to see whether we were violating the rules of escorting.

V.A.: Yes, discipline was very rigorous.

A.L.: Very rigorous indeed. That's what I'm trying to say: since we were treated so rigorously, I do not see why it was necessary. May I put the question in this way? Why was this necessary? In my view, it was necessary in order to protect these people because we would be needing them. Apparently, this was given some thought.

The End of the "Polish Experiment"

V.A.: Was the service hard?

A.L.: It was not at all easy.

V.A.: All the time on the road . . .

A.L.: All the time on the road, without proper sleep . . .

V.A.: Dry rations . . .

A.L.: No. We had a kitchen. We had a kitchen both on scheduled and on special itinerary convoys. We had our own kitchen and the prisoners were fed at certain stations where we stopped in a siding. A kitchen drove up to the train, the prisoners were fed, and then we proceeded further.

V.A.: And you remember Tatarenko, a section commander, if I'm not mistaken?

A.L.: There was a man by that name.

V.A.: Why did he shoot himself?

A.L.: I don't think it was Tatareko. Or was it? No . . .

V.A.: In August, 1940.

A.L.: Why Tatarenko . . .

V.A.: Yes, it was Tatarenko, Tatarenko, I know this from the documents.

A.L.: Yes, I remember that case. But why did he do it, I never went into details. I still don't see why.

V.A.: Tell me, what kind of arms did the escort guard troops have? They had pistols, didn't they?

A.L.: Yes, pistols were already in use.

V.A.: And even the soldiers had them?

A.L.: The soldiers had carbines.

V.A.: And who had pistols?

A.L.: Convoy commanders and their assistants.[13]

129

Chapter 2

V.A.: I'm asking about arms because I found the minutes of a YCL meeting which say that during an inspection the battalion displayed poor shooting skills precisely with pistols.

A.L.: I don't remember such a thing. It's quite possible. I myself wasn't a bad shot. The soldiers of my unit were also fair shots. And, anyway, what does it matter?

V.A.: It's just that I wanted to know what arms were in use then. So it was only commanders and their assistants who had pistols?

A.L.: Pistols and Nagant revolvers. There were few pistols then and it was mostly Nagant revolvers that were used. TT pistols were only just coming into fashion.

V.A.: As a matter of fact, judging by the documents, the battalion had a good reputation.

A.L.: Our battalion commander was Mezhov, a man with a revolutionary past, a member of the Party since around 1917, a very respected and disciplined man; he himself was disciplined and he demanded discipline of others. He was the commander of the battalion almost until the very beginning of the war.

V.A.: By the way, why was he replaced?

A.L.: He said what he thought and not what they wanted him to say. His political deputy was also replaced; he was very discontented.

A. Minko: Alexei Alexeyevich, how much time did it take to get from Kozelsk to Smolensk?

A.L.: From Kozelsk to Smolensk . . .

A.M.: One night? Less than one night? Or more?

A.L.: We took the train in the morning and arrived there in the evening. We had our dinner there.

130

The End of the "Polish Experiment"

A.M.: This was when you traveled by yourself. And when you escorted prisoners?

A.L.: When we escorted prisoners, that depended on the railway. But then, prisoner transports were let through just the same as passenger trains, because we had to have hot food sometime around midday. We traveled at night and made a stop during the day.

....

A.L.: I just cannot believe that the authorities especially decided to exterminate these Poles.

V.A.: So you don't even believe that . . .

A.L.: We did not talk about it. In my battalion I was not regarded as some kind of . . . philistine, so to speak; being a member of escort parties, I was invited to the sittings of the Party bureau where they made me answer for every minor breach of duty and demanded that I treat people better. And I just cannot believe that our men took part in any executions. As soon as Reprintsev arrived, his main task and the main question raised at every conference was: if you violate discipline and the rules for escorting prisoners, you will be severely punished. And violators were actually punished. They were discharged from the army. Thus, one lieutenant was discharged just before the beginning of the war because he allowed some passengers on his train, and for some other violation. He was immediately expelled from the Party and discharged from the army.

V.A.: Did he take any money for it?

A.L.: Apparently, he did. There was no sense in doing this without taking money. The situation with tickets was bad and so he tried to profit by it. The punishment was severe. I was never subjected to any punishment. And now . . . few of us have

131

survived to this day... it seems as if I am confessing, doesn't it, Vladimir Konstantinovich?

V.A.: Well, it's not quite that, Alexei Alexeyevich . . .

A.L.: So you say!

A.M.: I have received a letter from a man who tells a story about people who managed to escape from the Kozelsk camp. What do you think, was it possible to escape from that camp?

A.L.: Quite possible. After the war I met some Poles in Uzbekistan who were doing quite well there. This was in 1946 or 1947 when I went there to continue my service. And so one old man briefly told me his life story, or rather the life story of his son-in-law. Of course, he had been in the camp and then escaped from it in some way. Could it have been otherwise? No, it couldn't. And subsequently he joined Anders' army and left for Iran with Anders.

A.M.: But then there was an amnesty.

A.L.: Yes, there was, I know. We had several persons specially engaged in handling letters. When letters came to our battalion, they looked for those people in the camps and then gave them an opportunity to get in touch with their families. The families had been moved into the south, into Asia, to southern Kazakhstan and Uzbekistan. We turned them over to other escort parties at Ursatyevskaya. Do you know Ursatyevskaya? It's a junction where the railway branches off to Alma-Ata and Tashkent. It was there that they were taken and there they settled down to live. This was not very humane, but there was an instruction to move out all the osadniki, people from the belt which Pilsudski had set up near our border . . . He gave them 10,000 zlotys each, and plots of land and some timber for building houses, right? Do you remember this? This belt was, so to speak . . . . Later on it was dubbed an iron curtain. So all these people had to be moved out on the instructions of our government.

V.A.: Tell me, was the convoy going to Brest a scheduled one?

A.L.: From Brest?

V.A.: To Brest or from Brest.

A.L.: There were no convoys headed for Brest. People were being moved out of Brest.

V.A.: And were there any convoys going from camps to Brest?

A.L.: No.

V.A.: For exchange.

A.L.: For exchange—yes, there were some. There were some for exchange. But they, those who were taken for exchange with the Germans, were located at some place nearer to Minsk. I did not take any part whatever in those operations. It was mostly the KGB that participated, it was KGB officers who handled this. We had nothing to do with it. We only escorted people whom the KGB selected. And we had a KGB commissioner traveling with each convoy. Made all of us sick to death.

V.A.: With what?

A.L.: With his incessant faultfinding. He behaved in an uncultured way. All of them were so full of conceit.

V.A.: What rank did those commissioners hold?

A.L.: They had their own ranks with insignias in the form of triangles or, rather, angles. Two or three angles; there were never less than that.

V.A.: And why did you not return to your regiment after hospital?

Chapter 2

A.L.: Those who were severely wounded were taken a long way behind the front lines. I got to Ufa. After spending three months in a hospital, I was sent to Sverdlovsk for an assignment. And in Sverdlovsk they basically did not ask me any questions.

V.A.: But you were not particularly eager to get back to your unit, were you?

A.L.: As a matter of fact, while in Sverdlovsk I was assigned to a division as an assistant communications officer. But when I was on duty at the division headquarters I got in touch with an acquaintance of mine who was serving in the Main Administration of our internal troops in Moscow. Oh, no, he was in the frontier guard troops. And so I got in touch with him by high frequency telephone, and as I was speaking with him the division commander entered the room. Ah, he said, so you want to be sent to the front! And he sent me to the front straight away.

V.A.: And where were you when the war ended?

A.L.: In Brest. We got as far as Krakow and then were ordered to return. The bandit formations in the Baltic republics were joining forces with the Ukrainian nationalists. Our task was to guard the Moscow, Minsk, Brest Highway, along which a great deal of material was being transported. It was there that we saw the end of the war.

V.A.: Was your battalion in direct contact with Moscow?

A.L.: There was a high frequency telephone line. I was the first to receive an order to open the packet of instructions and begin forming a regiment on June 22. At five in the morning.

V.A.: In other words, you could get in touch directly with Moscow, by-passing the brigade headquarters?

A.L.: Of course, I could.

The End of the "Polish Experiment"

V.A.: Alexei Alexeyevich, the NKVD committed such terrible crimes against their own people. What makes you think they were not capable of liquidating the Poles?

A.L.: I heard nothing about this. Nothing.

V.A.: But then the procedure might have been as follows: the escort party would bring the prisoner transport to a certain station and then turn it over to the KGB.

A.L.: That's exactly how it was. For example, I turned all of my prisoners over to another escort party. After that they were questioned about whether I had broken orders or abused them. And then I had a paper signed to my name saying that there were no complaints against me, checked by such and such. Subsequently, I submitted this paper to my commander.

V.A.: Yes, I've seen such papers. But could it be that the escort guards simply did not know what became of the Poles?

A.L.: I, for instance, heard nothing about this, honest to God, nothing.

V.A.: This was a top secret operation.

A.L.: It turns out that the secret was so closely guarded that few people knew about it. And now we are having to hear about it with regret after the event . . .

....

. . . There was General Serov and then General Lyuby, also from the People's Commissariat of Internal Affairs, it never happened that he made us do it or informed us about this. He never told us about it and never made us do it. Although sometimes shooting down an offender was simply a must.

V.A.: How so?

A.L.: Well, if a person with lots of gold and money in a suitcase was fleeing to the east he did not require even such persons as these to be shot. Such people deserved to be shot. It was not until we had stayed several days in Smolensk as part of

135

an anti-profiteer detachment and refugees began moving in large groups. There were such people among these. And yet no one forced us to shoot them down. Although it seems that they ought to have been shot.

V.A.: Marauders?

A.L.: They were regular marauders. We had them tried by troikas* and eventually shot them, but never by lynch law. There was nothing arbitrary about it. You see, it was terrible when refugees . . . . We had to meet them and they had such a look in their eyes . . . . It had to be seen, and as for describing it . . .

V.A.: And why did you apprehend them?

A.L.: Our job was not to let through this kind of luggage and to prevent marauding. All the shops, or at least very many of them, both in Minsk and in Brest had been cleaned out. There were many jewelry shops in Minsk. And so our job was to find these people and confiscate the gold.

V.A.: How did you single them out from among the refugees?

A.L.: We checked their belongings.

V.A.: But you didn't check the belongings of all of them to a man, did you?

A.L.: No, of course we didn't. There were specialists in that kind of thing working there. The anti-profiteer detachments consisted mainly of frontier guards and state security officers.

V.A.: And when were these anti-profiteer detachments removed?

---

*"Troika" was a popular name for a Special Board (Russian acronym: OSO), a three-man board of the People's Commissariat of Internal Affairs, with powers to sentence socially dangerous persons without trial; abolished in 1953.

The End of the "Polish Experiment"

A.L.: On July 17. On July 17 the Germans started firing on us. Our house was the first to be shelled; a brass band unit was staying in it . . .

V.A.: In Smirnov Street.

A.L.: Yes, in Smirnov Street. We dug ourselves in the square and it was there that we met the German motorcyclists.

This dialogue does not call for any special comments, except where it touches upon convoys headed west. When studying the log of orders to the 136th Battalion, I was surprised at the number of convoys that in April and May 1940, took the same route: Smolensk—western Ukraine—Byelorussia. At first, I decided that it was prisoners intended for exchange who were traveling in these convoys. And, since there were no other camps in the area where the battalion operated, it seemed that the only alternative was to assume that they were Kozelsk and Yukhnov prisoners. It was in this form that this information, certainly, not through me, subsequently got into the press (Ekho Planety, 1989, No.24) and was used for further manipulations. There were, however, too many facts established beyond doubt which ran counter to this interpretation. Lukin provided me with an explanation regarding his two convoys; according to him one had Kandalaksha ("there were already barracks there which looked new to us") and the other the Sukhobezvodnaya Station near Kirov ("quite a number of people had already been brought there") as their destinations. But then Kandalaksha and Sukhobezvodnaya are neither in Byelorussia nor in the Ukraine. The contradiction seemed insoluble until it dawned on me that these were convoys going not from Smolensk to the west, but from west to east, whereas the trips made from Smolensk were with empty wagons. Proof of this was soon found in the form of numerous documents concerning mass deportations of the Polish population.

POLISH NATIONAL AUTONOMY
IN THE USSR

A Historical Outline

The existence on USSR territory of Polish autonomous districts has been forgotten today. Yet the "Polish experiment" deserves attention if only because it was the first attempt to solve the problem of an ethnic minority on a democratic basis.

The beginning of the Polish experiment dates back to 1922 when Julian Marchlewski* and Felix Kon** addres-

---

* Marchlewski, Julian (1866-1925), one of the organizers of the Social-Democratic Party of the Kingdom of Poland and Lithuania (which united with the Polish Socialist Party in 1918 to form the Communist Workers' Party of Poland), alternate member of the Central Committee of the Russian Social-Democratic Labor Party in 1907, and one of the founders of the Spartacus League in Germany. In 1920 he was chairman of the Provisional Revolutionary Committee of Poland. Chairman of the Central Committee of the International Organization for Assistance to Fighters for the Revolution. From 1922, rector of the Communist University of Ethnic Minorities of the West. Member of the All-Russia Central Executive Committee.

sed a congress of the Comintern with a proposal to set up Polish autonomous territorial-administrative units in the frontier area. To this end, according to Polish intelligence, between 1923 and the end of 1925 over 30,000 Polish families from towns in Central Russia and Siberia were resettled in the so-called far eastern territories, above all, the Volhynia Region. They were settled on the lands of the former Polish magnates of the far eastern provinces. For Soviet Poles, two relatively large autonomous districts, a Julian Marchlewski District in the Ukraine (40,000 residents on an area of 650 square kilometers) and a Felix Dzierżyński District in Byelorussia (44,000 residents on an area of 1,000 square kilometres), were set up. These districts were popularly known as the Marchlewshchina and Dzerzhinshchina. All party bodies and state institutions in these districts, including the militia and law courts, used the Polish language.

The structure of the Polish Socialist national autonomy in the Soviet Union included a broad network of so-called Polish national local Soviets were set up anywhere where more than 500 Poles lived. More than 670 Polish primary and secondary schools, seven special schools with classes

---

** Kon, Felix (1864-1941), CPSU member from 1918 (actual Party member from 1906), one of the leaders of the Polish Socialist Party. In 1921, Secretary of the Communist Party (Bolsheviks) of the Ukraine, in 1922-1923, Secretary of the Executive Committee of the Comintern, in 1931-1933, Chairman of the All-Union Radio Committee. Member of the All-Russia Central Executive Committee and, subsequently, of the Central Executive Committee of the USSR.

conducted in the Polish language, two colleges (Minsk Polish Teachers' Training Institute and Kiev Institute of Public Education), and also several faculties for Polish--speaking students at a number of colleges in the Ukraine, Byelorussia, Moscow, and Leningrad were opened on the initiative of the Soviet government. A Soviet judicial apparatus conducting proceedings in the Polish language, three professional Polish theaters, 16 Polish district newspapers, six republican newspapers and one national newspaper in the Polish language were put into operation. Hundreds of titles of books in Polish were published every year, Polish radio and a number of Polish research institutes were established within the framework of the Academies of Sciences of the Ukraine and Byelorussia. In the constitution of the Byelorussian SSR, the Polish language was proclaimed one of the state languages of Byelorussia.

Such a large number of Polish institutions and administrative units were intended to serve the needs of some 1.2 million Poles (including 650,000 in the Ukraine and about 300,000 in Byelorussia).

Despite immense efforts by Polish Communists, attempts to instill the stereotype of "socialist thinking" in the populations of those territories failed. Marchlewshchina became a blank spot on the map of successes scored in the development of collective farms. Thus, in 1932, the share of collectivized farms was 61.5 per cent nationwide, as high as 72 per cent in the Ukraine and as little as 16.9 per cent in Marchlewshchina.

The resistance to collectivization brought about the mass-scale deportation of local *kulaks* (well-to-do peasants) and *podkulachniks* (persons aiding the *kulaks*), as well as other reprisals. By 1933, the population of Marchlewshchina had been reduced by nearly 23 percent. The entire Polish Communist leadership was also subjected to reprisals.

The Poles became the first major Soviet population group to be collectively repressed in 1936-1938 on the basis of nationality rather than class affiliation. They were moved on a mass scale from the towns and villages of the Ukraine and Byelorussia to remote parts of the Asian USSR (mostly to the Kokchetav Region of Kazakhstan).

The Marchlewski Polish national district was liquidated by a decree of 1935 while the Dzierżyński district remained until 1938. The most bitter trials that the Soviet Polish community was to live through, however, were yet to come. The disbandment by the Comintern of the Communist Party of Poland in 1938 brought only greater reprisals in its wake.

After September 17, 1939, 12 million Polish citizens, including some four million Poles, found themselves in the USSR. All of them were granted Soviet citizenship by a decree of the Presidium of the USSR Supreme Soviet of November 29, 1939. About 600,000 people were deported from these territories and between 1.5 and 1.8 million Poles were moved by force into the heart of the USSR during the years of Stalinism.

These calculations have been made by Polish experts, particularly from the Union of Siberians. Among the Soviet scholars who were members of the joint Soviet-Polish academic commission on the history of relations between the two countries, it was Valentina Parsadanova, leading research associate with the Slavic and Balkan Studies Institute of the USSR Academy of Sciences, who studied the issues of the deportation. She published more than once stories in the press about the touching concern for the deportees displayed by the Soviet government. According to Parsadanova, the members of the commission "excluded from the category of deportation the call-up for service in the Red Army in August 1939, the migration of Poles from the western areas of the Ukraine and Byelorussia to the Donbass coal-fields and the Urals in search of employment, and their evacuation from the border area where fortifications were being built." (International Affairs, 1988, No.6, p.150).[15]

The flow of deportees, or special resettlers in the terminology of the day, was biggest in the first half of 1940. Thus, in the first quarter of 1940 escort guard units of the NKVD transported 138,619 special resettlers and, in the second quarter, 59,419 special resettlers from the western regions of the Ukrainian and Byelorussian SSR. An instruction of January 17, 1940, gives us an idea of how they were transported and in what conditions. Trains for transporting deportees consisted of 75 carriages, each carrying 30 persons. Each train was escorted by 22 escort guards, one doctor, one doctor's assistant, and two nurses. Deportees were allowed to take with them not more than 500 kg of luggage per family. The daily food allowance was 2.50 roubles per person.

The End of the "Polish Experiment"

It goes without saying that the Polish special resettlers, having been moved into the heart of the country, found themselves in extremely difficult conditions. Here is a testimony by Vladimir Zlenko from Stavropol: "Late in the autumn of 1939," he writes, "my parents, salesclerks of the food supply system of the Salair gold mines, were assigned to work at the Gromotukha gold mine situated not far from Peak Taskyl on the border between the Kemerovo Region and Khakassia. In the spring of 1940, a large number of Poles, both single and with families, were brought to the mine. They worked in the mine and after work felled trees, stripped bark from logs and built houses for themselves. The Poles' destitution was obvious even to the children."

There was a separate "special contingent" comprised of defectors convicted on the strength of resolutions made by OSOs, Special Boards of the NKVD. Here is a quotation from a circular by Colonel Krivenko, acting chief of the Escort Guard Troops of the NKVD, of March 2, 1940:

People's Commissar of Internal Affairs of the USSR Comrade Beria has ordered the People's Commissars of Internal Affairs of the Ukrainian SSR and the Byelorussian SSR to send the defectors from the former territory of Poland convicted by a Special Board of the NKVD to the Sevvostlag (Administration of the Northeast, i.e., Kolyma Corrective Labor Camps.—Ed.) of the NKVD (Vladivostok) to serve their sentences.

The organization of the process of sending forth convicts has been entrusted to the prison and corrective labor colony departments of the NKVD.

143

Chapter 2

Escort of prisoners, who are to travel in transports of 1,000 to 1,500 persons, each under close guard, has been entrusted to the escort guard troops. A total of 6 to 8 transports shall be sent forth.

To ensure the said escorting, you are ordered:

(1) to contact the People's Commissars of Internal Affairs of the Ukrainian SSR and the Byelorussian SSR, respectively, and to begin preparations for this type of escorting;

(2) to bear in mind that the escorted persons will be striving to escape; the command of the units shall therefore select the entire personnel of the escort parties on an individual basis and in greater numbers compared with the existing standard;

(3) in order that the persons being escorted cannot determine the system of guarding and the numerical strength of the escort party, to increase and reduce the number of posts on a train along the itinerary in cases of necessity and depending on the situation, for which purpose to demand in the equipping of freight cars with twice as many cars with brave platforms as is usual;

(4) to prevent escapes of the escorted persons, thorough preparations must be made for the reception and use of agents;

(5) for catching escapees, to assign to the trains the best junior instructors of sentry dogs, together with dogs;

(6) to take into account the experience of work for escorting special resettlers . . .[16]

And so on, and so forth.

Now here is what Anna Rozina, a Leningrad resident, writes in her letter to me:

In 1939, a prisoner transport arrived at the camp in which I was confined (Mordovian Autonomous SSR, Potma

Station, settlement of Yavas, Temlag camp). They were young girls who had fled from Nazi-occupied Poland. They told me that, when they saw Soviet frontier guards, they rushed to them and began kissing them, for they regarded these frontier guards as their saviors. All of them were sent to the camp . . ."

Incidentally, I inquired specially of the author of the letter what had become of these Polish girls after the amnesty had been granted, whether they were released and restored to their citizenship. Anna Rozina's answer was in the negative: all of them stayed in the Soviet penal colony.

And so it was Mordovia, Murmansk, Khakassia, the Yamal-Nentsi Autonomous Dictrict, the Far East . . . . This is not just the geography of deportation: it is the geography of graveyards. Those who lie buried there died a "natural" death. Of course, there are no gravestones nor grave mounds there. This is also quite natural for the regime whose victims these people became.

In some places, however, the burial sites are marked. Here is a letter from Dilbar Islamova, a resident of the Uzbek town of Karshi:

"About 10 years ago I was shown a hillock 50 by 50 meters in area, fenced off by wire, on the outskirts of the settlement of Guzar. I. B. Chernyak, director of the Tekhslozhbytpribor factory, told me that this was a graveyard of Polish POWs, of whom there were quite a few here during the years of the war. He also told me how they died of hunger and disease. I have not stopped thinking about these people ever since."

Dilbar Islamova also quoted testimonies by other local residents, who confirmed I.B. Chernyak's story. "I am always ready to assist you in further searches," she wrote in conclusion.

Still another site of mass burial of Poles, located in Arkhangelsk, has been indicated by B. P. Zamorov (Arkhangelsk). At a spot on the bank of the Yenisei River in the Krasnoyarsk Territory there lie buried victims of the tragedy about which G.S. Shaidullin from the town of Dnestrovsk in the Moldavian SSR, told me: "During the war I served as a sailor on the steamships *Bagration* and *Mayakovsky*, which sailed on the Yenisei. One day we tied up at a half-sunk barge of the *Karskaya* type, which was moored at the bank. It was moored not far from the Pridivnaya landing stage, which is 100 to 110 kilometers downstream from Krasnoyarsk. There was a smell of putrefaction coming from its flooded holds." From eye-witnesses' accounts, G. S. Shaidullin goes on to write, it transpired that Polish POW's were being transported in the holds of the barge. The barge encountered a shoal, was holed and began to sink. The people in the holds rushed to the only hatch which was not battened down, but the guards opened fire on them. "The last door to safety was blocked up with corpses. About 20 people survived. The bodies of those drowned were taken out during the nighttime and buried in trenches, on which trees were planted. Stories about this were told in whispers at the time. People were afraid."

On July 30, 1941, an agreement on the restoration of diplomatic relations between the USSR and Poland was signed in London, and, on September 14, a military agreement was concluded between the two countries. On the territory of the Soviet Union a Polish army under the command of General Wladyslaw Anders began to be formed. The Polish POW's were granted an amnesty. When released from camps and prisons, they went to assembly points. These emaciated, famished people attracted attention, even though there was hardly anyone among Soviet citizens who was not suffering hardships at the time.

Anders' headquarters were located in the settlement of Koltubanka, Buzuluk District, Chkalov (now Orenburg) Region. Here is what Yevgeni Zarubin from Kuibyshev (now Samara) tells us about the conditions in which Polish servicemen lived there: "Whereas our troops being mustered built dugouts for themselves, the Poles went on living in tents. This cost them dear in the frosty winter of 1941–42, when very many of them froze to death. The only construction project on which they were working was a church. In it, they held funeral services for their dead. It pains me to write about this, but no gravestone has been put up on the site of their burial to this day, despite the fact that I have more than once raised this question with the proper authorities." Yevgeni Zarubin often visits the graveyard in Koltubanka—his parents are buried there—

and he ventures to show accurately the place where men and officers from Anders' army lie buried.

The deportation of the Polish population continued after the war. In the late 1940s Leonid Okhlopkov, who was a young officer with the NKVD at the time, moved former soldiers of Anders' army and their families from Byelorussia to the Aldan gold fields. There is also the following episode in the history of Soviet-Polish relations: some 4,520 "Anders' men," repatriated from Britain, were turned into special resettlers by the Soviet authorities and 74 men from the territory of Poland were interned in 1944-1945; these data have been supplied by V. Zemskov, Cand. Sc. (History).

When I asked Leonid Okhlopkov to name his unit, it turned out that it was the very same 136th Escort Guard Battalion, subsequently reformed into the 252nd Regiment, whose archives I had studied in the minutest detail. After the war, the regiment was once again stationed in Smolensk and it was the same Colonel Reprintsev who commanded it. Leonid Okhlopkov also happened to visit the special dacha at Kozyi Gory where he was told in strict confidence about the Katyn tragedy, and it was positively stated that the executions were carried out by "our men."

And there is something else," continues Okhlopkov. "Just in case. In 1944, I was studying at the Saratov frontier guards school. In October, the students of that school were suddenly sent to the Caucasus to reinforce the guards on the USSR's Turkish frontier. The objective of the operation was kept secret, yet nonetheless rumors leaked out: the

NKVD operative troops (there were such troops at the time) would be moving out Turks and Kurds early in November.

"My frontier station was situated at an altitude of 4,000 meters (at the point where Armenia, Georgia and Turkey met) and at night you could see clearly endless winding mountain roads lit by truck headlights; it was the 'operatives' moving people out.

"It was only recently that it became clear to me that the 'Turks' were the Meskheti Turks."

Chapter 3

MOSCOW, LUBYANKA PRISON

The search for the missing Polish officers began immediately after the establishment of diplomatic relations between the Stalin and Sikorski governments. Negotiations with high-ranking NKVD officers to this end were conducted on behalf of Anders by Józef Czapski, a former prisoner of the Starobelsk camp. An account of the events by Captain Czapski was once published by the author in *Literaturnaya Gazeta*. This material, which also included answers to the author's questions by Leonid Raikhman, one of the main figures in the account, triggered off a stream of letters from readers, and now I can supplement the publication with fresh details. At the same time, I will now fill in the gaps which had to be left then because of lack of space.

Czapski writes:

The formation of a Polish army in the USSR, began in September 1941, in Tatishchevo near Saratov, and also in Totsk on the Kuibyshev–Chkalov railway line. Every day hundreds of people arrived at the summer camp in Totsk . . . . We set up something in the nature of an information bureau. The task that I was performing was to question each new arrival thoroughly. Each person, whether from Vorkuta, Magadan, Kamchatka or Karaganda told me about themselves, and all of them spoke about two things: they told me about their attempts to find traces of their deported families and gave me whole lists of their colleagues who were still being confined in camps and who had not yet been released. Right from the start I began asking each of them whether they had worked together with anyone of our comrades from Starobelsk, Kozelsk or Ostashkov. We still believed that our colleagues being held there would arrive any minute now . . . . And yet not only did none of them arrive, no news from them ever came and we knew nothing about what happened to them apart from contradictory second-hand reports . . .

From the moment that General Anders began organizing the army, he persistently pressed the Soviet authorities for information about the missing persons, but kept receiving the same polite and vague promises by way of a reply. We forwarded reports on all information concerning the missing persons to the army commander and to our embassy in Kuibyshev . . .

We expected our colleagues to come any day now, supplementing and enlarging the list of missing persons in the meantime. A month passed, but none of the former Starobelsk, Kozelsk and Ostashkov prisoners arrived. By the time the commander-in-chief had come to Moscow in December we already had a list in excess of 4,500 names which General Anders brought with him to Moscow . . .

Early in January 1942 I was sent by General Anders to Chkalov as a commissioner for the affairs of nonreturned POWs in order to try to clear up the matter with General Nasedkin, head of the Gulag . . .

During our first meeting I took Nasedkin by surprise, and this made him more approachable. There was a large map of the USSR on the wall behind him on which major camps under his jurisdiction were marked. The greatest numbers of asterisks, circles, and other signs denoting large clusters of camps were to be seen on the territory of the Komi Autonomous SSR, on the Kola Peninsula and on the Kolyma River . . .

Chapter 3

I described the situation with the three POW camps to Nasedkin and added that further detainment in the camps of POWs who were to be released on Stalin's orders 'smacked of sabotage.' I had a feeling that my interlocutor actually had a vague idea about the business, or, perhaps, he was only pretending . . . . He told me that in the spring of 1940, in the period of the liquidation of these camps, he was not yet at the head of the Gulag and that he had only corrective labor camps for political and criminal prisoners, but no POW camps, under his jurisdiction. Perhaps, there were "also" some Polish POWs among them; however, he had no exact information about this. He said that he would try to clear the matter up and give an answer the following day. I asked him whether he had sent POWs to Franz Josef Land and Novaya Zemlya, something which I had heard about from many of the prisoners who had returned. The general assured me that he had sent no one to these islands and, if there were any such camps there, they were under the juristiction of some other authorities not subordinated to him; perhaps there were some POW camps there after all . . .

In my presence, the general gave the order over the telephone for an exact clarification of the question about the camps at Starobelsk, Kozelsk, and Ostashkov. In giving this instruction, he quoted General Anders' letter, repeating the words 'on the orders of Comrade Stalin,' which were in it. This was the end of my first conversation with General Nasedkin.

About 11 o'clock in the evening in the same day, I was received by Bzyrov,* head of the Chkalov Regional Department of the NKVD. Bzyrov was very courteous with me and expressed his readiness to help me. In the first place he told me that I would not be able to find out anything definite anywhere except

---

*An error: the person in question was State Security Captain Ivan Bzyrin.

from the central authorities, and only the highest at that (the conversation was taking place in the presence of two witnesses, also NKVD officers), and he gave me to understand that Merkulov or Fedotov could help me. (At the time, Beria was head of the NKVD of the USSR, while Merkulov was his deputy, and on the next rung down of the hierarchical ladder were Kruglov, Fedotov, and Raikhman). When I mentioned Novaya Zemlya and Franz Josef Land, not only was he not surprised, but himself showed me on the map the port of Dudinka on the Yenisei through which the biggest batches of prisoners were delivered to the islands. He said that there were no Poles in his region who had not been released.

Next day I was once again received by General Nasedkin. This time, I did not catch him unaware as I had the day before. He said that he had nothing to tell me and that clarification of the questions in which I was interested could only be provided by the central authorities. Once again I asked the general about Novaya Zemlya and said that I had some information about Polish POWs being held there. Once again Nasedkin responded in a much different way than he had the day before. 'It is not to be ruled out,' was what he said, 'that the northern camps under my jurisdiction sent some small groups to these islands, but as for the many thousands which you have told me about, this is completely out of the question . . .'

In the middle of January I was sent by General Anders to Kuibyshev and Moscow, to General Zhukov, with a letter of recommendation and a letter giving an outline of the case, in which General Anders wrote that our fruitless search for the missing POW's made the organization of an army very difficult, that it was greatly oppressive both to himself and to his associates and, since he was not in a position to look personally into the matter, he requested that the same assistance be provided for me as would have been provided for himself. The Soviet generals whom I went to see held very high posts in the NKVD, and had been charged with the special task of facilitating the organization of a Polish army. In the preceding two years, General Raikhman had personally interrogated many of our colleagues, and I was hoping that he and the other generals, who undoubtedly had full knowledge of our case, would be able and willing to help me—for example, that they would arrange for me to have an audience with the almighty Beria himself or with Merkulov. Neither Raikhman nor Zhukov was in Kuibyshev when I got there, so I went to Moscow and, while there, it was only on February 3, 1942, after a brief detention—ostensibly my mistake—that I finally got to see General Raikhman at the Lubyanka (Zhukov was not present).

As I was waiting my turn in Raikhman's small waiting room, I noted with surprise that before he received me Raikhman received Khodas, the former commandant of the Gryazovets camp. A quarter of an hour later I was admitted to his office. As usual, we had our talk in the presence of witnesses.

I asked Raikhman to help me get an audience with Beria or with Merkulov, but was met with a polite refusal. I then submitted to him a memorandum in which I described in great detail all we knew about the history of the three camps up until the time of their liquidation, that is, up to May 1940. Following this introduction, I wrote:

'Nearly six months have passed since August 12, 1941, the day when an amnesty for all Polish POWs was announced. Polish men and officers released from prisons and camps are coming singly and in groups to join the Polish army. Despite the 'amnesty,' despite the firm promise given to ambassador Kot by Stalin himself in October 1941, to return the POWs to us and despite the categorical order given by Stalin in the presence of

Moscow, Lubyanka Prison

General Sikorski and General Anders on December 3, 1941, to find and release the prisoners of Starobelsk, Kozelsk, and Ostashkov, we have not received a single call for help from the POWs being held in the above-mentioned camps. In questioning thousands of our colleagues returning from camps and prisons, we never got any reliable confirmation of the whereabouts of the prisoners moved out of these three camps. We have only heard rumors that in 1940 between 6,000 and 12,000 officers and NCOs were transported to the Kolyma by way of Nakhodka Bay, that over 5,000 officers were concentrated in the mines on Franz Josef Land and many of them were also deported to Novaya Zemlya and the Kamchatka and Chukotka Peninsulas, that Polish officer POWs were taken in huge tow barges (1,700 to 2,000 in each) to the northern islands and that these barges sank. None of these rumors has been reliably confirmed.

We know now thoroughly and precisely the NKVD works, 90 none of us prisoners of war admits the possibility that the highest echelons of the NKVD may be unaware of the whereabouts of 15,000 prisoners, including 8,000 officers. Doesn't the solemn promise of Stalin himself and his strictest order to clear up the fate of the former Polish POWs enable us to entertain a hope that we will at least learn where our comrades-in-arms are and, if they died, how and when this happened?'

This was followed by a list which was compiled as accurately as possible. General Raikhman read it attentively . . . . Not a muscle in his face moved nor did his countenance change even for a second . . . . He answered me that he knew nothing about the fate of these people and that this question was beyond the competence of the departments subordinate to him, but, wishing to do General Anders a favor, he would try to clear the matter up and inform me of the results. He asked me to wait in Moscow for his telephone call. We parted rather coolly. I waited for 10 days, after which there came a call at night: it was **Raikhman** himself who made the call; he informed me in an unexpectedly amiable—even extremely amiable—tone of voice that, unfortunately, he would have to leave the next morning and that, unfortunately, he would not be able to see me and that he advised me to go to Kuibyshev, since all materials relating to our case had been forwarded to Deputy People's Commissar for Foreign Affairs Comrade Vyshinsky. I only had time to answer Raikhman that I was well aware that Vyshinsky would tell me nothing, for up until the day when my conversation with Raikhman took place Polish Ambassador Kot had already applied eight times to Comrade Vyshinsky without result. This ended my mission to Moscow.

We still had a grain of hope skillfully kept up by the NKVD officers assigned to our army. We were hoping that our colleagues would join us in July or August, that is, at the only time when navigation was possible in those seas. They often whispered in our ears in the strictest confidence: "Just don't tell anyone anything, be patient. Your comrades will join you in July or August." Yet July and then August came and passed, but still no one returned.

Of the three generals named by Józef Czapski, I had a chance to put queries to only one, Raikhman. Leonid Raikhman gave me a very courteous reception. It was the time when the whole nation was sitting glued to the TV watching the debates at the First Congress of People's Deputies of the USSR. I remember that my interlocutor was particularly interested in the Gdlyan case.

Leonid Raikhman disappointed me immediately. He said that he did not know Czapski and had never met him. On the other hand, he had met General Anders himself. As

far as I know, there is no record of this fact in the literature on Katyn. This is what Leonid Raikhman told me (the
text has been authorized by him):

Early in November 1941, I flew to Kuibyshev, where, as we
know, the embassies had been evacuated from Moscow. My task
was to ensure the safety of diplomats. It was there that, on the
instructions of the leadership, I had my only meeting with
General Anders. It took place in a separate room at a restaurant.
Anders was accompanied by an aide-de-camp and another Pole.
I had with me two members of an operative group of the
Kuibyshev counterintelligence department. Anders handed me a
list of Polish officers which took up less than one page, and asked
me to take measures to find them. I immediately passed the list
on to one of the operatives who were there with me and promised to call Anders in a fortnight. Before the expiration of this
period of time, however, I flew to Moscow. Before my departure,
l called Anders and informed him that it was the same operative
to whom I had handed over the list in his, Anders', presence who
was handling the case of the officers being searched for. At the
People's Commissariat of State Security all matters relating, at
least to some extent, to the Poles, were the sole responsibility of
Georgi Sergeyevich Zhukov* (State Security commissar 3rd class),
who had been the State Defense Committee Commissioner for
the formation of the Polish army since September or October
1941. He had a mandate signed by Stalin and he alone had the
right to meet with Poles without express permission from the
leadership of the People's Commissariat. Since I was deputy head

---

*Not to be confused with Marshal Georgi Konstantinovich
Zhukov, the prominent Soviet military leader.

of counterintelligence, Zhukov's department was subordinated to me; not so Zhukov himself and not in respect of Polish matters. Apart from the meeting with Anders, I did not subsequently take part in any meetings with any of the Poles. I have never heard the name of Czapski.

I also asked Raikhman about his participation in the preparation of witnesses to the Katyn events for the Nuremberg Trial. This is a separate subject. One of the Soviet archives has the minutes of the sittings of the so-called governmental commission for the Nuremberg Trial, in which Raikhman appears as one of three members of the team that was working with the Katyn materials. Besides him, judging by the minutes, the team included A. N. Trainin and L. R. Sheinin (more about this will follow later). Here is what Leonid Raikhman said in reply:

I had absolutely nothing to do with the Nuremberg Trial. There was yet another episode relating to the Poles: in the summer of 1946 (I do not remember the exact date, I only remember that I was wearing a tunic, not a greatcoat) Merkulov called me and ordered me to come to Molotov's office. He did not specify what question would be discussed; he just said: "You are to give me your opinion." This was the only time that I spoke with Molotov personally. Besides Molotov, Vyshinsky was also present in his office. It turned out that a decision on the status of former Polish citizens in the USSR was being prepared. I offered a number of comments on the subject.[2]

I was acquainted with Sheinin. We sometimes met at home, but I never came across him in the line of duty. As for Trainin, I did not know him at all, I never saw him and his name was not familiar to me.

Moscow, Lubyanka Prison

From April, 1946 through June 5, 1951 (I was called to Moscow because of my father's death), I stayed in the western regions of the Ukraine where I participated in operations to combat the OUN (Organization of Ukrainian Nationalists.–Ed.) banditism, and therefore I could not take any part in the work of the governmental commission for the Nuremberg Trial. How did my name get into the minutes? Perhaps Vyshinsky named me because, as I said, Zhukov's department was subordinated to me. Zhukov himself was already out of Moscow by 1946.

Naturally, during our conversation we touched upon the publication which had just appeared in *Moscow News*.*

As for the report to Generals Zarubin and Raikhman published in *Moscow News* on May 21, 1989, this is a blatant fabrication, if only because I held the rank of major in 1940.[3] Besides, such a report could only be addressed to Nasedkin, head of the Main Administration of Corrective Labor Camps. The only NKVD officer by the name of Zarubin whom I knew to be working at the intelligence department held the rank of captain, if I am not mistaken.

---

*A. Akulichev and A. Pamyatnykh. "Katyn: Confirm or Refute. *Moscow News*, May 21, 1989. Among other things, this publication includes a summary of a report by Tartakov, head of Minsk NKVD, of May 10, 1940, to generals Zarubin and Raikhman, in which Tartakov informed them of the liquidation of the officers' camps.

Chapter 3

At the time of my acquaintance with Raikhman I knew little about his service records. Gradually, as more and more fresh details came to light, I became aware that I was dealing not just with an eyewitness and immediate participant in many of the events in which I was interested, but, above all, with an extraordinary personality.

He began his career in Leningrad (possessed of a phenomenal memory, Leonid Raikhman even gave me the number of his office in the "Big House"* in Liteiny Prospekt : Room 626). He dealt with the Mensheviks** and, in particular, he exposed the "Union of Marxists-Leninists."[4] According to Leonid Raikhman, before the assassination of Kirov, the atmosphere and methods of work in the organs were absolutely different from the way they look from articles by today's journalists. The initiative to make arrests came from below, and the investigation was conducted by the operative himself. This rule was adopted in order to withdraw agents from work on cases. There was no need for slander or fabrication of investigation materials, because, with well organized operative work, a person summoned for interrogation "did not know things about himself which we knew about him." Under Yezhov, real

---

* Popular name of the headquarters of the Leningrad Department of the NKVD (now the KGB).
**Mensheviks, the democratic faction of the Russian Social Democratic Labour Party; split in 1903 from the Bolshevik majority; repressed after the October Revolution of 1917.

professionals worked in the organs. It took not less than five or six years to master methods of recruiting agents and working with them. After Beria was put at the head of the NKVD, investigation departments were set up within its structures into which party functionaries, "who were only good at one thing, beating," came pouring in. I could not refrain from asking him: Did they never beat anyone under Yezhov? "Sometimes," said Raikhman with a frown. "But then, doesn't it happen nowadays too?" Leonid Raikhman told me about the conference in Moscow, during which Yezhov read out the text of Stalin's well-known directive sanctioning the use of torture. According to him, Yezhov was utterly perplexed and looked depressed at that conference . . .[5]

Subsequently I learned many highly interesting details about Raikhman's pre-war past from Boris Bespalov, a former military procurator, who at one time worked in the commission for rehabilitation headed by Shvernik : "toiled in the working apparatus," to quote his own words. Here, for example, is one of the episodes:

Late in the summer of 1939, the idea of appointing Andrei Vyshinsky as Deputy Chairman of the Council of People's Commissars of the USSR was conceived somewhere from above. This brought about the need to "screen" the candidate thoroughly and establish what was on his mind, whether he was trustworthy enough and whether he could be admitted into the inner circle of Stalin's retinue. And, of course, what his attitude to Stalin himself was, whether it was hostile or not, and whether the newly appointed deputy head of government might not develop a wild

161

desire to stick a sharp knife into Stalin's chest or shoot a bullet at him during a meeting.

Sources that could provide the most reliable answers to all these questions were needed. L. Sheinin, who treated Vyshinsky with filial reverence, was an accepted guest in his family and, undoubtedly, knew a lot about him, was selected as one of the sources.

Sheinin was staying in the resort of Sochi at the time. Raikhman was sent to see him. Why Raikhman? Because the purpose was not to interrogate Sheinin, but to have an intimate, candid, heart-to-heart talk with him, during which every bit of information had to be gleaned from the respondents inner mind. Raikhman was quite skilled in this: he had passed an examination in doing such things back in 1936 during preparations for the trial of the Anti-Soviet Trotskyite Centre.[6] Also, this mission called for a person who was on very friendly terms with Sheinin and shared his trust.

Raikhman told me that, in order to avoid giving Sheinin a heart attack, which might have happened if he had been summoned for a conversation to the city department of the NKVD, he was informed at the sanatorium that there was a high frequency telephone call for him from Moscow. Sheinin would certainly have felt offended if there had been as much as a hint that someone could "play a practical joke" on him in this way and so he explained that his meeting with Raikhman had taken place on the beach by mere accident.

The heart-to-heart talk continued for several days and resulted in the appearance of a 10-12 page, double-spaced, typewritten document. In view of the special secrecy, both of the mission itself and of the content of the document, all names were written in by hand. The document was signed by Raikhman. I cannot give you a summary of its content, but, to be brief and

give you an overall idea, I will say that it was a prayer offered by
Vyshinsky to a divinity by the name of Stalin.

Thus, Raikhman's relations with Sheinin can hardly be
described as a brief acquaintance. Bespalov also told me
that during his stay in Leningrad, Raikhman, besides the
cases that were already mentioned, was directly involved in
investigating the Safarov case,[7] the case of the Moscow
Center,[8] and the case of the Anti-Soviet Joint Trotskyite-
Zinovyevite Bloc.[9] His investigatory activities were so
successful that he was promoted to the rank of state
security captain ahead of time, clearly skipping over the
rank of senior lieutenant.

As early as October or even the end of September 1939,
Raikhman, together with his team, arrived in Lvov where,
using some fictitious scientific institution as a cover, he
searched for approaches to Metropolitan Sheptitsky, head
of the Uniates. I believe it possible that his mission included also preliminary selection of POWs for the needs of
counter-intelligence. (Incidentally, Anders was among the
POWs concentrated near Lvov). In his own words, Raikhman subsequently had absolutely nothing to do with the
destiny of the Polish POWs. We may very well remember,
however, that he had a meeting with Anders and, later on,
discussed the problem of Polish citizenship with Molotov
and Vyshinsky.

Among the archive documents Raikhman's name is not
to be found in any papers relating to the POWs, but, on
the other hand, you can see in them the name of his

163

immediate commander, Fedotov. The POWs who were of operational interest to the 2nd Department of the Main Administration of State Security were placed at his disposal.

During the war, Raikhman's main task was to clear the liberated areas of enemy agents. In this connection he even quoted a few lines by Tvardovsky with great emotion: "And yet, and yet, and yet . . ." (meaning how many fine people perished). He also recalled several thrilling episodes from his own experience.

After the text intended for publication was thoroughly edited and signed, Leonid Raikhman gave me a number of additional details about his meeting with Anders. I shall retell the most essential points. When Raikhman arrived in Kuibyshev, Serov and Merkulov were already there. It was one of them who ordered him to meet the Polish general.

Which of the two was it? Most likely it was Serov, an ardent believer in subordination. Leonid Raikhman recollects that military ranks were used as an argument. Since both Merkulov's and Serov's rank was higher (three rhombs) than that of Anders and Raikhman (two rhombs), he was just the man to go to the meeting.

In what language did they communicate? Anders had a good command of Russian and Raikhman spoke Polish (he studied the language in Lvov where he stayed for the whole of 1940 and later visited several times in 1941).

What did they drink? Lemonade.

What did they talk about? About Kutuzov, for example.

Was this in any way connected with the situation at the fronts? (A barely perceptible pause). Not directly. Anders was using a walking stick, he was limping. He behaved calmly and with great dignity. They returned from the restaurant on foot. Raikhman and Anders led the way, their escorts bringing up the rear. On November 7, during the grand meeting at the theater, Leonid Raikhman ran into Anders' aide-de-camp as he left the restroom. The aide did not go into the restroom; instead, he did an about face and vanished, apparently wishing to bring Raikhman and Anders, who was waiting to hear from him, together. Leonid Raikhman, having no sanction to such a meeting, decided that the best thing for him to do would be to leave the theater without delay.

Immediately after the war, as we already know, Raikhman went to Lvov once again, where he supervised operations against the OUN detachments. (In the type-written text, Raikhman substituted "participated" for "supervised," but this is how it was in the original version). Were they just against the OUN or against the Armia Krajowa as well? Once again I could not refrain from asking, to which Leonid Raikhman replied very sharply: "We had no Armia Krajowa there." Raikhman did not hide his dislike for Greek Catholics from the Western Ukraine, who were holding their first rally in the Arbat demanding the revoking of the decisions of the Lvov Church Council of 1946 just as we were having our meetings. It was then that a vague idea flashed through my mind: Was Leonid Raikhman by any chance the one who organized this

Chapter 3

church council? I put this question to the late Vladimir Belyayev, a writer, who witnessed the developments in Lvov both before and after the war. Without a moment's hesitation, Belyayev phoned Pavel Sudoplatov in my presence and received an affirmative answer. (They spoke pure Ukrainian).

I also have the following letter in my file on Katyn:

I am writing in connection with your article "Round Katyn" published in *Literaturnaya Gazeta*(No.36 of September 6, 1989), in which Lieutenant General L.F. Raikhman, one of the heads of the country's counter-intelligence of the war and postwar period, was mentioned.

Many times I have heard the name of this highly experienced counter-intelligence officer and honest man from my father (he died in 1977), who was deputy head of the department of the MGB of the USSR in Kislovodsk in the period from 1947 to 1952 (all cases conducted by my father, Lieutenant Colonel Z. M. Koltun, during his work with the state security service were examined by a competent commission after the 22nd Congress of the CPSU and not one—not one!—violation of socialist legality was found). That is why I believe my father, who thought that such men as Raikhman outplayed German Intelligence and made a substantial contribution to our victory over Hitlerism.

Indeed, Beria, Merkulov, Kobulov, Dekanozov, Meshik, Tsanava, Ryumin, Goglidze, and their whole gang of torturers and murderers have compromised the NKVD and MGB of the USSR. Yet I will repeat this once again: there were such Chekists as General Raikhman (who, incidentally, if my memory does not fail me, was repressed in the late 1940's to early 1950's and who lived through a personal tragedy when his wife, People's Artist of

166

the USSR L., renounced him because of his arrest), as my father and thousands of Chekists who valiantly fought against Nazism without violating the laws of the country.

My request to you is as follows: while such Chekists as L. F. Raikhman are still alive, you must use your journalistic methods to get them to talk and offer them an opportunity to tell from the pages of newspapers and magazines about brilliant counterintelligence operations which they triumphantly carried out, because it was only highly educated professionals in their field who could beat the Abwehr and the SD intelligence.

Few of these people are left and they are departing from this life daily. We must hurry. We are indebted to them.

> Sincerely,
> Colonel M. Z. Koltun,
> Internal Troops,
> Stavropol

Colonel Koltun's memory does not fail him. In October, 1951, Leonid Raikhman was arrested. The not unknown Lev Shvarsman testified against him; he represented Raikhman as an active participant in a Zionist conspiracy inside the MGB. Raikhman spent eight months in solitary confinement in Lefortovo prison, chained with manacles; he could not recall this other than with undisguised and unquenchable fury. Until the end of his days, Leonid Raikhman's attitude towards his chief, Abakumov, remained that of the greatest piety. He admired Abakumov for his native intelligence and high professional qualities. And, quite naturally, he hated Beria and his henchmen.

As for the activities of Soviet intelligence and counterintelligence during the years of the war, they undoubtedly deserve the highest marks. This is, however, a subject for separate discussion. Incidentally, it was precisely these successes which were the cause of Beria's violent hatred of Abakumov, and Raikhman became yet another victim of their deadly feud.[10]

It should be stressed once again that Leonid Raikhman was quite a complex personality; in any case, he was far from primitive. I'm sure the reader would like to know who the People's Artist of the USSR called in M. Z. Koltun's letter by the mysterious letter L. actually was. It was Olga Lepeshinskaya, the famous ballet dancer, a soloist of the Bolshoi Theatre and winner of the Stalin Prize 1st Class for 1941. According to the information that I have, Olga Lepeshinskaya used to be Leonid Raikhman's secret agent and one day, just like in an inferior Soviet melodrama, the Chekist fell in love with his agent. In accordance with the principles of socialist realism (take, for example, *Lyubov Yarovaya** or *The Forty First***) the hero must sacrifice his love for ideology. To do him justice, Leonid Raikhman did just the opposite, and this got him into serious trouble. (Raikhman was very angry at A. V. Antonov-Ovseyenko, who wrote in one of his articles*** that NKVD generals had a weakness for ballerinas: "To me this was no mere weakness: I was married to a ballerina!")

---

*A play by Konstantin Trenyov.
**A story by Boris Lavrenyov.
***Teatr Iosifa Stalina (Joseph Stalin's Theatre). *Teatr*, 1988. No.8.

Moscow, Lubyanka Prison

And, lastly, yet another absolutely uncharacteristic and unusual feature. During the last years of his life, Leonid Raikhman acquired a passion for cosmology and achieved some striking results in this field. He wrote two books, *Dialektika nebesnykh tel* (The Dialectics of the Being of Heavenly Bodies) and *Mekhanizm solnechnoy aktivnosti* (The Mechanism of Solar Activity), and became quite well known among specialists. My amateurish attempts to expound Raikhman's theory will hardly be adequate. I will therefore refer the reader to the article *Prognoz bedstviya - vozmozhen!* (The Forecast of a Catastrophe Is Possible!) in *Moskovsky Komsomolets* of May 19, 1989. In introducing his interlocutor, Alexander Polikarpov, the author of the material, writes: "Leonid Raikhman is not a professional scientist in that he does not hold any degrees or titles. His amateurishness, however, is akin to the amateurishness of the piano tuner from London who discovered Uranus and the movement of the solar system in space.* Or of the school teacher from the provincial town of Borovsk, who laid the foundations of rocket dynamics and cosmonautics.**" I wonder whether Polikarpov knew about the grim past of the amateur without degrees or titles and if he did not know, whether he would have written his article if he had known. Incidentally, he was absolutely right about Raikhman's titles. Despite the arrest and absurd case of a Jewish conspiracy, Raikhman was not reinstated in the

---

*William Herschel (1738-1822), English astronomer.
**Konstantin Tsiolkovsky (1857-1935), Soviet scientist and inventor.

party nor were his general's privileges given back to him.

One interesting and unexpected fact rounds off this character sketch. Professor Kryzhitsky, the translator of Mackiewicz's book, who kindly offered me his assistance when mentioning Raikhman in one of his letters, wrote in parentheses: He is Zaitsev. Why is he Zaitsev? I asked and received in reply two articles signed by Prince Alexei Shcherbatov, published in *Novoye Russkoye Slovo* on July 5, 1988, and on May 8, 1990, and also a copy of the prince's letter to Professor Kryzhitsky.

Alexei Shcherbatov served at the headguarters of the 22nd US Army Corps in 1945. It was then that he first heard about Raikhman and his occasionally using the alias Zaitsev. Shcherbatov was told about him by Captain Lisowski, a representative of the Polish government in London attached to the HQ. Lisowski was a resident of Polish (London) intelligence in Plzeň and did quite a lot to save the servicemen of the Armia Krajowa from repressions. Lisowski's successful activity attracted the attention of the Lubyanka. Raikhman was sent to Plzeň where he contacted the civilian governor of the city and recommended that he complain to G2, US military intelligence, about the intrigues of the anti-communist underground, and the governor promptly carried out this recommendation. As a result, Lisowski was recalled by the London Poles. It was Lisowski who pointed Raikhman out to Alexei Shcherbatov as the immediate organizer of the Katyn executions.

Unfortunately, I cannot verify Shcherbatov's information (I have no reason not to believe him, yet this is second-hand information and certain inaccuracies, especially considering that a substantial period of time has elapsed since then, are not to be ruled out), but the situation that he described appears quite verisimilar.[11]

On the day the newspaper with the article "Round Katyn" came out, I brought Raikhman a freshly printed copy of the issue. Raikhman read the publication with the greatest care and on the whole seemed to be happy with it. Then he suddenly expressed doubt about the medal "For Gallantry," saying that this was an undesirable coincidence, since the period in question was precisely April 1940. He began scrutinizing the xerox copy of the decree on the decoration which I had with me. "There is no Raikhman here!"

He offered the following fresh arguments against Czapski and *Moscow News*:

– No foreigners ever entered the NKVD building.

– He recalled the existence of an Abwehr intelligence training center, at Katyn (the very same "Saturn" which is "almost indiscernible"*) because it was special force units which had to execute the Polish POWs.

– How he read it and with what facial expression: what does this matter if the very fact of the meeting was non--existent? ("Scum!")

– The expression "liquidation of camps" may be under-

---

*An allusion to *"Saturn" pochti ne viden* ("Saturn" Is Almost Indiscernible), a popular novel by Vassili Ardamatsky.

stood in two ways (this is a favorite argument which I have heard more than once from adherents of the Soviet version).

Leonid Raikhman died on March 16, 1990, in Moscow.

* * *

Georgi Zhukov began his service in the organs in Smolensk. Having heard about this for the first time from Raikhman, I decided that he must be the very same head of the investigatory section of the Smolensk Department of the NKVD who was sentenced by the military tribunal of the Kalinin military district in assizes to 3 years of imprisonment conditionally in November, 1939, for dereliction of duty (this dereliction boiled down to faults in paper work relating to the cases of those shot by decisions of troikas: even indictments were not infrequently lacking in the files). I remember that I wondered at the grim irony of fate; investigator Vassilyev, Zhukov's partner in the case, was defended during the trial by none other than the lawyer B. G. Menshagin, whose name was subsequently used by the Burdenko commission and from whose reminiscences I took this fact. This was what I wrote about in *Literaturnaya Gazeta*, having noted, however, that the initials of the other Zhukov had been lost.

Soon I received a letter from a reader by the name of B. M. Gzovsky, from Minsk. He informed me that there were two or perhaps even three Zhukov brothers working at the Smolensk Department of the NKVD. Gzovsky, who was a member of the Dynamo sports society, used to play volleyball on the same playground as they. Later on, this information was confirmed to me by L. V. Kotov, a historian from Smolensk. The first name of the investigatory section head was Nikolai, and he was the middle brother. In 1940, he was brought to trial once again and sentenced to 6 years of imprisonment.

Subsequently I read the following in *Izvestia TsK KPSS (1989, No.ll)*:

G. S. Zhukov, being head of the railway transport section of the NKVD of the Western Railway, made illegal mass arrests and also created trumped up charges against Comrade G. A. Rusanov (a Party member since 1916), former chief of the railway, who refused to give false evidence and was driven to suicide by Zhukov. Zhukov's criminal actions resulted in the arrest and sentencing without grounds of Comrade I. P. Astafyev, head of the political department of the Smolensk section, Comrade Bolotovsky, head of the political department of the Western Railway, and Comrade N. Kh. Katz, head of the department of the railway workers' supply, who have now (in January 1956– *V.A.*) been rehabilitated and restored to Party membership.

Most likely, it was in connection with this same transport case that I.V. Stremousov, head of the industry and transport department of the Smolensk Regional Committee of the All-Union Communist Party (Bolsheviks), and his wife, N.I. Avtukhova, head of the secretariat of the chairman of the regional executive committee, were arrested in 1937. They were sentenced under Article 58-10 of the

173

Criminal Code of the RSFSR to 10 years in camp without the right to correspondence, and in 1957 were rehabilitated (posthumously) for lack of *corpus delicti*. Their son, V. I. Stremousov, now living in Volgograd, wrote to me about this. According to his information, the investigation was conducted by Lieutenant (State Security Lieutenant?) Zhukov.

At the 2nd Department of the Main Administration for State Security of the NKVD, G. S. Zhukov headed the Central and Eastern Europe section, which of course included Poland. In my view, Leonid Raikhman's explanation that Zhukov himself, particularly as regards Polish affairs, was not subordinated to him, sounds unconvincing. To put it mildly, we already know that Raikhman himself was also interested in Poland.

According to Raikhman, it was Zhukov who was the first to recall the existence of the graves at Gnezdovo immediately after the publication of the German report about Katyn. Therefore, he is the author of the initial and obviously absurd version published in *Pravda* two days later, which has not been repeated since:

In their clumsily concocted lie about numerous graves allegedly uncovered by the Germans near Smolensk, the Goebbelstrained liars mention the village of Gnezdovaya; however, as befits cheats, they pass in silence over the fact that it is precisely near the village of Gnezdovaya that the site of archeological excavations of the historical "Gnezdovaya burial ground' is located.

Moscow, Lubyanka Prison

There is an obvious mistake here in the name of the village—its correct name is Gnezdovo and not Gnezdovaya. This shows that the rebuff was written in a hurry. Lieutenant General Zhukov's career ended abruptly and absurdly. Raikhman told me that, when speaking to Khrushchev one day, Zhukov had the imprudence to offer an unflattering opinion of Wanda Vasilevskaya, a noted Soviet writer, for which he was transferred to Novosibirsk and assigned the post of lieutenant colonel. B. M. Gzovsky writes that he met one of the Zhukov brothers in Novosibirsk in 1943. Looking very imposing and wearing general's shoulder straps, he was taking a stroll in company with a great dane. An acquaintance of Gzovsky's told him that he was chief of the Siblag (Administration of the Siberian Corrective Labor Camps). The acquaintance was mistaken: Zhukov was section head at the Novosibirsk Department of the NKVD, incidentally, in charge of the affairs of POWs and internees.

I learned some very interesting things about the Novosibirsk period of Zhukov's service from Anatoli Tretyakov, a non-staff correspondent of *Izvestia*, who was on friendly terms with Zhukov's son, Vladimir, who subsequently became a writer on international affairs. Among other things, Tretyakov gave me a hint upon which I have not elaborated to this day. In the late 1940's, a certain Medical Service Lieutenant Colonel Kazantsev, a forensic medicine specialist, who was said to have taken part in the exhumation of corpses at Katyn, visited with G. S. Zhukov. In response to Tretyakov's cautious question about who actually shot the Poles, Kazantsev, who was quite drunk, gave him a stern look and said, pronouncing

175

his words carefully: "You must fix this in your mind once and for all: the Poles were shot by the Germans." Anatoli Tretyakov had a feeling that, in saying this, Kazantsev wanted to make him understand something absolutely different. Kazantsev's name does not appear in the list of experts who worked at Katyn, but then, first of all, this in itself does not mean anything and, second, the talk here may well be about the later, postwar opening of the graves. Zhukov appears in this episode as well . . . . (More on this subject will follow in the next chapter).

Georgi Zhukov ended his days in the mid-1970s, working as director of the Tourist Hotel in Moscow. He was appointed to this responsible post in 1956 on the eve of the World Festival of Youth and Students, for it was here at the Tourist Hotel that progressive-minded youth then stayed. Anatoli Rubinov, my colleague and associate in *Literaturnaya Gazeta*, knew him well in this capacity; he told me that the Lenin Library had several brochures on the theory of the hotel industry written by Georgi Zhukov.

As for Pyotr Fedotov (P. V. Fedotov and not P. F. Fedotov, as Jerzewski named him), in 1940 he held the rank of state security commissar 3rd class and headed the 2nd Department of the Main Administration of State Security, that is, counter-intelligence. By the decree of April 1940, which is already well known to us, he was awarded the order "Badge of Honour." By a resolution of the Council of Ministers of September 7, 1946, Pyotr Fedotov was appointed Deputy Minister of State Security of the USSR and, later on, when the MGB was transformed into the KGB, became head of the 2nd Main Administration of the KGB. Interesting information about his activities and, in particular, about his methods, is to be found in the same issue of *Izvestia TsK KPSS*:

. . . Serving in the brigade of the NKVD of the USSR directed by Malenkov and Litvinov, he fabricated charges against many Party functionaries and government officials of Armenia, and used physical force against them. Using torture, he forced those unlawfully arrested (a list of these persons follows) to confess to crimes against the state. Testimonies obtained by this criminal method were used as the grounds for arresting all the commanding and political officers of that (76th Armenian Rifle.– *V. A.*) division, many of whom were shot. Fedotov fabricated material against a number of other prominent figures such as Comrade A. A. Bekzadyan, former USSR envoy plenipotentiary to Hungary, N. A. Popok, former first secretary of the Party regional committee of the Republic of the Volga Germans, M. K. Amosov, former first secretary of the Central Committee of the Communist Party of Kirghizia, and others. On his initiative, a so-called 'false foreign land' was set up in the Khabarovsk Territory on the border with Manchuria where many innocent Soviet citizens died as a result of lawless actions and provocation.

Here is what this "false foreign land" was. The Khabarovsk Territorial Department of the NKVD recruited people to operate as agents in Manchuria. Subsequently, such agents crossed the border and, as a result, fell into the hands of a Japanese district military mission where White Guards wearing Japanese uniforms would beat confessions to connections with Soviet intelligence out of the frontier violators and sometimes even prevailed on such people to become double agents. Then the agent, this time on a mission from Japanese intelligence, would cross the border in the opposite direction. As soon as he got on to Soviet territory, he was immediately put in the prison of the Khabarovsk Department of the NKVD and charged with espionage for Japan. This "false foreign land" functioned from 1941 until 1949. During that period a total of 148 Soviet citizens, who were subsequently sentenced to long terms of imprisonment, passed through it. There actually were a number of cases where people became double agents. There was, however, no border crossing by the "agents." The whole intrigue was cooked up by NKVD officers. It was they who posed as White Guards clad in Japanese military uniform. It is to be presumed that they used physical force to their hearts' content!

This episode describes splendidly the ways of the organization whose loyal servants Raikhman, Zhukov, and Fedotov were. I will repeat that the idea of the "false foreign land" was conceived by Fedotov. Polish POWs selected by the special sections of the camps were placed at the disposal of this monster. The previously mentioned directive from Beria "on the operative Chekist service of prisoners of war" emphasized as a top priority task the organization of a network of informers in the camps, and the purpose of setting up such a network was not so much "finding out the POWs' political sentiments" as the exposure of the "counter-revolutionary element," namely:

(a) persons who had served in the intelligence, police and security organs of former Poland (. . .);

(b) agents of the above-listed organs undercover and detective agents);

(c) participants in military fascist and nationalist organizations

Moscow, Lubyanka Prison

of former Poland (. . .);

    (d) staff members of law courts and procurator's offices;

    (e) agents of other foreign intelligence services;

    (f) participants in foreign White emigre terrorist organizations (. . .);

    (g) agents provocateurs of the former tsarist *okhranka* (secret political police) and persons who served in police and penitentiary agencies of pre-revolutionary Russia;

    (h) agents provocateurs of the *okhranka* in the fraternal communist parties of Poland, the Western Ukraine and Byelorussia;

    (i) *kulak* and anti-Soviet elements who fled from the USSR to former Poland.

To find and "register for operative purposes" this whole "element" was necessary, in particular, "to expose the foreign connections of those being worked on." Further steps were also worked out:

"The special sections of the military districts shall aim their investigatory activities at exposing the anti-Soviet connections of arrested POWs and persons who may be used for sending on missions abroad.

"To recruit agents intended for sending abroad only with the preliminary approval of the head of the Special Section of the NKVD of the USSR, of the People's Commissar of Internal Affairs of the USSR."[12]

Poles got to the Lubyanka either through the special sections of military disricts or directly from the camps. Here they were served with a warrant for arrest. As a general rule, they were charged with a crime under one of the paragraphs of Article 58. For example, Professor Swianiewicz was charged under Article 58-6 (espionage).

"Besides," writes Swianiewicz, "they explained to me that I was now regarded as a criminal and no longer as a POW, and that now I would be treated as such with all the rigors of the Soviet law applied to me." Swianiewicz said about this that he was not a USSR citizen and was given the sensible reply that the Polish state no longer existed and that, therefore, there no longer existed such a thing as Polish citizenship (the reader has probably already noted that Poland was mentioned as "former Poland" in all NKVD documents. In the territories incorporated in the USSR, Polish citizenship was abolished by a decree of the Presidium of the USSR Supreme Soviet of November 29, 1939). It is interesting to note that proceedings against the professor were instituted under the Criminal Code of the RSFSR, although he had lived and worked in Vilno and was therefore not subject to the laws of the Russian Federation. This formal shortcoming, however, was rectified later on. I have already had an opportunity to publish, in connection with a different subject, a decree of the Presidium of the USSR Supreme Soviet of November 6, 1940 (*Rodina*, 1989, No. 12), which introduced the application of RSFSR codes on the territories of the Baltic states, and even all cases with sentences already pronounced but not yet carried out were to be revised in accordance with these codes. Of course, the laws were used retroactively here, there, and everywhere, and thus such harmless organizations as the Polish Lawyers' Union or the Union of Reserve Non-commissioned Officers, not to mention the Polish Socialist Party, which united with the Polish Workers' Party in 1946 to form the Polish United Workers' Party, fell under the category of "military fascist and nationalist organizations."

Moscow, Lubyanka Prison

It was, of course, former intelligence officers who were of the greatest interest to Fedotov's department. (I will refer here to the testimony, published by M. M. Freidenberg, that specialists in radio communication were selected at the Ostashkov camp in early 1940). These people could subsequently be used quite effectively as identifiers and participants in radio deception operations. Besides, it should be noted that the list of foreign White emigre organizations included the OUN, the subject of Raikhman's particular concern. Undoubtedly, the work in the NKVD of agents provocateurs of the tsarist *okhranka* could also be of some use; I am at my wits' end, however, to figure out what Beria needed former jailers for. For sharing experiences with them, perhaps . . .

Even though Fedotov, Raikhman, and Zhukov did not take part in deciding the fate of the Poles in principle, they certainly had the right to influence individual destinies. Among former high-ranking NKVD officers, however, no one has better knowledge of this matter than Pyotr Soprunenko, former head of the NKVD Administration for the Affairs of Prisoners of War, who was a state security captain in 1940 (awarded the Badge of Honor by the April 1940 decree). I made an appointment with Pyotr Soprunenko. He arranged to meet me at a district military commissariat and then, all of a sudden, Lebedeva's article appeared in *Moscow News*. Soprunenko, who had just come through a serious oncological operation, took to his bed. I was first informed about this at the military commissariat, and then his daughter confirmed this in a telephone conversation.

Chapter 3

He really did have something to remember. Soprunenko's signature is to be found on a great many archive
documents relating to the fate of the Polish POWs. For
fairness' sake, it should be noted that among them there
are texts describing Pyotr Soprunenko's activities favorably.
For example, the department which he headed suggested
to the NKVD leadership that civilians, rank-and-file
policemen and frontier guards, "and also reserve officers
from among the working intelligentsia," who used to live
in Eastern Poland, be released and returned to their
homes. This initiative, however, did not meet with understanding among top officials. Then there appeared yet
another document, dated February 20, 1940, and signed by
Soprunenko and the department's commissar, Nekhoroshev:

> Top secret
> To People's Commissar
> of Internal Affairs
> of the USSR
> State Security Commissar
> 1st Class
> Comrade L. P. Beria

For the purpose of reducing numbers in the Starobelsk and
Kozelsk camps, I request your orders to carry out the following
measures:

1. To release and send home all those gravely ill, completely
disabled, tubercular, and old men aged 60 and over from among
the officers, of whom there are about 300.

2. To release and send home persons from among reserve
officers residents of the western regions of the Byelorussian and

Moscow, Lubyanka Prison

Ukrainian SSR agronomists, doctors, engineers, technicians and teachers, against whom there are no compromising materials. According to a preliminary estimate, 400 to 500 persons falling under this category may be released.

Quite humane, isn't it? Even though it is not quite clear why there were so many completely disabled persons and tuberculars in the Polish army. Following, however, is a paragraph that is highly unpleasant:

3. I request your permission to make out files on officers of the KOP (Korpus Ochrony Pogranicza - frontier Guards Corps), staff members of judicial bodies and procurator's offices, activists of the POW (Polslka Organizacja Wojskowa—Polish Troop Organization) and Zwiazek Strzelecki (Strelets in the text, a case of NKVD illiteracy) parties, officers of the 2nd section of the former Polish General Staff, and information officers (about 400 persons) for consideration by a Special Board of the NKVD."[13]

This was precisely what was done. (It will be recalled that by a decree of the Presidium of the USSR Supreme Soviet of January 16, 1989, approved by the Supreme Soviet of the USSR on July 31, 1989, all citizens repressed by decisions of extrajudicial bodies, excepting traitors and members of punitive squads, were rehabilitated, and these bodies themselves declared anti-constitutional). When Polish POW's interned in Lithuania and Latvia were brought to the Kozelsk camp, Soprunenko already knew what was to be done, because he had proposed that files be made out on them for consideration by a Special Board. Yet he missed the point this time as well, because Lavrenti Beria, who was charged with the construction of new

aerodromes, for which purpose a special administration*
was set up within the framework of the NKVD, decided to
transfer them to Construction Project No. 106 (which I
have already mentioned) at Ponoi or, which comes to the
same thing, beyond Kandalaksha where, as we remember,
Alexei Lukin transported POW's; this, however, was
already May, not April 1940.

Pyotr Soprunenko is keeping quiet, preferring not to
enter into polemics. One feels obliged to give Leonid
Raikham his due, for he, contrary to his colleagues'
custom, decided on taking up a public argument! True,
some information from Soprunenko has nonetheless leaked
into the press unfortunately, not into the Soviet press.

No sooner had Lord Nicholas Bethell, a noted British
historian, flown out of Moscow than his article, gloomily
entitled "The Executioner," appeared in the newspaper
Mail on Sunday of June 17, 1990. As the reader has,
perhaps, already guessed, the article centers on Pyotr
Soprunenko. Accompanied by a photograph of the block of
flats in Sadovaya-Samotechnaya Street in which he lives,
with the windows of his flat marked with a circle, it offers
a comprehensive picture of Soprunenko's role in the Katyn
issue in a word, it is a true masterpiece. The message of
the article is given in the subheading: "As Russia hits at
Britain over the vote on war criminals, its mass killer lives
openly in a Moscow flat."

---

*Main Administration of Aviation Construction of the NKVD.

Moscow, Lubyanka Prison

Among other things, the article includes a telephone monologue by Soprunenko's daughter, Yelena. She flatly turned down Lord Bethell's attempts to speak with Pyotr Soprunenko himself, saying that "these terrible stories" were very upsetting for him. "My father served his country," she said. "He was a coalminer in the Donbas, and he was drafted into the army academy because of his good worker's background. He never wanted to go into the NKVD. He just did his duty as an officer according to the rules."

What she said next is the most interesting thing.

"I can tell you one thing. The order about the Polish officers came from Stalin himself. My father says he saw the actual paper, with Stalin's signature on it. So what was he to do? Get himself arrested? Or shot himself? My father is being made a scapegoat for things that were decided by other people."

So the order was signed by Stalin himself. How similar our glorious "veterans of the invisible front" appear to the Nazi war criminals! In the case of the latter, Hitler alone was the culprit and the rest of them just did their duty as officers. Now what about Soprunenko's proposals that were cited above? I know that he will argue that "consideration by a Special Board" does not mean "execution." The members of a Special Board, if they came back to life, would say that they passed their resolutions on capital punishment on the basis of materials submitted by Soprunenko. (Incidentally, it is still not known today whether such Special Boards had the right to pass death sentences.) No, this will lead us into a blind alley. There is no sense in asking an executioner why he killed. To him, this question is meaningless. It is his profession and he does not by any means regard his work as killing.

So the order was signed by Stalin. Where is it? Has it been lost or destroyed? And what if we begin looking for it? This, I am afraid, will get us into an even more hopeless blind alley.

Now it is time to speak about the destiny of the archives of the Smolensk Department of the NKVD and here I will once again refer to Prince Shcherbatov. His particular interest in these documents is explained by the fact that his uncle, Sergei Shcherbatov, his two cousins and his *grande tante,** Princess Khovanskaya, were shot by the Smolensk Department of the GPU in 1922. The Swedish journalist G. Axelson, a correspondent of the Stockholm newspaper *Aftonbladet* and of the London *Evening Standard*, visited Smolensk in 1943 and saw the Shcherbatov's file there, about which he subsequently informed Alexei Shcherbatov. Let me, however, put first things first.

"In Smolensk," writes Shcherbatov, "the Germans captured the archives of the regional department of the NKVD where documents dated December 1918 through July 1941 were kept. These were the only Chekist archives to have got into German hands in their entirety. As I wrote previously, their earlier part was housed in the building of the Church of St. Peter and St. Paul (documents dating from 1918-1936) and the rest of them were in the NKVD

---

*Great-aunt

building (the former district court). An NKVD officer by the name of Alexander Engelgart, together with another agent, was given a mission to blow up and set fire to the first part of the archives. Engelgart did not carry out the order; moreover, he killed his partner. When the Germans entered Smolensk, he came to the headquarters of von Bock's army* and volunteered information about the archives and also about the killing of the Polish officers. After the fall of Smolensk, the Soviet side several times sent small airplanes to drop incendiary bombs on the buildings that housed the archives but to no avail."

I have something to add in this connection. L.V. Kotov, an expert on the history of the Smolensk underground, who has studied the ins and outs of all the available Smolensk archives, told me (this was before I became acquainted with the information provided by Prince Shcherbatov) that the archives were actually housed in a chapel; during the retreat it was set on fire, but the flames soon died down for lack of the necessary draught. The catalogue was burnt. The German occupation authorities found several former archivists, who made a new catalogue. All this is true, but the fact is that the archives in question were Party archives, those very archives which are now kept in the United States. As for the archives of the NKVD department, according to Kotov, they were evacuated, and only one of the railway cars in which they were transported suffered. It got bombed. According to Kotov's

---

*Army Group

187

information, which he obtained from I. Nozdrev, former Centerhead of these archives, who is still alive today, this happened on the Kardymovo-Yartsevo leg.

I have also succeeded in obtaining an indirect confirmation of the fact that the NKVD archives are safe and sound. Vladimir Stremousov, whom I have already mentioned, is in possession of a letter of February 15, 1988, signed by A. Nikonov, head of the secretariat of the Military Collegium of the USSR Supreme Court. The letter says that the file on Vladimir Stremousov's father is "kept at the Department of the KGB of the USSR for the Smolensk Region and is classified 'secret'." It will be recalled that Ivan Stremousov and his wife were convicted in 1937.

It is still not quite clear how Axelson could have seen the Shcherbatov's file in the Party archives. It is either one thing or the other. Either it was something in the nature of a summary prepared by OGPU officers for their Party bosses and not a file on a criminal case, or the materials of the case had been requested by the archives for temporary use in connection with their own needs.

Whichever of these, there are sufficient reasons to believe that searches in the archives of the Smolensk Department of the KGB may bring some positive results, though there is no one to carry on these searches. Independent historians are not allowed to come anywhere near the documents, and the KGB officers themselves cannot find anything in their own archives. Let us recall, for example, how the Kharkov KGB officers kept searching and finally came to special archives where they were given documents which they subsequently passed off as their own find.

Incidentally, why is it the KGB that is carrying on these searches, and what are the legal grounds for their searches? Its chiefs are repeating all the time that the present day State Security Committee headed by Kryuchkov has nothing to do with Beria's People's Commissariat of Internal Affairs. Who was it, then, that authorized them to examine the Katyn issue? The only thing that the KGB can and must do to facilitate the investigation is to ensure free access to their archives.

True, quite a few people are in doubt as to whether the papers have survived. For example, Ovidi Gorchakov, formerly a resident of Soviet intelligence and now a noted writer, stated in an interview to *Komsomolskaya Pravda* (May 22, 1990): "And, besides, I have no hope that archives will be of help. When we remove all the seals from special depositories, we will find little in them. In October 1941, when the Germans were approaching Moscow,the archives at the Lubyanka were burnt down–so much so that smoke came up in columns." True, archives were being burnt down, but not without exception. I have already written about this: certain categories of documents were destroyed and the rest were evacuated. Somehow I believe that the Katyn papers have survived. The summaries on Polish POWs prepared at the NKVD at the request of the leadership date from a later period than that mentioned by Ovidi Gorchakov; in particular, one of them dates from December 1943. This means that in December 1943 there existed documents on which that summary was based.

As for the possibility of instituting proceedings against the surviving participants in the Katyn action, here is what Valentin Alexandrov, a high-ranking functionary of the

Chapter 3

CPSU Central Committee who, incidentally, did quite a lot to achieve a political solution of the problem, said to Nicholas Bethell:

We do not rule out the possibility of a judicial investigation or even a trial. You must understand, however, that Soviet public opinion does not wholly support Gorbachev's initiative in respect of Katyn. We at the Central Committee have received a great number of letters from veterans' organizations in which they ask us why we are discrediting the names of those who just did their duty against enemies of socialism.

There is still another, weightier obstacle preventing a trial of the executioners, which was pointed out to me by the late Revolt Pimenov, People's Deputy of the RSFSR, a well-known human rights champion: bringing Beria's henchmen to trial would mean using the law retroactively.

And now here is something else about archives. I will quote an excerpt from a letter whose author has requested me not to reveal his identity:

"A file (falling under various categories of operational records) was opened on every person who got into the orbit of the organs' activities. It was kept regardless of whether proceedings or an investigation were instituted. Personal record cards were also filled in. After the liquidation of the Beria terror regime, his henchmen, who were initially at the head of the KGB, destroyed most of the archive files and card catalogues. However, statements confirming the destruction of these files, and also logbooks with lists of such files must have been preserved in the organs where these records were kept. People usually have no time for dealing with these purely bureaucratic documents, whereas bureaucrats guard them better than the apple of their eye, for you could get put in prison for the destruction of a secret document without making out an appropriate statement. "And then, further on:

"It is impossible that archive personal files on generals and officers of the organs dating from the 1930s and 1940s could be lacking.The service records in the files offer a comprehensive picture of their careers and the professional certification records, that of their practical activities."

As I promised, in order to make clear what should be searched for and where, here is a continuation of the list of the NKVD-NKGB officers who were directly involved in the Katyn action:

Bashtakov, Leonid Fokeyevich*	Head of the 1st Special Section of the NKVD of the USSR, State Security Major
Begma, Pavel Georgiyevich	Head of the special section of the Byelorussian Military District, State Security Major
Belyanov, Alexander Mikhailovich	Deputy head of the special department of the Main Administration of State Security of the NKVD of the USSR, State Security Major

* L. F. Bashtakov is still alive today; not long ago he gave testimony to investigators of the Chief Military Procurator's Office of the USSR about the shooting of Maria Spiridonova and a group of Soviet military commanders in Orel prison in October 1941.

191

Gertsovsky, Arkadi Yakovlevich	Deputy head of the 1st Special Section of the NKVD of the USSR, State Security Captain
Granovsky, German Markovich	Head of the 2nd section of the Gulag (Main Administration of Corrective Labor Camps) of the NKVD of the USSR, State Security Lieutenant
Zilberman, Konstantin Sergeyevich	Deputy head of the Main Technical Administration of the NKVD of the USSR, State Security Major
Kalinin, Anatoli Mikhailovich	Assistant head of the 1st Special Section of the NKVD of the USSR, State Security Captain
Kornienko, Trofim Nikolayevich(?)	Head of the 1st section of the 3rd department of the Main Administration of State Security of the NKVD of the USSR, State Security Senior Major(?)
Makov	Head of the 4th section of the 1st Special Section of the NKVD of the USSR, State Security Lieutenant

Maslennikov, Ivan Ivanovich	Deputy People's Commissar of Internal Affairs of the USSR, Corps Commander
Nikolsky	Head of the Main Technical Administration of the NKVD of the USSR, State Security
Ratushny	Deputy People's Commissar of Internal Affairs of the Ukrainian SSR,
Reshetnikov	Deputy People's Commissar of Internal Affairs of the Byelorussian SSR
Rostomashvili, Mikhail Yenukovich	Head of the special section of the Kharkov Military District, Colonel
Safonov, Pyotr Sergeyevich	Deputy head of the Gulag of the NKVD of the USSR, State Security Captain
Sakharova	Senior operative of the 1st Special Section of the NKVD of the USSR, State Security Lieutenant

Smorodinsky, Vladimir Timofeyevich	State Security Captain
Fitin, Pavel Mikhailovich	Head of the 1st Department (intelligence) of the Main Administration of State Security of the NKVD of the USSR, State Security Senior Major
Tsanava, Lavrenti Fomich	People's Commissar of Internal Affairs of the Byelorussian SSR, State Security Commissar 3rd Class
Chernyshov, Vassili Vassilyevich	Deputy People's Commissar of Internal Affairs of the USSR, Division Commander
Yatsevich	Head of the 2nd section of the 2nd department of the Gulag of the NKVD of the USSR, State Security Junior Lieutenant

Here now is a separate list of staff members of the NKVD Administration for the Affairs of Prisoners of War and Internees:

Soprunenko, Pyotr Karpovich	Head of the administration

Nekhoroshev, Semyon Moiseyevich	Commissar of the administration
Khokhlov, Ivan Ivanovich	Deputy head of the administration
Polukhin, Iosaf Mikhailovich	Deputy head of the administration
Slutsy, Mark Aronovich	Deputy head of the administration
Vorobyev, Nikolai Alexeyevich	Deputy head of the political department
Lisovsky, Dmitri Ivanovich	Senior instructor of the political department
Pronin, Nikolai Timofeyevich	Instructor of the political department
Senkevich, Illarion Ivanovich	Instructor of the political department
Romanov, Nikolai Ivanovich	Deputy head of the 1st section
Bashlykov, Ivan Mikhailovich	Secretary of the administration

Chapter 3

Seifullin, Minnigalim Yakubovich	Senior inspector
Goberman, Max Yefimovich	Senior inspector
Surzhikov, Fyodor Vladimirovich	Senior inspector

Chapter 4

PSEUDOEXPERTS

The subject of my concern in this chapter will be the forensic examination or, to be more exact, the examinations of the bodies exhumed in Katyn. This is one of the most important aspects of the problem, because it is the expert's findings that underlie the two mutually exclusive versions of the Katyn executions. Today, when the issue of the culprits of the Katyn massacre has been settled and, consequently, the conclusions of the Soviet Commission headed by N.N. Burdenko officially disavowed, such an analysis may appear redundant. Yet to me it seems indispensable, for two reasons at least.

First, we must know how the false Soviet version arose, how it was formulated and adjusted, and who fabricated it; the history of fabrications is history, too. Second, to judge from the TASS reports, the basis for a revision of the official Soviet viewpoint has been provided by the recently discovered archival documents meaning that there has been no such basis until now. For 46 years Soviet historians, lawyers, politicians and party functionaries, who sang in tune with the Establishment, referred to the Burdenko Commission's "authoritative opinion" as conclusive evidence of Nazi guilt while the records of preceding examinations have once and for all been declared provocative and false, or at least biased. So let us now see how irreproachable the document signed by the members of the Soviet Special Commission was and, on the other hand, how well-founded the charges against the experts whose findings defy Burdenko's.

To begin with, let us make one thing clear: there were not just two Katyn commissions, as many believe, but three, each of them recording its findings in the appropriate document. The first to unearth the graves was Gerhard Butz, who headed the forensic medicine laboratory Army Group Center. Professor Butz also submitted his report.

Besides this, there are two texts dealing not with the questions of forensic medicine, but with the circumstances of the Katyn slaughter: a report by the Secretary of the Secret Field Police, Ludwig Voss, and the communication of the Special Commission under Burdenko, comprising the findings of the expert examination carried out by Professor Prozorovsky and his colleagues. I am not going to review these documents here.

Finally, I have a good deal of material at my disposal which sheds further light on the conditions and methods of work of the experts.

Basically, it should be acknowledged that the exhumations of 1943 are well documented. When selecting the material for this chapter, I decided to base myself, first and foremost, on some sources which have recently been discovered or are hard for the Soviet reader to come by.

It is not difficult to divine the main argument of the adepts of the Soviet version: that all those who went to Katyn forest under the Germans or who were sworn enemies of the USSR, lied deliberately or were forced to distort the facts under the pressure of circumstances or, at the very least, were misled by the organizers of expert examinations and excursions. One thing that has been invariably pointed out is the composition of the International Commission—only one of its 12 members was a representative of a neutral country, the rest having arrived from countries Germany occupied or was allied with. For the same reason a Polish Red Cross commission was not trusted; it was the proposal of the Germans that was accepted, that is to say, that of collaborationists (accomplices, as they were known in Soviet parlance of those years). Nor, in Burdenko's fellow-thinkers' opinion, can we rely on accounts by members of public delegations and prisoners of war; they had been forced into participating in the propaganda campaign. Furthermore, what was totally disregarded under the circumstances was the desire to find out the actual fate of the captive officers, quite natural for any Pole, or such a moral category as the professional duty of a medical man.

Let me begin with the document first published in 1989. Its author is Ferdynand Goetel, a man of letters, who was on the first Polish delegation which flew from Warsaw to Smolensk on April 11, 1943, that is, before the official German Pronouncement about the Katyn graves. The report was written in London in 1946; the first version of the report of April 1943, handed over by Goetl to the Polish Red Cross, must have been lost. In December 1945, Goetel emigrated from Poland as he was being hunted by security forces. The original copy of the document is at the Sikorski Museum in London.

Early in April 1943, I had a call from the Secretary of the Society of Writers and Journalists, Władysław Zyglarski, who had been a member of the so-called Literary Commission of the Main Board of Guardians during the occupation and told me that I was being urgently looked for by Dr.Grundman from the "Propaganda Department of the Administration of the General Gubernia." Since I thought it had something to do with the kitchen at the Union of Writers' club, I set out for the city, chiefly to find out whether anything had happened in the kitchen. At the same time, Grundman, on learning that I lived at 56 Mickiewicz St. in Żoliborze came to my place by car. Not finding me at home, he repeated to my wife that he had some very urgent business to talk over with me and jotted down the telephone number of the nearest shop. I used, however, not that telephone but the one belonging to the photographer who lived in the basement of our house, only Zyglarski and a few more persons knew about it.

Realizing that something out of the ordinary was going on, I went to see Grundman before lunch the same day. He told me that the German army intelligence had discovered huge common graves containing Polish officers in a place called Goats' Mountains, not far from Smolensk. The graves had already been partly dug, producing extraordinary results. The victims must have numbered several thousand. The city authorities, shocked by the discovery, intended to send a delegation of Poles to the site, which was to be given every manner of assistance and to be spared the trouble of any joint propaganda statements with the Germans.

Pseudoexperts

Struck by the news, I thought at once that the Goats' Mountains might reveal a trace by which to unravel the mystery of the disappearance of the Polish prisoners of war in the camps of Kozelsk, Starobelsk, and Ostashkov. On reflection, I asked Grundman why he was not addressing himself to the Polish Red Cross - the most appropriate institution in this context both from the standpoint of its status and from that of the weight of its opinion in Polish society. Grundman replied that, in his view, the Polish Red Cross should indeed concern itself with this, but there were some circumstances which complicated relations between the German authorities and this institution. He presumed that I was aware of those circumstances.

I was, indeed, aware of the Germans' attitude to the Polish Red Cross. The Polish Red Cross was the only institution in the General Gubernia to have survived since the days of the sovereign Polish State and was the only trace of it. Protected as it was by international law, the Polish Red Cross had tenaciously resisted the numerous attempts of the Germans to get rid of it. In consequence, it existed only nominally because its only activities were the guardianship of those injured during the 1939 hostilities.

Realizing that the position of the Polish Red Cross could become unexpectedly strengthened if the news about the Goats' Mountains turned out to correspond to reality, I declared that in the event of leaving for the Goats' Mountains, I reserved the right to report the results of my observations to the Polish Red Cross, but, however, I would first like to know who was to form part of the delegation. Grundman replied that representatives of the Main Board of Guardians and its Warsaw branch, as well as representatives of the clergy, the city administration and the judiciary authorities of Warsaw had been invited to join the delegation. They were to attend a briefing in the Propaganda Department the following morning. The delegation was to leave for the scene of the accident by air in two days. I replied that in this case I would also join the delegation but I laid down as a condition the full freedom of judgement on what I would see as well as the freedom of distribution of this information. Since I, a representative of Poland, intended to inform Polish society in every way about everything I would search the Goats' Mountains, rather than sit confined in my own room. Grundman accepted my terms.

When I left him, I quickly began to look for a meeting both with representatives of underground organizations and those mentioned by Grundman. I was in the ranks of the Camp of Fighting Poland and editor of the *Nurt* (Current) newspaper. I had no direct contact with my chief, Julian Piasecki, and the liaison named Coral was to see me only a few days later. Therefore I chose a different course. Through a man who lived next door, Marian Buczkowski and his liaison, Martha, I passed on the news about my conversation with Grundman to Hubert, the then chief of the Propaganda Department of the Armia Krajowa in the Warsaw district.

Hubert, according to Marian Buczkowski, reacted to my report with contempt and said that "the Germans want to dupe Goetel." However, he agreed to my trip, calling on me to submit a report to him on my return from Smolensk.

Besides this, I contacted Chairman Kulski and Machnicki of the Main Board of Guardins by telephone. Neither denied that they had been called upon to do the same, but, like Hubert, they somewhat neglected the subject and showed, it seemed to me, even some apprehension in the face of such a delegation. Their position and that of Hubert angered me because I found that mere revulsion about any co-operation whatsoever with the Germans was not enough in this case. Of course, I knew that Katyn would become a tormenting and dangerous business for anyone who had anything to do with it. Whatever we might see over there, we were likely to be attacked either by the Germans or by the Bolsheviks. The latter presentiment was evident in Warsaw already.

We landed on the airfield near Smolensk at about noon. In the afternoon, escorted by Germans, we went round the city and in the evening we were introduced at the officers' casino to three officers from the Smolensk army Propaganda Department, two lieutenants and a captain. The Katyn issue was set out to us by Słoweńczyk*, a reserve lieutenant and apparently a journalist by trade from Vilno. Of the other two, one introduced himself as a sculptor from Innsbruck. Our conversation was eavesdropped from time to time by another lieutenant carrying the insignia of the Geheimpolizei**. I think it was Voss, who I was yet to find out about.

Słoweńczyk acquainted us with the "Katyn affair" in greater detail. He showed us some photographs of the forest and bodies as well as some documents found on them. He also showed us

---

*Commander of the Propaganda Company (Aktivpropaganda-kompanie).
**Geheimpolizei—Secret police (to be exact, Geheimpolizei—, GFP—secret field police).

some authentic documents, already decontaminated. A few points in his story are worthy of note. First, the detail about the way the graves had been struck upon. References to them had reached the field police which were engaged in intelligence work among the local population. People living in the vicinity of the Goats' Mountains (part of the big Katyn Forest stretching along the Dniepr by the Smolensk-Vitebsk Highway), asserted that *thousands* of Polish officers had been shot dead and buried in the Goats' Mountains, guarded by the NKVD, which had long served as a place for executions. The graves had been discovered by Polish workers who served with the Todt organization. They had carried out minor excavations on that territory and, having found that it was indeed Polish officers who had been interred in the graves, put up a wooden cross on the site. There is a picture of it, but the cross itself has not survived, having been pulled down as the exhumation work was started. In any event, it served as a signpoint to indicate where the excavations should be started. To our question as to whether those workers had been found, he said they had not as yet.

The second point, which was far more interesting, was that Słoweńczyk, although inclined to present the matter in the most dramatic way the Poles would see it had no idea where so many Polish officers had come from, and the only thing he had learned from the local population was that transports carrying them had arrived there from Smolensk. Since, furthermore, he had copies and even original letters and maps which had been found on the bodies, he asked why so many pages of those letters had the Kozelsk address? I told him in brief at the time what I knew about Kozelsk as well as about Starobelsk and Ostashkov, watching his reaction intently. This proved to be very quick, and convinced me completely that it was only now and from us that Słoweńczyk had learned about Kozelsk.

The following morning we drove to the Goats' Mountains. Turning into a forest, we stopped near a huge excavated pit. It was a long trench dug, apparently, as long and as deep as the grave, but not as wide, to witness the heads and feet of the bodies sticking out on the sides from the ground. A cross-section along the entire length of the pit provided clear evidence that the bodies had been buried in strict order and laid layer by layer, one on top of the other, in several tiers. The grave had been dug out in hilly terrain and in its upper parts the earth was dry, it was sand clay, while the lower parts were flooded by ground water. A second grave began to be unearthed not far away but it was only the first layer of bodies that could be seen so far. The excavations of both graves were made by local inhabitants, Russians. There was a roughly-built little house near the graves accommodating the exhumation group under Doctor Butz, Professor of Forensic Medicine at Wrocław University. Professor Butz wore a colonel's uniform. The group had just set about its work. Bearly 200 bodies taken out of the grave were lying in a forest clearing not far from the grave, waiting for a forensic necropsy in the order in which they had been dug out. The bodies were numbered and laid in several rows. About a score of bodies, apparently, already examined by Doctor Butz, were lying near his house in several places. Bits of military uniforms taken off the bodies hung from tree branches and shrubs. Everything around produced the impression of work that had just been begun and was not yet very tidy. Doctor Butz asked us to point to any corpse in the grave, and he would order it excavated at once and perform an autopsy on it is our presence. We pointed to some bodies in the middle of the grave. The autopsy showed that the skull had incoming and outgoing bullet holes, and the doctor tore up a pocket on the uniform with his knife and took out a postcard addressed to a captain whose name I do not remember. The postcard had been written by the captain's wife and mailed to Kozelsk from the Grodno district.

The remains of Generals Smorawiński and Bohaterewicz had already been identified among the bodies laid around the house. At my request, Doctor Butz cut off a general's shoulder strap from Smorawiński's uniform and took the "Virtuti Militari" order ribbon from General Bohaterewicz's greatcoat. I took that shoulder strap, the order ribbon, several buttons from the uniform of other officers and a pinch of earth from the graves with me to Warsaw. I kept those relics until the Warsaw Uprising when they were burnt with my flat in my house.

We did the rounds of the entire area and quickly learned to identify graves which had not yet been opened. Their edges were sunk and the surface rough and, besides this, there were little pine trees planted on top of them, no doubt on purpose; the small and even rows of these trees stood out against the background of the rest of the wild and forlorn forest, although it was not a very old pine grove as yet. The pines planted on the graves gave the impression of being robust and deep-rooted shrubs which must have been growing there for over a year.

From Doctor Butz I also received a list of names of those whose bodies he had already examined and identified. There were thirty of them. I checked the list and added to it in Grushenki, on my way back.

During our stay in the Goats' Mountains, German correspondents broadcast their comments on the affair and pleaded with us to go on the air to confirm that the crime discovered there had been committed by the Bolsheviks. In the end, weary of these importunities, I said just one phrase into the microphone to the effect that, in my opinion, the remains of prisoners from Kozelsk, about whom there had been no news since April 1940, lay in those graves.

Before our departure, I asked the Germans for permission for us to stay on by the graves alone since we wanted to pay homage to the dead without anybody else present. The Germans walked away and Doctor Seyfried* said the following at the graveside: "I call on the Polish delegation to observe a minute's silence in tribute to the memory of those who died so that Poland might live." I wrote those words down on the protocol sent to the Polish Red Cross (PRC), a copy of which was sent to the Propaganda Department at my request.

Apart from radio correspondents, none of the Germans disturbed us; we had complete freedom of action and our conversations with local residents took place without any hindrance from the Germans. Local inhabitants unequivocally confirmed the German version regarding the fact that the Goats' Mountains was a place which had long been known as an execution site and that the Polish officers had been shot by the Bolsheviks. I was not directly involved in the conversations because the circumstances they were held in and the haste of the questioning and the nervous atmosphere prevented us from putting on the more precise questions and having them answered."[1]

This text has spared me the trouble of speaking about the relationship of the PRC to the occupying authorities and setting out the details of the discovery and excavation of the burials. Goetel's description faithfully corresponds to other sources.

---

*Edmund Seyfried was Director of the Main Board of Guardians.

Chapter 4

It is interesting that Słoweńczyk, the co-ordinator of all the propaganda activities in Katyn and, consequently, the local German authorities, had not even the slightest notion about the officers' camps in Kozelsk, Starobelsk, and Ostashkov. Wasn't it the author of this report that let the Germans see everything with their own eyes? The delegation, including Goetel, had arrived, let me remind you, in Smolensk on April 11. In the morning of April 13, German radio told the world about the graves in Katyn Forest. By that time the Germans had a more or less authentic idea of the number of missing officers; the documents and personal belongings found on the bodies indicated that those who had been shot were the prisoners of war from Kozelsk alone.

It is no secret that the top people in the Reich had done everything to derive the greatest propaganda effect from their discovery of Katyn. Yet that required an independent expert examination. As soon as original information had been pieced together it led to an idea originating from Berlin about inviting the International Red Cross Committee to take part in the excavations.

Berlin, April 13, 1943.
Chief of the Cultural and
Political Department of the
Ministry of Foreign Affairs,
F.A. Six, in the Minister's Office.

At 22:30, April 13, Ministerial Counsellor Gregory, Deputy Chief of the Foreign Department of the Reich's Ministry of Propaganda, and shortly after him the Ministerial Director, Berendt, called up Professor Six at the Cultural and Political

Department, and, on instructions from Reichs minister Goebbels, notified him of the following:

. . . a place where the NKVD carried out executions has been discovered in the environs of Smolensk. Common graves in rows have been discovered with 12,000 Polish officers in them. They were all ones who had fallen into the hands of the Soviets when they occupied Eastern Poland. At that time there were 12,000 officers and 300,000 soldiers. Of those 300,000 men, 10,000 got to Iran, but without officers. The soldiers who had arrived in Iran know nothing about the whereabouts of their officers. Now the officers were originally confined in the camp for prisoners of war at Posbelsk.* The Polish authorities had maintained communication with them until April 1940, when it was broken. As for their subsequent whereabouts, we now had statements by railwaymen and townspeople who had watched the officers' arrival. According to those testimonies, officers were brought in daily in large groups and then shot. The exhumation showed that all the officers remained in their uniforms and with their insignia on, and had their decorations and documents on them, which enabled them to be personally identified. The exhumation was carried out by members of the Polish Red Cross, delegations of Polish scientists, physicians, creative workers, and industrialists. The Führer ordered that occasion to be used for propaganda around the world, with assistance by all means we have at our disposal. On April 14, Dr. Goebbels will announce that in the press and in a film, and the only thing the Reichsminister asked was that the Ministry of Foreign Affairs invite the International Red Cross to take part in the exhumation of these large common graves, insisting on it sending its commission there to that end. Since the work of exhumation has gone well ahead already, and the time of the year does not favor this work, it should be taken into the

---

*So it was in the text

account that the corpses were decomposing. Therefore, it is necessary to hurry up with inviting the International Red Cross. Please give me your instructions.

Signed: Six.[2]

Such an invitation was not long in coming, yet the IRCC never sent its delegation to Katyn.

On April 15, Moscow radio broadcast a TASS statement blaming the Katyn shooting on the Germans, and on April 17 the same text (mentioning the Gniezdowski graveyard) was published by *Pravda*.[3] In a communiqué, also on April 17, from the Council of Ministers of Poland, the Polish Government announced its intention to appeal to the International Red Cross. At the same time, an appeal to the IRCC was issued by Poland's Minister of Defense, General Kukiel. At 16:30 on the same day Prince Stanislaw Radziwill, Deputy Delegate of the Polish Red Cross in Switzerland, handed a relevant note to the IRCC representative Paul Rugger. It transpired at this meeting that a similar request had been addressed to the IRCC the day before, on April 16, by the German Red Cross. Moscow reacted to these events with an editorial article in *Pravda* of April 21, 1943, headlined "Hitler's Polish Collaborators." It referred to the Sikorski Cabinet in connection with its appeal to the IRCC. Sikorski did find himself in a difficult situation but he could not, afterall, remain indifferent to German propaganda reports. Whether any pressure had been brought to bear on the IRCC was not known. In any case, he did not respond until five days later, when he announced that he was ready to contribute towards establishing the truth, provided he was asked to do so by all the parties concerned, i.e., by the USSR as well. Such a response, coming as it did after the Pravda article, was tantamount to a refusal.[4] Stalin saw that he had his hands free. Late at night, on April 25, Molotov handed Ambassador Tadeusz Romer a note severing diplomatic relations between the USSR and the Polish Government in exile.

That dealt with the question of the IRCC's participation in the exhumation of the Katyn burials. It was then decided in Berlin to set up a special international expert commission. At the same time the idea of inviting Prime Minister Sikorski to Katyn was considered.

> Berlin, April 14, 1943.
> Bohle to Himmler on the question
> of inviting General Sikorski to
> Katyn in private capacity. Top
> secret.

Re: the murder of Polish officers near Smolensk.

One of the German party comrades living abroad expressed the following argument regarding the exploitation of the wholesale murder of Polish officers for propaganda purposes:

The Government of the Reich or the Minister of Propaganda of the Reich will make a public offer to the governments of hostile countries to send expert physicians or forensic physicians to see for themselves the evidence of the unparalleled cruelty committed by the Bolsheviks. Naturally, guarantees of inviolability must be given to this end. Besides, it is worth considering the question of granting Mr. Sikorski—also with guarantees of security provided—an opportunity to participate as a private individual in the identification of the slain Polish officers.

Chapter 4

There is no doubt that the governments of the hostile countries will not accept this offer, nor will they allow Mr. Sikorski to go there although, in all probability, he wants to do so. I presume, however, that the propaganda impact of such an offer on world public opinion would be extremely great, all the more so since Mr. Sikorski, for all his attempts to find out the whereabouts of the captive Polish officers, has received no answer from the Kremlin. Besides, that would bring a great propaganda dividend in terms of the effect it would have on the relatives of the slain, a considerable number of whom have, unquestionably escaped abroad, the identification of the slain would make certain the fate of their next-of-kin.

In any case, I do not consider it possible to ignore the thoughts expressed here and fail to pass them on to you.

Signed: Bohle

Field Headquarters, April 22, 1943.
Himmler to Ribbentrop on the
question of inviting Sikorski to Katyn.

Concerning Katyn Forest—one idea that bothers me is that we could be putting the Poles into a terrible situation if we invite Mr. Sikorski and the persons he will have chosen to fly to Katyn via Spain, with guarantees of inviolability provided, to see the facts for themselves.

That is just an idea of mine which is, perhaps, unworkable. However, I wanted to tell you about it.

Signed: Himmler

Field Headquarters. April 24, 1943.
Himmler to Bohle on passing the proposal
to invite Sikorski to Katyn to the Minister of
Foreign Affairs. Confidential.

Re: the issue of the murder of Polish officers near Smolensk.

Pseudoexperts

I thank you heartily for your letter of April 14, 1943. Your initiative regarding the murder of Polish officers appeared to me to be all the more interesting since I had already referred exactly the same idea on my own behalf to the Herr Reichsminister of Foreign Affairs. Whether it is workable or not I of course do not know.

Signed: Himmler

Fuschl, April 26, 1943.
Ribbentrop's reply to Himmler on the
question of inviting General Sikorski
to Katyn. Confidential.

I thank you heartily for your letter of April 22 in which you consider whether to invite Mr. Sikorski to fly to Katyn. I must confess that the idea seems tempting at first from the propaganda point of view. However, there is a position of principle over how to consider the Polish problem, and this position, ruling out any contact whatsoever with the Head of the Polish Government in exile, is too important to disregard even in the case of so seemingly tempting an act of propaganda.

Signed: Ribbentrop[5]

While the question of inviting the IRCC was being decided and an international commission formed, a technical commission of the Polish Red Cross got down to business in Katyn. In February 1989, Professor W.Kowalski discovered and published the so-called "Secret Report" prepared by the General Secretary of the PRC, Kazimierz Skarżyński. Incidentally, it is this item that started off a flood of Katyn publications in the censored Polish press, which has not as yet subsided.* The document, of which there is an only copy, was passed on in June 1945, to the chargé d'affaires of the British embassy in Warsaw, but in London it was made "top secret." In anticipation of that publication, Professor Jarema Maciszewski wrote that Skarżyński's testimony made it possible to show and remind everyone once more of the civic position of the PRC officials, who carried out their difficult and tragic mission with a sense of patriotic and humane duty. They did not allow themselves to be drawn into the ambit of German propaganda, realizing that while the Soviet Union was waging war against Hitlerite Germany, no service of any kind could be rendered to German propaganda, whatever the course of events and their own view on the developments of 1940-1941. The Polish Red Cross, conscious as it was of its full responsibility for the situation,

---

*This item was mentioned in a live Mayak broadcast at the time, in February 1989, and was immediately reported by Western media. It came to light that the authors of this scoop, A. Zhetvin and S. Fonton, were ordered by the chairman of the State Broadcasting and Television Committee of the USSR, A. Aksenov, to be barred from live broadcasting and transferred to low-paid jobs for three months. The order qualified Zhetvin's and Fonton's act as a "gross political mistake" which "damaged the interests of this country." After the official Soviet recognition, the victims appealed to Aksenov's successor, M.Nenashev, to cancel the order. Nenashev admitted that the order had been unfair but refused to cancel it simply to avoid creating a precedent. (*Argumenty i fakty*, No. 30, 1990).

emphatically declined to inform the Nazi authorities of the date of the crime in any form, in spite of all the potential unpleasant consequences.

The report contained the following basic conclusions:

1. There are partly uncovered common graves of Polish officers in the locality called Katyn, not far from Smolensk.

2. The examination of nearly 300 exhumed bodies allows it to be stated that these officers were killed with shots to the back of the head. The identical nature of all these wounds attests, beyond all doubt, to a wholesale massacre.

3. The murder did not have robbers as its object because the bodies were still in their uniforms, with decorations and footwear on, and a large number of Polish coins and banknotes have been found on them.

4. As suggested by the papers found there, the murder was committed in March-April 1940.

Proceeding from an investigation of the bullets extracted from the officers' bodies and the cases found in the sand, it is possible to say, Skarżyński writes, that the shots were made with 7.65-mm pistols, apparently of a German make.[6] Fearful lest the Bolsheviks should take advantage of these circumstances, the German authorities carefully made sure that not a single bullet or case were hidden by members of the PRC Commission.

In conclusion, Skarżyński emphasized the selfless work of the members of the technical commission who had taken the bodies out of a flooded ditch using their own hands. "I saw that ditch myself when I was in Katyn. It was formed by the lower edge of one of the seven huge graves terracing down to a narrow gully. The ditch was filled with ground waters and parts of the bodies stuck out of it. The Germans promised to provide pumps and the ditch remained uncleared right up to the last days of work.* And then Mr. Wodzinowski noticed once that Russian workers were filling up the ditch. He stopped that work at once, but got word that because of continuous Soviet air raids and the firefighting alert, the army could not provide the pumps. The workers could not be asked to take out the bodies in such conditions. Then five members of the technical commission of the Polish Red Cross, led by Mr. Wodzinowski, entered the ditch and extracted 46 bodies of Polish officers from the water in the space of 17 hours."[7]

An international committee of experts, on which the Nazis pinned their own particular hopes, sat in Katyn from April 28 to 30.

As I have already written, the motives behind the participation of experts in the Katyn commission have been a recurrent topic in the intervening years. To my mind, the worthiest reply to the charge of collaborationism was given by Professor François Naville of Geneva University. The story behind this text is as follows.

In September 1946, when the Nuremberg trial was nearing its end, a member of the Swiss Grand Council, Mr. Vincent, of the Labour Party, asked the Council of

---

*The exhumation was suspended on June 3 "for sanitary and policing considerations."

State in an interpellation how they "proposed to judge the case of Dr. Naville, Professor of Forensic Medicine, who had agreed to act as legal expert at the request of the German Government in April 1943, where the origin of the 10,000 corpses of Polish officers discovered in Katyn Forest near Smolensk was concerned." The Head of the Geneva Cantonal Government, Mr. Albert Picot, answered Mr. Vincent's case, in particular by reading extracts from the report which Professor Naville had presented to the Government, at their request. Naville wrote, in part:

Mr. Vincent seems to be under the impression that I received a considerable amount of German gold. He can be relieved of his anxiety. I was certainly entitled to ask for a fee for such complicated work of such importance, on which I spent one month of my time carrying out various researches, after a journey taking eight days. But from the very beginning I decided to refuse it, on moral grounds. I did not want to obtain money either from the Poles or from the Germans. I do not know who paid the expenses of the journey of our committee of experts, but I personally never asked for nor received from anyone any gold, money, gifts, rewards, assets, or promises of any kind. If, at a time when it is being mauled simultaneously by the armies of two mighty neighbors, a country learns of the massacre of nearly 10,000 of its officers, prisoners of war, who committed no crime other than to fight in its defense, and when that country tries to find out how this came about, a decent man cannot demand fees for going to the place and trying to lift the hem of the veil which concealed, and still conceals, the circumstances in which this act of odious cowardice, so contrary to the usages of war, was committed.

Chapter 4

Mr. Vincent asserts that I was acting under constant pressure from the Gestapo, which prevented us from having a free hand. This is absolutely untrue. I do not know whether the police were represented amongst those who received and accompanied us (doctors and guides), but I can definitely state that we were able to proceed undisturbed with our work as experts. I did not notice any signs of pressure being exerted on myself or on any of my colleagues. We were always able to discuss all matters freely amongst ourselves without the Germans being present. On many occasions I told my co-experts and the Germans who received us certain "truths" which they considered rather outspoken. They seemed dumbfounded, but no one ever molested me. I did not conceal what I thought of the moral responsibility of the Germans in this matter, as it was they who went to war and invaded Poland, even if our conclusions should establish their innocence in the matter of the death of the officers.

We spent two days and three nights at Smolensk, about 50 kms from the Russian lines. I moved about quite freely at Smolensk, as in Berlin, without being in any way accompanied or shadowed. As two of us could speak Russian, we were on several occasions able to talk to the peasants and Russian prisoners of war. We also contacted the medical personnel of the Polish Red Cross, who cooperated at the exhumation, and were specially detailed to identify the bodies, make nominal rolls and inform the next-of-kin. We assured ourselves that everything possible was being done in that respect.

We freely carried out about ten post mortem examinations of bodies which had been taken, in our presence, from the lower layers of the unexplored common graves. Undisturbed, we dictated reports on the post mortem examinations, without any intervention from the German medical personnel. We examined,

218

superficially but quite freely, about one hundred corpses which had been disinterred in our presence. I, myself, found in the clothes of one of them a wooden cigarette-holder engraved with the name "Kozelsk" (one of the three camps from which the doomed officers had come), and in the uniform of another I found a box of matches from a Russian factory in the Province of Orel, the region where the three camps concerned were situated.*

At the examinations, being concerned with the forensic medicine aspect, we paid particular attention to the transformation of the fatty substances of the skin and internal organs, to changes in the bones, to the destruction of joint tendons, to changes and atrophies of various parts of the body, and also to all other signs which would testify to the time of death.

Examination of the skull of a lieutenant, undertaken specifically by Professor Orsós, from Budapest, at which I was present, brought to light a condition that virtually excluded the possibility of death having occurred less than three years previously, according to scientific works already published on that kind of mutilation . . .

We experts were also at liberty to discuss amongst ourselves all our findings as well as the wording of our report. After having examined the graves and the corpses on Thursday and Friday, 29 and 30 April, all the experts met on Friday afternoon to discuss and decide on the composition of the report. Only medical personnel took part in that discussion, but without any interference. Some of us made a draft of the final report and it was submitted to me for signature on Saturday, May 1, at 3 a.m.

---

* Only Kozelsk was in fact situated in the region of Orel.

Chapter 4

I offered several comments and asked for some changes and additions, which were immediately made. I do not know whether the same consideration was given to the observations and criticisms made by Dr. Markov of Bulgaria; I do not remember whether he intervened during our discussion at the meeting, but I was present when he signed the report on May 1 about noon, and I can state that he did not then make any objections or protests. I do not know whether he was subject to any constraint by the authorities of his own country, either before the journey to Katyn or at the time he revoked his signature, on being charged with collaboration and when he declared that he had acted under pressure; but he was certainly not under any pressure or constraint while the committee of which he was a member was at work. In any case, he made in our presence a post mortem of one corpse and quite freely dictated the report on it, of which I have a copy...

As for us, the forensic medicine experts, it is our right and our duty in our modest sphere to seek above all to serve the truth in conflicts where the parties sometimes serve other masters, it is the tradition and the pride of our profession, an honor sometimes dangerous. We must do this without yielding to pressure, from whatever quarter it may come, without regard for the criticism and hostility of those who may be put into an awkward position by our unbiased impartiality. May our motto always remain that which honors certain tombs: *Vitam impendere vero.**

Albert Picto concluded his report to Vincent with the following words:

----

* Give life to the truth (Juvenal).

220

Pseudoexperts

The State Council considers that there is nothing with which to reproach Dr. François Naville, distinguished man of science, excellent forensic medicine expert, who acted on his own responsibility and who did nothing to infringe on any rule of professional conduct or of the code of honor. Dr. Naville's report contains a statement justifying the conclusions of his original report of 1943. He may publish it when he wishes. The Grand Council is not entitled to make any pronouncement on this matter.

On the other hand, the Grand Council agrees with us that it is in accordance with the ideal of science and the moral principles of our country that a scientist should seek the truth by means of thorough investigation.[9]

Soon after the war, two experts disavowed their Katyn reports, Professor Markov of Bulgaria and Professor Hajék, who represented the Protectorate of Bohemia and Moravia in the Committee. The rest turned out to be out of the reach of Soviet or pro-Soviet authorities and could afford to defend their honor the way François Naville did. Fresh evidence on the subject in question has, however, appeared from time to time.

In March 1989, *Vecherne Novosti*, a Belgrade newspaper carried a noteworthy item about Professor Orsós of Budapest University, a former member of the international commission. In an interview in that paper, a former Yugoslav intelligence agent, Vladimir Milovanović told of his acquaintanceship with Orsós in Germany in 1947. "Being sure that he was dealing with an avowed opponent of the 'Reds'," Milovanović said, "Doctor Orsós, whom I

221

already knew as a member of the international commission formed bv the Germans of representatives of Quisling countries in 1943, opened his heart to me once." Then came Orsós' monolog (in quotes), boiling down essentially to the allegation that the Katyn crime had been committed by the Germans. Milovanović admitted that there was little he had understood of the "special aspects." Nevertheless, he sent a report about his conversation with Orsós to Belgrade there and then.

The item in the Yugoslav paper passed almost unnoticed, while there is an important nicety about it. Professor Orsós was not just one of the experts invited by the Nazis; his findings played an important, if not paramount, role in the Committee's conclusions. This was mentioned in passing in François Naville's report we have just mentioned. Here is what another member of the Committee, Professor Palmieri, probably the last alive at that time, told the Polish political journalist Gustaw Herling-Grudzinski in Naples in January, 1973:

"None of the twelve members of our Committee had any doubts or reservations. The case was clinched by the dissection of a cranium made by the Hungarian Professor Orsós. On the inner wall of the skull he discovered a neosubstance which forms three years after a person's death."[10]

Something fundamentally new was demonstrated to the Nuremberg tribunal by Professor Markov of Bulgaria who disavowed his Katyn report soon after the war. Asked by the Soviet member of the prosecution, Smirnov, during the court proceedings on July 2, 1946, what the term "pseudocallus" meant, he replied:

"Professor Orsós understood by this phenomenon the deposition and stratification of the insoluble salts of calcium and other salts on the interior of the skull, and Professor Orsós argued that, according to his experience, such a phenomenon had been observed in Hungary to occur in cases where a body had been interred for at least three years."

Asked whether there had been many skulls with evidence of so-called pseudocallus presented to the members of the commission, Markov replied that he, for one, had "not noticed" any pseudocallus on the only body he had examined. As far as other experts were concerned, they, according to his observations, had discovered no pseudocallus either and knew nothing about this phenomenon.

References to pseudocallus were made also during the testimony given by the Soviet expert, V. I. Prozorovsky.

Smirnov: Have you heard of the term pseudocallus?

Prozorovsky: I found out about it, when I was given a book in the library of the Institute of forensic medicine. That was in 1945 . . .[11]

Smirnov: Speak slowly, witness.

Prozorovsky: Until then not a single expert in forensic medicine, notably, in the Soviet Union, had observed such phenomena.

Smirnov: Were there many cases of pseudocallus along the 925 skulls dissected?

Chapter 4

Prozorovsky: None of the experts in forensic medicine
discovered any lime deposits on the interior surface of the skull
or in any other section of the cerebrum during the examination
of those 925 bodies.

Milovanović's information should not be overestimated,
still less so since there is no possibility whatever of checking it. Yet it is difficult to dismiss it either. It is indicative,
however, that it appeared right after the publication of
Kazimierz Skarżyński's "Secret Report" in Poland.

Now let me come back to the findings of the international commission. Here is an excerpt from the protocol
signed by all its 12 members. (I quote this from the translation kept in the records of the ESC*):

The cause of the death of all the Polish officers so far taken
out of the graves was without exception, a shot in the head. They
were all killed with a shot in the back of the head and these were
all single shots. Only in rare cases have double shots been found,
and there is a single triple one. The shot passed deep into the
back of the head and on into the occipital bone. The out hole was
for the most part close to the hairline over the forehead. They
were, for the most part, revolver bullets of a less than 8-mm
calibre. The cracks on the skull and the traces of the powder on

---

*ESC - Extraordinary State Commission on Establishing and
Investigating the Atrocities of the German Fascist Invaders and
Their Accomplices. Formed by Decree of the Presidium of the
Supreme Soviet of November 2, 1942. Chairman: N. M. Shver-
nik. Members: N. N. Burdenko, B. Y. Vedeneyev, V. S. Grizodu-
bova, A. A. Zhdanov, Metropolitan Nicholas, T. D. Lysenko, Y. V.
Tarle, A. N. Tolstoy, I. P. Trainin.

the occipital bone near the in hole and also the invariably recurrent localization of the shot indicate that it was made at close range or in direct proximity, with the direction of the shot being everywhere identical with just a few minor deviations. The amazing uniformity of the wounds and localization of the shot within a very restricted part of the occipital bone warrant the conclusion that the shot was fired by a skillful hand.

The results of the commission's activities were summed up in his letter to Ribbentrop by Leonard Conti, the Chief of the Health Services of the Reich:

> Berlin, May 3 1943. Dr. L. Conti
> to the Minister of Foreign Affairs
> of the Reich on the results of the
> work of the international medical
> commission in Katyn.

With your permission and at my invitation, leading experts in forensic medicine from various European countries have carried out a forensic examination of mass burials in Katyn.

The protocol, signed by all of these most respectable foreign specialists, bears out the arguments put forward of all points.

In accordance with the wish of these foreign scientists, I venture to pass this over to you and also to inform you that the undersigned agree to have this protocol used for identification and publication of the truth by the competent agencies of the German Reich.

> Signed: Dr. L. Conti.[12]

Altogether, 4,143 corpses were taken out of the Katyn graves in 1943, and 2,815 of them were identified. There were no more than 200 bodies left in the last, eighth grave discovered on June 1, by the time work was terminated. The bodies were found to have 3,184 documents on them, the latest being dated May 6 1940, as well as a multitude of personal belongings. Besides this, numerous mass burials of Soviet citizens, victims of the NKVD, were found and opened up in the Katyn Forest.

Was it possible, in principle, that the story described in the communication of the Special Commission had been stage-managed?[13] Eyewitnesses were unanimous in asserting that they had observed no traces of any preliminary exhumation of the remains. The bodies had been pressed together tightly, the pockets were buttoned up and had to be ripped open to take the documents out. Aside from everything else, the Germans, in order to have stage-managed the whole affair, would have had to have procured hundreds of copies of Soviet newspapers from March-April 1940. For it was improbable that the captives should have kept these papers for eighteen months.

Of course, by no stretch of the imagination could anyone have expected Goebbels and his propaganda machine to have been objective. The number of those interred was doctored up to 12,000 (yet even the Soviet communication contained the false figure of 11,000). Floods of clamorous rhetoric were brought down on the "Jewish hangmen of the NKVD." But here is a curious detail which seems to have first been pointed out by Józef Mackiewicz: there were quite a few Jews in the list of identified victims, although this was manifestly at variance with the anti-Semitic Nazi version. This fact, in Mackie-wicz's opinion, indicates that the Nazis, for all their pathological anti-Semitism, tried not to interfere in the process of identification for the benefit of the cause.

As I have already said, the 1943 exhumations have been described in many sources, and yet there is still a certain gap to fill. There are no accounts by Soviet citizens, although the Germans are known to have arranged special guided tours for local residents. In my files, this episode has a modest reflection; nevertheless, I presume that certain details of the evidence that follows are noteworthy.

V. V. Kolturovich of Daugavpils relates his conversation with a woman who went with her co-villagers to see the uncovered ditches: "I asked her: 'Vera, what did people talk about among themselves when they looked over the graves?' The arguments were: 'Our careless bunglers would not have done a job like this—it is much too neat.' The ditches had been dug out ideally, lined up, and the bodies stacked just as ideally. That was, of course, an ambiguous argument and a second-hand one at that. It is, however, indicative that local residents were in no doubt about the possibility of Poles being shot by the NKVD.

A somewhat different picture of the exhumation was drawn by Lyudmila Vassilieva (née Yakunenko) now living in Krasnodar. She also participated in a guided tour. As she said, the trip had been carefully organized. Three or four Soviet witnesses had spoken before the inspection. Three graves altogether had been opened by the time the group arrived, and yet another was cut to show a cross-section exposing the roots of the spruce saplings planted on the surface; the German guide explained that the trees, to judge by the length of the roots, were at least three years old. Soviet prisoners of war were digging up the graves, and there was an unbearable stench. The body of a general was brought up from the grave in Lyudmila Vassilieva's presence. The documents taken out of his map-case contained what she remembered most: pictures of a handsome general with his wife and two children; his name impressed itself on her mind: Mieczyslaw. That is to say that Lyudmila Vassilieva had been present at the exhumation of General Mieczyslaw Smorawiński. She could not have found out that name anywhere else because it had not figured in any Soviet publications by the time we met. Later on, Lyudmila Vassilieva fought with a guerrilla detachment, saw a great deal of bloodshed, was more than once wounded herself, and still the Katyn exhumations were her most horrible memory of the war.

*   *   *

Let us now speak of the Burdenko Commission. Incidentally, its full name was "Special Commission of Inquiry and Investigation into the Circumstances of the Shooting of Polish Captive Officers by German Fascist Invaders in Katyn Forest." As you see, the very name unequivocally defined the purpose of the investigation and the criminals. The forensic examination carried out by the Special Commission was directed by Professor Prozorovsky.

Pseudoexperts

V. I. PROZOROVSKY

Biographical Note

Extract from the record of the interrogation of V. I. Prozorovsky. June 17 1946 (October Revolution Central State Archives, stock 7,445, inventory 2, storage unit 136, page 332):

Victor Ilyich Prozorovsky, 1901, Russian, a native of Moscow, has a clean record, a son, higher medical education (graduated from the 2nd Moscow Medical Institute), is professor of forensic medicine, Doctor of Medical Sciences, senior expert in forensic medicine at the Ministry of Health of the USSR, and Chairman of the Forensic Medicine Commission of the Academic Medical Council of the Ministry of Health of the USSR.

Let me add that Prozorovsky became Director of the State Forensic Medicine Research Institute in 1939, and senior expert in forensic medicine of the Ministry of Health in 1940. After the war he received yet another title, that of *Honored Scientific Worker.* The system of forensic medical examination was thoroughly reorganized in the Soviet Union while Prozorovsky was senior expert in forensic medicine (this structure was still in place) and specialist documentation was standardized. Under Prozorovsky, the *Rules of Forensic Medical Examination of Corpses,* which had been in force since 1928, were supplemented with a number of other documents such as *Instructions for Material to Be Used in Forensic Medical Examination for the Necropsy of Persons Who Died From Infectious Diseases for Subsequent Bacteriological Investigation* (1952), *Order of the Day N.452* of the Ministry of Health of the USSR; *On Medical Registration of the Causes of Death* (1954), circular N.1440; *On Blood Testing of Corpses* (1955); the instructional letter *Gauging the Stature by the Skeleton Bones of an Adult Person* (1958), et al.

There were two specialist debates on matters of principle, also under Prozorovsky. The first arose from the drafting of the new penal code, which came into force in 1960. The debate saw scathing criticism of the *Rules for Assessing the Gravity of Damage,* published in 1928. Professor Prozorovsky brought up a draft of new Rules which, however, was never adopted. One point that turned out to be in dispute was that of defining puberty. In the end, the necessity of defining puberty was laid down by the Penal Legislations only of six constituent republics, while the codes of the other republics indicated the actual age of a person with whom sexual intercourse was punishable. The other debate dealt with the limits of the competence of experts and began in 1945. The point is that the above-mentioned *Rules*, endorsed by the People's Commissariat of Justice and the People's Commissariat of Health, obliged experts to qualify bodily damage under the respective Articles of the Penal Code. A group of forensic doctors spoke out against that provision, seeking to prove that an expert had no legal right to produce statements on the kind of violent death (murder, suicide, or accident).

Unable to reconcile his colleagues, Prozorovsky turned to the Ministry of Justice, the Supreme Court, the Public Prosecutor's Office, and the Ministry of the Interior of the USSR for an explanation. In consequence, circular N.306

was published in 1956, whereby an expert had the right to produce a judgement on the kind of violent death "only when this judgement follows from the specialist knowledge of the forensic medicine expert concerned (theoretical training and expert practice) and the results of a forensic examination of the corpse in question." Yet that was not the end of the debate. (S. Shershavkin. *A History of the National Service of Forensic Medicine.* Moscow, Medicina Publishers, 1968, pp. 155-171 - in Russian). *The Rules of Forensic Assessment of Bodily Damage* (in force since April 1 1979), whereby an expert may not determine whether the damage is conditionally or unconditionally fatal or decide the question of the existence of a disfigured face, qualify injuries as being consequent on torture and torment, or establish the fact of beatings, etc. In accordance with Article 78 of the Code of Criminal Procedure of the RSFSR, he must refrain from answering questions outside his specialist subject or competence (*Forensic Medical Examination.* Yuridicheskaya Literatura Publishers, Moscow 1980, pp. 11, 111, 116–118, 219—in Russian).

Why am I writing about this? Simply because three of the five conclusions in the report of the Katyn forensic examination did not fall within the competence of the experts. Without going into extra detail, let me mention what are, in my view, the most essential shortcomings of the Act.

The report was signed by five experts. The exhumation and examination of the bodies were carried out, according to the Act, between January 16 and 23 1944. In his testi-

mony at the Nuremberg Tribunal, Professor V. I. Prozorovsky put January 14 as the opening date of the work in
Katyn Forest. Let us accept this latter version: in the course
of 10 days the Commission examined 925 corpses, that is,
every member of the Commission dissected and studied
185 corpses, or 18 corpses a day. It does not seem likely
that the expert examination carried out at such a pace was
sufficiently thorough. True, the report mentioned the
names of six more specialists in military medicine who
participated in the Commission's work; two of these were
experts in forensic medicine, and one, a pathoanatomist.
However, as they were not on the Commission, all they
could do was work as assistants, not make the final conclusions. Besides, one of the members of the Commission,
M. D. Shvaikova, a Professor of Forensic Chemistry, as
Prozorovsky testified, "was invited for consultation on
forensic chemistry and forensic chemical investigations"
and could not concern herself with the exhumation and
examination of corpses.

According to the report, the "expert examination has
produced appropriate material for subsequent microscopic
and chemical investigations in laboratory conditions." The
report makes no reference to the results of these investigations; they were never published or submitted to the court
in Nuremberg.

Furthermore, the objective data of the exhumation,
recorded in the statement of Prozorovsky's expert examination, just about textually coincided with the protocol of
the international commission. There is no paradox here

whatsoever. The point is simply that these findings were insufficient for the final and definite dating of the execution. So what came up then was material evidence, that is, documents taken from the graves. Now, the documents discovered by Prozorovsky and his colleagues were absolutely unconvincing. Altogether, there were only nine documents found on the 925 corpses. Two of them were items of mail from Poland dated September 1940. Naturally, they cannot be taken as evidence that the senders were alive by the time these were posted, and, besides, the text of one of the documents has faded. Five receipts of the acceptance of gold watches and money, two of them dated from December 1939, (records of the sale of watches to the Juvelirtorg dated March 1941) and three from April and May 1941, do not indicate anything either because they could have been antedated. A little paper icon, dated April 1941, is not a document at all, and it is only in view of a dire shortage of weightier evidence that anyone would think to produce it at all. What remains then is the unmailed postcard of June 20 1941, to Warsaw. Just imagine, there were 925 bodies and one postcard. The point is that the writer of the postcard, Cavalry Captain Stanisław Kuczyński, was never in the Kozelsk camp. According to Moszyński's lists, he was held in Starobelsk, from where he was taken in December 1939.[14]

The experts, moreover, with Prozorovsky at their head, came to the conclusion on the basis of these documents that the "German fascist authorities who undertook an examination of the corpses in the spring and summer of

1943 did not do so properly," and also, considering the absence of any signs of expert activity, that "the Germans carried out an extremely negligible number of exhumations in 1943." How could the experts learn about the examinations and exhumations since no evidence of them was ever discovered?

Finally, there is one more method that Prozorovsky applied to grave dating. He compared them with the state of the corpses in other common graveyards near Smolensk, referring to his own report in doing so. It follows from this, first, that the bodies of the Poles had likewise been interred about two years previously, and also, the method of shooting them was completely identical.

Thus, the Katyn executions were blamed directly on the Germans. Yet that is precisely what the experts had no right to do, by modern legal standards anyway.

It is, however, the Special Commission's working papers that stand out among the numerous Soviet archive sources capable of adding to what we know about the Katyn tragedy. Unfortunately, the greater proportion of these papers is still kept secret under current public record regulations. However, some isolated documents are quite accessible and need no declassification. It is these that I shall bring to the readers' notice. But first, a word of comment about the significance of these texts.

It is perfectly obvious today that the Burdenko commission's communication holds no water. Some of the contradictions it suffers from have been corrected in subsequent publications. Substantial corrections were made in Burdenko's version at the Nuremberg trial. Those who studied the records of preliminary interrogations of the witnesses for the prosecution, carried out in Moscow in June 1946, must have certainly noticed a multitude of minor divergences compared with the depositions of the same persons a year before. It is likewise noteworthy that the records of examination by Soviet experts in forensic medicine were written by the persons questioned. Finally, even in the course of the legal proceedings, the Soviet prosecution twice departed and in a most fundamental fashion at that, from the original formula (I shall turn to it again in greater detail in the next chapter). All these circumstances make the following texts particularly valuable. Apart from everything else, one cannot rule out the possibility of the official documents, not being subject to public disclosure, revealing the details which did not figure in the final text of the communication.

The earliest document is N. N. Burdenko's letter of September 2 1943, to V. M. Molotov.

Most esteemed Vyacheslav Mikhailovich: I address myself to you because of the following circumstances: last April you, as People's Commissar for Foreign Affairs, published the Soviet Government's note breaking off diplomatic relations with the Polish Government. In the note, you referred to the false charge, provocatively laid against our public authorities, of the execution of several thousand Polish officers. On reading the German Government's report about Polish officers having been shot in the Katyn Forest and the findings of the International Commission, I studied the text thoroughly. In spite of the pretentious title of the report "Culprits Exposed by Experts in Forensic Medicine," the Germans produce some quite peculiar arguments to put the blame on the Soviet authorities—the reference is, above all, to the shooting method. I, while in Orel as a member of the Government Commission, exhumed nearly 1,000 corpses and found that 200 Soviet citizens who had been shot had the same wounds as the Polish officers.

In conclusion, Burdenko expressed the hope that he would have an opportunity to go the environs of Smolensk before long, and reported that as the ESC was proceeding with its investigations, he collected 25 skulls of Soviet citizens executed by the Germans and was ready "to establish the unquestionable identity of wounds" and "to present them, if need be, to the representatives of our allies in advance."[15]

There are at least two conclusions to be drawn from this letter. First, Burdenko had started working on the Katyn business long before the exhumation. Second, he believed *a priori* that the guilt of the Germans was beyond doubt.

The following document is unsigned and undated. It is entitled: "Characterization of Cranial Wounds of the Bodies from the Katyn Forest Graves." To judge by all accounts, that is one of the first professional conclusions to have been drawn up for sure after an examination of exhumed remains.

The inholes, the first phrase says, "are, as a rule, in the occipital bone, above the large occipital opening, mostly in the vicinity of the median line." The diameter of the opening is indicated: from 0.6 centimeter to 0.8-0.9

centimeter, with openings of 0.8 cm in diameter predomi-
nating. Next there is a reference to a small percentage of
blind wounds with bullets of a 0.6-0.7 cm caliber having
been found inside the cranium, and in one skull, an
"irregularly shaped piece of metal, probably the jacket of
an explosive bullet." The document ends with the following
statement: "In some cases cranium damage with cold steel
has been observed. The wounds of the bone in these cases
had the form of tetrahedral openings with smooth edges
and were multiple.[16]

What can be said about this text? The conclusion has
been compiled quite objectively and, besides, by someone
having nothing to do with the army, otherwise the caliber
of the openings would have been indicated in millimeters.
What strikes the eye is the existence of punctured wounds
tetrahedral in shape, not mentioned in the communication.
The same wounds, on the bodies, not on the skulls, were
discovered by Gerhard Butz. The fact of the matter is that
it was the Soviet bayonet that was tetrahedral, while the
German was, of course, flat. It is not surprising that the
Soviet experts preferred to omit that detail.

A further document was Burdenko's letter of March 21
1944, to the ESC Chairman, N. M. Shvernik. Here is its
full text:

"Most esteemed Nikolai Mikhailovich! According to what
seem to be some fairly credible rumours which I have
received from military physicians, there have been some
wholesale murders carried out by the Germans in Vinnitsa.
The Germans are provocatively ascribing these murders to

the Soviet authorities. To establish the technique of killing, it would be good to send Professor L.I. Smirnov, patho-anatomist of the Central Neurosurgery Institute, who is a cranium examiner. I am making so bold as to write this to you because past experience of grave exhumation has not always been valuable." The letter carries Shvernik's resolution: "Accept Cde Burdenko's proposal to send Professor Smirnov to Vinnitsa. March 23."[17]

Of course, it is Vinnitsa that is the main point here. Mass interments of NKVD victims were revealed by the German authorities in Vinnitsa in the summer of 1943. An expert committee was formed, like that in Katyn, to carry out an identification of the corpses with the participation of local residents, and the findings were published in the occupation and world press.[18] It proved impossible to ascribe these executions to the Germans, although, as you may see, such attempts were made. One thing that follows from the date of the letter is that the Special Commission continued to function after it had published its communication.

Finally, in his letter of May 29 1944, Burdenko told Shvernik that he offered to "complement the material on the Katyn affair with the authentic testimony by physicians involved in the German expert group." And further on: "The testimony to be furnished by the parties to the German show, whose names we know, would finally expose the foul provocation of the German fascist hangmen in Katyn."[19]

So the Commission carried on working in May 1944. Did Burdenko feel his communication to be indequate? In any case, he presumed it necessary to supplement it. Burdenko's offer has been followed up only in part, as we know.

I have already stated that the Burdenko Commission's activities had been directed right from the start towards accusing the Germans rather than acquitting the NKVD agencies (which were, of course, presumed never to have been involved at all). For example, the first thing Burdenko seized upon on reading the International Commission's judgement was the method of shooting. The report of the Soviet expert group also underscored the "complete identity of the method of shooting Polish prisoners of war with the method of shooting Soviet civilians and prisoners of war, widely practised by the German fascist authorities on the temporarily occupied territory of the USSR." But, indeed, the one does not rule out the other. We know very well today that this method—shooting in the back of the head—was widely applied on the territory of the USSR not only by Einsatzcommandos of the SS but also by the NKVD, as conclusively evidenced by the exhumations, notably in the Curopathians.[20] Foreign correspondents invited to Katyn were sure as early as 1944 that it had all been a preposterous and unworthy farce. Here is, for instance, how the Englishman Alexander Werth described what he had seen there in his generally quite complimentary book *Russia at War. 1941-1945*:

Chapter 4

On January 15 a large group of Western correspondents, accompanied by Kathie Harriman, the daughter of Averell Harriman, the United States Ambassador, went on their gruesome journey to look at the hundreds of bodies in Polish uniforms which had been dug up at Katyn Forest by the Russian authorities. It was said that some 10,000 had been buried there, but actually only a few hundred "samples" had been unearthed and were filling even the cold winter air with an unforgettable stench. The Russian Committee of Inquiry, which had been set up, and was presiding over the proceedings, consisted of forensic medicine men, such as Academician Burdenko, and a number of "personalities" whose very presence was to give the whole inquiry an air of great respectability and authority; among them were the Metropolitan Nicholas of Moscow[*], the famous writer Alexei Tolstoy, Mr. Potemkin, the Minister of Education, and others. What, qualifications these "personalities" had for judging the "freshness" or "antiquity" of unearthed corpses was not quite clear. Yet the whole argument turned precisely on this very point: had the Poles been buried by the Russians in the spring of 1940, or by the Germans in the later summer or autumn of 1941? Professor Burdenko, wearing a green frontier guard cap, busy dissecting corpses, and, waving a bit of greenish stinking liver at the tip of his scalpel would say "Look how lovely and fresh it looks."

And further on:

---

[*] This is inaccurate: Nicholas was the Exarch of the Ukraine, Metropolitan of Kiev and Galich.

Pseudoexperts

Altogether, the Russian starting-point in this whole inquiry was that the very suggestion that the Russians might have murdered the Poles had to be ruled out right away; the whole idea was insulting and outrageous, and there was, therefore, no need to dwell on any facts which might have led to the Russians' "acquittal." It was essential to *accuse* the Germans; to *acquit* the Russians was wholly irrelevant.

Nevertheless, Kathie Harriman, who had led the team of foreign correspondents, declared on her arrival in Moscow that she had found enough trustworthy evidence to bear out the Soviet version. One must presume she had special reasons for doing so.

In April 1990, I happened to see one more person who had travelled to Katyn, the *Sunday Times* correspondent Edmund Stevens. Here is an excerpt from his dispatch of November 29 1989, on the occasion of the visit of Prime Minister Tadeusz Mazowiecki of Poland to Moscow:

I have followed the Katyn story since February 1944, when I was one of a group of war correspondents invited to the spot by the Soviet Press Department. As Kathie Harriman, daughter of the American ambassador, had asked to be included, we had a luxurious sleeper and wagon restaurant well stocked with caviar and other goodies for which we had scant appetite after our visit to the forest. We were bussed from heavily damaged Smolensk, some 15 kilometres to the forest, which mainly consisted of spruce saplings about three years old, planted before the Germans invaded and Stalin and Hitler were jointly carving up Poland.

Chapter 4

The corpses we were shown lay on the frozen ground, presumably where they were shot. The corpses were in great-coats, indicating they had been shot in wintertime, each with a bullet in the back of the skull.

Our guide on the visit was Nikolai Burdenko, the Soviet Union's most distinguished surgeon. His thankless, not to say impossible task was to persuade us that the Germans were responsible for the massacre. Burdenko and his assistants had doubtless been coached but their accounts seemed somehow artificial and unconvincing.

In his conversation with me, Mr. Stevens gave me some additional details. The group proceeded to Moscow immediately on the following morning. He did not remember whether journalists had been shown any documents whatsoever. Finally, the deputy mayor, who spoke at a news conference in Smolensk, had, in Stevens' opinion, been prepared in advance and read a "crammed" text.

Let me draw your attention to two points. First, Edmund Stevens assured me (I asked him expressly to confirm that assurance) that the group had never been present to watch any exhumations at all; the corpses were already lying on the ground. Let me remind you that this all happened in January and the foreigners, as Stevens told me, had been warned to put on warm clothes for the trip. I cannot understand how the experts could have managed to dig out the corpses from the graves in biting frost without damaging them. And the second point: the greatcoats. The fact that the bodies had winter uniform on surprised the correspondents very much, because they had been told that the Poles had been shot in August and September when there was obviously no need for great-coats to be worn as yet, and, on the contrary, it was, as a rule, cold in the Russian midlands in March and April. The foreigners' puzzling questions disconcerted the Soviet officials. In consequence, Prozorovsky wrote down in his report that the killings had been carried out "between September and December" and it was, apparently, too late to alter the witness' accounts, so the reference to August and September was left as it stood in the texts.

*　　*　　*

Some of the letters I received after my publications about Katyn referred to the Burdenko Commission. For example, Vera Zvezdayeva of Smolensk told me that her father, Andrei Kozlovsky, had observed the work of Soviet experts in 1944 and noticed, among other things, this important detail: "The family lived under occupation from 1941 to the day of liberation, so it had studied the German ways quite well. So my father told me that when the bodies of Polish officers had been dug up, they were all found to have retained their gold teeth, wedding or other finger rings. However, the Germans never left any gold in any shape or form on people they shot, under any circumstances." This fact was indicated in the expert commission's conclusion and Professor Butz's report. Now, the Special Commission's communication had no mention whatsoever of any articles made of precious metals.

Chapter 4

There is yet another piece of evidence. An expert criminologist Georgy Rybnikov, a former member of staff of the Institute of Criminology of the Ministry of the Interior of the USSR, writes that a member of the Special Commission, P. S. Semenovsky, approached him for consultations in the summer of 1947. He showed Rybnikov a score of spent bullet cases and asked him to identify the type of weapon. Rybnikov established that all the cartridges had been fired from a Schmeisser of the 1939-1940 model and one from a Parabellum. The cartridges, Georgy Rybnikov recalled, were rusty, and had lumps of fresh soil and yellow leaves sticking to them. Naturally, that fact alone did not prove anything as yet; for the cartridges could have been extracted from an entirely different burial. It is likewise well known that the Burdenko Commission had found no cartridges in Katyn. Yet it is also well known that that Katyn graves were opened again after the war. As for P. S. Semenovsky, as an expert, he has recently been established to have never distinguished himself at all by anything like professional honesty. It is none other than Semenovsky who produced the conclusion within the terms of forensic medicine regarding the notorious sensational affair of Semenchuk-Startsev, framed by Vyshinsky and Sheinin. The author of publications on this subject, Alexander Larin, a doctor of law, writes: "Doctor Semenovsky produced his judgement on the merits of the cases without so much as examining the body. I knew him personally. It was not by chance that Vyshinsky had picked him, rather than anybody else, as an expert. He was a mediocre professional but a very tractable and obedient man. Vyshinsky manipulated him as he wished. In his zeal and desire to justify Vyshinsky's trust, Semenovsky had managed to produce purely legal conclusions even in the report of the expert examination: like stating premeditation, ulterior motives and so on and so forth."[21]

Having read through the *Collected ESC Reports on the Atrocities of the German Fascist Invaders*, I never found the name of Semenovsky among the experts. Smolensk was the only exception. So where did the cartridges, given to G. I. Rybnikov in 1947, actually come from?

Now for the last point. The vast archival stock of the ESC, for which the Burdenko Commission had worked, contains a small, yet telling document, which serves as the best imaginable evidence to illustrate the style of work of that government institution. In a letter of August 18 1944, to the ESC Secretary, P. I. Bogoyavlensky, Professor I. P. Trainin, an ESC member, expressed his extreme surprise over the fact that the outline communication *On the Atrocities of Finnish Fascist Invadeders on the Territory of the Karelo-Finnish SSR* had been sent to him the night before the day of the publication and so no corrections were possible any longer.[22]

Chapter 5.

NUREMBERG VERSION

The Nuremberg trial of the major German war criminals was the most important episode of the Katyn affair. It was in Nuremberg that Stalin's version showed itself to be totally and legally inconsistent. Yet another reason why it is worth dwelling on Nuremberg is that the students of the Katyn problem still produce certain inaccuracies in summing up the course of the legal investigation. For instance, Czesław Madajczyk writes in his *Katyn Drama* that in the course of the trial, Professor Bazilevsky "repeated the testimony he had given to the Soviet Special Commission.[1] This is not quite true, as we shall see in a moment. A more glaring mistake was made by the author of an editorial insert to the well-known commentary by N. S. Lebedeva in *Moscow News*, of March 25 1990 . . . . "These contradictory findings resounded at the Nuremberg trials. None of the sides presented definitive and convincing proof." But the point is that the defense presented no version *of its own* at the Nuremberg trial: its object was solely to disprove the version of the prosecution. Any attempt at presenting a counter version would have been nipped in the bud, since the charges against the USSR were obviously at variance with the status of the International Military Tribunal (IMT).

At first, the Soviet prosecution was so far from being in any doubt about the favorable outcome of the legal investigation of Katyn, and so made a very serious correction just before the publication of the indictment. The number of victims was arbitrarily increased from 925 to 11,000.[2] The number 925 was that of the corpses exhumed by the Burdenko Commission. Eleven thousand was the final figure of Polish prisoners of war listed as missing. The Soviet leadership sought to legitimize its version and in that way close the book on the issue of those responsible for the Katyn killings, as well as on the subsequent fate of all captive Poles. That task, however, proved to be difficult to accomplish.

I have already chanced to write about the blank spots of Nuremberg.[3] At issue with me were P. I. Grishayev and B. A. Solovyov, former officials of the Ministry of State Security of the USSR who carried out their own specific functions in the trial. Among other things, they charged me with having insulted the memory of the dead and the honor of those representatives of the Soviet prosecution still alive. I think I might ask them whether they consider the numerous publications about the Sinyavsky–Daniel trial, which L. N. Smirnov, the former Chairman of the Supreme Court of the USSR presided over, as an affront to his memory? Perhaps they would presume the memory of R. A. Rudenko to have been insulted by recent commentaries on the unlawful expulsion of Alexander Solzhenitsin from this country or the banishment of Andrei Sakharov, and all kinds of reprisals against human rights activists and dissidents? All that happened while Rudenko was Attorney General of the USSR, the office he held from 1953 to 1981, incredible though it may seem. Of course, it would be right and proper, perhaps, to put the matter even more emphatically in this case. Do the teaching staff and undergraduates of the Sverdlovsk Law Institute still want their college to be named after Rudenko, and isn't this fact an insult to the memory of those who were persecuted on political grounds with Rudenko's direct participation, and an affront to the very idea of a law governed State?

"It turns out," the veterans of the Ministry of State Security write, "that it was not the only object of the Soviet prosecutors who arrived in Nuremberg to represent the USSR with dignity in the International Military Tribunal and to exert the greatest possible effort so that the major German war criminals faced a fair sentence based on tangible evidence, but for some other sinister and shady objective . . ."

The subject is an unpleasant one, but since Grishayev and Solovyov touched upon it, let me explain my position. Of course, the object of the Soviet prosecutors was to represent the USSR with dignity, but the point is that the involvement in the organization of wholesale reprisals over the years, the unlawful methods of Soviet investigation and legal proceedings could not fail to tell on the quality of their representation. These men had long forgotten what real contestant evidence, impartiality of courts, and legal investigations are like. The Soviet prosecutors had a fundamentally different *concept* of the trial of the major German war criminals from that of their Western colleagues. They presumed that the trial would boil down to pronouncing some spectacular indictments, and that was something they really could do, as they had been taught by their boss, Vyshinsky, and they least of all expected to have to deal with a subtle and highly professional defense. That is the reason why the full array of Nuremberg records has never been published in the Soviet Union, in spite of the IMT decision.

I can well expect many readers to be shocked by this judgement of mine. Perhaps, I may even be charged with attempting to call the IMT verdict into question. That is nonsense, of course. It is a different point I am trying to make; on reading this chapter through, the reader will, I hope, see what I mean. But to begin with, here are a few more preliminary comments.

The documents I am going to quote further on are best expressive of the atmosphere in which the Soviet delegation worked at Nuremberg. Few will know today (and, indeed, few knew in those days either) that apart from the official Soviet delegation, there was one agency directly involved in the proceedings of the International Military Tribunal, which has been variously named in various sources. Either it was a Government Commission on the Nuremberg Trial or Government Gommission on the Organization of the Trial in Nuremberg or else the Commission to Direct the Nuremberg Trial. It was led by Andrei Vyshinsky, Deputy Minister of Foreign Affairs of the USSR at the time.

The Government Commission, unlike many present departments, not only took decisions but was very demanding of those who failed to carry out or carried out inadequately its instructions. There is nothing surprising about

Chapter 5

this. It comprised, along with the Attorney General of the USSR, K. P. Gorshenin, the Minister of Justice I. T. Golyakov, the Chairman of the Supreme Court N. M. Rychkov, and also such odious figures as B. Z. Kobulov, V. N. Merkulov, and V. S. Abakumov. Obviously, they all applied their particular methods of conducting investigation. The minutes of November 16 included this dialogue, for instance:

Vyshinsky: . . . Cde Rudenko still has no plan by which to conduct the trial. Rudenko is not prepared for the prosecution. (The trial began on November 20.—*V. A.*). I sent the introductory speech which we had compiled with you for the Central Committee.

Kobulov: Our men, who are now in Nuremberg, are reporting to us about the behavior of the defendants in the interrogation sessions (reads out a note). Goering, Jodel, Keitel and others are arrogant. Their replies often contain anti-Soviet remarks, and our examining judge, S. D. Alexandrov, is too weak to respond to them. The defendants manage to pose as ordinary officials and mere servants of the High Command. When the English questioned Reder, the latter declared that the Russians wanted to recruit him and that he had given his testimony under pressure. That statement of his was recorded on tape.

Vyshinsky: The prosecutor must, whenever necessary, cut short the defendant's speech and give him no opportunity to make anti-Soviet remarks."[4]

"Our men" are Grishayev and Solovyov, but there are in fact more.

How did the incident with Alexandrov end? How did he try to justify himself? Perhaps he had explained his connivance with the enemies by tactical considerations. He objected reasonably that it would be difficult, after all, to expect Goering to make pro-Soviet statements. Here is his explanatory note to Gorshenin:

1. Colonel of Justice Rosenblit and, as a rule, Colonel of Justice Pokrovsky were present at all interrogation sessions, as well as myself.

2. There were no charges against the USSR or personal charges against me either from the defendants interrogated or from the witnesses questioned.

3. The incident which has been reported to you as one that supposedly happened to me actually occurred in my presence during the questioning of defendant Frank by American Lieutenant Colonel Hinkel on October 28 (a.c.) At the end of the session Frank did call Hinkel a swine. (. . .)

While reporting the previous, I consider that in this case the government agencies were misinformed about the actual setting in which the interrogations of the defendants took place.

I ask for a special inquiry to establish those responsibile for such misinformation and to call them to account under strict terms. Along with this, I ask for an end to be put to all kinds of misconstructions regarding the interrogations of the defendants that have been carried out, as all this is creating unsurable situation and hampering further work.

And so Alexandrov was left alone.

Let me, however, come back to the Katyn affair. I left off at the point where the Soviet prosecution had corrected the figure of 925 in the indictment to 11,000. This was done imprudently and led to an undesirable disclosure. That was where all the trouble with Katyn started.

Let me now turn to the book of the parties to the trial, Mark Raginsky, *Nuremberg: Before the Trial of History*. Here is what it says on page 22.

" . . . contrary to the Charter[5], the Tribunal did not accept the minutes of the interrogation of Paulus, carried out in Moscow in January 1946, and called, on solicitation from the lawyers, some war criminals into the witness box, whose testing could supposedly have disproved the report of the investigation of the Extraordinary State Commission on the atrocities of the Hitlerites in Katyn."

On page 49 you find:

At the organizational sitting of the Tribunal, Francis Biddle[6] not only supported the unlawful solicitations of Goering's defense counsel for calling the witnesses he had selected who, supposedly, could have refuted the Soviet Commission's Report, but started a lengthy discourse misinterpreting Article 21 of the. Charter in favor of the Nazi criminals.

Now turn to page 92:

"Frank attempted in every way to fence himself off from Katyn as well, yet the International Tribunal had been presented with indisputable evidence of the crimes of the Nazis in the Katyn Forest (near Smolensk), where Hitler's occupying authorities carried out mass killings of Polish prisoners of war in the autumn of 1941."

These quotations call for a word of comment.

Article 21 of the IMT Charter reads: "The Tribunal shall not demand evidence about the commonly known facts and will consider them proved. The Tribunal shall likewise accept without evidence the official government documents and reports of the United Nations, including protocols and documents of the committees created in various allied countries for an investigation of the war crimes, proceedings and sentences of military or other tribunals of each of the United Nations." In February 1946, Colonel Y. V. Pokrovsky, Deputy Chief Prosecutor on behalf of the USSR, presented the court with the report of the Soviet Special Commission on Katyn, which did not need, according to Article 21, additional information.

In his turn, Goering's defense counsel, Otto Stahmer, filed a request for German witnesses to be summoned and also an additional plea for the summoning of Professor François Naville of Geneva University, intending to disprove the charges on Katyn with their testimony.

Apparently, the Soviet prosecution was absolutely sure of a negative response to Stahmer's request and, therefore, made no moves right up until March 12 1946, when the request was granted, after all, in spite of Pokrovsky's vigorous protest.

Let me turn to the minutes of the IMT's organizational sitting concerned.

The chairman of the Tribunal Lord Justice Geoffrey Lawrence read out Stehmar's solicitation and then Pokrovsky's statement for the benefit of the Tribunal. It said essentially that "it was wrong, in point of principle, to check the incontestable evidence with such contestable evidence as the depositions of the persons listed in Dr. Stahmar's solicitation." There is no need in Pokrovsky's opinion, either in summoning Professor Naville who "was involved, deliberately or inadvertently, in Hitler's mystification regarding Katyn" since "the time of the killings made by Hitlerites in Katyn has already been established with perfect accuracy by the authoritative expert commission." Besides, the whereabouts of the witnesses for the defense is unknown and so an "actual summons would have been pointless." (According to Stahmer's supposition, four of the six witnesses were in captivity, two of them in Soviet captivity.[7])

The matter came under discussion. Judge Nikitchenko, invoking Article 21, offered to decline Stahmer's solicitation. Lawrence objected. It did not at all follow from the text of Article 21 that the documents it mentioned were *incontrovertible** evidence. "Of course," he said, "it would take time to consider counter documents, but it does not follow from this that the defense cannot try (*though I doubt that it will manage to do so*) to prove that the facts reported by the Government Commission are incorrect. We cannot obstruct the defense in this case, for we have no grounds for doing so." Justice Biddle supported him: "Government documents include also testimony by individuals, for example, soldiers who could appear as eyewitnesses. It was

---

*Emphasis here and hereafter is mine.–V. A.

wrong to interpret Article 21 to mean that other persons are not permitted to disprove this document. Subsequently, we would be in a position to say that the Soviet Commission's impressive report does not allow the Swiss Professor's testimony to be regarded as convincing." (It is not difficult to notice that Lawrence and Biddle were trying to persuade Nikitchenko and let him see that they would give their preference to the Soviet document anyway). French Justice de Vabres shared the opinion of his colleagues.

Nikitchenko put forward a different argument. "Whenever it was *the commonly known historical facts* that were quoted, the Tribunal accepted them without evidence and found them proved." It occured to de Vabre that the Russian text of Article 21 did not, perhaps, accord with the English. However, Lawrence and Biddle declared that the Russian text coincided with the English. "The prosecution could just as well have avoided touching on the question of killings in the Katyn Forest," Justice Parker remarked.

"If we ban the defendants from resorting to the help of witnesses, *we will not, therefore, give them the right of defense.*" De Vabres presumed that the rejection of the solicitatation "would not correspond to the provisions of international law and would provoke an unfavorable reaction from public opinion." To this Judge Volchkov objected that "not a single legal example can challenge the documents of another example. This is precisely what was consistent with international law". (It was, of course, an obvious overstatement. The Burdenko commission was not a legal example.) Then comes a yet more striking argument by Volchkov:

"An act of a sovereign State cannot be disproved by 2–3 witness dispositions." Biddle offered to vote. Nikitchenko declared that he could not take part in the voting because the question of amending the Charter was outside the Tribunal's competence. Biddle said that the point that was at issue in this case was not one of *amending* but one of *interpreting* the Charter. Lawrence seconded Biddle. Nikitchenko stood pat on his point. Biddle, who was sick and tired of this exhausting and fruitless discussion, once more offered to vote (the Soviet judge was clearly in the minority). Then Nikitchenko (it was also clear to him) said that one thing that should be done before considering the solicitation was to decide on Article 21, in principle. "If there are divergent opinions on that issue," he said, "I would not be able to share in deciding on the solicitation. Now, if we agree that, by being guided by Article 21, we will take our decision with regard to the solicitation." That is to say that Nikitchenko agreed to participate in the voting only in the event of the rejection being guaranteed. The discussion continued, nobody had any fresh arguments to advance, and everybody just repeated the old ones. Justice Biddle offered to vote for a third time. Three were for, while Nikitchenko abstained from voting. His dissenting opinion was recorded in the minutes. The session was closed.[8]

The judgement of the Tribunal came as a complete surprise to the Soviet delegation. In a strongly-worded letter of March 18 to the Tribunal, Lieutenant-General Rudenko wrote:

This question is one of great fundamental importance for the entire trial and the Tribunal's judgement of March 12, and constitutes an extremely dangerous precedent, since it gives the defense an opportunity to drag out the trial interminably by attempts to disprove evidence which was considered incontestable under Article 21. Regardless of the above-stated position of principle, which is one of basic and decisive significance for the matter at issue, one cannot pass over the fact that the Tribunal deemed it possible to call in as witnesses such persons as Ahrens, Rex, Hott, and others, who as one can see from the communication presented to the Tribunal, are the actual perpetrators of the atrocities committed by the Germans in Katyn and, in accordance with the Declaration of February 1 1943, by the Three Heads of Government, must be brought to trial for their crimes by the court of the country on whose territory these crimes have been committed.

On April 6, the court reverted to the issue of Stahmer's solicitation, but left the original verdict standing. The viewpoint of his colleagues was explained in detail by Justice Biddle ("He indulges in lengthy discourse, misinterpreting the issue"—M. Raginsky).

In the meantime, the Vyshinsky Commission got down to the business of coaching the witnesses for the prosecution. We read in the minutes of March 21:

1. Coach Bulgarian witnesses, for which purpose our representative must be sent to Bulgaria. Responsibility for this lies with Cde Abakumov.

2. Prepare three to five witnesses of ours and two medical experts (Prozorovsky, Semenovsky, Smolyanikov). The man in charge is Cde Merkulov.

3. Prepare Polish witnesses and their testimony. Cde Gorshenin (acting through Cde Safonov with Cde Savitsky) to be responsible.

4. Prepare authentic documents found on the corpses, and records of the medical examination of these corpses. Cde Merkulov to be responsible.

5. Prepare a documentary film on Katyn. Cde Vyshinsky to be responsible.

6. Cde Merkulov is to prepare a German witness involved in the Katyn provocation.

So it is Abakumov, Merkulov, and Vyshinsky all over again! I hope there is no need for me to explain what "preparing witnesses" means in their parlance.

The witnesses who had given the most essential testimony to the Burdenko Commision were summoned to Moscow at once. There it was Assistant Senior Prosecutor L. N. Smirnov, who had subsequently conducted the Katyn case in the court proceedings, who worked with them there in June 1946. He questioned, in particular, B. V. Bazilevsky, A. M. Alexeyeva, S. V. Ivanov, I. V. Savvateyev, P. F. Sukhachev, and also experts in forensic medicine, V. I. Prozorovsky and V. M. Smolyaninov. Written testimony was given in his own hand by the Bulgarian expert, Markov. If you look up the minutes of the Vyshinsky Commission's sitting of June 11, you will find that they contain a list of eight names, with the executants, Reichman[9] and Sheinin, being enjoined on the following day to dispatch witnesses to Nuremberg. However, there were only three of them to face the court. When was the final choice made? By whom? Nobody knows. This detail, I presume, speaks of the involvement of even higher placed personalities than Vyshinsky in the preparation of the Katyn case. Only Stalin, Molotov, and Beria could be such personalities.

In the meantime, in Nuremberg, Nikitchenko once more turned to the question of the Katyn witnesses. He proposed in a secret sitting of June 19 "that evidence on the Katyn case should be presented in writing, without any witnesses being summoned to the court." But the Tribunal eventually declined even this proposal. The only thing that the prosecution managed to achieve was the IMT decision to hear no more than three witnesses on behalf of each party. These were Bazilevsky, Markov, and Prozorovsky. One could not call that a happy choice by any means. Only Victor Prozorovsky, senior expert in forensic medicine at the Ministry of Health of the USSR, possessed a certain respectability. He, however, had directed the forensic medicine examination by the Soviet Special Commission and therefore could not show himself to be totally impartial.

As additional documents, the prosecution presented the court with records of the interrogation of the witnesses who had never come to Nuremberg.

Comparing the text of the Special Commission's communication with the records of the interrogations carried out by Smirnov in June 1946, you can easily see that the witness accounts had been edited. For instance, the former chief of the "Special Camp No. 1,"[10] Major V. M. Vetoshnikov (Security), interrogated by the Commission, testified: "I asked the Traffic Director of the Smolensk section of the Western Railway, Cde Ivanov, to provide the camp with carriages to take out the Polish prisoners of war." (*Collected ESC Reports on the Atrocities by German Fascist Invaders.* Moscow 1946, p. 104 [in Russian]). Now, there is no Vetoshnikov in the 1946 record of the interrogation of S.V. Ivanov, which stated, instead, that he had been visited by a serviceman with the rank of captain who introduced himself as the camp commandant. The point is, however, that you can never confuse a general service captain with a security major. So, we conclude: the Soviet prosecution strove to clear the witness accounts of any mention of the fact that the camps were under NKVD control. Another striking fact concerns the record of the interrogation of Alexeyeva. It had been written, as it should be in fact, in Smirnov's hand, as in their own. (To complete the confusion, each page bore their signature of confirmation).

Yet another document presented by the prosecution was the record of the interrogation of Ludwig Schneider, a prisoner of war, dated June 19 1946. Senior Corporal Schneider, a chemist by profession, had worked in Professor Butz's laboratory when he exhumed Katyn corpses. In his testimony he mentioned two cases of the results of laboratory tests being doctored. In the first case, Schneider had been called upon to determine the percentage content of ferrous oxide on the blade of a knife taken out of a grave, which turned out to be a little over 23%. However, Butz, according to Schneider, "had changed the figure with his own hand, tripling it." In the second case, Butz ordered the laboratory assistant Müller to expose a piece of uniform fabric to heat at a temperature of up to 80° C and to treatment with calcium chloride; Schneider knew that from Muller.

Finally, yet another strange document had been prepared (apparently, by Abakumov) which should be considered to have been of negligible legal significance. That is a record of the examination by Franz Joseph Ferdinand Hervers of the Netherlands. He had once overheard a conversation between two SS-men from which he inferred that the Katyn killings had been the handiwork of the Germans. The Hervers examination was dated May 2, but the record reached Nuremberg, as could be understood from the accompanying letters, only at the very end of July, when the legal investigation regarding Katyn was over.

True, Smirnov had an indisputable trump card at his disposal, and I shall come back to this again.

What about the progress made by Otto Stahmer?

According to the communication by the Soviet Special Commission, the execution of the Polish prisoners of war had been carried out by a "German military institution code-named 'Staff of the 537th construction Battalion' commanded by Lieutenant Colonel Arnes and his staff Senior Lieutenant Rex and Lieutenant Hodt." It transpired that the staff of a unit of this number had indeed been stationed in the Katyn forest in what had been once a country house belonging to the Smolensk Regional NKVD Department, though, to be exact, it was commanded by Colonel Ahrens, not Lieutenant Colonel Arnes. (The names of these men and of the military unit had been written down by the Soviet Commission as told by A. M. Alexeyeva, who had worked in the headquarters). Colonel Friedrich Ahrens was named first in Stahmer's list. Apparently, it was his presence at Nuremberg that compelled the Soviet prosecution to refrain from calling in Alexeyeva. She had testified that the execution had been carried out in August and September 1941, while Ahrens took over the command from Colonel Bedenk only in the second half of November. Rex could not be found, while Hodt was found too late. There were still Ahrens' immediate chief Lieutenant General Oberhäuser[11] and Professor Naville. It was a purely casual set of circumstances that helped Stahmer. A certain Reinhard von Eichborn presented himself in the office of Munich notary Hans Nobis on March 7, and declared that he had read the speech of the Soviet prosecutor (Pokrovsky) in *Süddeutsche Zeitung* of February 19 and wished to give testimony on the Katyn case. In a notarially certified affidavit, Eichborn testified that it was the headquarters of the 537th liaison regiment, not that of the 537th construction battalion, as stated in the Soviet Commission's record, which was stationed in the area of Katyn Forest in the autumn of 1941. The regiment had "received no orders to carry out any activities of the kind the prosecutor had spoken about" and "self-determined activities of this kind by the regiment are inconceivable"; the regiment's equipment precludes its involvement in such executions. In conclusion, von Eichborn referred to the Intelligence Chief of Staff of the Center Armies, Major General Rudolf Christoph von Hersdorff, as someone who could confirm the testimony. Von Hersdorff did actually confirm Eichborn's words in full. His testimony was presented to the court. Eichborn was summoned to Nuremberg for a cross-examination. Subsequently, however, the Tribunal resolved to limit itself to three witnesses on behalf of each party. Stahmer forewent the services of Professor Naville.

Let me note that the defense had presented the final list of witnesses within several weeks of the court session, while the prosecution kept its list secret. It was Rudenko who read it out only on the very day of the trial, which he did only on the insistence of the defense.

Friedrich Ahrens was invited into the witness box on July 1 1946.

"Shortly after I arrived—the ground was covered in snow—one of my soldiers pointed out to me that at a certain spot there was some sort of a mound which one could hardly describe as such, on which there was a birch cross. I did see that birch cross. In the course of 1942, my soldiers kept telling me that in the wood, shootings were supposed to have taken place . . . . I was able to confirm quite by accident that there was actually a grave there. During the winter of 1943—I think either January or

Chapter 5

February—I saw a wolf in this wood, but at first I did not believe that it was a wolf. I followed the tracks with an expert. We saw that there were traces of scratchings on the mound with the cross . . . . The doctors told me of 'human bones.'

Stahmer: It has been alleged that an order had been issued from Berlin according to which Polish prisoners of war were to be shot. Did you know of such an order?

Ahrens: No. I have never heard of such an order.

Q. Did you posssibly receive such an order from any other unit?

A. I have already told you that I never heard of such an order; I therefore did not receive it, either.

Q. Were any Poles shot on your instructions?

A. No Poles were shot on my instructions. No one at all was shot on orders given by me. I have never given such an order in all my life.

Q. Then, you did not arrive until November 1941. Have you heard anything about your predecessor, Colonel Bedenck, having given any such orders?

A. I have not heard anything about that. I was on such intimate terms with my regimental staff, with whom I lived closely together for nine months, that I am perfectly convinced that this deed was not perpetrated by my predecessor, nor by any member of my former regiment. I would undoubtedly have heard rumors of it, at the very least.

Q. Then, how did the exhumation take place?

A. I do not know about all the details. Professor Dr. Butz arrived one day on orders from the army group, and informed me that, owing to the rumors, exhumations were to be carried out, and that he had to inform me that these exhumations would take place in my wood.

Q. Did Professor Butz later give you details of the result of his exhumation?

A. . . . I cannot remember much about them now; but I do remember some sort of a diary which he passed over to me in which there were dates followed by certain written remarks which I could not read because they were written in Polish. In this connection he explained to me that these notes had been made by a Polish officer regarding events of the past months, and that at the end—the diary ended with the spring of 1940—the fear was expresssed in these notes that something horrible was going to happen. I am only giving a broad outline of the meaning.

Q. It was alleged that in March 1943, lorries had transported bodies to Katyn from outside and these bodies were buried in the little wood. Do you know anything about that?

A. No, I know nothing about that.

Then it was the turn of Kranzbühler, the defense councel of Denitz, to take the floor.

Kranzbühler: Colonel, did you yourself ever discuss the events of 1940 with any of the local inhabitants?

Ahrens: Yes. At the beginning of 1943, a married Russian couple were living near my regimental headquarters,[12] they lived 800 yards away and they were beekeepers. I, too, kept bees—and I came into close contact with this married couple. When the exhumations were taking place, approximately in May 1943, I told them that, after all, they ought to know when these shootings had taken place, since they were living in close proximity to the graves. Thereupon, these people told me it had occured in

Chapter 5

the spring of 1940, and that at the Gnesdowo station more than 200 Poles in uniform had arrived in railway trucks and were then taken to the woods in trucks. They had heard lots of shots and screams too.

Kranzbühler: Apart from mass graves in the neighborhood of the Dnieper castle,* were there any other graves found?

Ahrens: I have indicated by a few dots on my sketch that, in the vicinity of the castle, there were found a number of other small graves which contained decayed bodies; that is to say, skeletons which had disintegrated; and these graves contained perhaps six, eight, or a few more skeletons, both male and female. Even I, a layman, could recognize that very clearly, because most of them had rubber shoes on which were in good condition, and there were also remains of handbags.

Kranzbühler: How long had these skeletons been in the ground?

Ahrens: That I cannot tell you. I only know that they were decayed and had disintegrated. The bones were preserved, but the skeleton structure was no longer intact.[13]

It was the episode involving the encounter with a wolf that the Soviet prosecutor, Smirnov, seems to have found most interesting in Ahrens' testimony. He started working up to it from a distance, so to speak, as if casually:

Smirnov: By the way, did you personally see the Katyn graves?

---

*This is what the Germans called the country cottage of the original NKVD Department.

Ahrens: Open or before they were opened?

Q. Open, yes.

A. When they were open I had constantly to drive past these graves, as most of them were approximately thirty meters away from the entrance drive. Therefore, I could hardly go past without taking any notice of them.

Q. I am interested in the following. Do you remember what the depth of the layer of earth was which covered the mass of human bodies in these graves?

A. That I do not know. I have already said that I was so revolted by the stench which we had to put up with for several weeks that when I drove past I closed the windows of my car and rushed through as fast as I could.

Q. However, even if you only casually glanced at those graves, perhaps you noticed whether the layer of earth covering the corpses was thick or shallow? Was it several centimeters or several meters thick ?

Ahrens patiently explained everything all over again:

As commander of a regiment, I was concerned with a region which was almost half as large as Greater Germany, and I was on the road a great deal. My work was not entirely carried out at the regimental battle headquarters. Therefore, in general, from Monday or Tuesday until Saturday, I was with my unit. For that reason, when I drove through, I did cast a glance at these graves, but I was not especially interested in the details. (. . .) Therefore, I can not remember what you are asking me about.

Smirnov: According to the material submitted to the High Tribunal by the Soviet prosecution, it is obvious that the bodies were buried at a depth of one and a half to two meters. I wonder

267

where you found such a wolf which could scratch the ground up to a depth of two meters.

That was Smirnov's homework. However, Ahrens remained unperturbed. I did not find this wolf, but I saw it.

The prosecutor's last question was:

Q. Tell me, please, why, after having discovered the cross and learned about the mass graves in 1941, you only started the exhumation on these mass graves in March 1943?

Ahrens: That was not my concern, but a matter for the army group. I have already told you that in the course of 1942 the stories became more widespread. I frequently heard about them and . . . . I reported what I had seen and heard. Apart from that, this entire matter did not concern me, and I did not concern myself with it. I had enough worries of my own.

Next to appear in the witness box was Reinhardt Von Eichborn, a telephone communications expert attached to the staff headquarters of the Center Armies. He assured the court:

" . . . It is quite out of the question that if such a number of officers had fallen into the hands of an army group, it would not have reported the matter through the appropriate channel."

Besides, he denied emphatically the existence of an order for the execution of the Poles, explaining that all the orders for the 537th regiment had passed through his hands.

Next to take his place in the witness box was Lieutenant General Oberhäuser, liaison chief of Army Group Center:

"Such a task, however, would have been something unusual for the regiment, firstly, because a communications regiment has completely different tasks, and secondly, it would not have been in a position technically to carry out such mass executions."

And finally: "I consider that it is out of the question, certainly for this reason alone, that if the commander had known it at the time, he would certainly never have chosen as a place for his headquarters this spot next to 11,000 dead."

Smirnov kept asking what kind of weapons the 537th regiment had (carbines were of no interest to him). According to the general's estimates 150 pistols. "Why do you consider that 150 pistols would be insufficient to carry out these mass killings which went on over a period of time?" Smirnov asked.

"Because a single regiment of an army group deployed over a large area, as in the case of the Army Group Center, is never together as a unit," Oberhäuser explained.

The cross-examination of the witnesses for the defense was over.

Let us now take a closer look at the major witness for the prosecution, Boris Bazilevsky, who was now going to answer questions from Smirnov and Stahmer.

Chapter 5

B. V. BAZILEVSKY

Biographical Note

Boris Vassilyevich Bazilevsky (Kamennetz-Podolsk, 26.05.1885,—Novosibirsk, 1955?) graduated from the Physics and Mathematics Department of Petersburg University, majoring in Astronomy. In 1914 he taught mathematics, physics and cosmology at the 2nd Warsaw High School, in 1919 became a professor of Smolensk University, and from 1930 held the astronomy chair at the Smolensk Institute of Education. At the same time, he was the director of the local observatory. A political journalist, A. Z. Rubinov, who had lived in Smolensk before the war, told me that Bazilevsky had been in charge of an amateur astronomy group at the local House of Young Pioneers.

There have been some references to Bazilevsky having been arrested under Yezhov, but no documentary evidence bears this out so far. However, he certainly did suffer from some harassment. The Special Commission's communication says that Bazilevsky "was forcibly appointed" to the office of Deputy Mayor. B. G. Menshagin asserted that Bazilevsky had been Mayor in the early stages of the occupation and only later on did they change. He was then in charge of education, art, health, and housing in the municipal council. When a high school (a teachers' training seminary) opened in the city in October 1942, he became its headmaster. When Red Army units entered Smolensk, he lived in a home for invalids. According to

Gleb Umnov, former Smolensk police chief, he had been allowed to stay, "since he had a son still on the Soviet side." (*Novyi Zhurnal*, bs. 104, 1971, p. 276).

Further details of Bazilevsky's biography came to light later on. Gerald Reitlinger, in his book *The House Built on Sand*, set out the following story with allusion to Juergen Thorwald. In a memo sent to Hitler through Army Group Center Commander von Bock late in September 1941, the latter was asked to make Smolensk a self-governed capital of the occupied territories and a mobilization center "for all who want to fight Stalin." The memo was accompanied by a present, a museum gun abandoned by Napoleon during his retreat from Russia in 1812.[14] The memo had been written by none other than professor Bazilevsky. Was Bazilevsky, as Reitlinger presumed, a double agent? It is unlikely that this will ever be established. Umnov, in the publication quoted above, asserted that Bazilevsky had been an NKVD informer before the war and was dismissed from his post by the Germans for that reason. Menshagin denied this fact, however.

In January 1944, Bazilevsky testified before the Special Commission, headed by N. N. Burdenko, in the presence of a group of foreign journalists. Here is an account of that episode by one of the eyewitnesses, Alexander Werth.

While this is more than probable, if not *absolutely* certain, it must be said that the Russians conducted their publicity around the case (including the visit of the Western press to Katyn) with the utmost clumsiness and crudeness. The press was allowed to attend only one of the meetings of the Russian Committee of

Chapter 5

Inquiry, which questioned several witnesses. Among them were a Professor Bazilevsky, an astronomer, a doddery little man whom the Germans were said to have persuaded or compelled to become the assistant burgomaster of Smolensk; he declared that his chief, a quisling who had since fled with the Germans, had told him that the Polish officers were to be liquidated; a notebook said to belong to this ex-burgomaster was produced with this significant, if somewhat cryptic, entry: "our people in Smolensk talking about the shooting of the Poles?"[15] . . .

The whole procedure," Werth concluded his account of the interrogation, "had a distinctly prefabricated appearance."

Let me remind you also that according to Edmund Stevens (see the chapter on Pseudoexperts), Bazilevsky had read what was an unmistakably "crammed text."

The record of the preliminary interrogation of Bazilevsky, dated June 1946, contains the following personal characteristics:" Professor of Astronomy at the Institute of Education in Novosibirsk and the Institute of Engineers of Geodesy, Aerial Photography and Cartography, married, with one son."

Bazilevsky's original testimony must likewise have been edited. For instance, when testifying before the Special Commission, Bazilevsky was reported to have said that in his conversation with Menshagin he told Professor I. Y. Yefimov about it there and then, in the autumn of 1941, and the latter comfirmed this. In Nuremberg, Bazilevsky had named, apart from Yefimov, the sanitary physician Nikolsky, with whom he had also spoken about the fate of the Poles, "but it turned out that Nikolsky already knew about that particular atrocity from other sources." That is to say that the fact of the killings was at least rumored, if not commonly known. The Special Commission's communication had a special chapter devoted to these circumstances. They are extremely important but, even so, Smirnov interrupted Bazilevsky several times and asked him "not to dwell on details" and to be brief and, in general, they spoke so fast that Lawrence had to intervene twice.

Yet the subject in question was by no means of little importance. Here is the text of the Burdenko Commission's communication:

Early in September 1941, Bazilevsky asked Menshagin to plead with Commandant von Schwetz for the release of Zhiglinsky, a teacher, from prisoner of war camp No.126. In a move to meet this request, Menshagin turned to von Schwetz and then communicated to Bazilevsky that his request could not be granted . . . " and so on and so forth. Here is how the same episode was presented in Nuremberg:

. . . I learned that in this camp there was also a very well-known pedagogue named Zhiglinski. I asked Menshagin to make representations to the German Kommandantur of Smolensk, and in particular to von Shwetz, and try to liberate Zhiglinski from this camp.

Smirnov: Please do not go into detail and do not waste time, but tell the Tribunal about your conversations with Menshagin. What did he tell you?

Chapter 5

Bazilevsky: Menshagin answered my request with, "What is the use? We can save one, but hundreds will die." However, I insisted, and Menshagin, after a certain amount of hesitation, agreed to make such a demand upon the German Kommandantur.

Smirnov: Please be short and tell us what Menshagin told you about the German Kommandantur.

It is quite obvious that Smirnov was seeking to prevent a detailed account of Menshagin's motives. What was important to him was a refusal and the causes behind it.

But the point is that there was no refusal either. This circumstance was made a point of by Gabriel Superfin, the author of the commentaries to Menshagin's *Reminiscences*. In L. V. Kotov's book *Smolensk Underground* (Moscow, 1966, pp. 30-31) [in Russian] we read: "Zhiglinsky, taking advantage of his acquaintanceship with the Deputy Burgomaster, fixed himself up in the housing department of the municipal council." Bazilevsky's request was granted after all. Subsequently, Zhiglinsky became one of the underground leaders and was executed in September 1942 (of course, the spelling mistake in his name must be noted: "e" instead of "i." I do not think there is any particular motive behind it, as Kotov's book appeared 20 years after the Nuremberg trial. In all likelihood, the one who corrected the shorthand report just checked it against the text of the Special Commission's communication (it had some other mistakes too: for instance, "Rext" instead of "Rex" in one place, on page 108; in this case, however, it is surprising how it could have escaped the attention of the proofreaders, or perhaps that was a deliberate slip? Still, it referred to the same man).

At the very start of Bazilevsky's interrogation there was an incident which has been described many times in literature as an effective psychological device of the defense. Let me quote from the shorthand report:

Stahmer: Witness, when giving evidence, just before the recess, you read out your testimony, if I observed correctly. Will you tell me whether that was so or not?

Bazilevsky: I was not reading anything. I had only a plan of the courtroom in my hand.[16]

Q. It looked to me as though you were reading out your answers. How can you explain the fact that the interpreter already had your answer in his hands?

A. I do not know in what manner the interpreters could have my answers beforehand. The testimony which I gave was, however, known to the Commission beforehand; that is my testimony during the preliminary examination.

When the cross-examination ended, the American prosecutor T. Dodd took the floor.

Dodd: Mr. President, before this witness is examined, I would like to call to the attention of the Tribunal the fact that Dr. Stahmer asked the preceding witness a question which he understood to be as follows: How did it happen that the interpreters had the questions and the answers to your questions if you did not have them before you. Now that question implied that Dr. Stahmer had some information that the interpreters did have the answers to the questions, and I sent a note up to the

Chapter 5

interpreters, and I have the answer from the Lieutenant in charge that no one there had any answers or questions, and I think it should be made clear on the record.

Stahmer: I was advised of this fact outside the Court. If it is not a fact, I wish to withdraw my statement. I was informed outside the Court from a trustworthy source. I do not recall the name of the person who told me, I shall have to ascertain it.

Chairman (Lord Justice Lawrence): Such statements ought not to be made by counsel until they have verified them.

Smirnov: May I begin the cross-examination of this witness, Mr. President?"

That brought the incident to an end. Stahmer had achieved his objective, however. Bazilevsky spoke hesitantly and was nervous. Let us look at the way the interrogation began.

Stahmer: Do you know where the graves of Katyn were found in which 11,000 Polish officers were buried?

Bazilevsky: I was not there. I did not see the Katyn burial grounds.[17]

Q. Had you never been in the forest of Katyn?

A. As I already said, I was there not once but many times.

Q. Do you know where this mass burial site was located?

A. How can I know where the burial grounds were situated seeing that I had not been there since the occupation? . . .

Q. Therefore, you have no knowledge of the fact that here in the Katyn forest a sanatorium or a convalescent home of the GPU was located?

A. I knew that very well; that was known to all the citizens of Smolensk.

Q. Then, of course, you also know exactly which house I referred to in my question?

A. I myself had never been in that house. In general, access to that house was only allowed to the families of the employees and of the convalescents. As to other persons, there was no need and no facility for them to go there.

Q. The house, therefore, was shut off?

A. No, the house was not forbidden to strangers, but why should a stranger go there unless to recuperate. This was not a rest home for him.[18]

Q. Is this Russian who reported to you about the matter concerning the Polish officers, is this man still alive?

A. You must mean Mayor Menshagin.

Q. When you were reading out your testimony, it was not easy for me to follow. What was the mayor's name? Menshagin? Is he still alive?

A. Menshagin went away together with the German troops during their retreat, and I remained, and Menshagin's fate is unknown to me.

Q. Can you give us the name of an eyewitness who was present at this shooting or anyone who saw it?

Bazilevsky: No, I cannot name any eyewitness.

Bazilevsky's reputation, low as it had been, was finally wrecked by Stahmer's question on whether he had been victimized for his collaboration with the Germans. Bazilevsky had to reply: "No, I have not."

Q. Are you at liberty?

A. Not only am I at liberty, but, as I have already stated, I am at the present time a professor at two high schools.

Q. Therefore, you are back in office.
A. Yes.

The next man in the witness box for the prosecution
was Marko Markov, Professor of Forensic Medicine at Sofia
University. He was a supremely noteworthy figure, and
this is why. Some eighteen months before Nuremberg,
Markov had faced a Bulgarian court as a defendant under
Article 2 of the "Decree-Act on People's Trials of Culprits
of Bulgaria's Involvement in the World War Against the
Allied Nations and for the Misdeeds Related Thereto."
Together with them in the dock, there were five others
accused under the same article of the same act, namely:
Georgy Mikhailov, an expert in forensic medicine, and
three clergymen: Archimandrite Iosif Dikov, former chief
of the Cultural and Enlightnment Department of the Holy
Synod; Archimandrite Stefan Nikolov, former editor-in-
chief of the *Church Gazette*, Archimandrite Nikolai Kozhu-
kharov, former rector of the Sofia Ecclesiastical Seminary;
and former director of the National Propaganda Boris
Kotsev. Markov was charged with having been involved in
a similar examination in Vinnitsa. The rest had been to
Vinnitsa as members of the public and subsequently joined
the corresponding propaganda campaign. The most
striking thing is that Markov and Mikhailov were acquited
by the Bulgarian court while the clergymen and the
director of National Propaganda were convicted. I believe
that a deal was struck here and also that Markov had
examined only one corpse. Let me remind you also that

the Soviet prosecution had strongly objected to another expert from the international commission, Professor François Naville, being summoned by the defense. Yet, professor Naville was the only representative of a neutral nation on the commission.

Yet another aspect of the affair that made the records of the Sofia trial interesting is that the judges had come to a conclusion about the complete identity of the Katyn and Vinnitsa burials. As one of the documents says, "Vinnitsa is a copy of Katyn." And further on: " . . . the perpetrators of the killings in Katyn and Vinnitsa came from the same source, note the same killing—a shot in the back of the head and the same method of interring the bodies and disguising the cemetary—by planting trees."

As you see, Burdenko's idea of ascribing the Vinnitsa killings to the Germans materialized in the records of the Sofia trial where, however, the diametrically opposite effect had been achieved.

To be honest, I have not taken any time to explore Markov's subsequent fate. I can only refer to a letter from G. Superfin, who told me in September 1989: "After all his confessions, he still seems to have disappeared. The family is said to be living in Sofia and have no information about him."

From the protracted testimony of the Bulgarian expert, let me quote the replies of Stahmer's three key questions.

Stahmer: According to your autopsy report the corpse of the Polish officer which you dissected was clothed and you described the clothing in detail. Was this winter or summer clothing that you found?

Markov: It was winter clothing, including an overcoat and a woolen muffler around the neck.

Stahmer: In your autopsy report, witness, there is the following remark:

"Documents were found in the clothing and they were put in safe keeping under the folder No.827." Now, I should like to ask you: How did you discover these documents? Did you personally take them out of the pockets?

Markov: These papers were in the pockets of the overcoat and of the jacket. As far as I can remember, they were taken out by a German who was undressing the corpse in my presence.

Stahmer: "The documents found among the corpses (diaries, letters and articles from the autumn of 1939 up to March and April 1940). The latest date which could be fixed was the date of a Russian newspaper of 22nd April 1940." Now, I should like to ask you if this statement is correct and whether it is in accordance with the findings that you made.

Markov: Letters and newspapers were certainly in the glass cases that were shown to us. Some similar papers were found by members of the Commission who were dissecting the bodies, and, as I understood later, they described their contents, but I did not do so.

So Markov admitted the fact that the corpses had winter clothing on and,as we remember, these circumstances attracted the attention of foreign correspondents invited to Katyn and made them doubt the veracity of the Soviet version. He also admitted that the documents found on the body had been taken out right before his eyes. It is not clear what Markov meant when he said "I did not do that." Does this phrase mean that the contents of the documents did not correspond to the results of the exhumation, or that Markov showed no interest in the contents? In any case, he displayed laudable caution by not recording the fact in his protocol.

It was during the interrogation of Prozorovsky that Smirnov used his main argument. The telegram notifying the Warsaw authorities that the commission of the Polish Red Cross had discovered the German-made cartridges in the Katyn graves. This invaluable present was made to the Soviet prosecution by the Americans. Now Prozorovsky had every reason to assert that the Soviet Social Special Commission had also discovered cartridges thus marked. Apparently Stahmer had no time to make a careful study of the text of the Commission's communication (one of the protocols recorded his complaint about the delay of the translation),[19] otherwise he would inevitably have asked why there was no mention of that most important piece of evidence in the statement by the expert forensic examination. The document, "kindly provided to us by our American colleagues" (Smirnov), read: "Officials of thePolish Red Cross have brought with them cartridges used in the shooting of the victims in Katyn. They turned out to be German ammunition. They were made by the Geko firm and had a caliber of 7.65 mm. The telegram was sent from Krakow to the Government of the General Gubernia, dated May 3, 1943. In 1944, the Special Commission did not have this document, nor had it found any cartridges on its own.

Chapter 5

Prozosovsky had simply lied. It is interesting to note that
Pokrovsky, who also presented evidence on Katyn, did not
mention the telegram. The Americans, it must be presumed, passed it on to our delegation after Stahmer's plea
had been granted. Now, during the preliminary interrogations on June 17 and 18, both Prozorovsky and Smolyaninov confidently testified that they had discovered
cartridges with a company trademark. This is an example
of the professional honesty of the experts on the Burdenko
Commission.[20]

Otto Stahmer was clearly displeased with the Tribunal's
decision to interrogate only three witnesses during a court
session, because it had Professor Naville and Lieutenant
(by that time already senior-lieutenant) Hodt in reserve.
He had tried twice in the course of the proceedings to
convince the court to reconsider its decision and had had
his request rejected on both occasions. The first episode is
also interesting because it made it clear how Smirnov had
changed the original wording of the charge. Stahmer
seemed to be quite satisfied with this turn of events just
because it offered him an excuse for additional pleas.

Stahmer: Mr. President, before calling my third witness,
Lieutenant-General Oberhäuser, may I ask your permission to
make the following remarks? The prosecution has up to now only
alleged that Regiment No.537 was the one which had carried out
these shootings, and that under Colonel Ahrens' command. Today,
again, Colonel Ahrens has been named by the prosecution as
being the perpetrator. Now apparently this allegation has been
dropped, and it has been said that, if it was not Ahrens, then it

must have been his predecessor, Colonel Bedenck, and if Colonel Bedenck did not do it, then apparently, and this seems to be the third version, it was done by the SD. The defense had solely taken that Colonel Ahrens was accused as the perpetrator, and it has refuted that allegation. Considering the changed situation, and the attitude adopted by the prosecution, I shall have to name a fourth witness in addition. That is First Lieutenant Hodt, who has been mentioned today as the perpetrator, and who was with the regimental staff right from the beginning and who was, as we have been told, the senior of advance party which arrived at the Dnieper castle in July. I heard the address of First Lieutenant Hodt by chance yesterday. He is at Glücksburg near Flensburg, and I therefore ask to be allowed to name First Lieutenant Hodt as a witness who will give evidence that during the time between July and September such shootings did not occur.

Chairman: Dr. Stahmer, the Tribunal will consider your application when they adjourn at half-past three with reference to this extra witness.

For the second time, after the interrogation of Markov, Stahmer applied what was, to my mind, quite a subtle device, but this, however, proved just as ineffective.

Stahmer: Mr. President, I should like to ask a question concerning the legal proceeding first. Each side was to call three witnesses before the Tribunal. This witness, as I understand it, has not only testified to facts but has also made statements which can be called an expert judgement. He has not only expressed himself as an expert witness, as we say in German law, but also as an expert. If the Tribunal is to listen to these statements made by the witness as an expert on, I should like to have the opportunity for the defense also to call experts.

Chairman: No, Dr. Stahmer, the Tribunal will not hear more than three witnesses on either side. You could have called any expert you wanted or any member of the experts who made the German examination. It was your privilege to call any of them.

When the cross-examination sessions ended, Smirnov displayed unexpected initiative, although he could not fail to realize that he had lost. Stahmer seconded his request at once.

Smirnov: We had to choose from among the 120 witnesses whom we interrogated in the case of Katyn, only three.[21] If the Tribunal is interested in hearing any other witnesses named in the reports of the Extraordinary State Commission, we have, in the majority of cases, adequate affidavits which we can submit at the Tribunal's request. Moreover, any of these persons can be called to this Court if the Tribunal so desires. That is all I have to say upon this matter.

Chairman: Doctor Stahmer?

Stahmer: I have no objection to the further presentation of evidence as long as it is on an equal basis; that is, if I, too, have the opportunity to offer further evidence. I am also in a position to call further witnesses and experts for the Court.

But Justice Lawrence remained adamant.

Chairman: The Tribunal has already made its order; it does not propose to hear further evidence.

Stahmer: Thank you.

This comment betrayed ill-concealed satisfaction.

The Nuremberg Tribunal did not include the case of the Katyn executions in the final version of the sentence because of lack of evidence.

One of the American prosecutors in Nuremberg, Whitney Harris, reported in a letter to the author that Robert Jackson had recommended Rudenko to renounce the Katyn charge, "presuming the tremendous number of other crimes against which the Germans had no defense, to be sufficient to condemn them." Nevertheless, Rudenko had his way.

The only thing that could explain it was his absolute satisfaction that the truth of Katyn had always been buried under the ruins of the Second World War. However, it proved impossible to seal the Katyn issue at Nuremberg.

Chapter 6

WITNESSES

In the course of 50 years, the Katyn Case has drawn into itself a multitude of people. Some of them have had to pay dearly for their occasionally involuntary knowledge. One of those who fell victim to repression was S.A. Kolesnikov, a member of the Soviet Special Commission and Chairman of the Executive Committee of the Union of Red Cross and Red Crescent Societies—Solzhenitsyn met him at one of the GULAG transit centers. Soon after the war, Attorney Roman Martini of Krakow began an investigation into the Katyn crime. The Warsaw authorities called on him to prove the guilt of the Nazis. He proved the opposite and was killed in a "burglary" in his own flat on March 28, 1946. The only surviving inmate of the Kozelsk Camp, Professor Stanislaw Swianiewicz, told the *Gwiazda Morza* magazine in April 1989, that he had been attacked by unidentified individuals when he was writing his book *In the Shadow of Katyn* 10 years ago and had a miraculously narrow escape.

The fate of yet another Katyn witness, the American John Van Vliet, was described in *The New Russian Word* (of May 8, 1990) by Prince Alexei Shcherbatov.

Colonel John Van Vliet had been taken prisoner by the Germans in North Africa and stayed in a prisoner-of-war camp in Germany. The Germans took him together with another American officer, D. B. Stuart, to Katyn, where the graves of Polish officers shot by the NKVD were uncovered in 1943, and he was present to watch the exhumation of the corpses. Van Vliet came to the firm conclusion that it was Soviet executioners who killed the Polish officers.

At the very end of the war, Van Vliet got out of a German prisoner-of-war camp on the territory occupied by the Soviet army with difficulty.

On May 5, 1945, Colonel Van Vliet crossed the frontline and found himself within the area occupied by the 104th American division. He had some photographs taken in 1943 of the uncovered Katyn ditches. Van Vliet demanded to be put into contact with the Pentagon at once. He was dispatched to Washington (via London). Once there, Van Vliet was received by General Bissell (assistant chief of the G2 Department of Military Intelligence) to whom he handed an extensive report on Katyn, complete with all photographs. Bissell called on Van Vliet to keep quiet about everything he had found out and wrote on his report: "Top Secret."

In the subsequent five years, the world's political scene changed and the Cold War began. In April 1950, Van Vliet wrote a letter to General Parks in the Pentagon, asking him to tell him where he could find his report and the photographs he had turned over to General Bissell. General Parks replied that it was impossible to find those papers, and asked the Colonel to write up all he had learned about Katyn again. That was what Van Vliet did.

Let me interrupt this quotation. Van Vliet's first report got lost in unidentified circumstances. However, according to the information of Leopold Jerzewski, the traces led to the Soviet agent, Alger Hiss, Roosevelt's adviser at the

Chaper 6

Yalta Conference. The colonel's second report was published in September 1950.

Van Vliet was fighting with the 2nd Infantry Division in Korea at the time. A. P. Shcherbatov writes that he was captured and died in a State Security Prison. Fortunately, Shcherbatov was mistaken: Professor Zawodny met him in Omaha, Nebraska, in December 1988.

The fate of Soviet citizens who provided evidence for the Germans is of special interest, Two of them, as the Burdenko commission stated in its communication, had died before the liberation of Smolensk region by the Red Army. Three—Andreyev, Zhigulev, and Krivozertsev—"left with the Germans or were perhaps driven away by force." Another four were questioned by the Special Commission and testified that the Germans had forced them to give false testimony by means of intimidation and torture. One thing that could not be cleared up was the Gestapo's relationship with a former NKVD Department car park worker, Y. L. Ignatyuk, who, as he said, in spite of all his beatings, refused to give false testimony and yet was neither shot nor hanged, but waited for the Red Army to come back and reported to the Burdenko commission. The communication referred to another two men from whom the Germans extracted the evidence they needed—the former assistant warden of the Smolensk prison, N. S. Kaverznev, and an officer of same prison, V. G. Kovalev. Since there was no testimony of theirs in the communication, the only conclusion that remains to be made is that they did not live to see themselves liberated or did not actually exist. In any case, neither Vetoshnikov nor Ignatyuk, nor the other two, figured in any subsequent material; nobody makes any reference to their testimonies, and their subsequent fate is shrouded in mystery.

Ivan Krivozertsev is known to be one of those who went to the west. After the war he repeated his testimony under oath, changed his name, and settled in England, but either hanged himself or was hanged in 1947. In May 1990 L. V. Kotov published an account in the Smolensk Political information magazine (No. 5, 1990) about his conversation with Mihei Krivozertsev, the namesake of Ivan whom, incidentally, Zhavoronkov had been stubbornly passing off for his brother. So there is a Mihei Krivozertsev who asserts that Ivan Krivozertsev had collaborated with the Gestapo not because of Katyn at all; he "fled along with the Germans." Mihei Krivozertsev expressed the same opinion of Ivan Andreyev: "Ivan Andreyev was found after the war and tried for his misdeeds. He spent seven years in detention and was released under an act of amnesty. He lived here in Bateki, and worked at a factory near Smolensk. He died and was buried here." Incidentally, Leonid Kotov himself, when we met in January 1990, confirmed that Andreyev had not been subject to any punishment.

Traces of a railway engineer, Sergei Ivanov, disappeared in a strange way. In June 1946, he was, as we remember, questioned again, this time in Moscow, by the Soviet prosecutor at the Nuremburg Trial, L. N. Smirnov. The record of that interrogation indicated the witnesses'

Chaper 6

address; after the war Ivanov settled with his family in Vyshniy Voluchek. The local Registry Office to which I made inquiries about his fate told me that they had no record of the death of Ivanov (b.1882) between 1946 and 1989. Yet Ivanov's family, as the present landlady of the house informed me on checking the tenants' book, had lived in Vyshniy Volochek until the early 1950s. His wife, Olga, died in 1952 and his son Vitaly left for Kiev for a while in 1951. Where was Sergei Ivanov himself? It appears that he never came back from the Lubyanka prison in 1946.

Three girls who had been working in the country cottage testified before the Special Commission about what happened at the staff headquarters of the 537th battalion in the autumn of 1941. The latter was a friend of mine, Nikolai Ryzhikov, whom I met the summer of 1988. Zinaida Konakhovskaya did not greet the visitors in a friendly manner. Her first phrase was: "Who told you how to get here?" In the course of the conversation, Konakhovskaya strayed time and again, as if woolgathering, to 1941 and stubbornly refused to speak about 1940. It turned out, however, that it was well before the war that Zinaida Konakhovskaya, a medical nurse by trade, had begun working in the Goats' Mountains country cottages. After the war, she served 9 years in camps for "complicity" and then returned to the cottages where she continued working until she met Ryzhikov. Without having actually found out anything, Nikolai took leave of Konakhovaskaya who, on his departure, threatened to complain about him to the authorities. And she did; on the following day a messenger from the regional party committee came to see Ryzhikov at the hotel at 8 in the morning and promptly demanded that he should immediately go "to account for himself." As Nikolai described her, Konakhovskaya gave the impression of being a strong-willed yet tired woman who had an unpleasant life. In the middle of the conversation she suddenly declared that she had to take her medicine immediately and retired to another room. In Ryzhikov's opinion, she was hooked on drugs. After taking the medicine, Konakhovskaya plunged into a state of total prostration. Zinaida had the usual tattoo on her arm, and smoked Belomor cigarettes.

I have already mentioned that 56 people altogether had been questioned by the Special Commission. What kind of people were they?

Two of them (unless it was a hoax) were NKVD officials; one a police chief and the other three village elders. We know nothing about the ten witnesses beyond their names and initials; they had introduced themselves simply as "residents of Smolensk" or as nobody in particular. Their trades, carpenter, teacher, bookkeeper, and clergyman, were indicated in 28 cases, and in fact, there was also a "collective farm chairman" and even an "assistant public health officer of the Stalin District Health Department of Smolensk." Obviously, there were no collective farms, district health departments, let alone a Stalin department, under the Germans. In fact, even anybody else who continued teaching or working as a joiner, found themselves, with the coming of the Red Army, under the Damoclean sword of the implacable Soviet judiciary. The remaining 12 people, including those who had given the most valuable depositions, were inevitably treated as punishable under the decree on high treason and collaboration.

Few remember that decree today, and you can never inquire about it anywhere; it has never been published. Many ardent champions of the abolition of capital punishment must have marveled at the Amnesty International[1] report and discovered that what we have in this country today is just not a death penalty but death by hanging! It was the offenses punishable by the gallows that were dealt with in the Decree of April 19, 1943, by the Presidium of the Supreme Soviet "On Measures of Punishment for German Fascist Monsters Guilty of Murder and Torture of Soviet Civilians and Captive Red Army Men, for Spies, and Traitors from among Soviet citizens and for their accomplices."

A detailed reconstruction of the decree has been published by Gabriel Superfin, who was already mentioned in this book earlier on, so I am not going to repeat it. All I will say at this point is that the citizens of the USSR who were dealt with under that decree were those accused of offenses indicated in Article 58-1 of the Penal Code of the RSFSR (High treason)[2], notably, service with self-government bodies and fulfillment of the invaders' assignments for the collection of food, restoration of facilities essential for the invading army, and other offenses committed with the aim of aiding the enemy." It is perfectly obvious that a charge of high treason could be laid against a bookkeeper who had worked in a municipal council or a carpenter who had repaired the stool on which that bookkeeper had sat. Such things as washing linen for German soldiers, peeling potatoes in a German kitchen or washing floors in premises occupied by Germans were declared to be complicity with the enemy.[3] It follows from this that the Draconian decree applied to practically all the able-bodied population in occupied territories. For anyone as Solzhenitsyn writes, "can earn a potential" corpus delicti along with his daily bread: at least complicity with the enemy, if not plain high treason. Thank goodness that complicity was not punished by hanging, but only by hard labor!

Now, who of us today, in his heart of hearts, can charge those unfortunate people with perjury! Are there many of us among today's liberals and truth-seekers, who would have shown independence of judgement in the face of emergency circumstances when you have an abstract truth (in fact, not quite abstract, but one in favor of the invaders) on one scale, and your own life, the life and freedom of your family on the other? Soviet establishment historians lied about Katyn when, nothing threatened them any longer, and they lied with self-abandon. Whose guilt is greater? And then we do not know who of the witnesses found himself mentioned in communication and who did not. Perhaps, there were some fearless people among those who did not? (I believe there were.) Finally, what is to guarantee that the testimony has not been distorted and twisted or, at least, edited (it is just the opposite that we discovered in the preceding chapter)?

Since I have not yet mentioned the Decree of April 19, 1943, I should say, just to be impartial, that capital punishment in times of peace was abolished on May 26 1947, and replaced by a new sanction, 25 years of camp detention. However, capital punishment was restored on January 12 1950. "But they forgot to delete Article 4; it still stands," Solzhenitsyn remarked (for traitors and accomplices in 1955[4]—it is not difficult to work out that Zinaida Konakhovskaya probably benefitted from it), but it was applied selectively and discriminatingly so that many remained to serve their sentence to the end. I refer, in particular, to the testimony by Sergei Kovalev, a recent political prisoner, but now People's Deputy of the RSFSR. During a meeting of a group of deputies with KGB Chairman Kryuchkov, he cited the example of Mikhail Tarakhovich of Byelorussia who had been forcibly drafted into the German army, but deserted it 17 days after and subsequently fought with the Red Army all the way to Berlin and yet he was never forgiven those 17 days. When Andrei Sakharov attempted to secure a retrial of Tarakhovich, the Public Prosecutor's Office simply deceived him by announcing that there was no person of this name confined in Soviet camps. Tarakhovich is now at liberty but, according to S.A. Kovalev, this is not the only old man who served his sentence for "war crimes."[5] Nor were they covered by the recent decree of

Witnesses

January 16 1989, "On Additional Measures to Restore Justice . . . ," which revoked the verdicts of special conferences and troikas. It is beyond doubt that these cases must be revised on a strictly individual basis (it is, to my mind, wrong to rehabilitate everybody at once; one thing we see repeated again and again is that nobody, except the system, is personally responsible for the unlawful acts).[6] The trouble is that the mood of our law enforcement was dramatically opposite; it looks as if they were not going to revise anything at all. Here, for example, is what a department chief of the Main Military Prosecutor's Office, Major General of Justice V. G. Provotorov, said in response to a question from Sovetskaya Kultura (February 25 1989): "But were many real spies and enemies identified in the thirties?"

"I met few. But in the forties it was a different matter. There were policemen and punitive units, and those who joined the legions at their own free will. Some got into labor battalions from the camps. The Germans rewarded them by listing them for rationing and all kinds of benefits, such as 150 marks a month, two cigarettes a day, and wearable clothes. There were some who faced death by starvation in the camps and so opted for a labor army. However, it is they who built defensive structures, restored the bombed-out airfields, and formed part of some auxiliary, i.e, reinforced to a certain extent the enemy's military power. Those people have been punished and are not subject to rehabilitation as those who collaborated with the enemy."*

Don't you see a certain moral flaw in the soothing explanations of the Major General? Indeed, doesn't Vladimir Provotorov himself doubt his own rightness at all?" Benefits, defensive power—isn't it from indictments that this phraseology has been borrowed?

At the very start of my work on the Katyn affair, I set my priorities. One of them was to find out the fate of the witnesses. Not just in order to corroborate indirectly the mendacity of the Soviet version; I hoped to give them an opportunity to recant their testimonies and so relieve their consciences. That is why out of a multitude of readers' letters I immediately singled out two on the same subject as the most important.

Nikolai Neshev of Pyatigorsk, convicted under Article 58 of the Penal Code of the RSFSR and serving his sentence in Mordovia, writes that some prisoners had told him in a transit station in Totma in 1958 about an unnamed Katyn forester who had given evidence to the Germans and was sentenced for this to 25 years in prison; he was serving his term in the notorious Vladimir prison. The same thing was related to me by V. A. Abankin from Rostov-on-Don.[7] In 1974, he was transferred to the Vladimir prison from the

---

*This position in official Soviet circles is confirmed by the Decree of the President of the USSR of August, 1990 "On the Restoration of the Rights of All Victims of Political Reprisals of the 1920s - 1950s.

Perm political camp for striking. "It was rumored in the prison that a numbered inmate had been confined in one of the cells for several years. He was in solitary confinement, which is forbidden by the law in this country. Some said it was the Katyn Forest guard who saw Polish officers shot."

The Vladimir prison (the exact name is "OD Institution, Article 1-2, Vladimir") is a special kind of institution. Among those who served their sentences in it in various years were Vassily Stalin; Greville Wynne's helpmate Oleg Penkovsky; V. V. Shulgin, a former member of the State Duma; the American pilot Powers; Lieutenant General S. S. Mamulov, Deputy Minister of the Interior of the USSR; and other officials who had once worked under Beria; and also many Soviet human rights activists from the Brezhnev era. There is a version to the effect that Raoul Wallenberg was kept there for a time.* There is some reason to support the rumors about the Katyn forester.

The former mayor of Smolensk, B. G. Menshagin, served his term in the Vladimir prison from 1951 to 1970.

---

* Raoul Wallenberg, a Swedish diplomat spirited out of Budapest to Moscow by Soviet military counter-intelligence officials in January 1945, and officially declared by Soviet sources to have died in the Lubyanka prison on July 17 1947. He had saved thousands of Hungarian Jews by taking advantage of his diplomatic immunity.

Chaper 6

The reader must remember, of course, that Boris Bazilevsky, a professor of astronomy, one of the witnesses of the Burdenko Commission and later of the Soviet prosecution at the Nuremberg trial, referred to his conversation with Menshagin. Incidentally, the communication says that this testimony was of "particular importance." Menshagin's notebook was featured as material evidence.

"Bazilevsky's testimony," the communication says further on, "has been confirmed by I. Y. Yefimov, professor of physics, a witness questioned by the Special Commission, to whom Bazilevsky related that conversation of his there and then, in the autumn of 1941.

"Menshagin's notes, made in his own hand in his notebook, provide documentary evidence to prove Bazilevsky's and Yefimov's testimony. That the said notebook belonged to Menshagin and his handwriting has been certified by the depositions of Bazilevsky, who knew Menshagin's handwriting well, and by an expert graphological examination." So Bazilevsky's evidence is confirmed by the notes made by Menshagin, whose handwriting had been certified by Bazilevsky! Another confirmation of Bazilevsky's words was the deposition by Professor Yefimov to the effect that Bazilevsky had told him just what he had told the Commission!

There is more. During the interrogation session in June 1946 (we know this to have been the dress rehearsal before Nuremberg), Bazilevsky added some more details to the picture of Menshagin.

"It must be said that Menshagin quite quickly became 'their own man' in the German commandant's office. I find it difficult to comment on the reasons why Menshagin had so quickly earned the Germans' esteem. Perhaps, one thing that helped him was that Menshagin had been a hard drinker and very quickly found bosom companions in the German commandant's office, and struck up a particularly close relationship with one Sonderfuhrer Girschfeld, an Ostseer German who had a perfect command of Russian and was dealing with a number of questions connected with municipal self-government."[8]

When I read this record, I knew next to nothing about Menshagin, but even at that point I did not believe Bazilevsky's stories. Shortly afterwards Menshagin's recollections, the text he had taped in the closing years of his life, were published in Paris. At this point, I shall quote some of that book by courtesy of its commentator G. G. Superfin.[9]

B. G. MENSHAGIN

Biographical Note

Boris Georgiyevich Menshagin was born in Smolensk on April 26 (May 9) 1902. Upon leaving high school, he volunteered to join the Red Army, in which he served from

1919 to 1927. He was demobilized for his religious beliefs and regular churchgoing.

After demobilization, Menshagin completed a course of instruction at the extramural department of the Faculty of Law in Moscow. In 1928-1931 he was a member of the Bar at the Regional Court of the Central Black Earth Region, and in 1931, at the Aremz Factory (Moscow); and in 1931-1937, in the Second Moscow Freighters Depot.

From 1937 onwards, Menshagin worked for the regional bar in Smolensk right up until the city's occupation by German troops. He became mayor of Smolensk during the period of occupation, and held the same office in Bobruisk for a short time after the German retreat in September 1943. The end of the war found him with his family at Karlovy Vary, where he was interned by American troops. Freed from the camp several weeks later, Menshagin returned to Karlovy Vary which was already occupied by Soviet forces, but he did not find his family there. Mistakenly believing his relatives arrested, Menshagin presented himself of his own free will to the Soviet commandant's office on May 28, 1945.

By a ruling of September 12, 1951, of the Special Secret Department at the Ministry of State Security of the USSR, he was convicted under Part I of the Decree of April 19, 1943, to 25 years imprisonment. He served his term at Vladimir prison.

After serving his term, Menshagin was sent to a home for invalids in the Knyazhaya Guba (Prince's Bay) township on the White Sea. He spent the remaining years of his life in a similar home in Kirovsk near the town of Apatity where he died on May 25, 1984.

Boris Menshagin was not an ordinary lawyer, but one of the best in his profession in Smolensk. He most often defended "enemies of the people" and "wreckers," won several show trials and occasionally secured a revision of the ordinances of the Special Board which were known not to be subject to appeal. I hope there is no need for me to explain what cost and what risk this involved at the height of the Stalinist terror.

Today many who read the numerous commentaries in Ogonyok do not believe that effective defense of those in the dock was possible at all in those years and think of stories on that subject to be a legend. There is a rather fine nuance in this matter. Of course, if a defender in a public court sitting had declared that it was not a trial but a travesty of justice and that the case was a frame-up, and the prosecutor a hangman, he would not have defended anyone but would have surely ruined himself. Defense, however, could be built on an identification of certain contradictions in the record of the case (for it is common knowledge that examining magistrates cared little about making things tie together) and on those grounds to obtain a redefinition of the crime—say, using the word "negligence" instead of "wrecking activity"—such tactics were quite realistic. Taking into account the time spent in preliminary detention, the defendant could be released from custody right there in the courtroom. For it was not for nothing that Beria issued a directive in 1940 as illustrated by this document of July 12 1940, signed by V. M. Sharapov:

> According to Directive No. 76 of March 20 by the People's Commissar of the Interior of the USSR and the Orders of the Day of the People's Commissariat of Justice and the public prosecutor of the USSR No. 058, March 20, and 96/62c of May 9 1940, the persons arrested in connection with the cases raised by the institutions of the NKVD (besides the Workers' and Peasants' Militia), shall be released from places of detention, not in the coutroom, in the event of a court returning a sentence (ruling) of acquittal. (. . .)
> The prisoners involved in cases conducted by the institutions of the NKVD (besides Workers' and Peasants' Militia), should be brought back escorted from the courtroom to the prisons, from which they had been taken to the courtroom, regardless of the court verdict."[10]

Now, once the defendant had been brought back to prison, there was no problem starting a new case "in view of circumstances newly discovered."

Indeed, there must have been some reason behind that directive, there must consequently have been some sentences of acquittal in cases "raised within the security forces" and there were quite a few, I can assure you! Here is one more detail: the first charge that was laid against Menshagin in the Smolensk regional State Security Department was that he "incited the defendants to recant the testimonies which they had given during the preliminary investigation." And the man who laid the charge was none other than examining magistrate Belyaev*, whom Boris Menshagin had recognized by his handwriting; too many of the cases he had made out were returned for re-examination. Incidentally, the investigating judges themselves did not begrudge Menshagin's services either—remember the case of Zhukov and Vassilyev. That is to say they did in fact gave him his due.

Of course, Boris Menshagin took up the job of a mayor under the Germans; you cannot cross that fact out of his biography. But isn't it time to reconsider our long entrenched, unequivocally negative assessment of such an act?

By no means did everyone of that kind (village elders, mayors, overseers) take up those offices to carry out assignments from underground regional party committees. Yet it was by no means an out-and-out rascal that did not have such an assignment to carry out. For over and above regional party committees, there was such a thing as conscience. Would you say that a position of aloofness and non-intervention in the face of total evil was more morally sound? The fate of the intellectuals and professional people who stayed on in enemy-held territories is a vast subject. It will yet present itself in all of its tragic insolubility, and

---

* Belyaev was Junior Lieutenant of State Security and Deputy Chief of the Investigation Department, State Security Office, Smolensk Region, in February 1941.

it does not become us today to repeat the mendacious ravings of Stalinist propaganda.

Leonid Kotov was intransigent as regards Menshagin. He says that old people in Smolensk remember his activities as mayor perfectly well and for this reason the regional executive committee denied him the right of permanent residence when he applied for it straight after release in 1970. Kotov also asserts that the regional public record office has some documents proving Menshagin's direct involvement in the destruction of the Jewish ghetto. These papers intrigued me greatly and I asked Leonid Kotov to show me at least some extracts. There was a problem: nothing could be found except for some articles in the occupation press.[11] Indeed, the facts could hardly be squared. It is unlikely for anyone involved in murderous crimes to wish to settle where some witnesses of his misdeeds still live.

What did Menshagin know about Katyn? In April 1943, he traveled to the Goats' Mountains to have a look at the remains dug from the graves. He recalls:

On the following day* everybody assembled in the propaganda office in Roslavl Highway by 2 p.m. From there we drove in cars along the Vitebsk Highway to the Gnezdovo district. Traveling with me were Dyakonov and Borisenkov, officials from the Municipal Department, and the editor of the

---

* April 18, 1943.

newspaper published by the Germans, *Our Way** (perhaps I have not remembered right). Dolgonenkov** and some other propaganda officials—Russians.

Well, when we reached the post marked "15th kilometer" on the Vitebsk Highway, we turned left and immediately smelt the stench of corpses although we were driving through a pine grove and the smell there had always been good and the air always pure. A little further on we saw those graves. Russian prisoners of war were digging out the last remnants of its contents. Bodies were lying on the edges. They were all dressed in grey Polish uniforms with confederate caps on. All of them had their arms tied behind their backs and all had holes somewhere in the backs of their heads. They had been shot dead by single shots in the back of the head.

The bodies of two generals were lying apart. One was that of Smorawinski of Lublin and the other that of Bahaterewicz of Modlin, with their documents lying close by. Their letters were laid out near the bodies. The address on the letters were P.O. Box, either 12 . . .*** or 16, I don't remember any more; Kozelsk, Smolensk region. But all the envelopes carried the stamp of the Central Post Office, Moscow. There were about five and a half thousand corpses.

By the way they were shot dead you could not say that they had been killed by Germans, because they normally fired at random. But in this case, the men, with their arms tied, were

---

* The correct name is *The New Way*.
** Konstantin Dolgonenkov (1895-1980), once a Komsomol poet, member of the Union of Soviet Writers since 1934.
*** This is the correct number.

shot methodically right at the back of the head, while the Germans shot people without tying them, just spraying them with machine-gun fire. That is all I know.

Let me note that Menshagin had no sources except his own memory from which to find out the names of the Generals Smorawinski and Bohaterewicz, who were actually identified from among the Katyn corpses. Naturally, he had no access either to Polish or German sources.

Menshagin spent 22.5 years of his 25-year term in solitary confinement. For the first three years of his detention in Vladimir prison, he had no name and was listed as number 29, and wore a striped prison robe. Throughout his term he was banned from correspondence. The regulations barred him from having any contact with other inmates. When Menshagin appealed to Khrushchev with a letter pointing out that his solitary confinement was unlawful, at first he got Beria's Deputy Mamulov to "share" his cell with him. Then Colonel M. A. Steinberg of the Intelligence Department.

Following his letter to Khrushchev, he was escorted out for walks, also in the company of security officials. Apart from those just mentioned, there were P. A. Sudoplatov and B. A. Ludwigov, former Chief of Beria's Secretariat. In search of additional information about Menshagin, I turned to Elena Butova who had worked as public health officer in Vladimir prison in the 1960s. Here is her reply:

"I remember Menshagin very well. He gave the impression of being a modest and intelligent man. He was always polite in dealing with the medical staff. The physicians never talked about anything except health. Health was the only point of interest to us. Occasionally he digressed and began talking about his work on a catalog for a library. You could feel that work was close to his heart, and he showed a certain nervousness about it. He passed his requests on to library assistants through medical people. I observed no conflict between him and the administration. I think everybody treated him with some respect.

That is all I can tell you."

The library is a subject apart and I shall come back to it later.

The second testimony is by P. A. Sudoplatov, who had served his term, just like his colleagues, in the Vladimir prison, and been in contact with Menshagin for quite a long time.

Pavel Sudoplatov was, on the contrary, extremely hateful in speaking about Menshagin: The words "enemy" and "traitor" were among his comments. According to him, Menshagin had traveled to Berlin for negotiations with General Vlasov and the "churchmen," where he got a medal from the German authorities. In his youth, Sudoplatov stated, Menshagin had been a church elder and thoroughly knew the history of all the Moscow churches; the first thing he did in his capacity as mayor was to open the Assumption Cathedral.

The repairs to the Assumption Cathedral and the resumption of services in it on Menshagin's initiative had indeed taken place, and Boris Menshagin counted it as an achievement. Pavel Sudoplatov, on the other hand, did not approve of it, as he did not of Menshagin's religious beliefs in general. As to the medal (to be exact the bronze Service Order), it was presented to him not in Berlin but in Smolensk on July 19, 1943, the first anniversary of the taking of the city by the Germans (from Menshagin's unpublished recollections).

Kotov also said that there was a banquet on the occasion, during which Dolgonenkov recited the "poem of the Soviet Passport" (I don't know where Leonid Kotov had scooped up so sensational a detail). Whether Menshagin actually met Vlasov is not known.

I have spoken about Menshagin also with Revolt Pimenov, also a former inmate of the "Special Department, 1/Article 2." Revolt Pimenov did not know Menshagin, but had a lot of interesting things to tell about the Vladimir institution, in particular the prison library. That story has direct bearing on Menshagin. At one time, he had been making up the library catalog, as the reader knows by now from the words of Butova, earning 2 roubles 50 kopecks a month for it.

That the library in the former Vladimir Central was good has been noted also by Solzhenitsyn in his *Archipelago* ("Skripnikova was particularly struck by the regular dispatch of applications every ten days /she began writing to . . . the UN/ and the excellent library: you had a full catalog brought into your cell for you to make up a year's request." The fine choice of literature was for two reasons. First, almost any book could be passed into the prison from the outside world on the condition that, once read, it would remain there for good. Second, the prison was under the direct control of the security services so that it was safe from numerous withdrawals. Pimenov, for example, remembered that he had seen a Machiavelli with a preface by Zinoviev. He and P. A. Sharia, former Secretary of the Central Committee of the Communist Party of Georgia for ideology, had even enjoyed the right to order books by an interlibrary subscription service from the Lenin Public Library. True, Sharia had his right of subscription service taken away from him after the 22nd Congress when, according to Pimenov, the situation of Beria's associates worsened. It was by the efforts of the same Beriavites, Mamulov and Ludwigov, who had fallen for the Menshagin wage, that the golden age of the Vladimir library came to an end. They barred him from working on the catalog and were horrified to discover proscribed literature in the collection. The present chiefs, to avoid extra trouble, at first resisted their signals. Mamulov and Ludwigov began writing to Moscow and had their way in the end by having the library wrecked.[12]

You can see from this biographical note that the investigation of the Menshagin case went on for over six years. Throughout almost all this period he was kept in solitary confinement in the Lubyanka prison. At interrogation sessions, examining judges occasionally brought up the subject of Katyn, but in a rather lukewarm fashion. Menshagin also said that to the question "who killed?" in the book, he also replied that he did not know. However, his testimony was not to be found in any record. Every time the examining judge promised to come back to the subject later on. In January 1944, the Burdenko commission could afford to manipulate Menshagin's name at will. Even if it had occurred to him to protest, who would have believed him? Menshagin had been in Beria's stranglehold for a year by the time the judicial investigation got under way in Nuremberg. The witnesses, including Bazilevsky, were being coached on the spot, in Lubyanka, next to his solitary confinement cell. Nevertheless, the Vyshinsky commission had not only failed to bring him before the tribunal, but as can be seen from its proceedings, had never considered such a possibility. Why? It is Superfin's explanation that appeared to me to be most convincing: "Menshagin, already branded as traitor, could only be kept in custody and, consequently, in the tribunal he would have to be escorted by American military police." The only thing that remained to be done was to tuck Menshagin as far away as possible; that is why he served his term from start to finish. In 1955, the prison chiefs attempted to apply the amnesty decree to Menshagin. However, the Amnesty Commission of the Presidium of the Supreme Soviet, having come to Vladimir, refused to reconsider his case, declaring that it was not within its competence, and named A. B. Aristov, Secretary of the Central Committee of the CPSU, as the man to whom appeals should be made. The only effect that appeal had was to bring a response from the Public Prosecutor's Office of the USSR, to the effect that the amnesty would not be applied to Menshagin. No reason was given.

Half a year before Menshagin's term was due to expire, he was unexpectedly called out for questioning—on the Katyn affair. It turned out that one of the Vladimir inmates, Svyatoslav Karavansky, had tried to smuggle out, along with other texts, a message on Menshagin's behalf to the International Red Cross and to "all governments," first through his wife during a rendezvous and then through the prison barber. The document was addressed to Larisa Bogoraz. Karavansky was prosecuted under Article 70 of the Penal Code of the RSFSR (for anti-Soviet agitation and propaganda). Menshagin, who had not only had nothing to do with charging Karavansky with the job of making any appeals, but, in all probability, was not even acquainted with him, had been called on as a witness to the case. It was difficult to qualify the Karavansky case as anything short of an act of provocation. During legal proceedings behind closed doors, Boris Menshagin testified just as he had done in Lubyanka once, that he had first learned about the Katyn graves in April 1943, and saw the ditches uncovered just at the same time, and also that he (to quote the sentence in the Karavansky case) "was unaware of the circumstances of the massacre of captive Polish officers in 1941, but he was convinced that the Polish prisoners of war had been shot by German fascists." As we see, this version runs fundamentally counter to Bazilevsky's testimony recorded by the Burdenko commission and the proceedings of the Nuremberg trial. Nevertheless the investigation and the court were satisfied with Menshagin's depositions, while Karavansky was convicted, taking the term he had yet to serve into consideration, to 10 years of imprisonment. He spent three of these in prison and seven in a top security correctional labor colony.[13]

The Karavansky case is of interest to us also because the appeals he made referred to a certain "Katyn forester, Andreyev," who had also been sentenced to 25 years imprisonment and confined in Vladimir prison; his wife was supposedly serving her sentence there, too, although separately. Another source of the Karavansky case were the rumors which have been described in a letter to me from Neshev and Abankin. It is difficult to judge their authenticity, for certain details do not coincide: for instance, according to German evidence, Andreyev was not a forester, but a fitter—incidentally, I have already tried to explain this aberration. The only thing I can add is that according to what I have been told by Ivan Krivozertsev, Andreyev "supplied the Germans with food," and consequently could easily have been incriminated under the Decree of April 19 1943, ("concerning the invaders' assignments for the collection of victuals"). According to Karavansky's information, Andreyev was in 1966 serving the 22nd year of his 25-year term, that is to say the term had been counted since 1945. Now, according to Mihei Krivozertsev, Andreyev served about seven years and was released under an amnesty, that is, in 1955, and therefore, his term had begun in 1948. All questions, incidentally, are easy to resolve provided there is goodwill from the appropriate law enforcement agencies. Hence, we find one more reason why it would be interesting to see the Andreyev case is that it would enable us to find out whether he was a Gestapo agent, as Mihei Krivozertsev asserted.

To wind up my story about the fate of Menshagin, let me offer a few quotations which describe his life as a whole.

. . . I read the words "Car Park Lawyer" on one of the doors, I knocked and entered. I saw an intelligent-looking, neatly dressed man of about forty, wearing a necktie, sitting behind a table in a half-dark room partitioned off from another. His whole appearance was alien to the surroundings.

There was a vast amount of papers and folders for counter claims and judicial cases piled all over the table. Raising his head and glancing at me, he offered me a seat. I began telling him about myself, I said I had legal training and had worked in the Ukraine, and showed him my record of service indicating that I had been sacked as an "enemy of the people." It seemed to me that this reference did not frighten him but, on the contrary, made me an object of closer attention. His look commanded confidence and sympathy.

He told me that he had many cases of attempts to exact arrears for transportation and that he really needed an assistant, but that to go to the personnel department with my documents was a hopeless proposition. Let us try, as he said, to go over the head of the personnel officer . . .

The man who offered me a helping hand was Boris Menshagin.

From Grigory Kravchik's reminiscences

Chapter 6

. . . the man who was appointed city chief by the Germans was Boris Menshagin, the lawyer, who had subsequently left with them, a traitor who had the special confidence of the German Command, and notably von Schwetz, the Commandant of Smolensk.

Collected ISC Reports, Moscow (1946)

Having found himself in Karlovy Vary after the Americans, he went home, but found nothing other than a ransacked house with its doors* thrown wide open. He decided that the Bolsheviks had put his women in custody. He found a rope and climbed up into the mountains and forests to hang himself. But as he was making arrangements he was surprised by an elderly man with the armband (the Soviets issued armbands of all colors) of a local resident, who began persuading him not to do it. He then decided this meant that he was not destined to hang and, to make things easier for his next-of-kin, presented himself of his own accord to the Commandant's Office.

From Irina Korsunskaya's letter (1985)

Throughout his period of detention in places of confinement, following the personal record case, convict Menshagin has been given positive references.

He has been held in the Special Department-1/Article 2 institution in Vladimir and has recommended himself well, by and large, throughout the period of confinement.

When, earlier, an opportunity to work presented itself, he did it faithfully. At present, he is not taken out for work because of the absence of such a possibility. He occasionally demands special conditions of maintenance. There have been cases

---

* So runs the text.

of unjustified refusal to accept food. In his relationships with the administration and fellow prisoners he is arrogant."

From prison references (1970)

I do not feel myself to be lonely and basically believe it would be sinful to complain about the way of life I have enjoyed here. I had a good memory, built up a fairly large store of knowledge in various fields of the humanities, all members of my family loved me, I felt in my element in the army in 1919-1927, and later in the judiciary, and did my job successfully. Not everybody can credit himself with having saved eleven people from death at his own peril, not counting cases of the death penalty being commuted without such a risk; also, restoring freedom to thousands of people, including over 3,000 in war time, has always made me happy. As far as misfortunes are concerned, it is rare for anyone to escape them . . ."

Quoted from B. G. Menshagin's letter
(1980)

CONCLUSION

One simple question that inevitably arises for an author writing on Katyn is: *Why?* Why did Stalin kill the captives?

Western students (and until recently they alone were in a position to discuss the problem in real earnest) have failed to produce a convincing answer. All attempts to grasp the motives normally end in the supposition that the NKVD chiefs misinterpreted the order for dismantling the camps: Stalin, they argue, had no intention of having the Poles executed; it was his subordinates—they tried too hard. One can hardly fail to remember Reichman in this context with his aphorism "liquidation may have a double meaning!" And, indeed, none of the NKVD documents ever referred to "shooting" anybody. In all cases, you have euphemisms like "reducing numbers in the camps" and "referring the matter to the Special Secret Department." Perhaps, one wonders, Beria had no intention of shooting anybody either. It is perfectly obvious that this supposition brings you to yet another impasse. You find yourself wondering whether it was the NKVD itself which thought up the very idea of a "Nuremberg in reverse" (in that case, it was the author of criminal orders that was to blame, and in this one, it was the person who carried them out).

Some also recall that when the question of what was to be done with the German army after victory came up in an Teheran, Stalin simply suggested shooting 50,000 German officers without trial or inquest, thus throwing his Western counterparts into utter confusion. Even that episode, a telling one though it was beyond question, does not explain anything, but just proves that Stalin *could* order anyone to be shot. Does anybody doubt that at all?

I am afraid that we won't get out of this morass of small scale factology unless we find some new standard for generalization. In the long run, Stalinism is irrational, and since that is so, shouldn't Katyn (just like the whole of Stalin's rein of terror) be recognized as *murder without motive?*

Incidentally, here is one more conjecture not devoid of reason. Vojtek Mastny, in his book *Russia's Way to the Cold War,* having repeated the argument (one is already well familiar with) to the effect that Stalin has been "misunderstood," writes that the clue to the Katyn crime "can be found in its coincidence in time with the complaints of the Nazis that the Russians offered shelter to Polish officers with a hidden objective. But if Stalin's thugs killed the Poles to make Hitler favor Stalin, who was seeking just that with all his might at the time, Berlin was not informed about what had been done."

Any reference to contacts between NKVD and Gestapo boils down to the mention of rather low-key encounters, and even those are hypothetical. If you take a close look at the official news of Molotov's visit to Berlin, you will find that the Soviet delegation included Beria's Deputy Merkulov, never mentioned in the list of his retinue (*Pravda,* November 14,1940) and then you will understand why the welcome party included Himmler, and those who saw him

off, his Deputy Daluege. Let me remind you that the 1939
Soviet-German agreements included, apart from everything
else, a secret additional protocol on suppressing Polish
education and a phrase about mutual consultations.

So Mastny's reservations to the effect that the Katyn
action had no proper effect in Berlin because the Germans
never found out about it was not quite correct, afterall.
Small fries like Słoweńczyk may not have known, but what
about Hitler?

Now, the fact that the Germans had been silent right
up until 1943 does lend itself to explanation. First, it was
too serious a trump card to waste. Second, the burial itself
had to be discovered to make the whole thing look really
convincing. Friendship was all right, but Merkulov was
unlikely to have given the exact place of the execution.
What was really striking was the timing of the discovery of
the graves. It all happened after Stalingrad, when the
belligerents had reached a kind of parity and the outcome
of the war was quite unpredictable. Hitler had to change
the balance of strength in his favor at any cost and to that
end he had, first and foremost, to complicate the relationship of the USSR with the allies and to prevent the
creation of a second front in Europe.

A less urgent task was to provoke a rupture between
Moscow and the Polish government in exile, and this is
why.

Katyn was not the reason but only a formal excuse for
the Soviet overture. The real reason was that Stalin had by

that time already settled the Polish question his own way. Diplomatic relations were broken off late at night on April 25, and on May 8, the formation of a Kosciuszko division under the auspices of the Union of Polish Patriots on the territory of the USSR was announced, a prototype of the future Stalinist government of Poland. The announcement said that "the formation of this division has already begun." It is clear that the idea of cutting the Soviet Polish Gordian knot in that way had been formulated before, not after, the Katyn sensation. That is why Stalin declined the offers of the allies, self-righteously referring to the opinion of his "colleagues" and to "public opinion."

Personal and secret message from Premier Stalin to the Prime Minister, Mr. W. Churchill.

I have received your message concerning Polish affairs. Thank you for your sympathetic stand on this issue. I must tell you, however, that the matter of interrupting relations with the Polish Government has already been settled, and that today, V.M. Molotov delivered a Note to the Polish Government. All my colleagues insisted on this because the Polish official press is not only keeping up its hostile campaign but is actually intensifying it day by day. I also had to take cognizance of Soviet public opinion, which is deeply outraged by the ingratitude and treachery of the Polish Government.

As to publishing the Soviet document on interrupting relations with the Polish Government, I fear that it is simply impossible to avoid doing so.

April 25 1943

Conclusion

Churchill answered with the following message:

Mr. Eden and I have pointed out to the Polish Government that no resumption of friendly or working relations with the Soviets is possible while they make charges of an insulting character against the Soviet Government, and thus seem to countenance the atrocious Nazi propaganda. Still more would it be impossible for any of us to tolerate inquiries by the International Red Cross held under Nazi auspices and dominated by Nazi terrorism. I am glad to tell you that they have accepted our view, and that they want to work loyally with you . . .

The Cabinet here is determined to have proper discipline in the Polish press in Great Britain. The miserable rags attacking Sikorski can say things which German broadcasts repeat open-mouthed to the world to our joint detriment. This must be stopped and it will be stopped.

So far, this business has been Goebbel's triumph. He is now busy suggesting that the USSR will set up a Polish Government in Russian soil and deal only with them. We should not, of course, be able to recognize such a Government and would continue our relations with Sikorski, who is far the most helpful man you or we are likely to find for the purposes of the common cause. I expect that this will also be the American view.

My own feeling is that they have had a shock, and that after whatever interval is thought convenient, the relationship established on July 30th 1941, should be restored. No one will hate this more than Hitler, and what he hates most is wise for us to do.

We owe to our armies now engaged and presently to be more heavily engaged to maintain good conditions behind the fronts. I and my colleagues look steadily to the ever closer cooperation and understanding of the USSR, the United States, and the British Commonwealth and Empire, not only in the deepening war struggle, but after the war. What other hope can there be than this for the tortured world?

April 30 1943

All this rhetoric was wasted. In the long run, Stalin did just what Churchill had feared most and created a new Polish Government. Incidentally, our Western allies had played up the Polish issue throughout the world, but, however, whenever Stalin showed his mettle, they washed their hands of it.

It follows from what has been said that cause and effect often swapped places in Stalin's interpretation of the conflict. What was, after all, the role of the Germans? The communication of the Burdenko Commission says that by means of Katyn revelations they attempted to provoke a Polish-Soviet rupture. Granted, but why did that strategist of genius "fall for the provocation?" The point is, however, that Hitler could not fail to know, if only from reading the press, that Moscow's relationship with the London Poles was quite bad, spoiled as it was by Moscow itself. Now he was going to try to drive a wedge between Stalin and his new Polish partners, between the Soviet Union and the Poles as a nation. Katyn, which has reminded the Poles of the 1939 collusion, was the perfect means for this.

Now, the prospects of yet another collusion in 1943, after Stalingrad and, more particularly, after the Battle of Kursk, were quite practicable. Julian Semenov's admirers, watching with bated breath as Standartenfuhrer Stierlitz exposed the scheming of Karl Wolf and Allen Dulles in Switzerland, could hardly have suspected that the Soviet Government had been quite officially informed of Wolf's attempt to enter into separate negotiations (incidentally, it took place in Zurich, not in Berne) by none other than British ambassador Archibald Clark Kerr. Hitler and Stalin never reached the point of negotiation, but that idea was, to judge by all accounts, "in the air" both at the Kremlin and at the Reichschancellry. There was a mutual testing of the water which had no result, probably because Stalin was then counting not on Hitler but on the generals involved in a conspiracy against him, about whom Sandor Rado reported to Moscow as early as April 20, 1943. There is a version suggesting that Beria had maintained contact with Himmler throughout the war—incidentally, it could have been they who had caused the death of Raoul Wallenberg, who had happened to detect this channel of communication.

There is yet another circumstance mentioned by Frederick Shuman in his book *Russia Since 1917*. "It should be noted that Goebbel's original exposure, coincidental in time with the heroic insurrection of the Jews in the Warsaw ghetto, was designed to distract attention away from it." (Hence, the "Jewish commissars.")

Finally, there is one perfectly simple consideration: the Nazis had to respond in some way to the ESC communication, hence Katyn, Vinnitsa and Pyatigorsk.

Conclusion

It is only at this point that I see that the closing pages of this book look more like a prologue than a conclusion. That is just it: the Katyn problem is still there. The political solution has simply made full-scale work on it possible. Whoever may try to convince us of the opposite, the fact remains that no definite, unequivocal document has yet been discovered, nothing beyond indirect evidence and, of course, Soviet historical science is second to none in its interpretation of indirect evidence. We still do not know either the names of the criminals or the details of what was done; the information about the recently discovered burials is extremely incomplete and unconvincing. There is still no access to the archives of the State Security Committee, and yet it is there that the answers to all the outstanding questions can be found and it is this institution, rather than such a hypothetical concept as the "Soviet side" that must express its "deep regret" in connection with the matter at issue.

It goes without saying that the entire body of documents already identified must be declassified and published. Only then will there be a real opportunity to analyze them professionally rather than casually. I have already written about the inadmissible juggling of figures. It is difficult but necessary to relate them to each other. All information available should be fed into a computer, but it must be accessible for this and the appropriate officials and departments must make it a point of their concern.

Conclusion

One of the objectives which must be dealt with immediately is that of finding and questioning the witnesses while they are still alive. In addition to those I have mentioned, let me name one more: a war criminal. Alferchik, the former Smolensk police chief, has been identified in Australia. I am sure he has something to tell us about Katyn.

There is, incidentally, quite a large group of witnesses who have not spoken at all to this day. These were middle-level security officials at the time who know quite a lot but cannot reveal anything for the benefit of the public because they had once pledged not to disclose official secrets. One must presume that not only the Katyn problem but some other problems as well will be clarified if the pledges not to disclose official secrets, made, say, before 1953 inclusive, are found to be null and void. A decision on the matter could be made by the Supreme Soviet.

Turning the Katyn tragedy into a kind of myth has been one particular approach to the subject at issue. It has been kept quiet for much too long, and an entire legend has been built around it over the past half century. I think anybody who has ever ventured into places around Katyn must have come across some local residents who, without so much as a wink, have related fantastic details, indicating places of burial, and described the blood-curdling scenes of executions as if they had seen them with their own eyes. As a rule, it does not take any special effort to detect incongruities in these stories, yet the self-styled eyewitnesses stand pat on their versions, engage in extenuating discussions, and write to various institutions of the media. More involved cases demanding thorough verification take place.

There may also be some who are innocently misguided. I am afraid that now, as the sluice-gates of censorship have finally crumbled, the spinners of folk tales will have a chance to put the spotlight and perhaps even act as guides and give talks on behalf of the Znanie society. This kind of activity must be stopped. Once again, it is the publication of authentic documents that is the main antidote. With sources of information in his hands, any competent expert in local history can refute an impostor's tale, however sophisticated it might be.

Like any long-winded, exhausting, and multi-tiered subject, the Katyn affair has a periphery of its own, episodes which arise like a spin-off when dealing with the primary sources which have nothing to do with the key line and yet are capable of serving as an object of special investigation. For instance, while studying the records of the Main Administration for Escort Guard Troops of the NKVD of the USSR, I discovered the lists of about 200 interned servicemen from the British, French, and Belgian armies. In February and March 1941, they were escorted from the Butyrskaya prison to the Kozelsk camp where they were held right until the outbreak of the war. They were evacuated to Gryazovets in the closing days of June. The subsequent fate of these people is unknown. (Quite recently, this subject attracted the attention of Lord Bethel, who published a list of nine names I compiled in the British press and addressed an inquiry about them to the British Ministry of Defense. It must be presumed that the fate of the Englishmen, at least, will have been cleared up by the time this book is printed.) There are some particular problems of a different kind as well.

I also want to draw the readers' attention to the legal aspects of the Katyn affair which have come down to us from Stalin's and Hitler's times. The entire population of the territories incorporated into the USSR under the Soviet-German Treaty on Friendship and Frontier at that time, in 1939, was declared to be made up of Soviet citizens. Upon the conclusion of the war agreement with Poland in August 1941, citizenship was restored not to everybody but to ethnic Poles alone. In 1943, following the rupture of Soviet-Polish diplomatic relations, the Poles came once more to be considered as citizens of the USSR and those who refused this honor fell victim to reprisals. In consequence, one who was born in Lvov, say, in 1938, had "the Ukrainian SSR" indicated as his "birthplace" in his passport. In 1938, however, Lvov was a Polish city! Such strange cases, and even more involved ones, are very numerous! That is not to say that the Polish Sejm demanded compensation for Katyn from the Government of the USSR which is, understandably, a hard thing to settle, of course. However, to correct the entry in your passport is a simple thing but it has to be done and not just talked about, as we still try to do as we pass over inter-ethnic conflicts.

The legal responsibility of those responsible for the Katyn killings is another subject altogether. Whatever angle you approach it from, you have to speak of Stalin's reprisals in their totality, although there are certain shades and hues in this matter which must also be taken into consideration. Officials who may be expected to decide the matter on its merit usually refer their public pronouncements to the term of limitations which, they argue, has expired. However, any lawyer knows that Article 48 of the Penal Code of RSFSR leaves the question of application of the statute of limitations to a person having committed a crime punishable by death open for a court to decide. The Katyn affair should be qualified as premeditated murder under aggravating circumstances (Article 102 of the Penal Code of RSFSR), that is a crime punishable by death.

Furthermore, the Katyn affair, beyond all doubt, is a war crime. Such crimes, according to Article 6 of the Charter of the International Military Tribunal in Nuremberg, comprise a violation of the laws and usages of war, notably, the killing or torturing of prisoners of war. The Soviet Union is a party to the convention on the Non-Applicability of the Statute of Limitations to War Crimes and Crimes against Humanity, of November 26 1968, and, in December 1983, it voted for Resolution 38/99 of the UN General Assembly whereby the arraignment of individuals guilty of these crimes is mandatory for all members of the international community. Besides, Soviet legislation also stipulates punishment for war crimes (Articles 266-269 of the Penal Code of the RSFSR).

There is, moreover, a widely held view that there can be no trial of those responsible for the Stalinist reign of terror because they are no longer alive. However, this is simply not so. Under Article 5 of the Code of Criminal Procedure of the RSFSR, a criminal suit may be instituted against a dead person in cases "where a hearing is essential for the rehabilation of the dead person or resumption of a case in relation to other individuals in view of newly discovered circumstances."

Forced repentance is still not an absolution from the scourge of Stalinism. Only a court can declare Stalinism outlawed and order its propaganda banned de jure without prejudice to pluralism. Only the whole truth will guarantee our capacity for genuine moral regeneration.

The process of destalinization is only just beginning. The main thing is not to stop halfway. Otherwise, the blanks will remain as dirty as they are now. These are stains on the conscience of the people, not on history.

POSTSCRIPTUM

This book was published in Russia in January 1991. Now it is September, we have just lived through an attempt at a coup d'etat, and the KGB has a new chief, Vadim Bakatin. As Minister of the Interior, Bakatin did a great deal to help clarify the fate of Raoul Wallenberg. It is hoped that we shall soon get access to answer the last remaining questions on that subject, too. But much is clear even now.

First of all, the Main Military Procurator's Office of the USSR conducted an exhumation with the participation of Polish experts at Kharkov and at Mednoye near Tver. Both burials have released indisputable evidence of the shooting of Polish prisoners of war. The execution at Mednoye can be dated precisely to Apil 1940. Due to pecularities of the soil, the Mednoye burial ground has preserved in a condition fit for expert examination numerous documents and personal objects. Black greatcoats (which, as we know, were worn by policemen who made up a large proportion of the Ostashkov camp's prisoners) were very well preserved. The experts were astonished by the fact that the corpses had decayed to such a small extent. The graves found in the Kharkov forest park were in a much worse condition and consisted of a mess of human bones from which it was seldom possible to put together a whole skeleton. Yet, there can be no doubt as to the nationality of the victims on account of the numerous metal objects - buckles, buttons, and coins - found among the bones. The method of killing (shots in the head) is identical to that used in Katyn.

NOTES

Chapter 1
THE PROSE OF DEATH

1. See, in particular, the material *Proyasnyaya "belyie pyatna"* (Clearing Up Blank Spots) in *Mezhdunarodnaya Zhizn*, 1988, No. 5, and also the book: Kulkov, Ye. N., Rzheshevsky, O. A. and Chelyshev, I. A. *Pravda i lozh o vtoroi mirovoi voine* (Truth and Lies About World War II), 2nd enlarged ed., Moscow, Voyenizdat Publishers, 1988, pp. 272-275.

2. *TASS bulletin*, April 18 1989, AD series, sheet 4.

3. Central State Special Archives, stock 40, inventory 1, file 1, sheet 1.

4. October Revolution Central State Archives of the USSR, stock 353, inventory 3, file 661.

5. Central State Archives of the Soviet Army, stock 38,651, inventory 1, file 100, sheet 131.

6. October Revolution Central State Archives of the USSR, stock 353, inventory 3, file 678, sheet 1.

7. *Sbornik zakonov i rasporyazhenii raboche-krestyanskogo Pravitelstva SSSR* (Collection of Laws and Directives of the Workers' and Peasants' Government of the USSR), 1925, No. 77, Article 579, and 1930, No. 48, Article 497.

8. Central State Archives of the Soviet Army, stock 40, inventory 1, file 181, sheet 47.

9. *Ibid.*, file 69, sheet 60.

10. *Ibid.*, file 73, sheet 31.

11. *Ibid.*, stock 38,052, inventory 1.

12. Stefan Zwoliński. *Vooruzhennaya borba Polshi v gody vtoroi mirovoi voiny* (The Armed Struggle Waged by Poland in the Years of World War II). Interpress, Warsaw, 1989.

13. Central State Archives of the Soviet Army, stock 40, inventory 1, file 182, sheet 22.

14. Stanisław Swianiewicz. *W cieniv Katynia* (In the Shadow of Katyn). Overseas Publications Interchange Ltd., London, 1989, pp.97-98.

15. Central State Archives of the Soviet Army, stock 40, inventory 1, file 180, sheet 265.

16. *Ibid.*, file 74, sheet 2.

17. *Ibid.*, file 179, sheet 321.

18. *Ibid.*, sheet 153.

19. *Ibid.*, file 180, sheet 250.

20. *Ibid.*, file 181, sheets 71-72.

21. *Ibid.*, file 198, sheet 295.

22. *Ibid.*, file 180, sheet 276.

23. Czesław Madajczyk. *Dramat Katyński*. Książka i Wiedza, Warszawa, 1989, ss. 16-17.

24. Central State Archives of the Soviet Army, stock 40, inventory 1, file 191, sheet 246. The statement of July 9, 1941, attached to Sharapov's letter says that the commission of the Administration for Escort Guard Troops selected and destroyed 4,908 files and 15,590 copies of People's Commissar's orders. The remaining documents, packed into two boxes and 30 bags, were evacuated to Sverdlovsk.

25. *Ibid.*, stock 38,106, inventory 1, file 14, sheet 38.

26. *Ibid.*, file 182, sheets 49, 51, 53, 55.

27. *Ibid.*, file 88, sheet 18.

28. *Ibid.*, stock 38,052, inventory 1, file 74, sheet 45.

29. *Ibid.*, stock 38,106, inventory 1, file 7, sheet 14.

30. It should be noted that the prisoners were actually fed quite well. The diaries contain numerous mentions of the camp menu, which included *shchi* (cabbage soup), pea soup, goulash, fish, potatoes, semolina, and macaroni with sauce. A prisoner of war was given 30 grams of sugar a day, one pack of *makhorka* (rough tobacco) every five days, and a 200-gram cake of soap on every bath day.

31. In the plan drawn by Zawodny (Janusz K. Zawodny. Katyń. Editions Spotkania, Lublin–Paryż, 1989), this structure is marked "Circus" and the social center is in a wooden annex between the Cathedral of the Presentation in the Temple and the Church of the Kazan Icon of the Mother of God. "Circus," "Shanghai," "Philharmonic," "Indian Tomb," "Bristol," etc., were the POWs nicknames for the camp barracks.

32. Pamiętniki znalezione . . ., ss. 200-212. In Zentina's diary, the exact date when correspondence was permitted is also to be found: November 20, 1939.

33. The fact he was on good terms with the POWs got Valentin into serious trouble. A political report by Nekhoroshev, Commissar of the Administration for the Affairs of Prisoners of War, to Merkulov (Central State Special Archives, stock 1/п, inventory 1, file 1, sheets 145-153) says: "A small number of the POWs still do not believe that they will be sent home on the strength of the fact that all the persons being moved out are thoroughly searched by escort guards and that they are sent out in prison cars. The POWs are trying to influence the service personnel and

learn from them where they are being sent. It has been established that information about their transportation was leaked into the camp by projectionists Levashov and Gorshkov. In this connection, the service personnel have been given a severe warning." And then, further on: "To ensure maximum isolation of the POWs from the service personnel, the latter have been reduced to a minimum in the camp zone and access to the camp for the rest of the personnel has been restricted." I do not know whether the Levashov mother and son sensed they were being shadowed, a fact of which there is no doubt. The proof is in Beria's directive "on the operative Chekist (from the Cheka, the original name of the Soviet secret police.—Ed.) service of prisoners of war," whose Paragraph 7 says: "To ensure timely exposure and prevention of possible cases of prisoners of war using individuals from among the service personnel of the camp for criminal purposes (passing on messages and letters and bribing for the purpose of escape), on top of the briefing and political work being conducted by the camp authorities and political apparatus, the special sections of the camps shall provide the camp's warder and sentry personnel and the populated localities round the camp with agent service." (*Ibid.*, stock 451/п, inventory 1, file 1, sheets 17-20).

34. *Zbrodnia Katyńska w świetle dokumentów*. GRYF, London, 1986, s. 27.

35. Central State Archives of the Soviet Army, stock 38, 106, inventory 1, file 10, sheet 145.

36. As a report on incidents says, in June 1940, Tatarenko "deserted from the escort party of a scheduled

convoy and shot himself dead at his home." By an order of July 11, 1940, Mezhov, the commander of the battalion, and Snytko, its commissar, were reprimanded "for poor selection of the escort party."

37. Swianiewicz mentions "NKVD soldiers," but the fact is that the term "soldier", just like the term "officer" (instead of which the word "commander" was used), was not in use in the Red Army at the time. Further on, I shall correct this anachronism as need be without any additional comments.

38. Central State Archives or the Soviet Army, stock 38, 106, inventory 1, file 7, sheets 86, 87, 89.

39. Gustav Hilger and Alfred Meyer. *The Incompatible Allies*. New York, 1953, p. 268. In the years of the war, Oberlaender served as captain of counter-intelligence at the Soviet-German front and more than once spoke in favor of easing the occupation regime. Between 1953 and 1960, he was minister for refugee affairs in the German federal government. In one of his latest books, *Six Essays on the Brainwashing of the Soviet Population in the Years of World War II (Oberlaender, Th. Sechs Denkschriften aus dem Zweiten Weltkrieg ueber die Behandlung der Sowjetvoelker.* Ingolstadt, 1984), he expounds the methods of propaganda used among the non-Russian peoples of the Caucasus in 1942-1943.

Gerald Reitlinger in *The House Built on Sand* also writes about Koch and Oberlaender's pro-Soviet sentiments:

"As Reichskommissar for the Ukraine, it was from Hitler that Koch borrowed his jibes at 'nigger Peoples.' No such feelings beset the railway clerk from the Ruhr in the

1920s when he entered his future East Prussian Kingdom scarcely knowing what a Slav looked like. The proximity of Koenigsberg to the Soviet Union tended to increase Koch's radicalism rather than his German nationalism. In 1934, he published a small book called *Aufbau im Osten*. Printed in a peculiarly black-letter type, it contains a number of pretentious historical comparisons, which were said to have been written for him by a certain Weberkrohse.

"It also contains some of Koch's speeches. Whatever Koch's share in the authorship, the book does at least show the sort of thing to which Koch lent his name, such as, for instance the theory that German youth should throw in its lot with the hardened, classless youth of the Soviet Union, rather than with the decadent youth of the capitalist West; the theory that the great land spaces of the east were not, as he was later to preach, a place from which the natives should be evicted like Red Indians in order to create a grain belt, but rather the home of German and Russian pioneers living happily together.

"Still more significant was Koch's friendship with the Russophile professor from Koenigsberg University, Theodor Oberlaender, who was to work under Koch for a short time in the Ukraine. In the year of the publication of his book, Koch had been a party to a secret discussion between Oberlaender and the Old Guard Bolshevik Karl Radek, a Galician Jew. Both Oberlaender and Radek opposed the drift towards hostility of their governments. Radek, a strange figure indeed, showed himself to be an admirer of the SS and SA. This, above all things, Koch had to play down following his Ukrainian appointment." (Gerald Reitlinger. *The House Built on Sand. The Conflicts of German Policy in Russia. 1939-1945.* London, 1960).

In 1959, an allegation about Oberlaender's involvement in the assassination of Stepan Bandera was advanced (see, in particular, the newspaper *Krasnaya Zvezda* of October 20, 1959). In actual fact, Bandera was assassinated by KGB agent Bogdan Stashinsky.

40. Central State Archives of the Soviet Army, stock 40, inventory 1, file 74, sheet 99.

41. In the spring and summer of 1941, NKVD Construction Project No. 106 was engaged in building a military aerodrome in the Ponoi locality (Kola Peninsula). By a decree of the Presidium of the Supreme Soviet of November 28, 1941, I. I. Orlovsky and G. M. Prokofiev, heads of the construction project, and I. A. Tupolev, deputy head of the production department, were decorated with the "Badge of Honor" and senior mechanic I. G. Grigoryev, with the medal "For Valiant Labor." In an editorial published in the newspaper *Izvestia* on November 29, 1941, it was noted, in particular: "In quite a number of cases, particular so in the regions of the North with their harsh climate, the builders had to uproot forests, drain marshes and level off hilly land over a vast area. The novelty of the project and its particular complexity notwithstanding, the builders mastered the entire construction process within a short space of time, and with characteristically Bolshevik persistance and energy overcame the difficulties which faced them. All the facilities built in various parts of our boundless homeland we put up in

record time. In conditions of peace, the construction of a similar structure would have taken three years. In conditions of war, those dictated by the need to do everything possible to strengthen the defense potential of the homeland, it was built in less than five months."

42. Central State Archives of the Soviet Army, stock 38,106, inventory 1, file 14, sheet 44 and reverse.

43. *Ibid.*, stock 40, inventory 4, file 191, sheet 42.

44. Czesław Madajczyk. *Ibid.*, s. 17.

45. Central State Special Archives, stock 1/п, inventory 3a, file 1, sheet 288. Thus, the figure given by Madajczyk, from which 400 army officers should be subtracted, must be recognized as being very accurate. An even closer figure, 6,567, is given by Józef Mackiewicz. Thus, we can see that the calculations made by Polish authors are distinguished by a high degree of accuracy.

46. Central State Archives of the Soviet Army, stock 40, inventory 1, file 178, sheet 7 and reverse.

47. *Ibid.*, file 179, sheet 62.

48. See also an article about this in *Moscow News* of July 1 1990.

49. An even stranger thing happened at the 239th kilometer of the Moscow-Yaroslavl highway, where the local branch of the Memorial society found yet another mass grave of victims of Stalinism not far from the village of Selifontovo. Naturally, "a most active part in the excavations," reported *Izvestia* of July 15 1990, "was taken by officers of the KGB Department for the Yaroslavl Region and of the department of internal affairs of the regional executive committee, and by men and officers of military

units." V. Boyev, Business Manager of the Yaroslavl Regional Executive Committee, told the correspondent that, "incidentally, in the common grave were also found revolver bullets, one of them stuck in a skull." Soon, however, the exhumation had to be interrupted, because three unexploded shells were found in the graves. Sappers came and blew up the shells (let us hope that this was not right there among the bones). This information is extremely ambiguous. What kind of shells were they, whose were they, and where did they come from? Only their caliber, 76 mm and 36mm, is mentioned. M. Ovcharov, *Izvestia's* own correspondent, offers a hypothesis which in my view, is absolutely unrealistic: "Can it be that these shells were planted half a century ago by those who were directly involved in this criminal action and wanted by any means possible to hamper future excavations of the grave?" It is now too late to make guesses. "And the excavations of the common grave," the correspondent concludes, "have been suspended for reasons of safety." Q.E.D.

See also an article in *Sovetskaya Kultura* of July 28, 1990, which says that there is now nowhere to bury the exhumed remains.

50. Central State Special Archives, stock 1/п, inventory 3a, file 1, sheets 89-90.

51. Henryk Kokoszyński, a former Ostashkov prisoner, wrote to me and Minko that there was no canteen at the camp: skilly was poured into pails, which were distributed among the cells, ten liters of skilly per cell (50 persons). The colonists, however, could hardly have done without a

canteen. Apparently, there was a canteen, but not for the POWs.

52. Central State Archives of the Soviet Army, stock 40, inventory 1, file 74, sheet 217.

53. *Ibid.*, file 17.

54. Central State Special Archives, stock 1/п, inventory 1a, file 1, sheets 182-184.

55. The desecration of remains hardly comes as any surprise to us. I will refer the reader, for example, to the article *Obnazhenny yar* (Exposed Steep Bank), published in *Pravda* on May 11 1989, in which V. Chertkov, the newspaper's special correspondent, describes how the bones of people who had been executed came into view in 1979 on the site of a former NKVD prison in the town of Kolpashev, Tomsk Region. On the instructions of the local authorities, the corpses of these "enemies of the people" were washed out of the steep bank into the Ob River by streams of water created by ships' propellers, in order to avoid raising the question of their reburial. In this connection *Khronika* (No. 26, 1989) specifies that Yegor Ligachev was First Secretary of the Tomsk Regional Committee of the CPSU in the period between 1963 and 1983. In April 1990, a rally in support of candidates nominated by the Democratic Russia bloc was held in Novosibirsk; Paragraph 4 of the resolution adopted at the rally says: "We support the demand of the Novosibirsk and Tomsk Memorial societies for an open investigation into all the circumstances of the destruction of the grave of victims of Stalinism in the town of Kolpashev, Tomsk Region, in 1979. We believe it to be impermissible that citizen Ligachev, *who sanctioned this*

barbarous crime, is at present a People's Deputy of the USSR and demand his immediate resignation." (*Baltia*, 1990, No. 5).

56. Central State Special Archives, stock 1/п, inventory 2e, file 10, sheet 268.

57. *Ibid.*, sheets 283-284.

58. *Ibid.*, stock 3/п, inventory 1, file 1, sheets 145-153.

Chapter 2
THE END OF THE "POLISH EXPERIMENT"

1. Central State Archives of the Soviet Army, stock 40, inventory 1, file 180, sheet 201.

2. *Ibid.*, file 185, sheets 167-169.

3. *Ibid.*, file 186, sheet 23.

4. *Ibid.*, sheet 35.

5. A slip of the memory. As was previously mentioned, Vladimir Sharapov was head of the Main Administration of Escort Guard troops of the NKVD of the USSR. It was State Security Major Kadyshev who was head of the Yukhnov camp.

6. My mistake, A. Ya. Demidovich was head of the 2nd second section of the Kozelsk camp and not its commissar.

7. *Osadniki*–Polish resettlers in the territories which were incorporated into the USSR in September 1939.

8. Here and elsewhere during this conversation there are slips of the tongue. In this particular case, it should be

the MGB (Ministry of State Security) and further on, the NKGB (People's Commissariat of State Security.)

9. Brigade Commander Ivan Lyuby was awarded the Order of the Red Banner by a decree of the Presidium of the USSR Supreme Soviet of April 26 1940. I have no other information about this person.

10. For some reason, Alexei Lukin believes that in Katyn there was also a POW camp. Perhaps he is talking about the already mentioned Smolensk transit prison, but how does Lukin know the place name "Katyn"?

11. It was in a hospital that Lukin met with the anonymous political instructor. He told Lukin about an unmounted convoy departing a camp early in July 1941. The column was marching along a highway crowded with refugees and, as a result, according to the political instructor, some of the Poles scattered in various directions. The convoy's destination was Vyazma. Nothing else remains but to guess where the refugees seen near Kozelsk appeared from and why the convoy was heading for Vyazma, which is located to the west of Kozelsk. This was undoubtedly the evacuation of the prison of the Smolensk Department of the NKVD and not of a camp. As we know, this convoy departed on July 19 1941; it was, however, bound for Katyn and not for Vyazma. It was on the Smolensk-Vitebsk highway that it encountered refugees traveling in the opposite direction. Perhaps it was in order to carry out this action that Reprintsev, commander of the regiment, went to Katyn?

12. See the decree of the Presidium of the USSR Supreme Soviet of February 3 1941, on the division of the

NKVD of the USSR into the NKVD and the NKGB (*Pravda*, February 4, 1941).

13. Sentry dog guides also had to carry a pistol or a Nagant revolver. For example, in the order to escort guard troops "On the Attempted Suicide of T. S. Zibertov, a Sentry Dog Guide of the 146th Escort Guard Battalion," and the "Non-observance of the Rules for Handing Out and Keeping Personal Small Arms" of November 6 1939, it was said that the Nagant revolver of the 1895 model was a regulation personal small arm of the serviceman who tried to commit suicide (Central State Archives of the Soviet Army, stock 40, inventory 1, file 68, sheets 43-44).

14. State security ranks were introduced by the resolutions of the Central Executive Committee and the Council of People's Commissars of the USSR "On Special Ranks of the Commanding Staff of the Main Administration of State Security of the NKVD of the USSR" of October 7 1935, and "On the Approval of the Regulations for Doing Service by the Commanding Staff of the Main Administration of the NKVD of the USSR" of October 16, 1935. According to the regulations, two sleeve insignias in the form of truncated red triangles corresponded to the rank of state security sergeant, and three, to the rank of state security junior lieutenant. There did not, however, exist any insignia in the form of a single triangle, nor did there exist a corresponding rank. See *Sbornik postanovlenii i rasporyazhenii pravitelstva SSSR* (Collection of Resolutions and Directives of the USSR Government), No. 26 of June 4, 1936. Later on, the state security insignia of rank were brought into line with those adopted in the Red Army.

15. The letter by V. P. Moroz from the town of Jelgava published in *Sovershenno Sekretno*, 1990, No. 2, gives an idea of how the evacuation of the population from the border area proceeded. The author of the letter says that before the war he and his family lived at Bigosovo Station on the Western Railway. "My grandfather, Yemelyan Pavlyukevich, and my mother, Anna, were Poles. It became known that Poles were being arrested and Letts being evacuated from the frontier area, and so grandfather, who was awarded the order "Badge of Honor" in 1935, waited every day for them to come and take him. The chief of the frontier station summoned him in order to clarify his origin and nationality." It was Yemelyan Pavlyukevich's death that saved him from arrest.

16. Central State Archives of the Soviet Army, stock 40, inventory 1, file 179, sheets 181-182.

Chapter 3
MOSCOW, LUBYANKA PRISON

1. A laconic yet expressive description of these camps is to be found in *The Gulag Archipelago*: "There were also camps on Novaya Zemlya for many years, and the most terrible camps they were people were confined in them 'without the right to correspondence.' Not a single prisoner ever returned from there. Today we still do not know what these wretched people mined and built, how they lived and how they died. And yet it is to be hoped that we will live to hear a testimony about them one day!"

2. In his capacity as First Deputy People's Commissar of Foreign Affairs (appointed by a resolution of the Council of People's Commissars of the USSR of September 6, 1940), Vyshinsky actually dealt with matters relating to Poland. In the winter of 1941-1942, he, together with Stalin and Molotov, took part in the negotiations with General Sikorski and subsequently accompanied him during his trip across the country. This episode is touched upon by Ilya Ehrenburg in his memoirs *Men, Years—Life*: "Early in December, in the vicinity of Saratov, I was present at the review of General Anders' army recruited from Polish prisoners of war. Sikorski arrived accompanied by Vyshinsky. I do not know why the choice had fallen on Vyshinsky for this occasion. It may have been because of his Polish origin. But I remembered him in the role of prosecutor at one of the trials. He clinked glasses with Sikorski, smiling very sweetly. Among the Poles there were many grim-looking men, full of resentment at what they had been through; some of them could not refrain from admitting that they hated us. I felt that they would never be able to put the past behind them. Sikorski and Vyshinsky called each other 'allies' but hostility made itself felt behind the cordial words." It was Vyshinsky who held a press conference on May 4, 1943, on the causes of the breaking of diplomatic relations with the Polish government in exile during which he accused the staff of the Polish embassy, Ambassador Kot included, of espionage. It will be recalled that the formal reason for the Soviet demarche was the Sikorski government's appeal to the International Commit-

tee of the Red Cross to conduct an examination of the Katyn graves by experts.

Incidentally, there is an obvious discrepancy in Raikhman's statement. The minutes of the sittings of the Vyshinsky commission are dated May 24 and June 11, 1946. There was quite enough time during these three weeks to find out that Raikhman would not be able to work in the commission, since he was out of Moscow. Yet nonetheless he, being absent from Moscow, was ordered to arrange for the delivery of witnesses to Nuremberg. Indeed, from this very paragraph it transpires that Raikhman was not quite absent from Moscow, so to speak, and that he actually came to Moscow that very summer.

3. In 1940, Leonid Raikhman actually had the rank of major; he was, however, a state security and not an army major and wore collar pins in the form of one rhomb. This insignia corresponded to the rank of brigade commander or to that of major general of the Red Army, which had just been introduced in May 1940 (the decree of the Presidium of the USSR Supreme Soviet on the introduction of ranks of generals is dated May 7, 1940, and Tartakov's report, May 10, 1940, i.e., three days later). Raikhman regarded my reference to the decree of April 26, 1940, by which State Security Major Raikhman, as one of a large group of NKVD officers, was awarded the medal "For Gallantry," superfluous, although it seemed to corroborate his words. Readers, in their turn, decided that I was thus trying to "whitewash" Raikhman. In actual fact, however, I simply did not wish to quarrel with my hero ahead of time (every journalist will understand this); and

yet I mentioned his actual rank and thus incurred his displeasure.

4. In 1932-1933, extrajudicial proceedings were instituted against M. N. Ryutin, L. B. Kamenev, G. Ye. Zinovyev, and others (a total of 30 persons) by resolutions of the Collegium or the OGPU* on the case of the "Union of Marxists-Leninists." The commission of the Politburo of the CPSU Central Committee on the additional examination of materials relating to the repressions that took place in the 1930s, 1940s and early 1950s established that the investigation was conducted with gross violations of the law. In June 1988, the Supreme Court of the USSR repealed corresponding resolutions of the Collegium of the OGPU in respect to 25 people convicted in connection with this case for lack of corpus delicti in their actions. The other five people were rehabilitated earlier.

5. Kirov was assassinated on December 1, 1934. Yezhov was appointed People's Commissar of Internal Affairs on September 26, 1936. Prior to his appointment, he supervised the NKVD as Secretary of the Central Committee of the All-Union Communist Party (Bolsheviks). Beria became absolute master of the NKVD in December 1938.

6. The case in question is the case of the so-called "Parallel Anti-Soviet Trotskyite Center." On January 30, 1937, the Military Collegium of the USSR Supreme Court, which tried this case in full session, sentenced Yu. L. Pyatakov, L. P. Serebryakov, N. I. Muralov, and others (a

---

*OGPU — designation of Soviet secret police, 1922-1934; acronym for United State Political Administration.

total of 13 persons) to death by firing squad, and G. Ya. Sokolnikov, K. B. Radek, V. V. Arnold and M. S. Stroilov to various terms of imprisonment; the last two were subsequently also executed. The commission of the Politburo of the CPSU Central Committee has established that the materials of the case were fabricated. All the convicted persons have been rehabilitated.

7. A separate investigation of the case of the "Leningrad counter-revolutionary Zinovyevite Group of Safarov, Zalutsky and Others" was instituted in December 1934, in the course of investigations into the circumstances of the assassination of Kirov. There is no indictment among the materials of the case. In all, 77 persons were arrested and imprisoned or exiled by a decision of a Special Board of the NKVD of January 16, 1935, in connection with the Safarov case; subsequently, many of them were repressed for a second time on the same grounds when more severe punishment, including execution, was imposed on them. In a paper prepared jointly by the Party Control Committee under the CPSU Central Committee and by the Institute of Marxism-Leninism under the CPSU Central Committee it is noted: "The interrogations were in a prejudiced, biased manner and using physical compulsion." By riders of the Military Collegium of the USSR Supreme Court of August 23, 1957, February 8, 1958, and June 21, 1962, all the accused, excepting Safarov, were rehabilitated. The case of Safarov, who, as is stated in the paper, gave "provocative, false evidence against many people," is being examined.

8. In trying the case of the Moscow Center in January 1935, the Military Collegium of the USSR Supreme Court sentenced Kamenev, Zinovyev, and 17 others to various terms of imprisonment. As reported by the commission of the Politburo of the CPSU Central Committee, "the examination of the case has shown that its materials were falsified." The sentence in connection with the case of the Moscow Center has been repealed by the Plenary Meeting of the Supreme Court for lack of corpus delicti.

9. In trying this case in full session, the Military Collegium of the Supreme Court sentenced the 16 accused, including Zinovyev and Kamenev, to death by firing squad. As reported by the commission of the Politburo of the CPSU Central Committee, "careful analysis of the materials of the case has shown that they were also sentenced groundlessly." In 1988, the Plenary Meeting of the USSR Supreme Court satisfied a protest lodged by the General Procurator of the USSR and dismissed the case for lack of corpus delicti.

10. When this book was being prepared for publication, I learned about the existence of the reminiscences of A. L. Voitolovskaya, who appeared as a witness during the trial of Raikhman in August 1956. The collection *Zvenya* Links, prepared by the Moscow Memorial society, which includes a fragment of the book *Po sledam sudby moyego pokoleniya* (Following the Destiny of My Generation) by Voitolovskaya, has not yet come off the press. Which means that there was a trial! According to commentator N. Petrov (who, incidentally, refers to rumors), Raikhman was sentenced under Article 193-17a ("negligence") to 5 years

of imprisonment and, with the period of his preliminary detention taken into account, soon released.

11. I am talking about two aspects: an extremely involved political situation around Poland, and the terror employed by the Soviet organs against the pro-London underground. In that period Stalin showed a certain tolerance towards the London Cabinet. At any rate, he pretended that he was actually aiming at forming a government of national unity. To this end, a commission which included Molotov, Harriman, and Kerr was set up to implement the decisions of the Yalta Conference. The Western allies of the USSR were worried in the extreme over the state of affairs in Poland. In March 1945, Tomasz Arciszewski, Prime Minister of the government in exile, transmitted a summary of information about the latest developments to Churchill. The summary stated: "The Sovietisation of Poland is proceeding apace. . . . From 5th February Poles in important positions (professors, doctors, and so on) have been forced to sign a memorandum condemning the Polish Government in London . . . and praising the Lublin Committee. . . . The NKVD are keeping those arrested, in cellars, air raid shelters, and in every possible place. . . . In the course of interrogations, the NKVD beat prisoners, torture them morally, keep them in the cold without clothes. They accuse those arrested of espionage on behalf of the British and of the Polish Government in London, and of collaboration with the Germans. There is a high rate of mortality among the prisoners. . . . Please inform the British. Allied intervention necessary." The report concluded: "Most people in Poland

consider the present state of affairs as Soviet occupation."
As a result, at the fifth plenary session of the Yalta Conference, Stalin was compelled to say in reply to charges made
by Churchill that he did not see "why Great Britain and
the United States could not send their own people to
Poland." And yet, when Harriman and Kerr subsequently
brought the question of observers up before Molotov, the
latter replied that the Soviet government "had learned with
amazement" of this intention "inasmuch as this proposal
could touch the national pride of the Poles to the quick,
the more so since in the decisions of the Crimea conference this subject is not even touched upon." Stalin, in his
turn, kept accusing "terrorists instigated by Polish emi-
grants" of waging an armed struggle against the Red Army
(his telegram to Roosevelt of December 27, 1944). In
January 1945, the Armia Krajowa disbanded itself to be
replaced by the secret organization NIE (acronym for
'niepodległość', independence), headed by General Okulicki,
former Commander-in-Chief of the Armia Krajowa. In
March, Okulicki and his 15 associates were arrested, and in
June they were sentenced to various terms of imprisonment by the Military Collegium of the USSR Supreme
Court, presided over by V. V. Ulrikh (the so-called "trial of
16"). The fate of Okulicki, who was sentenced to 10 years
in prison, is still unknown today. (For details, see Eugeniusz Duraczyński, *Generał Iwanow zaprasza*, ALFA, Warszawa, 1989.) All the quotations in this note are from the
book *Roosevelt and Churchill: Their Secret Wartime Correspondence*, Saturday Review Press/E.P. Dutton & Co., Inc., New
York, 1975, pp. 667, 669, 684, 687.

12. Central State Special Archives, stock 451/п, inventory 1, file 1, sheets 17-20.

13. Central State Special Archives, stock 1/п, inventory 3a, file 1, sheets 274-275.

Chapter 4
PSEUDOEXPERTS

1. PT weekly, No. 21, 1989. Published by Pyotr Zharon.

2. Akten zur Deutschen Auswärtigen Politik, Serie E, Bd. V, ss. 579-580. Published after: Czesław Madajczyk. *Ibid.*, ss. 141-142.

3. In his memoirs, published recently, N. V. Novikov, who was then on the staff of the Fourth European Department of the People's Commissariat for Foreign Affairs, tells that right after the German communication on Katyn, he was urgently called in by Deputy People's Commissar A. Y. Korneichuk. Novikov quotes Korneichuk as having said: "I shudder to think of how this rotten fascist trick is going to be taken by my friends in the Union of Polish Patriots." Novikov replied: "They must be made to take it just as a rotten trick." "And we," the author of the memoirs writes, "went on to discuss the practical steps that would have to be taken in connection with this frame-up. It was necessary to contact top officials in the People's Commissariat for Foreign Affairs at once and find out what they knew about this business, and then outline how and in what form to hit back at the provocation and prepare proposals for the

People's Gommissar." It is a pity that Novikov does not
detail his contacts with top officials of the People's Commissariat for the Interior, but, of course, we already know
what way of "hitting back" was proposed by G. S. Zhukov.
Novikov tells us further on that the note about breaking
off diplomatic relations with Poland was written by Stalin
personally. (N. V. Novikov. A Diplomat's Reminiscences.
Politizdat, Moscow, 1989, pp. 124-125, in Russian).

4. A Swiss historian, Jean-Claude Favez, who spent
eight years studying the archives of the IRCC, has recently
published his book *An Impossible Mission? The IRCC, Deportations and Nazi Concentration Camps (Une mission impossible? Le
CICR, les déportations et les camps de concentrations nazis de
Jean-Claude Favez*, Payot Lausanne. 1989) in which he
writes, in particular, that in the course of World War II,
the IRCC "often, rather than looking for ways to act,
looked for ways to justify inaction."

5. Czesław Madajczyk. *Ibid.*, ss. 142-144.

6. In his report, Gerhard Butz says: "The executions
were carried out with 7.65 mm pistol cartridges, witness
the markings on their butts. These butts were in all cases
stamped "Geco 7.65 D." Pistol ammunition with this trade
mark, used in Katyn, had been made for years at the
Gustaw Genschow Co. in Durlach near Karlsruhe (Baden)."
The fact of cartridge-cases of German manufacture having
been discovered in Katyn was used by Soviet historiogra-
phy throughout the post-war years to corroborate Burdenko's version. Let us, however, quote more of Buhtz: "In
consequence of the Treaty of Versailles there was no
demand for ammunition in Germany and the Genschow

firm exported pistol cartridges to neighboring countries, Poland, the Baltic states and the Soviet Union (in fairly large quantities until 1928 and then in more limited quantities)." (Quoted from Jozef Mackiewicz. *Op. cit.* p. 290). See also the Voss report: "According to information obtained from the High Command of the Army (Ch. H. *Rust und Befehlshaber des Ersatzheeres,* letter of May 31, 1943), ammunition for pistols of this caliber and pistols themselves were delivered to the USSR and Poland. What remains unclear is whether the pistols and ammunition had been taken for the executions from Soviet depots or from Polish ones which had fallen into the hands of the Bolsheviks as a result of their occupation of Poland's eastern regions." (*Ibid.,* p. 280). Cartridge-cases of Soviet manufacture were also found in Katyn (Gracian Jaworowski. *Nieznana relacje o grobach katynskich.* "Zeszyty Historyczne," Paryż, 45, 1978, s. 4).

7. "Odrodzenie," 1989, nr.7.

8. Cf. a letter of 15.3.1943 from a member of the ESC and SC, the writer A. N. Tolstoy, to the ESC Chairman, Shvernik: "I have to be mobile. I beg you to give me the right to a daily ration of 300 liters of petrol." (October Revolution Central State Archives, stock 7021, inv. 116, file 324, p. 29). I do believe this is in fact a slip of the pen because Shvernik's letter of 24.3.1943 to A. I. Mikoyan says: "I ask you to permit a quota of 300 liters of petrol a month to Academician Tolstoy for his personal car." (*Ibid.,* p. 28).

9. Quoted from: Louis Fitzgibbon. *Katyn: A Crime Without Parallel*: London, 1971, pp. 155-161.

10. Quoted from: Leopold Jezewski. Op. cit., pp. 58-59.

11. Zewodny points out that Orsos had published his work on pseudocallus two years before Katyn (Janusz K. Zawodny, *Ibid.*, s. 33, przypisy).

12. Czesław Madajczyk. Ibid., s. 144.

13. "As well as looking for witnesses, the Germans set about the appropriate preparation of the graves in the Katyn Forest. This included clearing the clothes of the Polish prisoners of war they had killed of all documents dated after April, 1940, i.e., the time when, according to the provocative German version, the Poles were shot by the Bolsheviks, and removing all material evidence capable of disproving that provocative version." (Collected ESC Reports on the Atrocities of the German Fascist Invaders. Gospolitizdat, Moscow, 1946, p. 130). It has also been said, that corpses had been brought over to Katyn Forest "from elsewhere." (*Ibid.*, pp. 133-136).

14. Lista katyńska . . . , s. 294.

15. October Revolution Central State Archives, stock 7021, inv. 116, storage unit 326, pp. 13-14.

16. *Ibid.*, p. 56.

17. *Ibid.*, p. 57.

18. 9,432 corpses, including 169 female, were discovered in Vinnitsa; 679 of them were identified. Two of the Katyn experts formed part of the International Commission: Dr. Orsós and Dr. Birkle (from Romania), while the Special Commission of the Reich's Criminal Police Department comprised Professor Malinin of Krasnodar and Assistant Professor Doroshenko of Vinnitsa. The Germans revealed similar ditches in Pyatigorsk, for instance, also in 1943, as a reader, N. Neshev told me.

19. October Revolution Central State Archives, stock 7021, inv. 116, storage unit 326, p. 25.

20. In fact, this "identity of method" has yet to be determined. *See*, in particular, an article by the American historian, A. Ezergailis called *The Arais Team (The Jewish Culture Chronicle*, No. 4, 1990), where you can find a detailed description of the mass executions carried out by the Nazis in Latvia. Pistols, the author says, were used only for "coups de grâce," i.e. for finishing off the victims.

21. *Moscow News*, No. 36, September 3, 1989. See also the article "On Judicial Killings" by the same author in the *Chelovek i zakon* (Man and Law) magazine, No. II, 1988.

22. October Revolution Central State Archives, stock 7021, inv. 116, storage unit 326, p. 4.

Chapter 5
THE NUREMBERG VERSION

1. Czesław Madajczyk. *Ibid.*, s. 71.

2. Bradley F. Smith. *Reaching Judgement at Nuremberg*, New York, 1977, p. 71.

3. V. Abarinov. "In the Wings of the Palace of Justice", *Raduga* (Tallinn), No. 8, 1989 (enclosing the texts of archival documents); *Gorizont* (Moscow), No. 9, 1989. Katyn, "Facts and Arguments. Introduction and Commentaries by V. Abarinov, *Raduga*, No. 12, 1989. For P. I Grishayev's and B. A. Solovyov's letter and the reply to it see *Gorizont*, No. 5, 1990.

4. Passages from the verbatim report of the morning and afternoon sittings of the International Military Tribunal of July 1, 1946, have been reprinted from the official Russian text (October Revolution Central State Archives, stock 7445, inv. I, storage unit 64). Rudenko's protest was reprinted from the same source: inv. 2, storage unit 6, pp. 256, 257. Minutes of the Vyshinsky Commission, *Ibid.*, inv. 2, storage unit 391. Alexandrov's explanatory note, *Ibid.*, inv. 2, storage unit 391, p. 60. The minutes of the organizing sitting of the International Military Tribunal, *Ibid.*, inv. I, storage unit 2625, pp. 161-176. Records of the preliminary interrogations of witnesses for the prosecution, *Ibid.*, inv. 2, storage units 132, 134, 135, 136. A verbatim report of Smirnov's interrogations of witnesses for the prosecution has been published in a Soviet edition (*The Nuremberg Trial of Major German Criminals, Collected Proceedings in Seven Volumes,* edited by R. A. Rudenko. State Publishing House of Legal Literature Moscow, 1958, vol. III), duplication appears to be superfluous. In preparing the text for printing, the author has permitted himself to correct the punctuation of the original copy in accordance with modern rules as well as the transliteration of some names (Oberhäuser and Schneider), and also obvious misprints.

5. The reference is to the IMT Charter signed simultaneously with the agreement establishing the IMT on August 8 1945, in London.

6. A member of the IMT on behalf of the U.S. Supreme Federal Court, and a former U.S. Attorney General.

7. This argument reminded me of the trial of the Commander of the Armia Krajowa, General L. Okulicki, in

Moscow, a year before. Incidentally, Rudenko was one of the prosecutors. The Military Board of the Supreme Court of the USSR granted the defendant's request to summon witnesses for the defense. However, it was announced during the court proceedings on the following day that "because of meteorological conditions, the requested witnesses cannot be brought here by plane either today or tomorrow." The prosecutor immediately proposed: "Since it is not certain whether the witnesses of the defendant, Okulicki, can be brought over within the next few days, the prosecution sees no need to delay the hearing of the case, all the more so since yesterday, in view of the clarity of the circumstances of the case, the public prosecution forswore the interrogation of 11 witnesses listed in the indictment." The court agreed with the prosecutor. The sentence was announced later on the same day (*Pravda*, June 21, 1945). To my mind, this precedent deserves to be included in the appropriate reference books.

8. Katyn is far from being the only episode in the process which prompted the Soviet prosecution to appeal to Article 21 of the IMT Charter. For example, on June 20, 1946, Col. Karev, Assistant Chief Prosecutor for the USSR, lodged a protest against the court's decision to demand a statement from Wehrmacht General Jenicke about the drowning of civilians and prisoners of war in the Crimea. Karev declared that since there was un ESC report and Jenicke was responsible for war crimes in the Crimea, there was no need for his testimony. (October Revolution Central State Archives, stock 7445, inv. I, storage unit 358).

9. L. F. Reichman denies his involvement in coaching witnesses for the Nuremberg Trial (see Chapter 3).

10. Neither this camp, nor the other two listed in the "Communication of the Special Commission" ever existed. They are not mentioned in any documents of the Main Administration for Escort Guard Troops of the NKVD of the USSR.

11. Recently, by the way, the Soviet press has reproduced an important captured document referring, in particular, to Col. Bedenck and Maj.-Gen. Oberhäuser (see *Yoyenno-istoricheskiy zhurnal*, Journal of Military History, No. 51989).

12. The reference is probably to Parfen and Axinia Kiselev (see the communication). Among those who, apart from P. G. Kiselev himself, testified before the Burdenko Commission, were his relatives, his wife, his son, Vasily, his daughter-in-law Maria, and also their tenant, Timofei Sergeyev, a road repair worker. *Moscow News* of May 21, 1989, and some Polish sources call Parfen Kiselev Perfeniy Kozlov. Kiselev's testimony figured in the very first German reports about Katyn. The Burdenko Commission's communication presented Kiselev as a peasant who "resided in his own farmstead very close to the Goats' Mountains retreat." Obviously, he could not have had anything like "his own farmstead" in the dispossessed Smolensk countryside; there could have been nobody but foresters living in the woods, (hence the legend about the Vladimir prison, see Chapter 6) or collective farm bee-keepers. Local residents, notably one A. A. Kostyuchenko, remember that there was an apiary in the Goats' Moun-

tains, but there has been no way so far of finding out who kept it.

13. "Depending on the conditions of interment (type of soil etc.) the total decay of soft tissue and skeletization of a corpse take about 3-4 years." (*Forensic Medicine Examination*, Moscow, 1980, p. 158, in Russian).

14. Gerald Reitlinger. *Op. cit.*, p. 312. The allusion is to Thorwald: Thorwald Juergen. *Wen sie verderben wollen. Bericht des grossen Verrats.* Stuttgart, 1952, S. 80. The same subject is dealt with in Alexander Dallin. *German Rule in Russia. 1941-1945. A Study of Occupation Policies.* London, 1957, p. 529, with reference to the archives of the German High Command.

15. The communication of the Special Commission said: "Are there any rumors abroad among the population about Polish prisoners of war having been shot in the Goats' Mountains? (a question to Umnov)." In 1950, G.K. Umnov read the communication of the Burdenko Commission. Commenting on the entry in the notebook, Umnov said: "As I was Smolensk Russian Police Chief in the first months of the German occupation, I never received any orders from the city boss, Menshagin, to investigate the speading of rumors amongst the population about the shootings of Poles by Germans. The entire story about Menshagin's notebook, mentioned in the Soviet communication, seems to me to be a fake. Menshagin had an excellent memory and very seldom took notes. The Bolsheviks could have found his notebook, at both Menshagin's house and the city administration building were burnt down at the time of the German retreat from

Smolensk." (*New Journal,* book 104, New York, 1971, pp. 277-278).

16. This writer has no adequate explanation for Bazilevsky having the layout of the conference hall in his hands. One reason may be that after an incident between Goering and Back-Selewski (Goering called the latter "beast" when he passed the dock) witnesses were escorted into the courtroom so as to prevent them from coming into contact with the defendants, that is, by the door used by the simultaneous translators. In one of the booths for simultaneous translation at the time was Yelizaveta Shchemeleva (Stenina). As she said, before the proceedings began, she had asked her American colleague whether she had received the English text of the Burdenko Commission's communication. The American woman said she had not yet received it. Stahmer happened to be there and overheard this exchange. You can imagine how Yelizaveta Shchemeleva felt as she translated Stahmer's dialogue with Bazilevsky. She still shudders to think of it.

17. There are, however, different accounts, too. One S. Maximov, who participated in a German-sponsored tour, recalls:

"Worn out and crazed by the putrid smell, we trudged along towards our little truck, Bazilevsky, a professor of astronomy from Smolensk, slowly dragged his feet on my right. The professor, like the rest of us, didn't have a shadow of a doubt that the Katyn tragedy was Stalin's handiwork. He said with indignation that Russian history has never known a more dreadful epoch than the epoch of

Bolshevism." (S. Maximov. *I Was in Katyn, Na rubezhe, On the Frontier,* Paris, No. 3-4, 1952, p. 11, in Russian).

18. *Sovetskaya Rossia* of June 21, 1987, unexpectedly shed light on the present scene in Katyn Forest. That was at the height of the campaign against forest cottages. A. Semukov, a reader from Smolensk, mentioned the "fine villa and cottage country retreat in the Goats' Mountains" among private country retreats and hunting-grounds. The acting chairman of the Smolensk Regional Executive Committee, V. Bidnyi, replied in the same issue: "The places A. Semukov writes about will be open to everyone before long." (This was the subject of a comment by G. G. Superfin in *Russkaya Mysl,* Russian thought). I don't know anything about the other places, but the one in the Goats' Mountains is not open as yet.

19. According to a written statement by Yelizaveta Shchemeleva (Stenina), the text of the Burdenko Conmission's communication was translated by Soviet translators.

20. The *Voyenno-istoricheskiy zhurnal, Journal of Military History,* has recently (No. 11-12, 1990) also tried to play the same losing game. The material it published is interesting, incidentally, because it contains documents from the confidential archive inventory of the Special Commission. The publishers, apparently, do not suspect that these texts, because of a mass of minor inconsistencies, again discredit the communication of the Burdenko Commission.

21. Smirnov exaggerates. The Burdenko Commission questioned 56 people.

Notes

Chapter 6
WITNESSES

1. *When It Is the State That Kills*, Progress Publishers, Moscow, 1989.

2. The corpus delicti qualified as "betrayal of one's motherland" (Article 58-1, paragraphs a, b, c, d) was written into the Penal Code of the RSFSR in 1934, " . . . when the term motherland was restored to us . . ." (Solzhenitsyn), in pursuance of the Central Executive Committee's Resolution of June 8, 1934, "On Complementing the Provision Regarding Crimes Against the State (counter-revolutionary offenses and crimes against the order and administration, particularly dangerous to the USSR) with articles concerning the betrayal of one's Homeland." The resolution qualified spying, disclosure of military or official secrets, defection to the enemy, crossing, and flying over the border as betrayal of one's motherland. The punishment stipulated for civilians was 10 years imprisonment, involving the confiscation of all property, if there were extenuating circumstances, or death by a firing squad if there were none, and for servicemen, only death. Adult members of a serviceman's family, if they had known about the betrayal in the making and failed to report it to the authorities, would be jailed for 5 to 10 years, and all their property confiscated, or, if they did not know anything about it, would be deprived of suffrage and deported to the country's distant areas for 5 years (*Izvestia*, 9.6.1934). Later, the code came to be interpreted in a wider sense, and sanctions envisaged for members of servicemen's families

were applied not only to them. Let me remind you that Article 58 was repealed in December 1958 (*Vedomosti Verkhovnogo Soveta SSSR, Gazette of the Supreme Soviet of the USSR,* No. I, 1959).

3. N. Semenov. *The Soviet Court and Punitive Policy.* Munich, 1952, pp. 130-131. (quoted from G. G. Superfin).

4. The Amnesty Edict of 17.9.1955 did not apply to punitive organs, and one of the sources used by Superfin says that those convicted under the Decree of 19.4.1943 were not subject to amnesty at all. (V. S. Klyagin. *Some Questions of the Theory and Practice of Extra Dangerous State Crime Control.* Minsk, 1976, p. 95, in Russian).

5. *The New Times,* No. 16, 1990.

6. Strictly speaking, since extrajudicial institutions have been found to be unconstutional, *all* their rulings must be quashed and cases involving a corpus delicti beyond question retried. Consider what happened to G. G. Yagoda. He is the only one of those shot for their part in the "right-wing Trotskyist bloc" not to have been rehabilitated; this means that the Politburo Commission has acknowledged that the bloc existed and Yagoda was its only member.

7. Vitold Andreyevich Abankin, among other political prisoners, was mentioned in Andrei Sakharov's Nobel Lecture.

8. October Revolution Central State Archives, stock 7445, inv. 2, storage unit 132, pp. 263-264.

9. B.G. Menshagin. *Reminiscences.* Prepared for printing by Alexander Gribanov, Natalia Gorbanevskaya,

Gabriel Superfin. Commentaries by G. Superfin. YMCA-PRESS, Paris, 1989.

10. Soviet Army Central State Archives, stock 40, inv. I, f. 179, pp. 212-213.

11. The inquest led to Menshagin being charged with active involvement in *organizing* a Jewish ghetto, which is not the same thing, of course. Menshagin was away from Smolensk when Jews were shot (early July, 1942).

12. R. I. Pimenov's memoirs *Two Years with Beria's People,* constituting a chapter from the book *One Political Process* have been published under the pen name O. Volin in *Top Secret* (No. 6, 1989). This journal (No. 6, 1990) carried Pimenov's protest against a breach of copyright by the editors.

13. Soon after the verdict was returned, Karavansky called upon the public Prosecutor's Office of the USSR to sue the judge and the prosecutor under criminal law "for covering up the murderous bestial misdeeds of Beria, a foreign intelligence agent."

Appendix I

KATYŃ IN HISTORICAL PERSPECTIVE

A Chronology by Iwo Cyprian Pogonowski

1918-1921 In Poland six border wars were fought against neighboring powers including Soviet Russia. On July 4, 1920 the Soviet armies were ordered to advance "to the west over the corpse of Poland on the road to world-wide communist revolution." Polish victories over the invading Soviet armies in the battles on the River Vistula (Aug. 1920) and on the River Niemen (Sept.-Oct. 1920) ended the border wars and stopped the Soviet march to the west.

March 18, 1921 In Riga, Latvia, the Peace Treaty between Poland, Soviet Russia and Soviet Ukraine was signed. It defined the eastern frontiers of Poland. These frontiers were recognized by the Allies at the Conference of Ambassadors on March 15, 1923, according to the terms of article 83, paragraph 3 of the Versailles Treaty.

Feb. 9, 1929 In Moscow, renunciation of war as an instrument of national policy in form of a Protocol was signed between the USSR and Poland, Romania, Estonia, and Latvia.

March 17, 1930 In Berlin, Commercial Agreement was signed between Germany and Poland ending five years of customs war.

July 25, 1932 In Moscow, the Non-Aggression Pact was signed between Poland and the USSR. Poland promised not to oppose Soviet entry into the League of Nations any longer.

July 3, 1933 In London, the Convention for the Definition of Aggression was signed. Meanwhile the Germans added to their national anthem *Germany above all* the *Horst Wessel Song* on their future conquests including the words: "and tomorrow the whole world."

Jan. 26, 1934 In Berlin, the Non-Aggression Pact was signed between Germany and Poland.

May 5, 1934 In Moscow, the Protocol was signed between Poland and the USSR, extending until December 31, 1945 the Non-Aggression Pact of 1932.

March 10, 1939 Stalin's speech to the 18th convention of the Soviet Communist Party was broadcast on Moscow radio. Stalin accused Great Britain and France of trying to foment German and Japanese attacks on the Soviet Union in order to eventually dictate their terms to the exhausted belligerent. Stalin then suggested the possibility of cooperation between National Socialist Germany and the Soviet Union. This offer provided the Germans with the possibility of buying time by pretending to accept a permanent rapprochement with the Soviets.

An additional freedom to manoeuvre was important for Germany because Poland defended her sovereignty and refused to join Germany against the Soviet Union. By doing so, Poland deprived the Berlin government of the 40 to 50 well trained Polish divisions. Polish forces could have made up the deficiency in German manpower and, together with 100 German divisions, could have been used in a decisive attack on Russia. The Soviet Union was the main target of the planned conquest of Slavic lands in order to create a new Germany "for the next 1000 years." and thereby fulfill the doctrine of Lebensraum (or the future German "living space"). When Poland refused to submit to either the German Nazis or the Soviets, the Berlin government gambled on a fake rapprochement with Moscow, while both the Soviet Union and Germany wanted to eliminate the Polish State starting with its leadership. For the Soviets Polish leaders and state administration were "class enemies" while the Germans considered the Poles to be an "enemy race."

March 15, 1939 Firming up of British resolve not to allow a new Munich - also a widespread conviction that the Poles definitely would fight for their independence and that Polish leaders would not consider submission to Germany as an acceptable alternative. At the same time the German public was all out to fight Poland but was scared to fight Great Britain and France. It remembered the defeat in the first world war. However, the extraordinary support of the German people for Hitler was growing. They placed him in position to make key decisions alone and they were ready to carry out those decisions.

March 28, 1939 Poland's foreign minister, Józef Beck (1894-1944), stated in Warsaw that any change in the status of the free city of Gdańsk-Danzig would be an aggression against Poland. Commander-in-Chief of the Polish Army, Marshal Edward Śmigly-Rydz (1886-1941), ordered mobilization in Poland.

March 31, 1939 British Prime Minister Neville Chamberlain (1869-1940) stated in Parliament in London, after consultation with French Prime Minister Edouard Daladier (1884-1970), that Great Britain and France would fight on the side of Poland if the Polish government had to use its armed forces to defend its independence or its vital interests.

April 6, 1939 Common-defense treaty was signed in London by Great Britain, France, and Poland.

April 11, 1939 In Berlin Chancellor Hitler signed the White Plan (Fall Weiss) ordering preparations for a German attack on Poland on Sept. 1, 1939.

April 28, 1939 Germany declared its non-aggression pact with Poland null and void, after assurances of the Soviet ambassador in Berlin on April 17, 1939 that "there is no reason why the relations between Soviet Union and Germany could not keep on improving very much."

May 5, 1939 Poland rejected the German demand for a right-of-way through Polish Pomerania to East Prussia and the annexation of the free city of Gdańsk-Danzig, as a prelude to conversion of Poland into a German protectorate, and subordination of the Polish armed forces to Germany within an anti-Soviet military pact. Poland's foreign minister, Józef Beck, stated that "the Poles will not accept peace at any price." Beck confronted the German government with the fact that an attack on Poland would start World War II, and lead to an eventual German defeat.

Marshal Śmigły-Rydz felt that a Soviet attack on Poland was a strong possibility if a war was started by Germany. Polish mobilization eventually included 1,500,000 men of which 1,200,000 reached their units, and 900,000 eventually took part in the defensive battle of Poland in Sept.-Oct. 1939.

May 7, 1939 The French ambassador in Berlin reported that Germany needed Soviet help to attack and partition Poland.

May 17, 1939 The Soviet embassy in Berlin announced that there was no conflict between USSR and Germany and that the Soviet Union does not intend to enter into any new pact with the West. The German press stopped all attacks on the USSR.

May 27, 1939 Japan, alarmed by the German-Soviet rapprochement, notified the Berlin government that it does not want to be involved in the oncoming European war.

July 25, 1939 Poland gave to Great Britain and France each a copy of the deciphering electro-mechanical digital computer, complete with specifications, perforated cards and updating procedures for reading German military code *Enigma*. Breaking the *Enigma* code was one of the most important Polish contributions to the victory over Germany in WWII - it made possible the British *Ultra*.

Linguists, mathematicians, and engineers of the University of Poznań, working on a contract with the Intelligence Section II of the Polish General Staff, broke the *Enigma* code system in 1932-33 and developed an electro-mechanical deciphering digital computer for decoding of it. The Polish computer became operational in 1938. It appears to have been the world's first digital computer. It predated by six years the first American digital computer *Mark I* built in 1944 by Howard Aiken of Harvard University.

Aug. 14, 1939 The Soviet Union demanded an agreement for the Red Army to enter Poland and Romania. Polish foreign minister Józef Beck rejected the Soviet demand because such an agreement would lead to partition of Poland by Germany and the USSR as there was no guarantee that the entering Red Army would fight against the German aggression on the side of the Poles.

Aug. 22, 1939 Public announcement of next day arrival in Moscow of German foreign minister Joachim von Ribbentrop (1893-1945) to sign a nonaggression pact with Soviet Union valid for ten years. The pact was to encourage a German attack on Poland and therefore it did not include the clause used in all previous non-aggression pacts signed by the Soviet Union, which stated that the treaty would be invalid if either party attacked a third power.

The Soviets were soon to participate in the (fourth) partition of Poland and hoped for a long war of attrition on Germany's western front, as Great Britain and France would declare war on Germany in fulfillment of their common-defense treaty with Poland. The Soviet Union wanted to stay out of the conflict while capitalist nations of Europe would fight among themselves.

Appendix I

Aug. 22, 1939 In a secret speech Hitler referred to the imminent conquest and colonization of Poland and ordered his military commanders to use the utmost ferocity against both Polish armed forces and Polish civilians.

Aug. 23, 1939 In Moscow the German-Soviet Nonaggression Pact was signed for the purpose of bringing about the partition of Poland by the two signatories. At this point in time the Soviets have accomplished a number of their goals. They caused the Germans to betray Japan with whom Germany signed the Anti-Cominform Pact on Nov. 25, 1936. Thus, the Japanese military offensive against the USSR, then in progress, was derailed and the Japanese had to negotiate an armistice with the Soviets. Successful operations of the Red Army against the Japanese seemed to indicate that the damage done by massive purges of Soviet officer corps was healing. However, the Soviet government felt that it needed two more years to bring its armed forces to an adequate level of strength to embark on the campaign for world domination.

The German attack on Poland meant the beginning of the second world war because Poland, France, and Great Britain were members of a common defense alliance. The USSR unleashed Germany on France, Great Britain, and Poland to bring about a long war of attrition in western Europe after the certain defeat of the Polish army by a joint German and Soviet attack.

The pact with Germany was strengthening the Soviet position to negotiate for conclusion of an armistice with Japan and thereby to end the military confrontation, which Japan started in 1938. The Japanese, who signed with Germans the Anti-Cominform Pact in Nov. 1936, now were betrayed by Germany.

In the Far East the Soviet disengagement from hostilities against Japan was to deflect the Japanese forces towards aggression against the United States and European colonies in Asia and produce a war of attrition in the Pacific basin, while Germany was to fight a war of attrition in the Atlantic basin. Moscow hoped to sit out both of these wars until it would become the most powerful country on the globe. It is important to note that the Soviets postponed their attack on Poland until their armistice negotiations with Japan were successfully concluded.

The Soviets were anxious to get Germany entangled into a war of attrition as soon as possible. Moscow was aware that the Germans were discouraged by simultaneous difficulties with the Japanese, also because of the conflicting German ties to both China and Japan. (Stalin's disastrous miscalculation became apparent with the collapse of France in 1940, which freed the Germans to implement the doctrine of Lebensraum and attack the Soviet Union.)

Aug. 25, 1939 In response to the German-Soviet pact of Aug. 23, the government of Great Britain clarified and confirmed its commitment to the treaty of common defense with Poland and the inviolability of Polish borders.

Fall 1939 - Winter 1941 It was the high tide of German conquests in Europe. Germany, however, was completing the destruction of European power basis for the control of the globe. This process began with the first world war.

Berlin cherished the vain hope that German minorities in the conquered lands would replace casualties and add men for new divisions. In reality from 1941 Germany was short of 1,000,000 men per year for the rest of the war.

Appendix I

A severe problem for German armaments was inadequate transportation. Germany had too few personnel carriers, so that her infantry could not keep up with tanks. Also most German transport had to be based on horses, which perished in World War II in greater numbers than ever before in history.

Manpower shortage resulted in massive use of slave labor imported to Germany from occupied lands, especially from Poland and the USSR. These people were permanently prohibited from cultural Germanization and were destined for slave labor and eventual extermination.

Sept. 1, 1939 World War II started with the German attack on Poland. Mass killings of over six million Polish citizens began - almost half of them Jews.

Sept. 5, 1939 The German army (the Wehrmacht) conducted mass murders of 20,000 Poles in Bydgoszcz in Gdańsk Pomerania, where by 1945 over 50,000 Polish Catholics had been killed. In western Polish provinces the Germans started executing Poles immediately, using lists prepared well in advance.

With the events in Bydgoszcz the Germans initiated a new and total type of modern warfare. It took the form of a wholesale slaughter of the Polish civilian population, and especially the cultural elite, before German genocide of European Jews began.

Sept. 15, 1939 An armistice was signed between the Soviet Union and Japan. It was followed the next day by the Soviet government's order to the Red Army to attack Poland after Soviet Union was disengaged in the Far East.

Sept. 16, 1939 In Moscow the order was issued to the Soviet armed forces of about one million men to attack Poland along the one thousand kilometer long Polish-Soviet frontier.

Sept. 17, 1939 The Soviet Union invaded Poland using "hyena" tactics, stabbing the Polish army in the back. The Soviet government saw the attack on Poland as the beginning move on the road to the communist world domination.

At the same time the tempo of the German offensive markedly slowed down. The Germans were running out of ammunition, their cracked units were decimated and exhausted, while they lost about one-third of all tanks used in the invasion of Poland. The Poles still had some 26 full strength divisions and were locked in twenty five major battles, which were not going well for the Germans. Had the Red Army not invaded Poland at that time, the Polish-German war could have dragged on for several more weeks, as the Polish defense lines became shorter and the German striking capability was weakening.

Sovietization of occupied Poland was the main aim of the Soviets and according to it they conducted their extermination and exploitation programs. Soviet use of universal socialist slogans and subversion helped them to penetrate Polish society much more effectively than could the primitive ethno-centric German propaganda. The Soviets were by far more systematic than the Germans in collecting information on each individual in the newly occupied territory.

An immediate equalization of the value of Soviet rubles with Polish currency resulted in the wholesale robbery of goods in the hands of Polish citizens and institutions. Hospitals, electric power plants, power lines, apartments, private homes and businesses were stripped and their contents shipped to the

369

Soviet Union by trucks and by railroad. Poland, with her relatively low stand-ard of living, in comparison with western Europe, appeared to the newly arriving Soviet people, to be an extraordinary land of plenty.

Sept. 28, 1939 Conclusion of the Boundary and Friendship Treaty between governments of Germany and the Soviet Union included an agreement on a common program to exterminate Poland's intellectual elite and leadership com-munity as dangerous to both signatories.

The treaty contained secret provisions for a coordinated program of preven-tive measures for the mutual extermination of potential Polish opponents of both regimes. Germany and the Soviet Union were to take all necessary measures to contain and prevent any hostile action directed against the territory of the other partner. They committed themselves to crush any agitation within their part of occupied Poland and inform each other of means employed to achieve this goal.

A joint Soviet-German victory parade took place in Brześć (Brest Li-tovsk) on the Bug. A close cooperation of German Gestapo with the Soviet NKVD began. Zakopane and Cracow were frequently used till June 1941 as meeting places to coordinate German and Soviet extermination programs directed against Poles. (See Nov. 14, 1940 visit of Molotov to Berlin, p. 376-7.)

Oct. 3, 1939 In Moscow, the head of NKVD, Lavrenti Beria, assisted by his deputy Vsevolod Merkulov, started to prepare the largest execution of prisoners of war during the second world war. For this purpose Beria ordered the selec-tion of officers from the quarter of a million Polish prisoners of war in Soviet hands. After an authorization by the Central Committee led by Joseph Stalin, Beria issued order no. 4441/b on the handling of Polish prisoners of war:

"Until special orders are issued the camp in Kozielsk is to contain prisoners of war who were born in the area of German occupation of Poland. [Eventual-ly, the camp in Kozielsk contained Polish prisoners of war separated into two groups according to their birth place either in the Soviet or in the German zone of occupation of Poland.]

"The camp in Starobielsk is to contain Polish army generals, officers, high ranking administrative officers, both military and state.

"The camp in Ostashkov is to contain officers of Polish intelligence, counter-intelligence, prison administration and police officers...

"The commandants of all NKVD prisoner-of-war camps are to check thor-oughly the identity of each individual prisoner. The selection process is to be completed by Oct. 8, 1939..."

Each of the thousands of selected Polish officers was presented with a self-incriminating questionnaire which was to document that the Poles were enemies of the Soviet state. Each man was individually interrogated by NKVD officers and each individual dossier was presented to the NKVD headquarters. Eventual-ly, the dossier of each man included such items as:

    a. confiscated personal documents taken from the prisoner
    b. biographic notes on prisoner's past
    c. photographs
    d. official reports of the interrogations
    e. testimony of fellow prisoners
    f. reports and evaluation of NKVD camp authorities
    g. fingerprints

Appendix I

h. copies of each prisoners correspondence and letters detained by the NKVD censor. (This correspondence was used by the NKVD to locate, arrest, and deport to Khazakstan the families of the prisoners on Apr. 13, 1940.) Nearly 15,000 Polish officers (among them hundreds of doctors of medicine) held as Soviet prisoners of war were given a death sentence in absentia, without any attorneys present during the NKVD "court" proceedings. Paragraph 58 of the penal code of the Soviet Socialist Federated Russian Republic prescribed the death penalty for class enemies and counter-revolutionaries. It dealt with the enemies of the Soviet state and was used as the "legal basis" for the largest execution of prisoners-of-war during World War II. The NKVD special court, or *Osoboye Sovyeshchanye*, was also known as the *NKVD Troyka*. On all administrative levels the Troyka consisted of the local head of NKVD, the secretary of the communist party cell within the local NKVD, and of an other local officer of the NKVD, who served as an accuser. This administrative NKVD court obviously violated international conventions on prisoners of war (that of the Hague and of the League of Nations).

Apparently, there was some German participation in bringing Polish officers to the three POW camps mentioned by Beria.

Oct. 3, 1939 In Berlin, German government appealed for peace with Great Britain and France. Both of these countries rejected the German appeal two days later on October 5, 1939.

Oct. 31, 1939 In Moscow, Vyacheslav M. Molotov (Skryabin, 1890-1982), Commissar of Foreign Affairs, admitted openly in his speech to the Supreme Soviet that the military defeat of Poland was brought about by the attacks of German and Soviet armies.

Jan. 25, 1940 SS-Reichsfuhrer Heinrich Himmler selected Auschwitz, in southwestern Poland (newly annexed by Germany), as the site for a new concentration camp for Poles to be processed in accordance with the German-Soviet pact of Sept. 28, 1939. During World War II, German concentration camps became sites for mass extermination of prisoners, either gradually, by hard work on a starvation diet, or immediately, by execution by gassing or shooting.

Auschwitz originally was designed for the extermination of Poles and other Slavs at a rate of up to 5,000,000 per year. It was a major railroad junction centrally located in German-controlled Europe. It also was in proximity of major coal fields. Coal was a convenient fuel for the cremation of large number of bodies.

Feb. 10, 1940 Deportation from the annexed Polish provinces to the Soviet Union started with 220,000 former Polish officials and their families, then followed on April 13, 1940 by deportation of 325,000 relatives of previously deported or captured men, then followed in June, 1940 by deportation of 300,000 and then in June-July by deportation of 240,000 war refugees from western Poland.

Soviet deportation, internment, and resettlement programs during the second world war involved an estimated two million Polish citizens. Among first 1,140,000 civilian deportees taken from areas annexed by the Soviets, there were: 703,000 Poles, 217,000 Ukrainians, 83,000 Jews, 56,000 Byelorussians,

Appendix I

35,000 Polesians, and 20,000 Russians and Lithuanians; of the 336,000 Polish citizens, refugees from German occupied central and western Poland, 198,000 were classified by the Soviets as Jews and the remaining 138,000 as Poles.

Soviet authorities also deported about 210,000 Polish citizens in 1940-1941 after declaring them citizens of the USSR and drafting them into the Red Army. 250,000 Polish citizens were arrested individually in 1939-1941 and deported to prisons and labor camps in the Soviet Union, which then contained a total of 440,000 Polish citizens. About 240,000 deportees were children below fourteen years of age.

The Soviets acknowledged taking 181,000 Polish prisoners of war in 1939 and in 1940 deporting an additional 12,000 Polish prisoners of war who had been interned since 1939 in Lithuania - these figures are considered too low and the actual number of Polish prisoners of war deported to the USSR is estimated to be close to 300,000. Additional tens of thousands Poles were arrested and deported to the Soviet Union in 1944. As late as 1945, 9,877 Polish coal miners were deported from Silesia to the USSR.

It is estimated that by October 1, 1942 some 900,000 of the deportees, including 50,000 children, were dead. Over 2,500 books, publications, and articles were printed in Poland and abroad after the war on the subject of deportations of Polish citizens to the Soviet Union during 1939-1945.

Feb. 12, 1940 Headquarters of the NKVD ordered the liquidation of three prisoner of war camps in Kozielsk, Ostashkov, and Starobielsk. It was a decision which complied with the joint German-Soviet program of Sept. 28, 1939 to liquidate the Polish resistance, intellectual elite, and members of Polish leadership community. The liquidation of Polish officers became the largest execution of prisoners of war during World War II (1939-1945).

Prior to the execution, German representatives interviewed Polish officers of German descent and took twelve of them out of the Soviet POW camp in Kozielsk in exchange for their acceptance of German citizenship. Those officers of German descent who refused or were not classified as racial Germans were left to be executed. By June 6, 1940, the execution of 15,000 Polish officers (mostly reservists and college graduates) was reported by the NKVD as completed.

The Soviet report for the first quarter of 1940 by Major P. Soprunienko, the chief of NKVD administration of POW camps, listed imprisoned officers of Polish armed forces: one admiral, 12 generals, 82 colonels, 200 lieutenant colonels, 555 majors, 1507 captains, 13 navy captains, 2 commodores, 3 lieutenant commodores, 6049 lieutenants, second lieutenants, and ensigns. (Intelligence, police, and administrative officers were not included.)

4,443 officers from the camp in Kozielsk were murdered. (In 1943 the German Commission reported 4,143 bodies, while the Polish Red Cross Commission reported 4,243, plus 200 in partially excavated grave number 8.) They were buried in the Katyń Forest on the upper Dnieper River (near the Smolensk-Vitebsk Highway) between March 1, and May 3, 1940 under the supervision of the regional command of NKVD in Mińsk, Byelorussia. The 190th infantry regiment provided escort guard for the execution at Katyń (near the NKVD rest home). 262 of the victims buried in Katyń graves were Jews. Of the 15,000 Polish officers executed by Soviet security forces about 700 were Jews. (The chief rabbi of the Polish army, Major Baruch Steinberg (1897-

Appendix I

1940), a few Lutheran pastors, and a large number of Catholic priests were among the chaplains of the Polish armed forces executed by the NKVD on Dec. 24, 1939.)

The evidence, in the form of diaries and Red Cross forensic medicine reports, indicates that a vast majority of the victims were systematically murdered in Katyń at the grave site. A smaller number of Polish officers executed elsewhere were probably brought to Katyń graves by lorries. Most of the victims were handled in the following manner:

1. Polish officers and prisoners of war were searched and then driven in vans from the camp at Kozielsk to a railroad station. Immediately they realized that their new guards were grim and very brutal men -- much more so than the Soviet guards were so far.

2. The prisoners were loaded into a special prison train. Each prison car, called "Stolypinka" (after tsarist minister of interior and head of government Piotr A. Stolypin), was divided into compartments for six to eight people. These compartments were crowded with up to sixteen Polish officers.

3. The prisoners spent one or two nights in the prison train.

4. Most of the hungry and dehydrated prisoners arrived at the Gnezdovo (in Polish Gniezdowo) railroad station near Katyń. All prison trains passed through Smolensk and some of the prisoners might have been unloaded there and executed in the local NKVD headquarters in the execution chamber.

5. Upon arrival in Gnezdovo the prisoners were gradually transferred to a passenger bus with its windows smeared with cement. They were transported directly to the grave site at Katyń. During the transfer the railroad station was encircled by a large number of NKVD soldiers supervised by a Colonel of the NKVD.

6. In groups of thirty, Polish officers were made to file through the rear door of the bus, passing between NKVD soldiers standing with bayonets on the ready.

7. Each man was pressed into a small and very tight cubicle. (There were 15 cubicles on each side of a central corridor of the bus. It was returning to the train at half hour intervals.)

8. Hunched in a cramped position, the victims, in batches of thirty, were driven to the execution site.

9. Upon arrival to the grave site in Katyń, one at a time, the victims were ordered out of the cubicles. Each prisoner was directed towards the rear door of the bus.

10. Apparently at the exit door two NKVD men grabbed each prisoner by his arms. They quickly determined whether to tie his hands and put a choke knot on his neck or whether just to control him with the grip of their own hands while leading him directly to the nearby grave. Polish officers who were still strong enough to struggle were attacked by additional NKVD men. Some suffered crushed skulls, many had their overcoats tied around their heads, some were gagged by stuffing sawdust into their mouths. A number had their elbows tied tightly together behind their backs. Very many were stabbed with four-cornered Soviet bayonets.

All rope used by the NKVD at Katyń was manufactured in the Soviet Union and pre-cut to the same length. It was secured with metal clasps while the victim was held down. Some of the victims were searched and robbed of watches, rings, etc.

373

11. At the grave site each victim was apparently held by two men. A third NKVD agent, a skilled executioner, shot him from the back, at the base of his skull to produce minimum bleeding. The exit holes of most of the bullets were in the forehead of the victims. Uniformity of the fatal wounds inflicted on Polish officers indicated long experience of the executioners (usually trained with the help of doctors in the service of the NKVD).

In Katyń, the NKVD executioners were armed with German "Walther" 7.65 millimeter pistols and used German ammunition manufactured by "Geco." These pistols (known for a very small recoil and therefore were not tiring executioner's hand) were reloaded very quickly -- much more conveniently than Russian pistols and revolvers (all of which produced a heavy recoil). Among hundreds of 7.65 mm shells and bullets found at Katyń, there was a small number of 6.35 millimeter shells, made by the same German manufacturer.

12. Most of the victims were stacked in layers inside a large "L" shaped grave. There is evidence that bodies of men murdered in execution chambers were dumped from the trucks in a very disorderly manner.

13. Bodies of the victims were covered with dirt. Pine trees were planted on the mass graves. Some of the remain of the Polish officers ended up under an asphalt road built later.

The mass murder of the 3920 Polish officers held in Starobielsk was conducted under the supervision of the regional command of NKVD in Kharkov, Ukraine. As indicated by the very precise location of bullets a part of the victims was killed inside execution chambers in Kharkov while the rest were murdered at the grave site at Piatikhatki. Multiple wounds were inflicted at the grave site. Many skulls were penetrated by several bullets. Some had bullets wounds in the legs and other parts of the body as a result of a last minute struggle. The graves at Piatikhatki appear to have been dug and later covered by hand. If and when the exhumations will be completed the final forensic report will be prepared.

The 68th Ukrainian infantry regiment provided escort guards for the execution of Polish prisoners held in the camp of Starobielsk. Men murdered in the Kharkov prison and at the grave site were buried near the village of Piatikhatki. Today, the mass graves of Polish officers are within the 6th quadrant of parks and woods encircling the city of Kharkov, some 8 kilometers from the center.

Between six and seven thousand Polish officers imprisoned in the camp at Ostashkov were executed inside a special NKVD building, within special soundproof enclosures equipped with floor gutters for draining the blood. The execution was described in 1991 by the head of NKVD in Kalinin, Vladimir Tokarev. The chief executioner, mjr. Blokhin brought from Moscow German Walther pistols and ammunition in suitcases. He was helped by executioners named Krivienko and Semyanikov. The initial transport of 390 Poles was too large for one night killing. Blokhin decided that 250 executions per night was feasible. During the execution Blokhin had his hand massaged to relieve the stress of shooting. As in other NKVD executions Walther pistols were used to minimize recoil and overheating as well as to provide for very quick re-loading. Apparently all of the Poles held in Ostashkov were murdered inside the execution chamber in Kalinin (Tver).

The Ostashkov camp was actually located on the nearby lake island of Stolbnyj. Apparently the mass murder of all of the Polish officers held there

Appendix I

was conducted in Kalinin (now Tver) in the NKVD building (which now houses a medical academy). The execution chamber was padded for sound-proofing. A noisy ventilation electric fans muffled out the sounds of shots fired by the executioner. (During executions the Soviets often used the roar of truck engines run without mufflers.)

Each victim was asked, before entering the execution chamber, the year of his birth, his name and his father's Christian name. At that point the victim was shackled. Immediately upon victim's entry through the padded door the executioner fired his pistol. He aimed into the back of victim's head. In one study of 243 skulls 160 bullets entered precisely the occiput. Practically all other bullets penetrated the first or the second vertebrae. A few skulls indicated that the victim turned his head in the last moment.

Immediately after the executioner shot his pistol the victim's collar was pulled up to absorb the bleeding and victim's body was moved through an exit to the waiting fleet of trucks. After each night of killing the convoy of trucks was formed. The trucks loaded overnight with corpses proceeded to the grave site where the bodies of the murdered Polish officers were dumped in a disorderly fashion into the waiting grave at Myednoye. An earth moving machine was used there to dig the graves and later to cover them with dirt.

The 129th infantry regiment based in Vyelke Luki provided escort guards for the transport from Ostashkov and the execution in Kalinin (now Tver) under the regional command of the NKVD in Smoleńsk. The bodies of Polish officers were transported to Myednoye (near Kalinin, now Tver, 90 miles north of Moscow, on the Moscow-Leningrad highway). The NKVD built its resort in Myednoye and placed the watchman's house and a large latrine on the grave site. The rest of the grave site was covered with pine growth.

Deputy Minister of the Interior and a member of the Central Committee of the Communist party of USSR, Vsevolod Nikolayevich Merkulov was in charge of the entire operation of murdering Polish officers described above. For his performance in the execution of Polish officers Merkulov was awarded Order of Lenin on 27th of April of 1940. His entire team of 140 NKVD executioners (including truck drivers who transported the dead bodies of Polish officers) were awarded bonuses of money, advancement in rank and military decorations. Eventually, most of the executioners were sent to the front, many ended in psychiatric hospitals; some, including mjr. Blokhin, committed suicide.

The NKVD of Mińsk, Smoleńsk, and Kharkov had conducted mass murders since the civil war and Bolshevik revolution and developed skilled teams of executioners known for their cruelty and brutality. The total of 828,000 individual executions by Soviet security forces was admitted in Aug. 1992.

May 1940 Beginning of the "Aktion AB" (Auserordentliche Befriedungsaktion), the "extraordinary pacification program," was ordered by Himmler. It was a grand design to exterminate Polish intelligentsia, "the spiritual and political leaders of the Polish resistance movement" within German occupied Poland. This program, which involved an immediate arrest of 20,000 Polish professionals, was coordinated with similar operations within the Polish territory occupied by the Soviets. The immediate purpose was to contain and prevent the emergence of any hostile campaign directed against the territory of the other side.

375

Appendix I

June 14, 1940 Arrival at Auschwitz of the first 728 Polish prisoners - the official beginning of the extermination program in the camp. For the next 21 months Auschwitz was to be inhabited almost exclusively by Poles.

Oct. 1940 In Moscow, the government of the USSR was shocked by the collapse of France, which ended the hope of the Soviet Union of a protracted and continuous war of attrition on German western front. The unleashing of Germany on Great Britain, France, and Poland in 1939 became a most dangerous Soviet miscalculation.

The government of the Soviet Union decided to prepare for re-organization of Polish armed forces on its territory. A few Polish officers of the general staff, still surviving in the Soviet captivity, were brought to Moscow for talks with the Minister of Interior Affairs and head of the NKVD, Lavrenty Beria and his deputy Vsevolod Merkulov. Col. Zygmunt Berling was the senior among the Polish officers (he was known for his leftist leanings). Col. Berling demanded that all Polish prisoners of war in the USSR, of all political persuasions, be released to serve in the reorganized Polish army.

When Beria and Merkulov agreed, Col. Berling demanded an immediate release of the Polish officers held in the prisoner of war camps in Starobielsk and Kozielsk. Col. Berling stated that these officers would make excellent leaders in the reorganized Polish army. In the heat of the conversation, Merkulov said inadvertently, *no, not them. We made with them a major blunder.* ("Mi sdyewalee s neemee bolshoyoo oshibkoo.")

Nov. 14, 1940 The Soviet newspaper *Pravda* reported the official news of Molotov's visit to Berlin. His delegation included Deputy Minister of Internal Affairs Vsevolod Nikolayevich Merkulov, who was the deputy to the Minister of Internal Affairs and Head of the NKVD, Lavrenty Beria (1899-1953). Merkulov and his retinue were never officially identified. German welcoming party included Heinrich Himmler (1900-1945), Beria's counter part. Merkulov and Himmler met to inform each other about the progress made by German and Soviet governments in their joint program to destroy Polish leadership community as agreed in the secret clauses attached to the Treaty on Boundary and Friendship concluded by the Soviet Union and Germany on Sept., 28, 1939. Himmler's deputy Deluge was included in the German party which saw Molotov and his retinue off.

Molotov's visit to Berlin was not a success. Soviet demands for greater influence in the Balkans, especially in Bulgaria and Yugoslavia, were rejected by the Germans. While the Soviets had been making deliveries of oil, grain, and rough materials to Germany on schedule, the German side was defaulting on its commercial commitments. Most annoying to the Soviets was the steady increase in the number of German forces in occupied Poland as well as a recent tenfold increase of German overflights over the Soviet territory. The German excuse was that their troops were shifted to Poland for training purposes as far as possible from Great Britain.

The one bright spot in German-Soviet relations was the cooperation between the Gestapo and the NKVD. The German side had made progress in its Aktion AB (the extraordinary pacification of Poland) and opened the Auschwitz concentration camp for liquidation of Polish leadership community, while the Soviets completed the largest in history execution of officers prisoners of

376

war. By the end of July 1940 the Soviets completed the massive deportation of Polish officials, their families, and other "class enemies."

Within the framework of the German-Soviet Population Exchange Commissions there was a close cooperation between the Gestapo and the NKVD. Regular meetings were held at various localities controlled by the Soviets and by the Germans. German transports with Polish prisoners were arriving inside Soviet territory. While travelling in Soviet controlled areas, the representatives of the Gestapo tried to retrieve some Polish officers whom they classified as "racial Germans," or *Volksdeutsche*. Generally, Germans were familiar with the Soviet extermination procedures. German aerial war-time photos included the location of Katyń long before the announcement by the Berlin government that grave sites have been found there.

Dec. 18, 1940 In Berlin, completion of final plans of the German invasion of the USSR under the code name *Barbarossa*. The surprise attack was to be led by the German army helped by the armies of Finland, Romania, and Hungary in the direction of Leningrad, Moscow, and Donbas. The invasion of the USSR started on June 22, 1941 and ended in the collapse of Germany on May 9, 1945.

July 30, 1941 In Moscow signing of the re-establishment of diplomatic relations between Poland and the USSR by Gen. W. Sikorski and J.W. Stalin. Polish representatives inquired in vain about the missing officers who were imprisoned by the Soviets in Kozielsk, Starobielsk, Ostashkov, and other locations. Agreement was made to form a Polish army in the USSR. In 1942 about 80,000 Poles, mostly soldiers, were evacuated from the USSR through Iran to the Middle East as Polish-Soviet relations deteriorated.

Nov. 23, 1942 In Cairo, Egypt, the U.S. liaison officer to Polish army, Lt. Col. Henry I. Szymanski, reported to the U.S. government on the devastating results that Soviet exile had had on the Poles; Gen. Strong of army G-2 warned him to "avoid political involvement" -- Szymanski's report was suppressed.

Feb. 4, 1943 Germans were defeated at Stalingrad.

By the end of February 1943 the 537th German Signal Regiment reported finding mass graves of Polish officers. German authorities were informed by the Soviets about the execution of 15,000 Polish officers already in 1940. However, they did not know the precise location of the mass graves. Once Katyn graves were located the Germans were ready to proceed with exhumations and an international investigation for the purpose of driving a wedge between western allies and the Soviet Union. This operations were to end with the re-burial of the bodies of the Polish victims. (see Chapter 4, page 197)

April 11, 1943 In the Warsaw airport, a German plane was loaded with representatives of the Polish Red Cross for an inspection trip to the grave sites at Katyń. The Germans were prevented by the USSR from obtaining an investigation of Katyń graves by the International Red Cross. They therefore gathered an international medical commission composed of distinguished professors of forensic medicine from the following countries (without the participation of German doctors):

377

Appendix I

1. Belgium, Speelers, M.D., Ophthalmology, Gent University.
2. Bulgaria, Markov, M.D., Forensic Medicine, Sofia University.
3. Croatia, Miloslavich, M.D., Forensic Medicine, Zagreb Univ.
4. Czechia, Hajek, M.D., Forensic Medicine, Prague University.
5. Denmark, Tramsen, M.D., Forensic Institute, Copenhagen.
6. Finland, Saxen, M.D., Pathological Anatomy, Helsinki Univ.
7. Holland, De Burlet, M.D., Anatomy, Groningen University.
8. Hungary, Orsos, M.D., Forensic Medicine, Budapest University.
9. Italy, Palmieri, M.D., Forensic Medicine, Naples University.
10. Rumania, Birkle, M.D., Forensic Medicine, Ministry of Justice.
11. Slovakia, Subik, M.D., Pathological Anatomy, Bratislava Univ.
12. Switzerland, Naville, M.D. Forensic Medicine, Geneva Univ.
13. France, Costedoat, Medical Inspector, the official representative of the French Vichy Government, to Katyn examinations.
14. Germany, the exhumation work at Katyn was entrusted by the German High Command to Buhtz, M.D. Forensic Medicine and Criminology at Breslau (Wrocław) University, Silesia.

The International Medical Commission limited itself to:
1. Identification of bodies.
2. Ascertaining the cause of death.
3. Establishing the date at which death occurred.

Thus began the most timely and extensive scientific investigation of the mass murder of any of the 15,000 Polish officers.

April 13, 1943 German government radio announced finding the Katyń graves of Polish officers. Germans claimed that the Soviet Union, allied with the United States and Great Britain, murdered nearly half of all the army officers of Poland, which was an other member of the anti-German alliance. Even though the Soviets murdered Polish officers while allied and cooperating with Germany in 1940, now the Germans tried to use this Soviet crime to split the allies. Berlin's revelations about the graves at Katyn were used primarily to foment disunity among the allies.

April 14 to Aug. 4, 1943 In occupied Poland, German press and radio gave most of its attention to the Katyń massacre. German propaganda claimed that the mass murders of Polish officers were committed by Jewish agents of the NKVD. For example, the Soviet state security major Leonid Fedorovich Raikhman was identified as a Jew. He was decorated on Apr. 27, 1940 for his part in the murders of Polish officers. (Raikhman died on March 16, 1990 as a general in the NKVD-KGB since 1945.) The Germans blamed Jewish Commissars for the Katyń murders and claimed that Soviet Marshal Lavrenti P. Beria, who was in charge of the NKVD, was Jewish because allegedly he had a Jewish mother.

April 26, 1943 The Soviet Union broke diplomatic relations with the Polish Government-in-Exile under the pretext that the Poles refused to accept Soviet (false) claims that the Germans murdered Polish officers at Katyń. The Soviets cynically claimed that in this matter the Poles collaborated with the Germans and thus betrayed the anti-German alliance. Moscow complained that the Poles did not address pertinent questions about the Katyń murders directly to the Soviet

378

Appendix I

government and therefore insulted it. Thus, the Soviets not only committed the mass murder of 15,000 Polish officers, but also used the murder itself as a political weapon to gradually deprive Poland of independence.

Immediately, they succeeded in weakening the Polish position with the western allies despite the fact that allied governments in London and Washington were aware that the Soviets, and not the Germans, had committed the Katyń massacre and other mass murders of Polish citizens in Soviet held territory in 1939-1941. At this stage of the war London and Washington were willing to betray Poland rather than to antagonize the Soviets. Moscow wanted to have diplomatic relations with a new government of Poland which would be fully controlled by the Soviets.

April 30, 1943 In Katyń, 982 bodies had been exhumed, of these, about 70% were identified. Seven mass graves have been excavated. The largest, "L" shaped, contained stacked bodies of about 2,500 officers. All examined bodies were systematically laid face down and had the bullet entry at the nape of the neck and the exit in the forehead, generally, on the line of hair growth. The forensic study of the Katyń graves by the twelve renown scientists was the most thorough and reliable ever -- it never could be repeated.

May 3, 1943 In Katyń, twelve physicians, members of the International Medical Commission, published their signed report and stated in it that the Polish officers were murdered in the Spring of 1940.

May 13, 1943 Two American officers, prisoners of war, Lt. Col. John Van Vliet and Cpt. D.B. Stewart examined the Katyń graves.

July 4, 1943 Near Gibraltar, General Władysław Sikorski, Prime Minister of Poland and Commander-in-Chief of Polish Armed Forces, died in a sabotaged British airplane.

At that time the notorious Kim Philby served as the British security chief in Gibraltar. He was a Soviet spy, who later died in Moscow and was given a Soviet state funeral with full honors. He was one of the few foreigners who achieved a rank of a general in the NKVD - KGB. Philby was in position to sabotage Sikorski's plane by damaging the equipment or drugging its Czech pilot (possibly using an NKVD team, which was present in Gibraltar accompanying Soviet ambassador I. M. Majsky).

Already for several months, the Soviets had wanted to liquidate the legal Polish government headed by Sikorski. German radio called General Sikorski "the last victim of the crime of Katyń."

Among others, British Secretary of State for Foreign Affairs R.A. Eden exerted heavy pressure on General Sikorski, shortly before his death, to accept the false Soviet version of the Katyń crime "for the sake of unity of the anti-German alliance." Sikorski resisted British and American pressure to falsify the truth. Thus, Poland lost an able and dedicated leader who, more than any other head of government, repeatedly appealed to the conscience of the world on behalf of the victims of German terror, especially the Jews suffering in occupied Poland the unbelievable atrocities of the German "Final Solution."

379

Appendix I

July 4-10 Germans defeated in the battle of Kursk. Germans completed their exhumation at Katyń and by July 7 reburied the victims. The last of the seven opened graves were closed again at Katyń.

Sept. 25, 1943 Smolensk captured by the Soviet armies together with the region of the Katyń graves. Shortly afterwards M.N. Burdenko arrived to Katyń with a group of medico-legal experts. For a period of nearly four months they "made a preliminary study and investigation of the circumstances of all the crimes perpetrated by the Germans at Katyń."

Nov. 2, 1943 In Moscow, a Decree of the Supreme Council of the USSR establishing an "Extraordinary State Commission for Ascertaining the Crimes committed by the German Fascist Invaders and their Associates." The Extraordinary Commission set up a "Special Commission for Ascertaining and Investigating the Circumstances of the Shooting of Polish Officers by the German Fascist Invaders in the Katyn Woods." The new commission set up for the Soviet "investigation" was first mentioned in Moscow on Jan. 17, 1944 -- it was headed by M.N.Burdenko, surgeon and Academician.

Nov. 28 -- Dec. 1, 1943 In Teheran, Poland was betrayed by Churchill and Roosevelt as they recognized the Hitler-Stalin line of partition of the Polish state drawn along the Bug River on Sept. 28, 1939; they also secretly agreed to make the postwar Poland part of the Soviet zone of interest -- an agreement which left Poland to be subjugated by the Soviet terror apparatus. As a cover-up they agreed to call the Hitler-Stalin, or Ribbentrop-Molotov line the "Curzon Line" as of 1920 (the line proposed by the Allies' ambassadors on July 10, 1920; then it was falsified on July 11, 1920 in the Lloyd-George's office by shifting to the Soviets the region of Lvov before the proposal was delivered to Moscow). They also agreed to suppress the truth about the Soviet murders of the 15,000 Polish officers "for the sake of unity of the anti-German alliance." Poland was to become the most important Soviet conquest in World War II.

Jan. 1944 In Katyń, the Soviet Special Commission under N. N. Burdenko exhumed, investigated, and reburied the bodies of Polish officers murdered by the NKVD in the Spring of 1940.

Dec. 1944 - May 1945 On the eastern front there were the last frantic struggles of the disintegrating German state, dismantling of death camps and deadly evacuation marches of prisoners. German army's losses in 1944 were immense, and represented more than one hundred divisions.

The December 16 counter-offensive on the German western front in the Ardennes failed. The Americans, British, and French forced their way forwards over the Rhine River. The Soviet and Polish armies burst across the Vistula River and then cleared Pomerania and Silesia to reach the Oder-Neisse river line, which was to become the border between Poland and Germany.

By mid-March, the German government of Adolf Hitler had been directing operations from a bomb-proof bunker deep under the chancellery in Berlin, while the Allied forces progressed deep into Germany.

After the April 16 attack across the Oder River by the Russians and Poles, Hitler composed his political testament. He repudiated the German people as unworthy of him and he denounced the members of the German government as traitors. He believed that the Jewish-Bolshevik conspiracy had brought him down.

Hitler took his own life on April 30, 1945, when the news came that the powerful German army group "Mitte," ordered by him to rescue Berlin had been defeated by the 2nd Polish army near Bautzen (Budziszyn) on April 21-27. It was the bloodiest battle fought by Poles in World War II. 26,000 German elite soldiers of the Berlin rescue force were killed there and 314 of their best tanks and 135 self-propelled guns were lost. 27,000 Germans were taken prisoner, most of them wounded in combat.

The Germans were under the command of one of their ablest officers, Field Marshal Ferdinand Schoerner, and the Poles, mostly former soldiers of the Home Army, were led by General Karol "Walter" Swierczewski, who had commanded the International Brigade in Spain and was one of the heroes of Hemingway's *For Whom the Bell Tolls.*

In the final assault on Berlin, units of the Polish 1st Army took part and were the first to take the Brandenburg Gate (erected in 1791 during the partitions of Poland which were initiated by the Berlin government). The Poles were also the first to capture (on May 8, 1945) the Siegessaule, or the Victory Column (erected in 1873 to commemorate the defeat of France and the unification of Germany in 1871 as well as the establishment of the short-lived German Empire, which ended forty-seven years later, in 1918). Polish 1st Army units were the only non-Soviet forces in the Berlin operation.

Meanwhile the last act of the tragedy of the prisoners of German concentration camps was unfolding midst evacuations, disease, starvation and executions. The war, which had cost some fifty million lives, was coming to a close. The war started with the German-Soviet pacts in 1939; it led to mass murders committed by both totalitarian states.

By the end of 1944 the Soviet terror apparatus again was tightening its grip on Poland. Earlier Soviet plans to form the third Polish army, and thus complete a Polish front of three armies, were abandoned by Moscow. Instead, the NKVD resumed mass arrests and deportation from Poland of anti-communist able bodied men in order to weaken Polish resistance to the Soviet takeover.

The Poles fought the Germans throughout World War II. Nine hundred thousand Polish soldiers participated in the fall campaign of 1939. Over 350,000 took part in resistance units; 200,000 in Polish units of airmen, sailors, and soldiers fought under allied command on the western and southern fronts of Germany. 400,000 Polish soldiers fought alongside the Soviets on the eastern German front. Polish participation in campaigns in France and the Battle of Britain were followed by the attack on Narvik, Norway, then by victorious battles such as at Tobruk, North Africa, Monte Cassino, Italy, and at Falaise, France. Finally, in April 1945 the Poles defeated the main force of the last German offensive (ordered by Hitler in person) to rescue Berlin. Poles served in the only non-Soviet forces to press through to the conquest of the German capital. All these engagements made Poles feel that they had contributed significantly to the defeat of Nazi Germany.

Feb. 4 to Feb. 11, 1945 In Yalta, F.D. Roosevelt, W. Churchill, and J.V. Stalin agreed on the terms of unconditional surrender by Germany, the Soviet Union's entry into the war against Japan, and the structure of the United

Nations. The Teheran agreement to make Poland a part of the Soviet zone of influence was reconfirmed, as well as the line of the 1939 partition of Poland between Germany and the Soviet Union, along the Bug River, as the postwar Polish-Soviet border. The United States and Great Britain agreed to withdraw their recognition from the legitimate Polish Government-in-Exile in London and to accept a new, Soviet controlled government of Poland. Poland's territorial losses in the east were to be compensated by acquisition of smaller territories held by Germany in 1939. These were, centuries earlier, a part of the original Polish ethnic lands during the rule of the first Polish dynasty, the Piasts.

President Roosevelt felt uneasy about his treatment of Poland. He was a part of the western cover-up (in 1943-1945) of the 1940 Soviet massacre of 15,000 Polish officers. Especially embarrassing was the matter of the mass graves in Katyń Forest. He also was annoyed by the repeated demands of the Polish wartime government to put pressure on Germany to stop the murders of millions of Jews and Poles in occupied Poland. Churchill described in his *Triumph and Tragedy* how President Roosevelt was anxious to end the discussion about Poland with Stalin and made the incredible statement: "Poland has been the source of trouble for over five hundred years."

(President F.D. Roosevelt died two months later on Apr. 12, 1945 and the Yalta agreements, which never were ratified by the United States Congress, nevertheless became the corner-stone of the postwar Soviet empire for the next 45 years.)

When the outcome of the conferences at Tehran (1943) and Yalta (1945) was made known, the Poles were devastated. They considered themselves twice betrayed. They felt that the western allies had failed them in 1939, by neglecting to act on their declaration of war; and in 1943, by secretly agreeing to place Poland in the Soviet sphere of interest. Consequently, they perceived themselves to be among the foremost victims of the war. With six million of her citizens dead, her cities, industry, and agriculture in ruins, not only was Poland now to lose half of her territory, but she was also to be subjugated and thoroughly reshaped by the Soviet Union.

The second world war was entered in 1939 by Great Britain and France in defense of the freedom of Poland. The war was ending in 1945 with the betrayal and surrender of Poland to Soviet control by Great Britain and the United States of America.

March 24, 1945 In Washington, President Roosevelt issued a written secret order to George H. Earle, his representative in the Balkans, forbidding Earle to say anything negative about Soviet responsibility at Katyń.

May 22, 1945 In Washington Gen. Bissell, head of G-2, met alone with Lt. Col. Van Vliet and ordered him to write a report on Van Vliet's 1943 visit to Katyń. Van Vliet's report was immediately classified as "top secret." The report was never seen again.

July 17 - Aug. 2, 1945 In Berlin-Potsdam Conference of the Big Three represented by H. Truman for the U.S.A., W. Churchill and C. Attlee for Great Britain and J.W. Stalin for the USSR. It broadened the Yalta agreements, provided for Allied Commission for Control of the Occupied Germany, re-confirmed the June 28th transfer of international recognition from Polish Government-in-Exile to Soviet controlled Provisional Government of National Unity in Warsaw, and established the western frontier of Poland on the Rivers Oder (Odra) and Neisse (Nysa) and the northern frontier south of Koenigsberg-Kaliningrad, the new region of the USSR. Poland's territory was reduced by 30,000 sq. miles. The Western Allied Governments continued to suppress the truth about the Soviet mass murder of the 15,000 Polish officers in 1940.

Sept. 20, 1945 - Oct. 1, 1946 Trials were held in Nuremberg by the International Military Tribunal. 22 officials of the German wartime government were treated as war criminals. 19 defendants were convicted, 9 were sentenced to death, 8 were hanged on Oct. 16, 1946, the day after Hermann Goering committed suicide in prison. Soviet representatives falsely accused the German wartime government of the massacre at Katyń of 11,000 Polish officers.

American and British judges decided that Germans were not guilty of the Katyń murders and decided to drop this matter without reviewing available evidence, which clearly indicated that Soviet security forces were responsible. Allied trials of German war criminals continued in countries occupied during the war and in the four zones of occupation of Germany, until the incorporation of the West and East German states in 1949. Very few war criminals were tried in Germany after 1949.

April 26, 1950 In Washington, Col. Van Vliet was ordered to reconstruct his report on Katyń, which has been "lost" by the U.S. Defense Department.

Oct. 11, 1951 -- Dec. 22, 1952 a Special Committee of the U.S. Congress on Katyń Murders held hearings and unanimously concluded that the security forces of the Soviet Union were responsible for the Katyń massacre. It recommended that its investigations of the Katyń crime, depositions, evidence and findings "should be presented to the General Assembly of the United Nations, with the end in view of seeking action before the International World Court of Justice against the Soviet Union for a crime of violation of the law recognized by all civilized nations." (82nd Congress, Congressional Record 8864, 1952.)

July 1953 In Moscow, Marshal Lavrenty Beria was executed. An extensive investigation of his activities was recorded in over fifty volumes of files. These records, still kept secret, must include extensive information related to the Soviet execution of the 15,000 Polish officers in the spring of 1940.

Dec. 1953 In Moscow the execution of Vsevolod Nikolayevich Merkulov former Deputy Minister of Internal Affairs and a member of the Central Committee of the Communist Party of USSR, who received the Order of Lenin for his services by the time he was bringing to conclusion the largest in history execution of officers prisoners of war in spring of 1940. Voluminous records of Merkulov's testimony are still being kept secret.

February 1977. In Sweden, the arrival from Poland of Tomasz Strzyzewski, Polish censor no. C-36 of the Krakow Main Office for Control of Press, Publications, and Public Performances was noticed by the mass media. He risked his life by bringing with him some 700 pages of classified censors' documents. Strzyzewski exposed the falsification of history of Poland in general and

Appendix I

World War II in particular by the Soviet controlled Communist government in Poland. In particular, he was protesting against Soviet distortion of the truth of such events as the NKVD massacre of Polish officers in 1940. Strzyzewski's grandfather was one of the fifteen thousand Polish officers murdered by the Soviets at Katyń and other sites of mass murders. (Details about Strzyzewski's revelations are in "The Black Book Of Polish Censorship," translated and edited by Jane Leftwich Curry, Random House, New York, 1984)

April 13, 1990 The president of the USSR, Mikhail Gorbachev, officially admitted Soviet guilt in the killing of the 15,000 Polish officers who were held before their execution in three Russian Orthodox monasteries used as prisons by the Communists and located at Kozielsk, Ostashkov, and Starobielsk. Gorbachev turned over documents about the 15,000 Polish officers to Poland's President General Wojciech Jaruzelski. They were not complete and did not include a copy of Stalin's signed order to conduct the executions and other important documents. Gorbachev did not accompany Gen. Jaruzelski to a ceremony in Katyń, a part of the official visit.

Nov. 21 --23, 1991 In Katyń, twenty probing holes were drilled in the grave sites, which were in 1943 investigated by the Germans and in 1944 by the Soviets. The holes were drilled in presence of Polish and Russian representatives. No bodies of Polish officers were found. This confirmed the earlier results of the German aerial photographic survey. Soviet earth moving machines were photographed at Katyń by the end of April, 1944. They were used to remove the bodies of Polish officers and to destroy their graves.

The NKVD-KGB records indicate that all executed Polish officers from the camp in Starobielsk are buried in the village of Piatikhatki, near Kharkov. The KGB allowed exhumation of only 140 bodies in Piatikhatki. A conclusive report on the Piatikhatki grave site could not be prepared up till the Summer of 1992.

May 22, 1992 In Moscow, signing of the Treaty between the Republic of Poland and the Russian Federation on Friendship and Good Neighborly Cooperation by the Polish President Lech Wałęsa and the Russian President Boris Yeltsin. Additional documents on the murder of the 15,000 officers were given to the Polish delegation. However, President Yeltsin did not accompany President Wałęsa to the Katyń graves - a part of the official Polish visit.

In principle Bielorus, Russia, and the Ukraine agreed to excavate the bodies of Polish officers, properly re-bury them and then convert the grave sites into formal military cemeteries. In a way, these monuments and burials of Poles on the foreign soil would be similar to the Polish military cemetery in Italy, at Monte Casino, for example. Public collection was to be initiated to cover the expenses of proper monuments at each of the planed military cemeteries. The work on the Polish military cemeteries was considered to be of the highest priority.

In Warsaw a wall-monument is considered (similar to the Vietnam Memorial in Washington) inscribed with the 15,000 names of the victims of the mass execution of Polish military, intelligence, police, and territorial officers by the Soviet security forces in 1940. One of the locations mentioned for the wall-monument is the area of the Marshal Józef Piłsudski Square where it could serve as a backdrop of the monumental grave of the Polish unknown soldier.

Index

Index

Brest (Brześć) 40
Brikle, Dr. 385
Britain, battle of 390
British airplane, sabotaged 387
British pressure on Poles 388
British resolve 367
British security chief in Gibraltar 387
Brzeżany 395
Budapest University 395
Bug River 388, 391
Bukharin N.I. (1888-1938) 68
Bulgaria 395
bullets
    found at Katyń 236-7, 244, 281
    cartridges 353
    German "Geco" 281, 352
Burdenko, Dr. Nikolai N. 71, 197-198,
    242, 279, 387, 352, 358, 388
Burdenko Commission 17, 197, 228-245,
    258, 271, 273, 291, 310, 321, 358, 360
Burdenko's letter to Molotov 235
Burdenko's letter to Shvernik 237
Butyrka prison 76
Butz, Dr. Gerhard 16, 67, 205, 237, 248,
    260-1, 264-5, 352
Butz theory 70
bus with smeared windows 378
Bydgoszcz 371
Byelorussia (Białoruś, Belorus, Byelorus)
    70, 377, 394
Byelorussian S.S.R. 30, 80
Byelorussians 376
Bytom 406

Camp commandants 42-4
capitalist fight 369
Catechism of a Revolutionary 409
categories for extermination 365
Catholic priests executed 377
Caucasus 334
cause of death 385
Central Committee 247
Chamberlain, Neville 367
chaplains 377
Cheka 333
Chekist 333
Chelm Lubelski 402, 408
Chelyabinsk Tribunal 33
Chelyshev, I. A. 330
Chertkov, V. 339
Chmielewski, Julian Police Serg. 80
Chodkiewicz, Karol Scout Troop 405
choke knot 378

Chrzanowski, Gen. Pawel 405
chronology and annotations 7, 365
Churchill, Winston 54, 319-20, 350, 386,
    391-2
    message of Apr. 30, 1943 320-1
    Triumph and Tragedy 391
Cieszyn (Tesin) 405
citations given 31, 62
class enemies 367
class intuition 11
Class Struggle 409
coffins 88
collapse of Germany 384
collection of money 394
    for formal military cemeteries 394
    for proper monuments 394
    for a wall monument in Warsaw 394
Colonial Medicine, Paris 395
colonization of Poland 369
Commissariat for Military Affairs 22
common-defense treaty 368-9
Conference of Ambassadors 366
Congressional Record 393
conquest of "the whole world" 366
contacts punishable 32-3
Conti, Dr. Leonard 225
Convention on Aggression 366
cooperation, USSR and Germany 367
Copenhagen, Forensic Institute 385
corpses bumped 381
corpses loaded on trucks 381
correspondence used to deport 374
Costedoat, Medical Inspector 385
Cracow (Kraków) 398, 402
cremation of bodies 376
Crimea 350, 357
crime, international 7
Criminal Code of RSFSR 28, 374
criminology 385
Croatia 385
Cross of the Brave 397
Cross of Independence 395, 397, 399
Cross of Polish Legions 406
Cross of Merit 395, 399, 404, 408
Cross of the Polish Military Org. 406
crushed skulls 378
"Curzon Line" 389
cubicles in the bus 378
Curry, Jane Leftwich 394
customs war 366
Czapski, Józef 92, 150-156
Czarnek, Cadet Officer Stanislaw 408
Czarnek, Lawyer Witold 408

Index

Index

Index

Index

Ministry of Justice 398, 400
Minkiewicz, Gen. Henryk 55
Minko, Andrzej 12, 338
Minsk 79, 80, 363, 377, 382
Minsk Mazowiecki 398
Mołodeczno 65
Molotov, Vyacheslav M. 27, 158, 163, 211, 235, 344, 349-50, 375, 381 383
    unsuccessful visit to Berlin 383
Monte Cassino 390
Moroz, V. P. 343
Moscow 39, 343, 345, 348, 352, 354, 359, 374, 382, 388, 394
    shocked by the fall and collapse of France 8, 382
Moscow News 22, 159, 337
Moszyński, Adam 78-80
    Lista Katyńska 78
Munich 367
Muralov, N. I. 346
murder as a political weapon 387
murder method 378-380, 387
murder rate at Kalinin 380
murders after Spring 1940 77-81
Myślenice 406

Nagant revolver 342
Naples University 385
Narvik, attack on 390
nationalist arrogance 11
Naville, Dr. Francois 216-22, 253-4, 278, 385
Naville's letter 217-221
Nechayev 409-410
Neisse River (Nysa) 392
Nelken, Col. M. D. Jan W. 396
Nekhoroshev, Commissar 332
Nidelko, 57
Nikitchenko, Judge 254-9
NKVD 11, 135, 161, 166, 176, 186, 209, 227, 316-7, 374-5, 376-85, 387-388, 390-391
    administration of POW camps 374, 377
    camp commandants 374
    camp liquidation 377
    camps, POW 374, 377
    censorship of mail 374
    circulars 143, 144
    control of camps 260
    convoys 59, 77
    courts, special Troyka 375

dacha (rest home) 72, 96, 98, 358
Dnieper castle 266
documents 48, 118-22
dossiers contents 374
drownings 91-92, 146-7
-NKGB 44
execution at Cherven (Czerwień) 82
executioners, skilled 378
files 113
graves of civilians 266
hangings 109
interviews 123-137
investigation of prisoners 377
"Jewish hangmen" 226
Katyn list 191-196
listing of Polish officers 377
military supply of 25
numbers 40-1, 337
organs of 11,
P.O.Box 12 Kozielsk 49
P.O.W. Affairs 114
political dept. 114
prison 45, 80
prisoner's mail, use of 374
rank 63, 345
rumors 92
see: escort guard troops 22, 24-25, 62, 74, 82
Smolensk 43,
Ukrainian KGB- 108, 109, 110, 111, 112,
North Africa 390
Norway 390
Nowak, Waclaw 2nd lt. 80
Novograd Volynsky 29-0
Novikov, N. V. 351-2
Novosibirsk 339
Nurenberg Trial 17, 246, 285, 356, 392
    blank spots of 247
    concept of 248

Ob River 339
Oberhauser, Gen. 356, 358
Oberlaender, Prof. Theo. 68, 334-6
October Revolution Archives 354-5, 357
Oder-Neisse Line 389
Oder River (Odra) 389, 392
Office for Control of Press 393
Ogonowski, Józef, sr. patrolman 80
Ogrodnicki, Pedagogue Lt. Karol 402-3
Okhlopkov, Leonid 148
Okulicki, General L. 350, 356-7
Olędzki, Józef mjr. 79

Index

Index

School Aid Soc. 405
School Educational Soc. 405
Scouts' Radio Club 404
"Secret Report" 213-5
secret provisions, Sept. 28, 1939, 7
Selifontovo 337
Semenov, N. 363
Semenovsky, Dr. P. S. 244-5
Semukov, A. 361
Semyanikov, executioner 380
Sentry dog 342
Serebryakov, L. P. 346
Sergeyev, Jr. Lt. convoy comm. 81
Serov, I. A. minister 20-1
Shakhov, Lt. Staff of Gryazovets 44
Sharapov, V. Mjr. Gen. 24, 44-5, 331,
   340
Shchemeleva, Y. 360-1
Shcherbatov, Alexei 170-186
Shepetovka (Szepetówka) 38
Shergunov 24
Shkolnikov 32-3
Shoerner, Marshal Ferdinand 387
shooting method 239
Shulzhenkov, Jr. Lt. staff Yukhov 44
Shvernik, N.M. 237, 353
Sidorova, Maria 88-9
Siegessaule (Victory Column) 390
Siepiński, Prof. Wacław 407
Sikora, Andrzej 391
Sikorski, General Władysław 16, 210-13,
   320, 344, 384, 387-8
   died as Prime Minister of Polish
   Government-in-Exile and Commander-
   in-Chief of Polish Armed Forces 384
   "the last victim of Katyń" 388
Sikorski Museum 200
Silesia 389
simultaneous interpreting 405
Sinyavsky-Daniel trial 247
six border wars 366
Skarzynski, Kazimierz 213-15
Skarżyński Report P.R.C. 215, 224
skete 47
Skorobogatkov, YCL 46
Skrętowski, Witold pol. comm. 79
Skryabin (= Molotov, Vyacheslav M.)
Slavs 335, 375
Slavic lands 367
Słucz, battle of 395
Smirnov, V. I. 30, 266-9, 281-4
Smolensk 40, 58, 60-1, 66, 126, 204,
   361, 377, 382, 388, 390

Smolensk NKVD 43, 56, 341, 382
Smolensk-Vitebsk Highway 377, 381
Smorawiński, Gen. Mieczysław 206
   305-6
Snytko, M. Politruk 45, 334
Social Insurance Inst. 398
Sofia University 385
Sokolnikov, G. Y. 347
Sokołowski, Ph.D., 2nd. Lt. Stefan L.
   404-405
Slovakia 385
Solovyov, B. A. 355
Solski, Mjr. Adam 66, 72
Solzhenitsyn 23, 65, 94, 106, 293, 362
   The Gulag Archipelago 65, 308
Soprunenko, Pyotr 181-5, 194, 377
Sovetskaya Kultura 338
Sovetskaya Rossia 361
Soviet admission of attach 375
Soviet Army Archives 20, 59, 330-1, 333,
   337, 339-40, 342-3
Soviet Balkan demands 383
Soviet bayonets 379
Soviet "blunder" admitted by Merkulov
   382
Soviet conquest 389
Soviet execution of Polish officers
   completed 383
Soviet extermination procedures 384
Soviet false claims 386
Soviet-German Commission 29
Soviet-German Protocols of 1939 9
Soviet-German Treaty on Friendship and
   Frontier 7, 15, 326
Soviet guilt 394
Soviet miscalculation 8, 382
Soviet occupation 350
Soviet penal code, #58 375
   death penalty for class enemies
Soviet-Polish Gordian knot 319
Soviet re-organization of the Polish
   army in the USSR 382
Soviet security forces 7, 8, 365
Soviet slogans 372
Soviet Special Commission 16, 387
Soviet sphere of interest 391
Soviet subversion 372
Soviet takeover 390
Soviet terror apparatus 390
Soviet unleashing Germany 382
Soviet version 20, 388
Soviet wholesale robbery 373
Soviet witnesses 227

394

Index

Index